REFUGEES

REFUGEES

by

Diana Christopher

SEVERN HOUSE PUBLISHERS

This first world edition published 1987 by
SEVERN HOUSE PUBLISHERS LTD of
40–42 William IV Street, London WC2N 4DF

Copyright © F. Beermann Bv, 1987

ISBN 0–7278–1505–9

Printed and bound in Great Britain

PROLOGUE

July 1985

'Oh, Mrs Johnson, it is *such* a pleasure to meet you at last,' gushed Miss Sutton. 'I've read all of your books, you know.'

'Have you?' Stephanie Johnson asked in genuine surprise.

'Every one,' Miss Sutton insisted. 'And enjoyed them all. I just know *Where the Sun Never Shines* is going to be a great success.'

She passed on into the crowded reception room of the Waldorf Astoria in New York, and Ed Martinez wrinkled his nose. It was a large nose, situated in the centre of a set of equally large features, on top of a long neck and a heavy body – when it moved independently like that, it suggested a boulder coming loose on a mountain side, with the threat that the white hair above would become an avalanche of snow.

'It already is a great success,' he observed, 'no thanks to her. And she may have read all your previous books, but she sure didn't do much to help them along.'

'Who's she from?' Stephanie asked.

'*The Globe*. Oh, she's important, so we mustn't grumble. Mr Rutin . . . ' the publisher smiled at the next man in line, 'I'd like you to meet Stephanie Johnson. Mr Rutin represents *Midas Magazine*,' he explained to Stephanie, meaningfully. Her book had been intended to appeal to female readers, and to have a representative from a man's magazine attending the party was sheer icing on the cake.

Rutin shook hands. 'Fourteen weeks top of the bestseller list, eh? Congratulations. May I say that you look exactly as I had imagined you would.

Stephanie raised her eyebrows. 'Why, thank you.'

'I wonder how many dreams you have inspired,' Martinez said thoughtfully, as Rutin joined the throng.

1

His tone was both reflective and wistful. He had spent the occasional night dreaming of Stephanie Johnson himself. As she was one of his authors, he knew that she was forty-eight years of age – and remained a most beautiful woman who exuded a subtle air of restrained eroticism, which permeated her books as well, and was certainly partly responsible for her success. She was tall, a good five foot eight in her stockings, he estimated, and was slender without being thin. She had dark brown hair, which, on public occasions like this, was worn in a severe chignon, but was clearly long and luxuriant; her splendid features, high forehead, straight nose, wide mouth and firm chin, were only prevented from being bold by the warmth of the surprising blue eyes, huge and deep – and vaguely, attractively, sad.

Certainly a woman to dream about, more so because of the air of mystery she maintained about her personal life and background. Martinez had now known her for ten years, and had published eight of her novels. He took a great deal of pride in having, by patient encouragement, finally extracted from her the world bestseller he had always felt she could write. He knew that she was a comparatively recent American citizen, and that before settling in New York she had lived in England, yet although her accent was flawless he did not believe she was actually English. Then there was the complete absence of a permanent man in her life. But she must have loved, once – she insisted upon being called Mrs Johnson, and she had a son at Harvard, he knew.

He had often been tempted to pry, and equally, had been tempted to use the woman of mystery angle in promoting her books, but he had known that either course might have antagonised her, and he did not wish to risk that, and not only on professional grounds. So he dreamed, and looked, and listened whenever he was invited to dine at her Park Avenue apartment, and learned nothing, and realised he was falling in love, the very last thing a publisher wants to do with one of his authors.

Now he covered his self-induced embarrassment with a hasty examination of the next card. 'Elizabeth Latchman. Elizabeth Latchman? Must be a private invitation. The only Latchman I know of is the industrialist.'

He raised his head at the ripple of laughter from Stephanie, gazed at the features of the woman who had appeared in front of him, and gave Stephanie another hasty glance. He might almost have been looking in a mirror. Except that here the face was definitely bold, and the eyes dark, and this woman wore a dress which had clearly come straight from Paris, and jewellery to match. She flared, where Stephanie, in a quiet deep blue sheath, merely glowed.

'Ed,' Stephanie said. 'You've never met my sister, Beth.'

'Well, what do you know. I never even knew you had a sister.' Martinez shook hands.

'My pleasure, Mr Martinez,' Beth Latchman said. 'My little sister has told me so much about you.'

'Has she, now,' Martinez said delightedly.

'As publishers go, you are the best,' Beth said. 'Do try to spare me a moment, Stephanie, whenever you can.' She disappeared into the throng.

'I never knew you had a sister,' Martinez complained again. 'And Latchman . . . that wouldn't be *the* Vernon Latchman?'

'Right, first time,' Stephanie assured him. 'Unfortunately, Vernon does not care for literary gatherings, so he decided not to come.'

'He's been married before, hasn't he?'

'Yes. But so has Beth, three times, ' Stephanie said. But now she was restless, anxious to escape the guest line and find her sister. She hadn't been sure Beth would come, and she did so want Beth's approval, for everything she did. But it was another hour before she found her sister surrounded by nine men in one corner of the huge room. This was not unusual. Beth, even at fifty-five, attracted men of all ages like a magnet. At the

3

sight of her younger sister, however, she excused herself, and came over to Stephanie, a glass of champagne in her hand.

'Well, my darling girl, what does it feel like to have arrived with a capital 'A'?'

'Pleasantly insecure. I keep expecting to wake up. Did you feel the same?'

'Me? I've never arrived, in either a social or a financial sense. I've always sneaked in the back door. Is there really to be a film?'

'A mini series. Yes, this time they could just be serious, judging by the size of the option.'

'And are you really going to play the lead yourself?'

'You have got to be joking. That's a rumour put up by some rag. Beth . . . dinner?'

'I'd love to, darling. Whenever we can escape.'

They were already being separated. 'Can't have the two most beautiful women in the room tête-à-tête,' John Harper said, and drew Stephanie aside. 'Now tell me, what does a man have to do to have a word with his client?'

'Oh, I am sorry, John,' Stephanie said. He was her accountant, and in many ways her business manager, as well as being one of her favourite men. 'I've been so busy these past few days, what with the interviews and the TV stuff . . . is it urgent?'

'Whenever one of my clients approaches genuine millionairess standard I regard it as urgent,' Harper told her. 'You happen to have an inordinate amount of cash lying around right this minute, and I'd like us to think of something constructive to do with it.'

'How about spending it?'

'Some of it, by all means,' he agreed. 'But seriously, you know, now that you are not only rich, but famous, as well as single,' he added severely. Like Martinez, that was a situation he would like to change. 'All of those things immediately make you a marked woman for every fortune hunter in town.'

She blew him a kiss. 'Briefly, John. Nowadays a

4

novelist is only as rich, or as famous, as his or her last book.'

'Briefly can often be long enough. I happen to know there's a character in town making quite serious inquiries about you, right this minute.'

Stephanie frowned. 'Inquiries? About me?'

'And Beth. Questions at your banks, of your doorman, presumably of the Latchman hirelings as well.'

'How do you know this?'

'It's my business to look after both you and your finances, remember?'

'So what have you found out about this . . . man?'

'Man. Named Meyer. He could just be a prying reporter looking for gossip. Would you like to check into it?'

Stephanie Johnson looked across the room at her sister, once again surrounded by eager men. Name of Meyer, she thought. And asking about Beth, as well as me. Therefore he is not interested in my sudden fame as a novelist; he is far more sinister than a reporter or a fortune hunter.

'He's here tonight,' Harper went on casually. 'God knows how he got an invitation.'

Stephanie followed his gaze to the other side of the room, looked at the tall dark man with the rugged but unmistakably Jewish features. She remembered shaking his hand an hour ago, and even being attracted by him, but there had been so many names and faces his had not registered sufficiently.

Now he was suddenly an enemy. Anyone asking questions about Beth had to be regarded as an enemy.

'Yes,' she said. 'I would be grateful if you would find out everything you can about Mr Meyer. I would also like to meet him. Now.'

THE FIRST CHRONICLE

September 1984

'Bob! Good to see you. Come in, come in,' Isaac Stein held the door, while the two secretaries in the outer office exchanged glances. Robert Meyer did not often visit Jerusalem, but when he did, he got the red carpet treatment, even from Isaac Stein.

Stein closed the door, indicated the comfortable armchair before his desk and, seated himself in the even more comfortable swivel chair by the window, which looked out at the Church of the Holy Sepulchre. He was a short lean man, with sharp features. He looked like what he was, a predator. In front of him, Meyer, large and relaxed and sleepy looking, wearing a well cut blue suit and a quiet tie, suggested an unsuspecting victim – but Stein had no illusions as to which of them was the more dangerous: Meyer's record proved that.

'How was Paraguay?' he asked.

'Hot,' Meyer replied. 'And wet, and poor, and generally unpleasant.'

Stein nodded. 'And von Epps?'

'Cool, and dry, and rich, and extraordinarily pleasant.'

'And also, now, dead, I understand.'

Meyer nodded. 'He blew his brains out when he realised who we were.'

'You sound upset about that.'

'Dissatisfied. We'll never know if he was the right man, or just someone with a generally guilty conscience.'

'He was Heinrich von Epps, all right,' Stein said. 'His suicide just about proves that. And he had at least seven hundred deaths on his conscience. If he had a conscience. You have taken a holiday?'

'I went to the Seychelles and lay in the sun,' Meyer told him.

'Sounds pleasant.'

'It was lonely.'

6

'That's your trouble. Why don't you find a good woman?'

'In my job?'

'So tell her you're a travelling salesman.'

'I'd prefer to be lonely. Anyway, maybe I won't have to be lonely that much longer. For God's sake, Isaac, it's thirty-eight years since the War ended. There can't be many of the bastards left.'

Stein carefully lifted the cover of the folder on his desk, and then let it fall again. 'A few.'

'Meaning you've a new assignment for me.'

'A real sleuthing case,' Stein agreed, and began to fill a pipe, as he always did when about to talk business. 'Have you ever heard of a man called Josef Janski?'

Meyer frowned. 'Sounds Polish.'

'He is. Or was.'

'I was ten when I left Poland. 1946.'

'But you left a lot behind.'

Meyer returned his gaze. 'Yes, Isaac, I left a lot behind. But I have never heard of Janski. Should I have?'

'You're probably lucky you didn't, while you were in Poland. But your father and mother might have. In fact they probably did. Janski was a lawyer, and was in the people business, at the beginning of the War. He was a well-thought of lawyer, who handled a lot of Jewish clients. So naturally, when the Germans took over in 1939, and the nature of their takeover became apparent, as it soon did, Janski's clients turned to him for advice. He was prepared to offer them more than that. He told these people that for a fee, a considerable fee, he could get them out of the country, to some place safe, like Yugoslavia or Greece. A lot of them fell for it. One hell of a lot. And the evidence we have indicates that having fleeced them of everything they possessed, Janski simply turned them over to the Gestapo.'

He studied Meyer as he spoke, watched the changing expressions around the younger man's mouth and eyes.

'That's why I thought your parents might have heard of him,' he went on quietly.

Meyer raised his head. 'You know about them?

'It is my business to know about everything. And especially everything to do with my employees, Bob. You are one of my best investigators, because you're driven not only by a desire for revenge, but because you also suffer from a guilty conscience.'

'Sure,' Meyer agreed. 'I won't deny that I survived, thanks to Michael Sobieski. My parents went to Auschwitz.'

'They were arrested as they were about to leave Warsaw for safety in the south,' Stein said. 'I'm pointing no finger, Bob. Shit, had I been there and had the money, I would have done the same, tried to get out while I could. What I am suggesting is that it must have been Janski, or someone like him, who arranged their so-called departure. Can you remember anything of it?'

Meyer shrugged. 'I wasn't quite four, Isaac. I don't know what I actually remember, and what I think I remember because I've been told about it so often. I know I wandered away from Momma and Poppa at the station, while they were saying goodbye to various friends and relations.'

'You were going with them, of course?'

Meyer nodded. 'And I know that Uncle Michael came looking for me. He picked me up, and turned to take me back to the group, and saw men he recognised as the Gestapo coming towards Momma and Poppa. He realised there was nothing he could do about them, made an instant decision, and just walked away, with me in his arms. No one asked any questions, apparently. It seems that my parents never mentioned me to whoever set up the deal . . .'

'Josef Janski,' Stein suggested.

'Maybe. Anyway, the Gestapo were only looking for them. I suppose they reckoned they could just include me in the emigration without having to pay for me. Poppa was a little inclined to cut corners like that.'

'And Sobieski brought you up as one of his, a good Catholic. You owe him a great deal.'

'My life,' Meyer acknowledged. 'Do you know, I never saw him after I left Poland. I never went back, and he died, about three years ago. We corresponded, of course, and I'm still in touch with his son. But I never saw him again.'

'So will you look for Janski?'

'What have you got?'

'Just a hint that he may still be around. Janski and his entire family disappeared in 1945. It was quite a large family, three daughters and a son. All roughly about your age.'

He paused, but Meyer made no comment, so he continued. 'Well, a great many people disappeared around the end of the War, without any trace, from starvation or disease or just from being murdered and left to decompose in a ditch, and frankly we had assumed Janski and his family had all suffered some such fate. But you know we never actually close the file on anyone we're interested in until we have certain proof of death, so Janski's file, this file, lay on the shelf gathering dust until three months ago. Then something cropped up. An old boy named Rothmer died in Tel Aviv, and going through his effects, his family found a diary. Rothmer was a Polish doctor who emigrated to England before 1939, and indeed, served in the British Army during the War.

'In the mid Fifties he emigrated again, to America, and settled there, but he came to Israel for a visit in 1972, and decided to emigrate a third time, to Tel Aviv. But he had to return to the States first, to settle up his affairs, and in his diary there is an interesting entry, that he had, on that return trip to the States in 1972, travelled with a man named Janski, also with a Polish background.'

'Long odds,' Meyer commented. 'Janski isn't an uncommon name.'

'Granted. But this man's first name was Josef, and he was seventy-one years of age, which is exactly how old Janski would have been in 1972.'

'And he told all this to a casual acquaintance? Not the pattern of a fleeing war criminal, Isaac.'

'Hear me out. He didn't tell Rothmer anything. But he had a slight stroke during the voyage, and the man he was travelling with, a Frenchman named Mathieu, who seems to have been some sort of bodyguard, Rothmer recorded, was afraid to call in the ship's doctor, because Janski didn't want any publicity about his trip. So he approached Rothmer instead, and Rothmer helped the old man out.

'While doing so, he read his passport and the old man, rambling, also mentioned that he had had a very hard time since the end of the War, been stateless for a while, and broke, the perfect picture of a refugee. But now, apparently, one of his children had become successful in America, and he was on his way to join this child, and security at last. Rothmer, of course, although he recorded the incident in his diary – he was so meticulous he even recorded every meal he ate – thought nothing of it.'

'But it so happened that the Rothmer family *had* heard of him? That was a bit of bad luck, for Janski.'

'They hadn't heard of him, actually. But they took the diary along to old Moses Pressay, to see if it might be worth publishing. Moses waded through it, he adores jobs like that, as you know, and came across this passage. And he, of course, had heard of Janski as he picks our brains regularly. So he brought the relevant volume to my attention.'

Meyer scratched his chin. 'So what's difficult about finding him, if he's living with his children in the United States?'

'Simply that he landed in New York, and disappeared. He is recorded as entering the country on a six months' tourist visa. Then nothing. The visa was never renewed, and the entry card was never returned. So he undoubtedly remained in the country, illegally. That's not so unusual, of course. The States is full of illegal immigrants. Most of them are found, eventually, through looking for a job or applying for Social Security, or just plain getting ill and dying. There is no record of a Janski corresponding to our man doing any of those things after he set foot on American soil.'

'If he was 71 in 1972, then he's very probably dead by now,' Meyer commented.

'Maybe, but there's no record of it, so we don't know.'

'And the children?'

'No one named Janski we have been able to trace in America in any way corresponds to any of the children. We have some data on them. The mother, Elizabeth, died during the War. As I said, there were four children, the eldest, also named Elizabeth, was born 1930. Then there was a second daughter, Anna, born 1932, then a son, Antoni, born 1934, and lastly another girl, Stephanie, born 1936. That makes her roughly the same age as you, Bob.'

'Cheer me up. So what else have you got on them?'

'Nothing at all. They disappeared from Warsaw in 1945 with their father. But going on the diary, it seems certain that at least one of them made America by 1972, almost certainly using a false name, or maybe having married in Europe before emigrating. That suggests it could be one of the girls. But whether it was girl or boy, he or she seems to have prospered, and been prepared to look after the old man, whatever his crimes.'

Meyer studied the notes he had been making. 'It hardly seems likely any of them could have been involved in Janski's activities. They were kids during the war. Even the eldest could only have been fifteen when it ended.'

'I wouldn't feel too sympathetic for them if I were you,' Stein said. 'If they looked after Papa in his old age, they're probably tarred with the same brush. Do you think you can do anything with this?'

'Maybe,' Meyer said. 'I'm not promising I'll find your man tomorrow.'

11

'Take your time. Just find him. Or his grave.'

'Dan Sobieski is a big wheel in Warsaw now. He'll be a help. But I'll need the usual backup.'

'That won't be a problem. Even our Communist "friends" would like to lay hands on Josef Janski.'

'Well, then, I'll start at Warsaw. That's where he started, right?' His mouth twisted. 'I've always wanted an excuse to go home.'

CHAPTER 1

Warsaw 1944

'There's the bell. I'll get it, Savielly. I'll get it.'

Savielly the butler remained poised in his pantry doorway and watched the little girl run down the hall. Miss Stephanie was eight years old, inclined to plumpness, and moved in an untidy swirl of long dark brown hair and flying pinafore. She moved enthusiastically, excitedly – she found all life a delightful adventure. Now she slipped the bolt and pulled the heavy oak in, jumping up and down.

'Uncle Hans!' she screamed. 'Hello, Uncle Hans.'

Savielly carefuly stepped back into the pantry, leaving the door slightly ajar. From the recesses of the little room he could see and hear, without being noticed. So he watched the German colonel lift the little girl from the ground and hug her to his grey uniform jacket while she squealed happily.

'Now is my day complete,' Hans Riedeler said. 'Is she not a most adorable child, Joachim? They are all, adorable children.'

Stephanie peered over his shoulder at the stranger. Now her smile was nervous. No German officer, and no German soldier, had even been less than polite to Stephanie Janska, and the fact that they were the conquerors and she and her family the conquered, had never seemed of any importance: she did not even understand what the word conquest meant. But she did know that black uniforms were to be feared, because she had heard the servants, such as Savielly, whisper it. And this man had a little skull on his cap badge. She wondered if he was a pirate.

'This is Uncle Joachim,' Riedeler explained, setting Stephanie down.

'Hello, Stephanie,' said the man in black. But he was less interested in the little girl than in the high-ceilinged, walnut-panelled hallway, the Persian carpet on the floor, the brass horse furniture which decorated the walls, and the carved balustrade on the curved staircase. 'A Pole possesses all of this?'

'He has been of great value to us,' Riedeler said. 'Great value.'

Stephanie continued to smile from one to the other, although she was looking bewildered at the conversation.

'Is your daddy in?'

'No. But Mummy is.'

'Stephanie!' came the voice from the head of the stairs. Mummy was at this moment descending. 'Who is it?'

'Uncle Hans Riedeler, Mummy. And Uncle Joachim.'

Elizabeth Janska turned the corner and stood on the landing, the smile fading from her face as she took in the black uniform. She was a tall, regal woman in her middle thirties, with a good figure, apparently unaffected by being four times a mother, and with silky yellow hair to soften her strong, handsome features. Stephanie often wished she had Mummy's hair, but only Anna had been so fortunate. Although Stephanie did have Mummy's eyes, large and blue. Dreamer's eyes, Beth called them. But Beth was always saying things like that.

'Frau Janska,' Riedeler said, 'Elizabeth. I should like you to meet Joachim Kaltenbrunner. Joachim is the new Obersturmbannfuehrer of the SS here in Warsaw.'

Elizabeth Janska resumed her slow walk down the stairs, her features once again composed into a smile. 'It is my pleasure,' she said. 'Josef will soon be home. Why don't you gentlemen come into the conservatory, and we will see how close to real coffee we can get. Run along, Stephanie. Tell Beth she can bring you all in to say hello in half an hour.'

Stephanie hesitated, then obeyed, bouncing along the corridor to the playroom, where the children were supposed to spend their Sunday afternoons, and where they were now all gathered, peeping through the doorway.

'Isn't that black uniform wonderful?' Tony asked. 'And the death's head. I'm going to join the SS when I grow up.' Tony was ten years old, and like Stephanie, could not remember a time when Warsaw, all of Poland, had not been ruled by the Nazis. He thought they were the best thing that had ever happened to Poland, quite apart from the obvious fact that they were keeping the Russians from taking over the whole country. He was tall for his age, and lean, and already practised the goose step in front of his bedroom mirror, while he could click his heels with a deafening thud.

'If they'd have you,' Anna said scornfully. 'You have to be tough to get into the SS. And handsome,' she added dreamily, peering after Kaltenbrunner as Mummy escorted the two officers through the door to the conservatory. With her mother's magnificent blonde hair, and the handsome Janski features already taking shape, Anna, even at twelve, was a very pretty girl. And she was the biggest dreamer of all, Stephanie thought, even if she seemed to dream only of men.

'They'll have me. Of course they'll have me,' Tony declared. 'I'm Antoni Janski. They'll want me, won't they, Beth?'

'If you're unlucky, they might want you,' Beth Janska said, and returned to her book.

'Bless me, Father, for I have sinned.'

Father Simon made no reply. He had to suffer Beth Janska's confessions at least twice a week. He thought it a great pity that a pretty girl like Beth, who looked older than her fourteen years and already had the figure of a young woman, should have such a sombre view of life. But then, the War had driven her to such an early maturity, in both ways, perhaps. He could only try to help her survive these trying times as resiliently as possible.

'Yesterday I ate roast pork,' Beth said. 'With my mother and father and my brother and sisters. I overate. We all overate. And when I went out for a walk, afterwards, there was a boy picking through our dust-bins. He was starving, Father.'

'Did you have any food with you?' Father Simon asked.

'No, Father.'

'Then you could not give him any. Go on.'

'On Monday I rode my pony, with my brother and sisters riding theirs. It was raining, Father, but in our habits we were quite dry. We were happy, and we laughed. But when we left the paddock, there were children standing there, barefoot and shivering in the rain.'

'Go on,' Father Simon said.

'On Tuesday my mother bought all four of us new shoes, Father. But again on our way home we passed children who were barefoot on the street in the rain.'

Father Simon sighed.

'And on Sunday afternoon, I sat on the knee of Colonel Riedeler. I am ashamed of these things, Father.'

'Were your father and mother present when you sat on the Colonel's knee, Elizabeth?'

'Oh, yes, Father. They were both there.'

'Then we may conclude that you did so with their permission. Can you tell me why Colonel Riedeler visited your parents?'

'He often comes to see Father, Father. But this time, he wished to introduce Obersturmbannfuehrer Kaltenbrunner.'

'Indeed.' Father Simon's tone suddenly lost its paternal boredom, and became quite animated.

'They talked business for a while, and then we were called in to meet them,' Beth explained.

'Do you have any idea what business your father was discussing with these gentlemen?'

'No, Father. Is it important?'

'Hopefully, not to you, my child. This Kaltenbrunner, what is he like?'

'I hate him,' Beth said. 'I hate all the Germans.'

'I know, my child,' Father Simon said. 'But that is an

16

opinion you will voice only here in the confessional. Now, take your brother and sisters home.'

'But Father, I have sinned . . .'

'No, Beth, *you* have not sinned. It is not necessarily a sin to be more fortunate than other people, only to have come upon that fortune wrongly or illegally. *You* are innocent of those things. And because you worry so much about your good fortune, you have already done penance.' He reached round the confessional screen to to squeeze her hand. 'Now go home.'

Beth hesitated, then got up and left the booth. Anna, Tony and Stephanie waited for her, all very smartly dressed in their smocks and stockings, their new shoes, and all very impatient.

'Whatever do you do, so long in there?' Anna demanded.

'She has to confess all her wicked thoughts,' Tony explained.

'What are wicked thoughts?' Stephanie asked anxiously.

'Thoughts about men, stupid.'

'Oh. Is it wicked to think about men?'

'That depends on what you think, stupid,' Anna told her.

'I don't think about men at all,' Stephanie confessed sadly.

'Come along,' Beth snapped, and led them on to the street. Although it was six o'clock, the late July evening was still bright and would remain so for several hours, despite the constant rumble of thunder in the east. At least, the unceasing noise was officially called thunder, but Beth, and everyone else who thought about it, knew it was really gunfire, just as the planes which flew overhead nowadays were Russian reconnaissance machines, probing ahead of their armies as the Germans were forced steadily backwards from their once almost limitless conquests. What would happen when the Russians got here? That was a question no one seemed prepared to consider.

The street itself was almost empty. There were no motor cars, and only the occasional bicycle. And there was a great deal of rubble. It has become softened over the years. Grass sprouted from torn up paving stones through which they picked their way, and there were even small trees poking upwards from the ruins of the house across the way. Beth, who was fourteen, could remember the bombers as if they had come yesterday. They had all been herded into the cellar, and little three-year-old Stephanie had screamed and screamed. Yet oddly, she did not seem to remember it at all. Neither did Tony, very clearly. And if Anna, who had been seven in 1939, certainly remembered, she seemed to possess an oddly selective memory, and could shut out unpleasant events at will.

Of course, they really did not have all that much to remember. The noise, heard from the cellar, could have been a very severe thunder storm. Only a couple of the bombers had actually dropped their deadly loads on Wrakinow, a suburb several miles from the city centre. Only the street by the church had been badly hit; the Janski house had lost nothing more than a few panes of glass. Then, for several weeks, everything had been confusion, with Mother wanting to pack up and join the streams of refugees fleeing to the south and east, and Father refusing, insisting that to do that would be to lose everything, and that the Germans wouldn't be so bad to deal with, certainly far better than the Russians.

Mother had then wanted to lock the children in the secret chamber behind the upstairs fireplace in the spare bedroom, built by Father's grandfather to conceal his friends who had rebelled against their Russian overlords – Poland had then been a province of Russia – and had been on the run. Mother supposed this had to be 1863 all over again. But Father had laughed at her and told her these were Germans, not Russians, and that they were going to be here for a very long time; the children could not live in the secret chamber for the rest of their lives.

18

Father had had his way. Father had always had his way. Tall, and dark, and handsome, his brown hair neatly brushed back from his forehead, his big features always relaxed and confident, he always knew what was best. Beth was proud that she and Tony and Stephanie all took after him in looks – save for Stephanie's blue eyes – and she at the least, she was sure, in strength of character. Only Anna was entirely Mother's daughter, with her china doll prettiness and softly yielding personality. And the ability, apparently, to forget. Certainly Mother seemed to have fogotten the bombs, had obeyed Father in welcoming the Germans as friends, even if she had had to abandon her Polish friends to do so.

Beth had stood with her at the window, both to watch the untidy, dirty, crushed looking members of the defeated Polish army being marched away, and to watch the smart, confident, superbly fit and equipped young men who were the new German soldiers come marching in. Father had been contemptuous of the Polish army, which had disturbed and frightened her, but of course, Father always new best, and he had always said the antiquated Polish military system could never stand up to a modern war.

Father had always been against the 'colonels', the military junta which had ruled Poland since the death of the great Marshall Pilsudski several years before, although of course he had never dared say so except in the privacy of his own home – those who openly opposed the government took the risk of being arrested and beaten up by the police. Had he felt any change, except for the Russians, would have to be for the better. No doubt he had been right, but she had felt so sorry for the poor young men being taken away to captivity. Not one of them had ever come back again.

But Father had prospered. As had his family. And Poland? Beth could remember visiting Warsaw, a month after the surrender, and gazing at the ruined buildings, the great craters in the streets, the still shattered water mains and the dangling electricity cables. Could such destruction be good for Poland? Father had said, yes, because it would enable the city to be rebuilt, bigger and better and more modern. But that had never been done.

When she had stood on the road above Ujawdowskie, where the roses had always clustered on the gently sloping hillside in great banks, red and then white and then red again, Poland's colours, all the way down to the old royal palace, and seen nothing but a trampled mess, she had burst into tears.

Then there had been the rumours, and the deportations. It was said every Polish intellectual was being sent to a labour camp, and certainly her schoolmistresses had all disappeared and the school closed. For several weeks she had remained at home. Then, at the beginning of 1940, she had gone to a new school, one containing mainly German children and teachers. Father had arranged it. Only one or two of her old schoolmates had been there; the others had simply been moved out of Wrakinow, with their parents, and their houses commandeered by the Germans – no one knew where they had actually been sent, not even Father. But did that mean Father was not considered an intellectual? He had always seemed the most learned and intelligent of men to her. Or did it mean, as he said, that the Germans were merely cleaning Poland of all its weakening elements?

Anna, Tony and Stephanie had followed her to the school as they grew older. They had accepted that as natural and right. It did not seem to bother them that they were surrounded by half-starved Poles, their own people. Stephanie, of course, was too young to understand anything. She thought all the cities in the world were half rubble, and contained people who starved. Perhaps that was the most frightening thing of all, Beth thought: that Europe was becoming more and more filled with little Stephanies.

But Tony, and certainly Anna, should know better.

Although even if they did they would hardly know the worst. Beth had evesdropped on Mother and Father talking about what had happened in the Warsaw ghetto the previous year, when the Jews, finally wearying of constantly being deported to labour camps, had risen in revolt and been exterminated by the SS. By 'Uncle Joachim's' predecessor. From what Father had said, it had been quite horrible; Mother had been weeping. Yet here the four of them were, walking down the street, waving to the off-duty German soldiers they saw on the other side, without a care in the world.

And Father Simon said she had nothing to confess.

They were home, and Tony, Anna and Stephanie were chasing each other up the garden path, shouting and screaming. The Janski house was situated in a large block of elegantly appointed middle-class residences, each of which stood in an acre of ground, surrounded by gardens filled with shrubs and flowers – although since 1939 Father had replanted all the flower beds with potatoes and onions and cabbages – and by trees, elms and beeches. Wrakinow was a beautiful, quiet place. But during the five years since the German occupation it had become more and more strange. The Janskis' house had always been the largest in the neighbourhood, because Father had inherited a very successful law practice in Warsaw from Grandfather. But now it was the only house in the neighbourhood still inhabited by a Polish family; their neighbours had all left and their houses taken over by the Germans as living quarters for their officers and their wives.

Something else to feel guilty about, Beth thought, as she followed the others, even if Father had assured her all the people from Wrakinow had been sent to much pleasanter places down in the south.

She saw Savielly the butler watching her from the pantry window. Savielly was always watching, silently. Beth suspected that he felt just the same as she did about the Nazis, even if, like her, he was happy to be able to live in their midst in comfort and security. But

21

as Father Simon had reminded her, those were not thoughts to be shared, except in the secrecy of the confessional.

The children played croquet noisily. Beth and Stephanie partnered each other against Anna and Tony, and as usual were several hoops ahead; if Stephanie was erratic, Beth was very good, and neither Anna nor Tony could match her single-minded concentration. When Beth set out to do something, she always succeeded.

The lawn was situated behind the house, surrounded by huge trees growing out of a thick hedge which effectively shut out the rest of the world. It was a place of quiet beauty, the way Wrakinow had been years ago, but of sadness, too, at least to Beth. She could remember playing croquet here when she was Stephanie's age, with Mother and Father and various friends, while Jumbo the Alsation sunned himself under the trees. Now Jumbo was gone; Father had been 'invited' to make a present of him to the Gestapo. And the friends were gone, too; the only people who came to drinks or dinner at the Janski house now were German officers, and they didn't play croquet.

Presumably, those friend who had been sent away because the Germans didn't want them in Wrakinow were no longer friends. But were they also now enemies? If sad, that had not seemed important, down to about a year ago. Down to a year ago the Germans had clearly been in Poland to stay, and so were the people to be friendly with. But during the last few months there had been an air of insecurity, even amongst the Germans. And during the last few weeks, there had been that steadily increasing rumble from the East. Father had become more and more agitated.

Strangely, Mother had become less agitated at the sound of the Russian guns. During these last weeks she had achieved an air of calm contentment Beth had never known in her before. She wished she could ask her about it, but Mother was not an intimate sort of person, the way Father was. She kept her children, even her eldest daughter, at arm's length, left the details of growing up to Nanny, who had been around ever since Beth could remember. She could ask Nanny things, like what was going to happen to them if the Russians did capture Warsaw, but Nanny always said, 'Don't worry about it. Your father will know what to do.' Nanny worshipped Father, which was more, Beth was sure, than Mother did.

'You wretch!' Stephanie shouted at Tony. 'You kicked my ball. Beth, Tony kicked my ball away from the hoop.'

'I did not,' Tony protested.

'I think he's improved your lie,' Anna remarked.

'He hasn't. He kicked my ball away from the hoop. Mummy,' she shouted. 'Tony kicked my ball away from the hoop.'

Beth had not noticed her mother leave the conservatory doorway. Now she gazed at her in surprise. It was just after five o'clock on the first of August, and Mother was usually in the process of dressing for the evening at this time. But this afternoon she was wearing trousers, which Mother never did except for picnics; not only that but her hair was dishevelled, and her face flushed and devoid of make-up. 'Hurry, children,' she said. 'Come with me.'

'But Tony kicked my ball,' Stephanie insisted.

'You have to stop your game now, anyway,' Mother told her, and took her hand to lead her back to the house. 'Hurry, now.'

'I'll just put the things away,' Beth said.

'There isn't time for that,' Mother said over her shoulder. 'Do hurry.'

Beth gazed at her in renewed surprise. Mother was usually the tidiest of people, who insisted any game be entirely packed away when it was finished.

'Where are we going?' Anna panted, running behind them.

23

'To the cellars. You must spend the next few days in the cellars,' Mother told her. 'I've taken your things down.'

Beth, also hurrying behind them, stopped to look up at the sky. Bombers. It had to be bombers. Russian bombers? But the sky was clear, without a cloud in sight. It was a beautiful afternoon.

Then, as they reached the house, she heard a curious pop-pop-pop sound in the distance. Her heart skipped a beat, because it was a sound she had heard before, in 1939, just before Warsaw had surrendered.

'Balloons,' Stephanie shouted. 'Is there to be a party?'

'Yes,' Mother said. 'Later.' She took Stephanie into the hall, and abruptly halted, as they all did. Beth, bringing up the rear, looked at Savielly in consternation. Savielly had taken off his jacket – she had never seen him without his jacket before, even on the warmest day – and he carried a revolver, tucked into the waistband of his trousers beside his braces. Could it really be Savielly? Even his face seemed different.

But, even more surprisingly, there were two other men in the hall, also in their shirt sleeves, and they carried rifles slung on their shoulders, together with cartridge belts and the little sticks which Beth knew were grenades. Like the rifles and ammunition, they must have been stolen from the Germans, too. Beth had never seen them before, and she looked at her mother to see if Mother knew them, but Mother gave no indication at all.

'Quickly,' she said, ignoring the strangers. 'Down you go.'

'But what about supper?' Stephanie asked.

'I'll bring it down to you,' Mother promised. 'Oh, damnation.'

It was the first time Beth had ever heard Mother swear. She turned her head to look up the stairs, as Mother was doing, and saw Nanny coming down. The strangest Nanny she had ever seen, her hair loosened and untidy, her dress torn, and her normally plump, jolly face flushed and angry – and afraid. Behind her followed two more strange young men, roughly dressed and carrying guns. When Nanny hesitated on seeing the children, one of the men gave her a push, and she stumbled down the last few steps. Beth had to catch her to stop her from falling.

'Nanny? Are you all right?' she asked

'Miss Beth,' Nanny gasped. 'Help me. They mean to kill me.'

Beth stared at her, as did the other children. Nothing anyone was saying or doing this afternoon seemed to make any sense.

'Now really, Nanny, don't be absurd,' Mother said sharply. 'Just do as you are told and you will be quite all right.'

'You,' Nanny said, looking at Mother. 'You planned this. You will suffer. Oh, when the Germans ...'

'Be quiet,' Mother snapped. 'Oh, please get her out of here, quickly.'

The two men pushed Nanny towards the front door. 'And keep your mouth shut,' one of them warned.

But Nanny turned as she reached the doorway. 'Remember,' she said to Beth. 'They are going to murder me.'

One of the men hit her in the stomach.

'Oh, Nanny!' Beth shouted, and ran forward. Savielly caught her arm, and she turned and struck at him; Savielly had never touched her before.

'Beth!' Mother snapped.

Nanny had fallen to her knees, gasping, while the two men dragged her up again. Anna started to cry,

'You let me go,' Beth shouted at Savielly.

'Then do as your mummy says,' Savielly said, not calling her Miss Beth, as he usually did, and pushing her towards the cellar door.

'Mother!' Beth protested.

'Savielly, please,' Mother said.

'Get them downstairs,' Savielly commanded. 'This is no place for children.'

'Come along girls,' Mother said. 'Come along, Tony. Please do as you are told.'

Mother, obeying Savielly! The world seemed to be standing on its head. But Nanny had been dragged out of the front door, and there was clearly nothing to be done until Father came home. Beth followed the others down the steps into the cellar, where, in the big empty room next to the wine store, four beds had been arranged, made up with their own pillows and blankets and furry toys.

'Oh, goodie, Alice,' Stephanie cried, and threw herself on top of her favourite doll.

'Why did that man hit Nanny?' Anna asked.

Mother sighed. 'I'm afraid Nanny is really a very bad woman.'

Tony scratched his head. 'Nanny?'

'Yes,' Mother said. 'I've only just found out, and then . . . I had to get those men to help me get her out of the house.'

'But she said they were going to kill her.'

'That was nonsense. Just Nanny talking. Now I have got a huge number of things to do, so you will have to stay down here by yourselves. Beth . . . I want you and the others to stay here until I come for you. Please understand me, Beth. No one is to leave this room until I come for you.'

'What about supper?' Stephanie asked again.

'You'll get supper,' Mother promised again. 'Do you understand me, Beth?'

Beth suddenly wondered if she hated her mother as well as the Germans; certainly she was behaving in a hateful manner. And taking orders from Savielly . . .

'When will Father be home?' she asked.

Mother gave another little sigh. 'I don't know. I don't know if . . .' she obviously thought better about what she was going to say.

'Are the Russians coming?' Beth asked.

'Yes,' Mother said. 'Yes, the Russians are coming. Now I must go.'

Beth followed her to the stairs. 'Does Father know that Nanny is a very bad woman?'

Mother gave her an odd look. 'I'll tell him, when he comes home,' she said, and hurried up the stairs, closing the door at the top.

'What will happen when the Russians get here?' Anna asked.

'Mother seems to think it'll be a good thing,' Tony remarked.

'It'll be ghastly,' Beth said. 'Don't even think of it. Oh, I wish Father were home.'

'I'm hungry,' Stephanie announced. 'I wish Mother would bring supper down. And if you hadn't kicked my ball, Tony, we'd have walloped you.'

'Oh, shut up,' Tony snapped.

The electric lights went off.

Anna and Stephanie screamed, but Beth knew where the candles were, and soon had them alight and glowing. 'It's just a power failure,' she said reassuringly. 'It won't be long.'

She was wrong. The power never did come back, and when Mother finally came down with a frugal supper, she told them they must only burn one candle at a time, or they might run out.

'Can't we buy some more?' Anna asked.

'No,' Mother said.

Once again Beth accompanied her to the stairs. However oddly Mother was behaving, until Father came home she had to be humoured. 'Please tell me what's happening, Mother?' she asked, as winningly as she could.

Elizabeth Janska hesitated. 'There's going to be a battle,' she said at last.

'Here in Wrakinow?'

'I'm afraid so.'

'Between the Germans and the Russians?'

'Yes. But first, between the Germans and the Home Army.'

'What's the Home Army?'

27

'Us. The Poles. You saw Savielly and his friends.'

'Savielly?' Beth couldn't imagine stout, portly old Savielly in an army. Killing people?

But Nanny had said his friends were going to kill her.

'And this Home Army is fighting with the Russians?' She couldn't believe that, either. Every Polish child knew that the Russians were their hereditary enemies.

'Yes,' Mother said. 'The Russians are fighting against the Germans. So they are our allies, like the English and the Americans and the French.'

The world was becoming crazier every moment. Only last week Mother had entertained three German officers and their wives to dinner.

'The Russians are just on the other side of the river,' Mother went on. 'There is a rumour they are already in Praga suburb. So we are going to seize Warsaw and hold it until they cross the river to our aid.'

'We? You belong to this Home Army?'

'Yes,' Mother said fiercely. 'I have told them they can use this house as a headquarters.'

'Does Father know?'

Another hesitation. 'I don't know where your father is,' she confessed.

'But . . . aren't you worried about him?'

'We are going to fight for Wrakinow,' Mother said, ignoring her question. 'So you must keep the children down here for the next few days, and look after them.' She went up the stairs.

The children stayed in the cellar for nearly six weeks. Beth would not have believed it possible if it had not actually happened. The cellar was actually quite comfortable, having been fitted up as a servants' apartment; it was self-contained and had its own bathroom – but within twenty-four hours there was no water. She supposed she was the lucky one, in that she was allowed up at night, to take a bucket to the duck pond to get water for drinking and washing, and for flushing the toilet.

On the other hand, she could also see what was going on. It made her think of the end of the world. The house had been turned into a fortress, all the beautiful furniture, the mirrors and the pictures and the lamps, gathered in the centre of each room, and covered with the carpets. The windows had been barricaded with their shutters and boards nailed across the outside. And every room had become crowded with men and women, all armed with rifles and revolvers, some standing guard at the windows, some sleeping on the floors, others sitting against the walls and talking. They were all perfectly polite to her, but she sensed an air of hostility, no doubt because she still looked well-fed and they looked gaunt and hungry.

A machine gun had been positioned in the front hall, facing the closed door, and a radio station set up in her bedroom upstairs, constantly in use, while messengers kept arriving and hurrying away again. Several of the men in the house seemed to be in positions of authority, and it was disconcerting to see the way Mother did what she was told. She seemed to be everyone's servant. The real servants had vanished, and there was dust and dirt everywhere. The usual sweet smell of freshly cut flowers, polish, soap and lavender was gone; the house smelt like a sewer.

But at least it was still standing, where all around them was destruction. Wherever Beth looked she saw flames and smoke billowing up towards the sky. It was impossible to escape the stench of burning wood and plaster. And all the time, steadily getting closer, was the pop-pop-pop of the guns, and the deeper explosions of the shells.

'Where are the Russians?' she asked Mother at the end of the first week.

'They'll soon be here,' Mother said.

But Beth felt she no longer believed it. Just as she no longer believed this was really Mother. All the elegance was gone, her hair and clothes were stiff with dirt and sweat, her fingernails were cracked and unpainted.

Mother had always been surrounded by beautiful scents; now she moved, like everyone else, in a cloud of body odour.

It was like the longest of nightmares. Beth wondered that the others, trapped in the darkness, listening to the noise, did not go mad. She tried to alleviate their misery by inventing a succession of games, sneaking them outside at least once a day, whenever there was a lull in the firing, for fresh air and daylight. They really were very good, and in fact were too confused to be bad. They could understand that something terrible was happening, but as nothing terrible had ever happened to them before they were still not convinced they were in any personal danger, however frightened they might be.

Stephanie behaved the best, but then she was too young to understand what was happening. Even when a shell landed in the yard, and the whole house shook, while the chimney pots came crashing down and the cellar wall cracked and several wine bottles fell out of the rack and shattered to cover the floor with sticky red liquid, Stephanie thought it was all part of some mammoth if terrifying adventure, and busied herself with reasuring Alice, her doll.

Tony just sat and shivered most of the time; however much he dreamed of being a soldier, this was too close for comfort. He had his books and most of his toys, including his lead soldiers, but however hard Beth tried, he didn't seem able to concentrate on anything. He kept asking, 'Where's Father? Why doesn't Father come?' As if Father's coming would put an end to all this.

Beth didn't know what to tell him. She had a terrible feeling that Father was dead, and that Mother knew but was afraid to tell her. But she refused to allow herself to accept that. Because she, too, felt that if only Father could come home, they would be all right. There could be no chance of Father ever fighting for the Russians, or regarding them as friends.

Anna took it the worst, uttering hysterical shrieks whenever the house shook. But Anna had the severest problems, because in the cellar she started to menstruate for the first time. Fortunately, Beth had the necessary pads, but the pain caused Anna to have even more hysterics, and the presence of Tony and Stephanie was an embarrassing nuisance.

Beth felt it was a matter that Mother should take responsibility for, but when she mentioned it, Mother just looked at her vaguely and said, 'You'll have to see to it, Beth, dear,' and went on skinning the dead rabbit she was preparing for lunch. And Beth remembered that even before she had changed so alarmingly, Mother had shown no interest in such matters, and had left *her* menstrual problems strictly to Nanny.

Poor Nanny, she thought. Had she really been shot? But that was incredible. It would have meant Mother was a liar, on top of everything else.

They lost track of time, and grew progressively hungrier, as the meals became smaller and more irregular, and filthier, as the duck pond finally dried up. At least the weather was warm, often hot, even in the cellar, but the heat caused problems of its own, as they sweated profusely and even the little food they had went off so very quickly. But here again Mother was too busy to concern herself with their problems.

Beth had her diary, and at first kept it as meticulously as ever, but soon she began just to strike out the days, and then she stopped doing even that. She had no idea what day it was when Mother came running down the steps and called them to hurry up. For the previous two days she had not been down to them at all, and there had been no food for twenty-four hours. Now the noises of battle were very close, a continuous rumble punctuated by whines and heavy crashes.

'Where are we going?' Tony asked. 'To have a meal?'

'Yes.' Mother said. 'To have a meal. But we must hurry.'

31

'Can I touch your gun?' Tony asked. Mother had a rifle slung across her shoulder.

'Later. Come along.'

Stephanie grabbed Alice, and they hurried up the stairs. In the hall, they saw that part of the roof and the attic floor had been blown away, while a man was lying at the foot of the stairs, bleeding and groaning.

'Ugh,' Stephanie said. 'He's making an awful mess.'

'Don't look at him,' Mother said. 'Now, we are going to go out of the back door, and cross the garden, and run into the woods. Wait here a moment while I make sure it's safe.'

She went towards the back door, leaving them clustered by the cellar door. Suddenly down there was security. Beth looked around her. The crowds of men and women were gone, and the radio was silent. Only their odours remained, sweat and cordite, and fear. And the dying man at the foot of the stairs. Beth couldn't understand why no one, Mother, at least, was doing anything to help him. She felt she should, but he looked so dirty, and horrible.

They heard footsteps, and looked up to see a man and a girl, not much older than Beth, coming down the main staircase, carrying a machine gun between them.

'They're closing in,' the girl said, and even as she spoke there was a flurry of pop-pop-pops from outside, and a shattering sound. 'Oh, Lord,' the girl said. 'Oh, Lord. We won't make it.'

'Well, let's go,' the man said.

'What about him?' Beth asked, pointing at the dying man.

'Can't carry him. He's done, anyway.' The man gave a mirthless grin. 'Maybe he's the lucky one. You kids had better come with us.'

'Mother said to wait for her,' Beth explained.

The man shrugged. 'Suit yourself.' He and the girl lifted the machine gun to the back door.

Beth looked at Tony, then at the man, who had stopped groaning and did seem to be dead, then at Tony again.

'Let's go and find Mother,' she decided, and held Stephanie's hand. They ran to the back door, but as they reached it, they heard a barrage of shots. Beth dropped to the floor, taking Stephanie with her. Anna and Tony followed her example, Anna crying and screaming in terror.

The shooting stopped, but the children remained on the floor. The others were waiting for a lead from Beth, but she was incapable of moving. Something terrible had happened, was still happening, she was convinced of it.

The couple with the machine gun had closed the back door behind them. Now she watched it opening again, swinging back on its hinges with a tremendous crash. She gazed at German soldiers, standing there, automatic weapons waving to and fro.

Then she heard a shout, 'Don't shoot my children!'

It was Father. Beth rose to her knees with a scream of joy, and a moment later was in his arms, with the others.

'Oh, Father,' Tony sobbed. 'We have missed you so.'

'Have you found Mother?' Beth asked.

Josef Janski's handsome face was sad. 'Your mother . . . Beth, Mummy is dead.'

'Dead?' She stepped away from him. 'But . . . she was here, just fifteen minutes ago.' She ran to the door.

'Don't go outside,' Father shouted. 'Stop her.'

The German soldiers tried to catch her, but she wriggled through their grasp, and reached the doorway. At the foot of the shallow steps lay the man and the girl, curiously humped over their machine gun and surrounded by a vast pool of blood. A little further off Mother lay on the path. Blood was streaming from her body, already coagulating. Her rifle was still slung on her shoulder.

THE SECOND CHRONICLE

November 1984

'Bob! Bob Meyer!' Danilo Sobieski was a head shorter, but more heavily built; in his warm topcoat, scarf and slouch hat he looked enormous, his big, beaked features peering out at the world in apparent perpetual disapproval. But his eyes were smiling today. 'My God, but it is good to see you after all these years.'

The two men embraced, while the train behind them pulled away from the platform, and the snow drifted down to settle on their hats and coats; Warsaw Central is largely exposed to the elements. 'It is good to be back,' Meyer said.

'I have a taxi waiting,' Sobieski said, and hurried him through the barrier, carrying his suitcase for him. The two men were roughly the same age, had spent their childhoods as brothers. 'Sophie will be so pleased to see you, at last. She has heard so much about you, she is very excited. And the kids . . . you have never married?'

'No,' Meyer said.

Sobieski gave him a quick glance as he held the door of the taxi for him. He followed, settling himself into the warm interior. 'You have been too busy.'

'Yes,' Meyer said. 'Did you manage to arrange an interview for me with Dubrowski?'

'Oh, indeed. Our government . . .' he grinned. 'Even our government, Bob, is interested, if you have any information on Josef Janski.'

'Did you know him?'

Sobieski shook his head. 'He left Warsaw when I, when we, were just boys. But I heard of him after the War.'

'Do you have any idea what happened to him?'

Sobieski shrugged. 'You will have to ask Colonel Dubrowski. You are to see him tomorrow.' Again he glanced at his friend. 'I was under the impression that you knew what had happened to Janski.'

'I have some information and some ideas.' Meyer peered out of the window. 'Do you know, I could swear I remember all of this.'

'Of course you do. It is Warsaw.'

'Yes, but Warsaw was bombed flat.'

'Indeed, but it has been rebuilt almost exactly as it was in 1939. We have even retained some of the original pillars, where members of the Home Army were shot by the Nazis. You can see the bullet holes.'

'Rather gloomy,' Meyer observed.

'We do not intend to forget.'

'Of course,' Meyer agreed. The taxi was slowing. 'Isn't this the city centre?'

'You see, you remember everything, Bob. Over there are the bears. You will not remember them.'

'The bears?'

'They live in a pit in the centre of the square, and people gather to look down at them, and feed them. Would you like to?' Sobieski winked. 'It is good for our morale, as a people, to have at least a few bears, always caged.'

Meyer glanced at him. He knew that his old friend had decided to make the best of his situation, had not only joined the Communist Party but was an official in the very government he was poking fun at. Which was why he had been able to set up the interview with Colonel Dubrowski. 'But there are always more bears on the outside,' he remarked.

Sobieski nodded. 'It is not something we talk about. Look, Ujawdowskie.'

Meyer gazed at the red and white roses, filling the embankment as they had done before the War. 'It is good that some things never change,' he said.

Sobieski's face was sombre. 'All things change, Bob. Trying to replace them as they were once is a waste of time. After lunch, I will take you to see my father's grave. He would dearly have liked to have seen you one last time before he died.'

Meyer nodded. 'I know. I wish I had been able to come back before now. I feel guilty about that.'

'But you were always too busy chasing Nazis,' Sobieski observed.

Meyer looked at him. 'They murdered my parents, Dan. Helped by people like Josef Janski. Yes, I have always been too busy.'

'And when you find Janski, supposing you ever do, you will kill him?'

'I am not the executioner, Dan. I will arrange for him to be returned to Israel for trial.'

'And if he refuses to go?'

Meyer's eyes became hooded. 'That would be a different matter.'

'And what of his family? If they tried to protect him?'

'For them, too, if would be a different matter,' Meyer said grimly. 'If Janski is alive, I will get him, no matter who stands in the way. They can only get hurt.'

CHAPTER 2

Warsaw 1945

By the time they got back from the funeral, the German soldiers had removed the dead man from the foot of the stairs, much to the children's relief. The bodies of the young couple had gone from the yard, as well. Only their blood remained, scattered over the grass, while the man's blood stained the parquet floor of the front hall. But then, Mother's blood also mingled with the grass outside the back door.

Beth had been more distressed by the funeral than the fact of her mother's death; by the haste and starkness and brutality of the whole affair. She had only been to one previous funeral, that of her grandfather back in 1938. She remembered it vividly: the huge black hearse, the horses, the motor cars following behind, the weeping mourners – Mother among them – the church service and the eulogy, and the masses of flowers. And finally, the graveside ceremony.

Mother's funeral had been quite different. It had taken place that very afternoon, and there had not even been the plainest coffin, just a canvas shroud. Father and a man he had hired had placed the corpse on a hand cart and pushed it along the street to the cemetery. The four children had been the only mourners, and they had not been dressed in their best, only what they had been wearing for the previous six weeks. The priest had not even been Father Simon, but some man she had never seen before. He said no more than a perfunctory prayer as the body was lowered, because he was in a hurry – there were several other groups waiting to bury their relatives, and he was the only priest.

Worst of all were the German soldiers who surrounded the graves, armed with automatic weapons, staring at the families of the deceased.

'It was sad. More than sad. It was criminal.' Father

sat on the settee he had dragged from the furniture piled in the centre of the drawing room, Stephanie on his lap, Anna and Beth cradled in his arms, while Tony sat at his feet. 'The Home Army was composed of nothing but criminals. And now . . .' he rubbed tears from his eyes, 'now they have murdered my Elizabeth.'

'*They* killed her?' Beth asked. She was the only one of the four to have seen the body, before the man Father had hired had stitched up the canvas shroud. It was a sight she would never forget, even if she could not really relate that bullet-shattered corpse in the filthy trousers and blouse to the mother she had once known and loved. That mother had disappeared the afternoon this whole dreadful business had begun.

'No, the Germans actually shot her,' Father said. 'But what were they to do? They knew our house was being used as a headquarters for the Home Army, and when they attacked it they saw an armed woman leaving by the back door. They called on her to stop and surrender, and she didn't . . .' He wiped his eyes again. 'It was not their fault. It was the fault of the swine who made her join them. I hope they are all hanged. They all *will* be hanged, I know.'

Beth couldn't remember any evidence of Mother having been forced to join the Home Army, quite the reverse; she had sounded proud and defiant when she had claimed to be one of them. Besides, had she really been a prisoner they would hardly have given her a rifle. But she decided not to tell Father that; it would only distress him more.

'They killed Nanny, too,' Tony said.

'Did they?' Father asked. 'Oh, the swines. But that is not all they did. They murdered Frau Behting from next door. They just walked in there and shot her as she stepped out of her bath. Just because she was a German. Oh, they were the most terrible animals. And to think you were in their power for six weeks. I shall never sleep again.'

'They've made such a mess of the house, too,' Anna

complained. 'Are the workmen going to come and put it right?'

'No,' Father said. 'We are going to have to do that ourselves.'

'Where were you all the weeks we were in here?' Stephanie asked.

Beth held her breath. That was the question she had wanted to ask all afternoon, and hadn't dared.

'Trying to get back here to you,' Father explained. 'But the Home Army were shooting everybody who wasn't one of them.'

'You were with the Germans,' Tony said.

'Of course. The Germans are our friends. Now, we must plan what we are going to do about the house.'

'But aren't the Russians coming?' Beth asked. There didn't seem much point in repairing the house if it was going to be knocked down by the Russians. 'Mother said they were already in Praga, just the other side of the river.' But that had been six weeks ago. Oh, she wished she could understand, or that someone would explain it to her.

'The Russians will never get across the Vistula,' Father declared. 'This is one battle they are going to lose. We shall beat them now just as we stopped them in 1920. Now, before we start work, are you hungry?'

'Oh, Father,' Stephanie cried. 'I am so hungry I could eat ... Tony.'

'You just try,' Tony said. 'I'd eat you first.'

'Well,' Father said. 'You won't have to eat each other. Wait until you see what I have in that bag.'

There was an enormous amount of work to be done, and as Father had warned, they had to do it all themselves. To Beth's surprise, although it was time for the autumn term at school, they were kept at home; the school had closed down. All of Warsaw had closed down. The city had been wrecked all over again by the Germans rooting out the last pocket of Home Army resistance. It still smouldered in places, while there

39

were fewer people than ever on the street, except for German soldiers. Father told them not to leave the garden, but one day while he was out Beth went to the church. She hadn't been to mass or confession for seven weeks, and she wanted to ask Father Simon why he had not said the prayers over Mother's body. Father Simon, she thought, might even be able to tell her what had really happened.

But the church was wrecked. She stood and stared at the roofless walls, the shattered windows, the over-turned pews. Even the bombers in 1939 had not des-troyed the church; Mother had told them the church had been protected by God. But God must have been looking the other way when the Home Army had used it for a command post.

How far the other way she discovered when she went closer and stood in the shattered doorway. There were one or two cross timbers still in place, and from one of them Father Simon hung, swaying gently to and fro. It was clear he had been there for some time. Beth turned and ran as fast as she could, until she collapsed from sheer exhaustion, panting and nauseated. Father Simon would never hear her confession again. Nor would he explain to her what had truly happened. Instead his death was just one more ghastly mystery: who had hanged him, the Germans or the Home Army?

The streets were reduced to rubble, the paving stones having been torn up for barricades, and the lids on the manholes to the sewers all torn off. Father had said some of the Home Army 'criminals' had tried to escape from Warsaw by using the sewers, and had been forced to surrender by tear gas dropped down the manholes. Beth could still smell the gas when she looked down one of the manholes. It brought tears to her eyes. But the tears were already there. If only she could understand what was really happening, who was right and who was wrong.

She did not tell the others about Father Simon. They were content to put their faith entirely in Father.

He had come back to rescue them, had brought them food, and with his reappearance the fighting had stopped, at least in Wrakinow. He could not work miracles, such as restoring the electricity or the water, but every morning with Beth and Tony he went down to the stream which ran through the woods, half a mile behind the house, to fill pails so they could at least wash and drink.

On these visits to the stream they often saw other people, also drawing water, and several of them Beth even recognised. But they looked the other way whenever she spoke to them.

'Bah, they're all secret Home Army supporters,' Father said contemptuously. 'They actually want the Russians to come. They can't understand how bad that would be.'

Beth didn't altogether follow his reasoning. She didn't see what the Russians could do that would be worse than destroying the city and shooting everyone who opposed them – and perhaps hanging a priest. But it was just heavenly having Father back to reassure them and look after them. She didn't have to agree with everything he said.

It was great fun working with him at restoring the house, though it was hard work. He found some tarpaulin and patched the hole in the roof, letting Tony climb the ladder behind him, much to his delight – Mother had never let him climb ladders. Father put Beth in charge of the interior, telling her that she was the lady of the house now. That made her feel terribly important, and she set Anna and Stephanie to work just as she remembered Mother telling the maids what to do, cleaning and dusting and sweeping. They grumbled, but obeyed. It came naturally, after six weeks in the cellar, to obey Beth.

Gradually they replaced the furniture in its proper places so that the first two floors looked reasonable. There was nothing they could do about the servants' attic, which was full of rubble from where the shell had struck. And it was impossible to get any of the surfaces really clean, any more than they could get themselves really clean, because of the water shortage. But they polished away as best they could.

Father also told Beth that she could do what she liked with Mother's things. Beth didn't relish the idea – it seemed rather ghoulish. But Anna and Stephanie loved picking through the silk underwear and the fur wraps, and wearing them about the house, while Beth appropriated the fox fur jacket.

She continued to be surprised at the way the others had surmounted the tragedy of Mother's death. She felt sure none of them had understood the way Mother had changed during, or perhaps before, those terrible six weeks. But Mother had never been emotionally close to her children, the way Father always had. Thus Beth supposed they had steadily grown apart. Only Anna really seemed to feel an inordinate amount of grief. Tony was too self-centred, and Stephanie too full of bubbling good humour to feel grief for any length of time. Or to feel hatred for those who had been responsible, whether they had been Germans, acting instinctively, or those members of the Home Army who had forced Mother to join them. But had they forced Mother to join them? Beth felt the answer to that question was very important, but she didn't know how she would ever find out the truth.

Even Anna's grief, she was sure, was less about Mother's death than about everything that was happening, to them.

The days began to draw in, and the nights became cold. There was no fuel for fires, and the hole in the roof, even shrouded in canvas, could keep out neither the rain nor the chill. Sometimes, when Father was out, as he often was, all four of them would crawl into the secret chamber behind the first floor chimney breast and pretend to be hiding from the Russians, like Grandfather's friends so long ago, huddling together for warmth. They put on all the clothing they could find, two sweaters as well as their school blazers, and two pairs of thick stockings, on top of which Beth added the fox fur jacket and the others whatever else they could find, so that for all their constant hunger they looked terribly overweight. To this accumulation they soon even added their overcoats. Beth was afraid Father would comment, and perhaps make them take some of the extra clothing off, but he never did, perhaps because he seldom took off his overcoat any more, either.

As usual, when he came home from his forays, he had food with him, even if it was tasteless, uninteresting stuff, black bread and sausage which contained almost no meat and at which they would once have turned up their noses. But the stodge at least filled their stomachs. And usually Father was full of good cheer, and sometimes even had a bottle of wine or spirits with him. He would offer Beth and Anna a drink, and to Beth's concern Anna often took it; she did not like either the taste or the light-headedness which resulted.

But as November drew to a close, Father became less good humoured and confident. Now the sound of the guns was very close, just beyond the river, and every day Russian planes flew overhead. They never bombed Wrakinow, or even Warsaw; no doubt they could see that there was nothing there left worth bombing. But no one could doubt that they were in complete command of the skies. The Luftwaffe, which had destroyed Poland five years before, had just disappeared.

Father said nothing about his fears, however, until the day Beth and Tony went into the woods and cut a branch to make a Christmas tree. He was out at the time, and by the time he came home, the branch was standing in a bucket in the front hall. The Christmas decorations had been stored in the cellar, and were undamaged, and Stephanie and Anna were having a happy time hanging tinsel and multi-coloured streamers, while Beth and Tony padded the base with cotton wool from the storeroom. Beth knew there weren't going to

43

be any presents this year, but she didn't tell the others in the hope that Father might suddenly come up with something. To her concern, however, he merely stared at the tree when he came in, brushing snow from the arms of his topcoat.

Then he said, 'This is nonsense. Beth, we must leave Warsaw.'

They stared at him. They had always lived in Warsaw. 'I will go to Kaltenbrunner,' Father said, 'and arrange transport.'

'But where will we go?' Tony asked.

'We'll go to Lódź', Anna said. 'To Aunt Katerina.' Aunt Katerina was Father's sister.

'If the Russians take Warsaw,' Father said, 'they will certainly take Lódź as well. And they are going to be in Warsaw in a few weeks at the outside.'

'You said . . .' Tony began.

'I know what I said,' Father interrupted. 'But there are just too many Russians and not enough Germans. The Germans are having to fight on two fronts – the Russians on one side and the British and the Americans on the other. We must leave here, and travel west, to the British and the Americans. I will arrange it.'

No one said anything until after he had gone out again. Then Stephanie asked, 'Are we really going to leave Warsaw, Beth?'

'Father wants to leave Poland,' Anna said bitterly.

'He's not running away, is he, Beth?' Tony asked.

'He's one man,' Beth said loyally. 'He's not even a soldier. If the Germans can't stop the Russians, how can he? He wants to take us away so the Russians won't . . .' she hesitated. Even Father had never claimed the Russians shot children. He said they did far worse things to them, especially the girls, and she had no idea what he meant. What could possibly be worse than being shot? 'So they won't send us to camps,' she said. The Germans sent people they didn't like to camps, so the Russians probably did the same.

'Won't the English and the Americans send us to camps?' Tony asked.

'Oh, no,' Beth said confidently. 'They don't have camps.'

'I don't want to go to a camp,' Stephanie wailed.

Anna began to cry.

'We're not going to a camp,' Beth shouted. 'That's what Father is arranging.'

But Father came home as angry as Beth had ever seen him. 'Not enough transport, for Poles,' he said. 'They are all packing up, like frightened rats. They are taking their mistresses and their bastards with them. But they cannot take me, Josef Janski. There has been no more loyal supporter of the Führer in all Poland. Not enough transport!'

'What will we do now?' Beth asked. She felt almost relieved.

Father put his arm round her shoulders and squeezed her against him. 'I'll just have to organise some transport of our own, that's all. Don't you worry. I'll sort it out.'

Christmas was the most miserable the children had ever known, because Father was out all day, and there were no presents, after all.

'Oh, I wish Father were here,' Tony grumbled.

'He's arranging transport for us to leave Warsaw,' Beth explained.

'I don't want to leave Warsaw,' Stephanie complained. 'I want to stay here.'

'We all want to stay here. But we are going to do what Father says,' Beth declared fiercely. 'And that's it. Now come on, let's sing a carol. I'll play.'

But the piano had been hit by a bullet during the battle, and made only odd sounds.

Father didn't come home for two days, and then arrived, unshaven and exhausted. He sat on the settee with his feet stretched in front of him while the children stood around. To Beth's dismay, she saw that he had not brought the usual loaf of bread and long sausage, and there was no food left in the house.

'When are we leaving, Father?' Tony asked.

Josef Janski opened his eyes. 'Soon,' he said. 'If we have to walk.'

Beth looked out of the window at the snow.

Father sat up. 'So I want you all to start packing,' he said. 'Just what you can carry. No toys, I'm afraid. I'll buy you new toys when we get where we're going. Just take warm clothing and toothbrushes and things like that.'

Then he went to bed and slept for twenty-four hours, while the children grew hungrier and hungrier. They were now all sleeping in one bed for warmth. They used the big double in the master bedroom, where Mother and Father used to sleep, because Father wouldn't sleep in it any more. They never took off their clothes, huddling together beneath the blankets, Beth and Anna on the outside, Tony and Stephanie cocooned in between them. And still they shivered, and their noses ran, as they all had colds. Partly, Beth knew, that was the result of the continual hunger, but their empty stomachs had become such a natural state, that even Stephanie no longer complained about it.

She started them packing, but it was a slow business. Tony and Stephanie couldn't bear the thought of being separated from their toys, despite Father's promise, and Anna wanted to take every dress she owned. Beth had to abandon most of her things to make sure there was room in her suitcase for Stephanie's clothes – Stephanie was not going to be able to walk very far carrying a suitcase.

In the New Year, Father left them again. Before going, he went out and brought back a big store of food, several sausages and loaves of bread. Then he took Beth aside and warned her that he might be gone for some time. 'It's to do with our leaving Warsaw,' he explained.

Beth believed him and kissed him, begging him to come back. But when he was gone she cried. They were all terrified. The fighting was very close. The dreaded pop-pop-pop could be heard quite clearly, and the roar

46

of artillery was constant. Occasionally misdirected shells even burst in Wrakinow, although the Janski house escaped another direct hit. Now when they went to the stream they saw no people at all, save for groups of German soldiers marching or driving on their way to new positions. Everyone else had fled.

But Father didn't come home.

'Oh, I wish he would,' Anna grumbled. 'There's only a little of that sausage left.'

I wish he would too, Beth thought. Now she really did want to leave Warsaw as rapidly as she could. She had the strangest feeling that they were the only people left alive in the world, that even the German soldiers were mere robots, carrying out orders and manoeuvres without the slightest reason. While the Russians seemed to be only guns, moving inexorably foreward.

But still Father didn't come home, and after more than a fortnight, Beth knew a terrible fear, that he might have been killed. Life without Father just could not be contemplated. Yet she was surprised, and ashamed, that that was all she actually felt. Just a fear of being left alone with her brother and her sisters to look after. No real grief at the thought that Father might be dead.

On the evening they ate the last sausage, Beth knew that he had to be dead. Of course he had been gone for six weeks in the summer, but then Wrakinow had been under siege. Now ... Wrakinow was not under siege, at least by the Germans. Wrakinow was ... she lay awake, staring into the darkness, knowing it was just before dawn, listening to the growling of hundreds of engines. From the steady breathing beside her, she gathered the others were still asleep. Carefully she pushed back the blankets and went to the window, parted the tattered curtain and looked out. There were no lights to be seen save for the constant flickering just beyond the houses, accompanied by the roar of the guns. But the street was crowded with vehicles, from huge trucks to command cars and even private automobiles, making their way through Warsaw and its suburbs to the west.

Her heart leapt. Perhaps Father would be among them. But all the voices she heard were speaking German, and if Father was there he would certainly stop for them. And it was very cold standing by the window in the pre-dawn. She went back to bed; Father would know where to find her, if he was ever coming.

She awoke with a start several hours later, to daylight, her arm being shaken by Tony.

'Beth,' he said. 'Beth! Listen, the fighting has stopped.'

Beth sat up, pushed hair from her face, frowning. It was very quiet. Of course, it was never truly quiet. There was always the rumble of gunfire in the distance. But the uproar which had dominated their lives for the past fortnight was gone.

'It's as if the whole world has died,' Anna said.

'Perhaps Father will be able to come home now,' Tony said illogically.

'Beth, what are we going to eat?' Stephanie asked, practical as ever.

Beth got out of bed, going over to the window again. The street, so crowded just a few hours before, was absolutely empty. But it was also torn and rutted by the tyre tracks, the snow scattered and discoloured. It had been no dream. And now ... the silence had ended. There were no fresh gun shots, but slowly, seeping across the January morning, there was sound, gradually increasing in volume.

'I hear automobiles,' Anna announced. 'Lots and lots of automoblies.'

'Automobiles,' Tony said scornfully. 'Those are tanks.'

Perhaps the Germans were coming back, Beth thought. Oh, how she hoped the Germans were coming back. Because if it wasn't the Germans ...

'Beth, what do we have for breakfast?' Stephanie asked again.

It wasn't the Germans. The noise was coming from the east, and suddenly Beth saw a sight she would never forget. A man stood in the middle of the street, wearing a green uniform with a brown fur cap on his head. With his topcoat and his thick boots and his gloved hands he looked totally warm and comfortable, even in the snow – and with his automatic rifle, and the grenades hanging from his belt, he looked exceedingly dangerous.

She had an overwhelming urge to run, and did so, across the room and the hall into Tony's bedroom at the back of the house. From his window she looked out over the shattered garden towards the wood. The wood promised security. But it looked so cold and desolate . . . and even as she watched, she glimpsed movement in the trees. The men in green were there, too.

The others had trailed behind her and now stood watching her anxiously.

'Beth?' Anna asked. 'What is the matter?'

For the first time in months, Beth felt warm, as an enormous surge of blood pounded through her arteries from her quickened heartbeat. Those men were Russians. The vague threat which had hung over her life, all of their lives, ever since she could remember, had finally arrived. Not only were they the hereditary enemies of all Poles, but they were the sworn enemies of all Germans, and of all Poles who might have helped Germans. And now they were in Wrakinow, all around the house. They were trapped.

She went back into the front room. The lone soldier had been joined by several others, and now some of them had gone into the garden of the house next door. A moment later she heard a crashing noise, followed by a sudden chatter of rifle fire. That house had been empty since last summer, she knew, when the Home Army had murdered Frau Behting as she had been stepping from her bath. So what were they firing at?

'Those aren't Germans.' Tony stood at her elbow.

Beth chewed her lip, listened to more crashing and banging from down the street, splintering wood and high-pitched laughter. The Russians were tearing that house apart. They would tear this house apart too, and they would shoot ... Perhaps they meant to shoot everybody they found.

'Beth ...' Anna's voice shook, and she was weeping again. 'Will those men harm us?'

'Maybe they'll feed us,' Stephanie suggested, as optimistic and hungry as ever.

'I think we should hide,' Tony said.

'Yes,' Anna agreed. 'We can hide in the secret room. Mother always said that was the thing to do. We can hide in there until they go away again.'

Father had said they couldn't hide in the secret chamber because the Germans were going to be in Warsaw a long time, and he had been right: the Germans had stayed more than five years. And the Russians were going to stay a long time, too, Beth knew. But just to stand here and wait for those men to come in ... Yet it had to be done. They had to surrender, and hope. At least, one of them had to surrender, and hope. But maybe it could be done in such a way that some of them would be safe, anyway. It was her responsibility to see that the others were safe. Father had said she was the woman of the house now, and she was determined she was never going to let them down the way Mother had. So there was no use shirking it. And if the men, after all, turned out to be friendly, then nothing would have been lost.

'Yes,' she said. 'You must all go into the secret room, and stay there for at least twenty-four hours, or until I come for you. You must promise me this.'

'But what are you going to do?' Tony asked. 'Are you going to find Father?'

'Will you bring us food?' Stephanie asked.

'Yes,' Beth promised them. 'Yes. But I may not be able to do it right away so you will have to be very brave and very patient for perhaps twenty-four hours.'

'That's an awful long time to be in that hole,' Anna complained.

50

'It may be a lot less than that,' Beth said. 'And if I don't come for you after twenty-four hours, Tony will tell you what to do.'

'Me?' Tony cried in alarm.

'You're the man of the house until Father comes home,' Beth told him. 'But I'll be back. Now hurry. What time does your watch say?'

'Mine says half past nine,' Tony said.

'That's not right. Mine says twenty past nine,' Anna said.

'Mine only says half past eight,' Stephanie said sadly. 'Maybe I forgot to wind it.'

'It's just coming up to quarter past nine,' Beth said. 'So you'll stay inside until nine o'clock tomorrow morning. Now remember, it's just a continuation of that game we were playing last week, pretending we were revolutionaries hiding from the Russians.' If only they knew, she thought. 'Now you must hurry.'

The Russian soldiers had left the house next door and were pointing at the Janski house, which was by far the biggest in the street.

Beth pushed the others into the tiny aperture and closed the spring. There was another spring on the inside, so they could let themselves out if she didn't come back. If she didn't come back! Her heartbeat had slowed, but she was clammy with sweat.

She stared at herself in Mother's full length mirror. She looked a sight. Her hair was a tangled mess and her body a shapeless mass beneath the top coat and the fox fur and the blazer and the two sweaters over her dress. She wondered if she should make herself look pretty for the Russians, but knew that was impossible – she was utterly filthy beneath all of her clothes and there was no water.

There was no time, either. Hearing the voices on the front path, she went to the stairs, and saw the four suitcases, stacked neatly side by side in the upstairs hall, waiting for Father to arrive with transport. She seized them and thrust them under the big bed, panting and sweating, then ran down the stairs to stop the soldiers from breaking down the door. She was too late. They were already attacking the door, emptying their rifles into it. Some of the bullets passed clean through the wood, and Beth didn't dare go down to the hall for fear of being hit. Then the shooting stopped, and the door shuddered as they heaved against it. A moment later it gave way, crashing to the floor.

The men stumbled inside, weapons thrust forward. Beth stared at them, incapable of movement. They were young, in their early twenties, she estimated, and had strangely Mongoloid features, reminding her of pictures she had seen of the Chinese.

They stood in a group, looking about them and then saw her. For a moment they stared at her in equal surprise, then moved forward in a rush, shouting at her. She had no idea what they were saying, or what they were going to do to her, but she knew it was going to be something unpleasant. Her nerve failed, and she turned to run back upstairs, but was seized by her hair and shoulders from behind. She stumbled back down the stairs in their midst, feeling hands pulling and prodding at her. Presumably they were searching her.

'I'm not armed,' she shouted, but they didn't seem to understand her. Her overcoat was pulled off, and then the fur and the blazer, and the fingers were plucking at her sweaters, hurting her through the thick material, while others were raising her skirt and pulling at her stockings.

'No,' she shouted, because that had to be indecent. 'No.' But the fingers probing into her chest and stomach were making her breathless.

Then there was another sound, and Beth, suddenly released, fell to the floor. She sat up straightened her dress, stared at the two men who had just entered the house. One was a private soldier, dressed like the men who had just manhandled her, but was clearly of a different race, tall and heavy and with a drooping moustache. He was laden with knapsacks and bags.

The other man was an officer. His uniform was smarter and better cut, he had badges on his collars and shoulders and sleeves, and medal ribbons on his breast, and he was armed with a revolver instead of a rifle.

He spoke to the men brusquely, as they stood to attention on either side of Beth. They sheepishly picked up the rifles they had discarded in their anxiety to get at her, and clattered up the stairs to continue their search of the premises. But as long as the others kept quiet, Beth was sure they would not be found.

And perhaps it did not matter, now that the officer had arrived. He looked about thirty, round faced with a stern but not unkindly expression. She scrambled to her feet as he turned his attention to her.

'I speak Polish,' he said unnecessarily, as he was speaking Polish. 'What is your name?'

Beth drew a long breath. 'Elizabeth Janska,' she replied adding, 'Sir.'

'Where are the owners of this house?'

'My parents,' Beth said. 'I think they are both dead.'

'Then you are an orphan. War is a terrible thing.'

Beth felt a glow of warmth. Everything was going to be all right. She opened her mouth to tell him about the others.

But the Russian officer continued speaking. 'We will requisition this house as a mess for the officers of my company. You will remain here with us. There is much work to be done.' He turned to the man beside him, spoke rapidly in Russian, then turned back to her. 'Show my orderly the kitchen, and help him prepare a meal for four. Hurry, now.'

Beth nodded and ran into the kitchen, the orderly behind her. The others could wait for a little while longer, until she had prepared the meal – they might even be invited to join in eating it. The one thing she must not do was make the officer angry with her in any way.

Then she checked herself. 'We have no food,' she said. 'No food.'

The soldier might not understand Polish, but he knew what she meant. He grinned, and from his shoulder took the various bags and haversacks. He opened them, and on the kitchen table emptied a whole ham, a leg of lamb and a heap of carrots and potatoes. Beth could not believe her eyes and her mouth began to water. It was months and months since she had seen food like that: she could have eaten the lot, raw. She was again tempted to ask him if she could call her brother and sisters, just for a nibble. But she made herself be patient, helped the man chop everything up and place the pieces in a large pot he took from another knapsack. 'But we have no fuel,' she said.

The Russian soldier next produced an iron stand, like a large trivet, which he placed outside the back door, setting the cooking pot on it. Then he looked around, grunted with satisfaction, and seized one of the kitchen chairs, breaking it into pieces with a few twists of his hands. Beth watched in consternation as he stacked the wood under the stand, and struck a match to set it alight. She was wondering what would happen if the Russians stayed more than four days – there were only four kitchen chairs.

But the smell from the pot was instantly delicious. She was glad she had waited, because there was so much food she was sure there would be lots left over for them.

She heard a voice, and turned. Another officer stood in the doorway, addressing her in Russian. She felt she should acknowledge him but curtseying seemed rather silly, so she bowed instead. The man said something else, and jerked his thumb at the hall. Obviously her presence was required. She glanced at the orderly, but he didn't seem concerned at losing his assistant as he stirred his stew.

She hurried into the hall, checking at the freezing blast of air coming in the shattered front door. The five soldiers were walking down the path, having apparently completed their search. Suddenly she was seized by the shoulder and thrust towards the stairs. She regained her balance and hurried up, her heart pounding as she wondered if after all the others had been found. She reached the first floor gallery, and stared at the master bedroom in horror. The door was open, and there were three other men in there, presumably all officers, because her Polish-speaking acquaintance was one of them. But they were all in various stages of undress; one of them was entirely naked. Beth knew what a naked man looked like; at least, she knew what Tony and Father looked like, because Father had been a sun worshipper in happier days, and the whole family, even Mother, had gone bathing in the nude on their summer holidays – but she felt this was something one should only do with family.

Far more to her concern, however, was the fact that the room was warm, because there was a roaring fire in the grate, made by breaking up two of Mother's favourite chairs and setting them alight.

'Oh,' she cried, and ran forward, pausing in distress as the flames drove her back.

The man who had brought her upstairs closed the door, and the Polish-speaking man grasped her arm and drew her away from the fire. She wanted to curse him and tell him what an awful thing he had done, but didn't dare – he had finished undressing himself.

'You,' he said. 'Take off clothes.'

She stared at him. 'Me? But ...'

'Take off clothes,' he said again. 'Or ...' he looked at the fire and gave a bellow of laughter. 'We burn you in fire.' He spoke to the other men, who also laughed, and the first naked man got off the bed. Beth gasped. If she had seen the male penis often before, she had only ever seen Tony's erected, and then only once.

'Hurry,' the spokesman said. 'You will not be cold. The fire will warm you. And if it does not, we will warm you.'

Beth didn't know what to do. It was unthinkable that she should take off her clothes in front of four strange

55

men, but she had a terrible feeling that they *would* burn her in the fire if she refused. And she was actually less afraid of undressing than of having them discover how dirty she was. But she knew she had to obey.

She tore at her clothes, pulled off the sweaters and dress, and paused at her vest. The men had been talking and laughing as they watched her.

Now the spokesman said, 'Good. Very good. You have good figure. Take off the vest.'

Beth drew a long breath. It had never occurred to her that she had a good figure. She knew she had long legs and a handsome face and luxuriant hair. But her breasts were small, although the nipples were large, and distended as she took off the vest – despite the fire, the room was still chilly.

She stooped to roll down her stockings, half turning away from them, and was seized from behind by a pair of arms which went round her waist to lift her from the floor, while a naked man came hard against her drawers. She screamed, and kicked, and the man laughed as he carried her to the bed and threw her on it. She still wore her boots, and her stockings, now collapsed around her ankles, but the men didn't seem to mind.

She hit the bed and was held there by her shoulders while her drawers were pulled down to her ankles and over her boots. She screamed again, and tried to kick, and a man caught each of her ankles. The two others took a wrist each and lifted her from the bed. She was so surprised by the suddenness of the attack that she still wasn't sure what was going to happen to her. She only knew she was at once angry and terrified and humiliated, and that her eyes were shut. She opened them again as she was carried across the room and felt the growing warmth of her skin: they were going to burn her after all.

'No,' she screamed, wriggling desperately. 'No. Please!'

The spokesman smiled at her. 'We are just going to

toast you a little,' he said, and they held her in front of
the fire, twisting her to and fro. Her flesh seemed to be
scorching, and she moaned, gasping in relief when she
was carried back to the bed and laid on it again. Then
she gasped again as a naked man sat on her chest and
thrust his member at her face. They had released her
wrists and she struck at him with her nails. Her wrists
were seized again, and she was slapped twice across the
face with such force it made her head spin. Her mouth
sagged open and the penis was thrust inside. She
thought of biting it but realised he would beat her
again, and by now other things were happening to her.
The men were holding her legs apart and one was
thrusting into her. The pain was excruciating, and
inadvertently she bit the man in her mouth. The offend-
ing flesh was withdrawn with a roar of pain, and his fist
came crashing down to send her racing away into
welcoming blackness.

Beth could only have been unconscious for a few
seconds, because when she came to the men were still
going at her, another between her legs now, one suck-
ing her nipples, and another even kissing her mouth,
the stubble of his chin scraping across her cheek. That
she hadn't bathed in weeks didn't seem to bother them
at all, mainly, she realised, because they hadn't bathed
in weeks, either. She gasped, but made herself lie still,
her head swinging and banging with pain from the blow
on her chin, her body aching from the assault, filled
with anger and humiliation and, above all, disgust.

She had no idea how long she lay there before there
was a knock on the door, and the orderly shouted
something. Instantly the men leapt off the bed, and
hurried for the door, not bothering to dress.

'You come too,' the spokesman said. 'We eat, eh?'

He had been the first between her legs. Had she had
a gun she would have shot him first. But the suggestion
of food was stronger even than her sense of outrage.
She rolled out of bed and reached for her clothes, but
he shook his head.

'You come, so,' he commanded.

She obeyed, discovering to her surprise that she still wore her boots and stockings. Shivering, she hobbled downstairs, and found that the dining room was also warm, several of the chairs having been thrust into the grate. She wanted to scream with anger. Mother had loved that furniture. Sometimes it had seemed she loved it more than her own children. But then, she remembered, these were the men Mother had wanted to come and rescue her from the Germans.

The cooking pot had been set, without a mat, on the polished mahogany table, and was already scorching the surface. Five large spoons had been provided, although no plates or bowls; each man simply dug his spoon into the appetising stew. Beth did not hesitate; afraid they would eat it all. But there was enough for several people.

The men were laughing and happy. Yet they were also bestial animals. Then what did that make her, eating with them? When one produced a bottle of clear white liquid from the knapsack he had discarded in the corner, and they each drank from the neck before offering it to her, she took a swig with the rest of them. She knew it wasn't water, but she was quite unprepared for the burning sensation which filled her mouth and throat, and then her chest and stomach, or for the way the room suddenly revolved around her. Nothing Father had ever offered her had tasted like this. Yet at the same time the day became instantly brighter, the pain in her head and between her legs seemed to lessen, and when the men burst into song, she found herself insensibly beating time with her spoon.

Was this what Father had meant when he had said the Russians would be far worse than the Germans? Of course, being assaulted and manhandled the way she had been was much worse than anything she had ever imagined – but she knew it couldn't be as bad as being shot and lying sprawled on the floor oozing blood. And now the vodka and its good cheer . . . She remembered

58

something Father had said to a guest at this very table, back in 1939 when there had been talk of the Russians allying themselves with Poland against Nazi Germany. Father had declared, 'Never. Better be beaten by the Germans than have the Russians in our country, even as allies. Believe me, my friend, the Germans will only possess our bodies; the Russians will want our souls, as well.'

Beth supposed that was what was happening to her, because after three swigs of vodka she was quite drunk, and didn't care what they did to her. This was just as well, because after the meal she was dragged back up to bed, although her Polish-speaking assailant, with much grumbling, had to put on his clothes and go out, apparently to check on the billeting of their men.

The other three went at her indiscriminately for about half an hour, rolling her to and fro to get at whichever orifice they desired, while she lay in a drunken stupor, absolutely relaxed, hardly aware of what they were doing. She even fell asleep when they did, to awake a little while later, her head pounding but her brain quite clear.

On either side of her lay a snoring man; the third was sprawled across the foot of the bed. On the street outside she could hear the sounds of engines and of voices, to indicate that the Russians were occupying Wrakinow in force, but the house itself was quiet. Cautiously she eased herself out of the bed on to the floor, staring in horror at the sight of the blood staining the inside of her thighs; they must have hurt her more than she realised. But she was not prepared to worry about herself at this moment.

She took off her boots to make less noise, but did not dress herself; if she met anyone she would say she was going to the bathroom. But she met no one, as she hurried along the upper hall to the servants' staircase, and then down to the kitchen. She froze as she heard movement, but a moment later there was a snore, and she cautiously stepped inside. The orderly lay fast asleep on the floor, and the cooking pot was on the table. She held her breath, in sudden fear that he might have eaten it all. But it was still at least a third full. Gasping with delight, she hugged the pot against herself. It was very heavy but she was a strong girl, and she ran back up the stairs and into the spare bedroom with it. A moment later the spring was released and she was kneeling in the midst of her brother and sisters.

'Oh, Beth!' Anna burst into tears.

'Beth!' Stephanie screamed.

'Hush,' Beth said, and emptied most of the stew on the floor. The floor was dusty, but she wasn't prepared to worry about that.

'Food, oh my!' Tony crammed some into his mouth. 'We heard so many noises, we didn't know what was happening. It sounded as if they were breaking up the furniture.'

'They were,' Beth said.

'Oh, this tastes so good,' Stephanie said, also cramming food into her mouth.

'Well, chew it properly, or you'll be sick.'

'Beth,' Anna observed, nibbling more daintily, 'you have nothing on.'

'And you're all sticky and smelly,' Stephanie remarked.

'Yes,' Beth agreed.

'Aren't you cold?' Tony asked.

'Yes,' Beth said. 'I must take the pot back.'

'But you can't walk about the house with nothing on,' Anna pointed out. 'Especially with strange men around.'

'They like me with nothing on,' Beth explained. 'They think I'm very pretty. Now you must stay here until I can come again. Maybe tonight.'

'But Beth . . .' Tony began.

'No questions,' she said. 'I'll come again tonight.'

She gathered the pot into her arms, and left them scraping food from the floor. Running back down the stairs, she replaced the pot on the table. She hesitated, supposing she should get back into bed with the three men and pretend she had been there all the time, and saw two buckets of water by the back door, obviously drawn by the orderly before he went to sleep. Water! And she *was* all smelly and sticky ... and with blood on her thighs.

She went outside, shivering, and emptied the water over herself. There was still soap in the kitchen, even if it hadn't been used for some time. Now she was nearly blue with cold, but after rinsing in the second bucket she was almost clean for the first time in weeks, and there was a towel in the pantry. She rubbed herself vigorously to get her blood circulating ... and the door opened to admit the Polish-speaking Russian.

'What are you doing?' he demanded.

'I came down to wash myself,' she said. 'I was all dirty.'

The officer peered into the pot, and then at the still sleeping orderly. 'The swine has eaten it all,' he growled. 'Never mind, I have our supper.' He held up two rabbits. Both had been shot with a high velocity rifle, and were mangled looking messes, but there was still a lot of meat left on them. He threw them on the table and put his arm round her. 'Now come,' he said. 'You have amused those fellows long enough. Now you can amuse me.'

She went willingly enough. She knew how to survive now; just do as they wished and keep thinking. He walked her into the hall, making for the still warm dining room, then released her and stood to attention as another man, older and from his badges obviously senior, walked through the broken front door. At his side was Josef Janski.

THE THIRD CHRONICLE

November 1984

'You go down these steps here, Mr Meyer,' Colonel Dubrowski said, leading the way to the heavily eroded stone staircase. 'And there is the corridor.'

Cautiously Meyer descended, and found himself holding his breath. The place, well below the ground, smelled of disinfectant. But he would have held his breath anyway. Twenty-five Szucha Avenue, Warsaw, was where the Gestapo had had its headquarters during the war, and was now a museum.

Although he had not come to Warsaw to sightsee, he would have wished to come here, even if Dubrowski, a tall, humourless man, had not been so clearly determined to bring him here. Here was the true story of what this remarkable, heroic, talented and yet self-destructive nation had suffered during the longest six years of its history. And it was just possible that his own parents had been made to walk down these steps.

The Colonel indicated what appeared to be a school-room, with hard benches arranged in rows facing a blank wall. 'This they called the tram,' he explained. 'Prisoners brought down here were placed in these seats to await interrogation. Often they sat here for forty-eight hours, without food or water, forbidden to move. If they moved, the guards beat them with their truncheons. Well, you know, it is impossible to sit still for forty-eight hours.'

He led Meyer farther along the corridor and opened a door. 'In here, they were finally interrogated. They were whipped and beaten, and given electric shocks. You will observe that outside in the corridor there was a large radio. That was kept playing loudly, all the time, so that the screams of the men and women being tortured would not be heard on the street above.'

He showed the way down a narrower corridor, leading away from the interrogation room. 'After interrogation, the prisoners were put in these cells.' He opened a door, showed Meyer the rough cot, and behind it, the pitted wall. 'Sometimes they were excecuted right here – those are bullet holes. They never knew when the peep-hole here would slide open, and a gun barrel come in. Here, do you see these inscriptions? They were scratched on the walls by the prisoners.'

Meyer peered at the rough letters cut into the stone. 'B-O-Z-E-J-A-K,' he read. 'And then, B –'

'Translated,' Dubrowski said, 'it reads, "Oh Lord, how they do beat."' He opened another door. 'Here is one which reads, "Nobody thinks of me and nobody knows I am so alone girl twenty-one years of age and must die guiltless 12:IX: 43 Sunday ZR."'

To Meyer's relief, they returned to the street level and the comfort of the Colonel's automobile.

'I thought you should see that,' Dubrowski said, 'to understand what we have to remember. But of course, Mr Meyer, you were here during the War. You are a Pole yourself.'

'Was,' Meyer said. 'I am an Israeli now.'

The Colonel preferred not to comment on that, and led Meyer up the stairs to his office. On his desk a file lay open. 'Sit down.' He sat down himself. 'Josef Janski is one of those Poles we are determined to remember, so that we may be able to recognise them should their sort ever appear again. But at least he seems to have met his just deserts.'

'What do you have on him?' Meyer asked.

'Not a great deal. He undoubtedly collaborated with the Germans, right from 1 September 1939. He may even have been in their pay before then. The exact form of the collaboration has never been established, but the evidence is overwhelming. He was allowed to remain living in his house in Wrakinow suburb, and his children were allowed to attend the German school there. That was a very rare privilege. The Polish people as a whole were treated like animals.'

'As you have just reminded me, I was here during the War,' Meyer said. 'We have evidence to indicate his collaboration took the form of betraying his Jewish clients to the Gestapo.'

Dubrowski gave a cold smile. 'Hence your interest. I do not know about that. I am sure he worked more widely with the Germans than merely betraying Jews. After all, by the end of 1943 there were hardly any Jews left to betray, eh? We do know for certain that he chose the German side during the uprising of 1944. It was an unfortunate choice for him; his family were trapped in Wrakinow when the Home Army seized that area.'

'What happened to them?'

'His wife was killed in the fighting. His children survived. Do you know, I think I remember them. Three very handsome girls. Very young, you know, but very handsome. Of course, I was only a teenager myself, then.'

'You fought with the Home Army?' Meyer asked in surprise.

'Indeed not,' Dubrowski said. 'I was with the Red Army.'

'But you saw the Janski children? And Janski himself, after the Russians took the city. Then they were still here at that time.'

'Yes. I did not know who they were at that time, of course. I only found out afterwards.'

'And he was not arrested by the Reds?'

'When I saw him, he was certainly acceptable to the Russians. He possessed a safe conduct signed by Marshal Rokossovsky himself. It seems he claimed to have turned against the Nazis after the death of his wife. I personally do not believe that. I believe he was always looking out for number one. So when the Germans retreated from Warsaw, he changed sides, pretended Communist sympathies, and gained himself acceptance by betraying other Nazi collaborators. They tried to finger him in return, but the Russians, and our people, I am afraid, believed Janski. He was a plausible

rogue, by all accounts, tall, handsome, charming ...
oh, yes, plausible.'

'So what was his reward for betraying his fellow
traitors?'

'What he wanted. Merely a pass to take his family to
Lódź, where he said a sister lived. It was a strange
request. As you know, Lódź is farther to the west than
Warsaw, and although our advance was then very
rapid, the city had only just been taken. However, he
was given a place in a convoy, and for his children, as
he wanted. It was then I saw them, the girls, pale,
frightened little things, but still handsome. And there
was a boy as well, as I recall. All gone. War is sometimes a sad business. Whatever the crimes of the father,
they were handsome children.'

'What do you mean, all gone?' Meyer demanded.

'I mean that Janski just disappeared. He and all his
family. The convoy could not drive right into Lódź, you
see, because of the shell craters in the road. So we
stopped and disembarked, and formed up to march the
last couple of miles. The Janskis were with us when we
left the trucks, but they just walked into the darkness
and vanished. They never appeared in Lódź and were
never heard of again.'

'So what do you think happened to them?'

Another shrug. 'They were killed. Or just died. You
must remember that Poland, Germany, Czechoslovakia,
Austria, were all in a state of complete chaos at that
time, the winter of 1944-45. German resistance was
collapsing everywhere, the roads were packed with
refugees as well as deserting soldiers, there was no
food, people would kill each other for a loaf of bread.
And it was very cold. Thousands, perhaps millions, of
people just collapsed and died. Janski and his children
were clearly amongst them. They must have missed the
road in the darkness, and wandered off and got lost,
and either been murdered or froze to death.'

'So the file was closed.'

Dobrowski tapped the folder. 'Our files are never
closed, Mr Meyer.'

'Is it possible for me to see the old Janski house?'

Dubrowski gave a cold smile. 'I'm afraid not. It was pulled down thirty years ago, to make way for the erection of a block of workers' apartments. I have told you, all trace of the family has been lost.'

'Suppose I told you that we have pretty good evidence that Janski survived. And at least one of his children?'

'I would have to be pessimistic about the truth of your evidence.'

'Millions of refugees did survive.'

'Oh, indeed. Some fled from Poland into Germany. They were all Fascist swine, of course. Janski was certainly a Fascist swine, as presumably were his children. It is possible he got to Germany. Possible.'

'Did you look for him in Germany?'

'My dear Mr Meyer, we didn't look for Janski at all for some two years, when the facts of his crimes came to light. I had just joined the police then, but of course I was not involved at that time.'

'And your superiors heard that he had disappeared outside Lódź and assumed that he must be dead.' Meyer stood up. 'My thanks. You have been very helpful.'

'Where will you go now?'

'Why, to Germany, Colonel, because I am sure that is where Janski went.'

CHAPTER 3

The Road 1945

'My dear girl. Oh, my dear girl. What have they done to you?' Josef Janski held Beth against him and glared past her at the Polish-speaking officer.

'Nothing,' Beth said. She had already resolved that she would never tell anyone what had been done to her, and she had washed the blood from her thigh.

'Nothing? But . . . where are your clothes?'

'They made me take them off,' Beth said. 'They wanted to look at me. They said I was pretty.'

'And they didn't rape you?'

Beth didn't know what the word meant exactly, but she assumed that was what had happened. 'No,' she said.

'And those bruises on your body? That mark on your face? Your lip is cut.'

Beth stared at the officer, who was staring at her. 'I tried to run away, and fell down the stairs.'

Father gazed at her for several seconds, then looked at the senior Russian officer, who was waiting patiently, and spoke in Russian. Beth had never known her father could speak Russian. He turned back to her. 'You must get dressed. You will catch cold, and besides, it's not decent for you to be naked in front of these men. Where are Tony, Anna and Stephanie?'

Beth looked at the Polish-speaking Russian again. He still seemed bemused at not having been denounced, but he was undoubtedly listening. 'Are we safe now, Father?'

'Of course we are safe,' Father told her. 'These men are our friends. If they made you strip it is because they thought you were German.'

Beth knew they hadn't thought she was German, and she also remembered how the Nazis had been their friends, just a fortnight ago. But she believed that if

Father said the Russians were friends, then they were, at least for the time being. 'They are in the secret chamber,' she said. 'I hid them there.'

The Polish-speaking man's jaw dropped, and the Russian colonel asked a question. When Father explained, the colonel gave a roar of laughter.

'He wants to be shown,' Josef Janski said. 'Let's go and find them, and find you some clothes, too.'

Beth wasn't sure it was a good idea to show the Russians the secret chamber, but Father was in charge now. She took them upstairs to the master bedroom, and had the satisfaction of watching the colonel kick his drunken subordinates out of bed. She dressed, hurriedly and took them all into the spare bedroom, where she released the spring and let the wall recede. Tony, Anna and Stephanie blinked at them. Once again the colonel roared with laughter, while his officers looked more embarrassed than ever. The colonel said something, and Father tousled Beth's hair.

'He says you are a very brave girl, and that if you wish to join the Red Army he would be happy to enlist you.'

'Girls can't be soldiers,' Tony objected enviously.

'In Russia they can,' Father said.

'I don't understand,' Stephanie said, as usual putting into words what the rest of them only dared to think. 'The Russians . . .'

'Are our friends,' Father hastily interrupted. 'Just as Mother always said they were.'

'Are they going to give us back our house?' Beth asked. 'Before they burn all the furniture?'

'Ah, no,' Father said. 'They need the house. So we can't stay here. But they have given us permission to go to Aunt Katerina in Lódź.'

'Aunt Katerina,' Anna shouted. 'Oh, I knew we'd go to Aunt Katerina. I so like Lodź.'

'When are we leaving?' Beth asked. Not for the first time during the past six months, she felt totally bemused. And not only by Father's amazing volte-face.

It was difficult to understand what had happened to her that morning and afternoon. But for the bruises and the fact that she could still feel their fingers, and the memory of the blood on her thigh, she would not have believed it had actually happened. And now . . . Lódź?

'This evening,' Father said. 'There's a convoy leaving this evening, and we have places in it.' He waved a piece of paper with an official stamp on it. 'This is our pass, signed by Marshal Rokossovsky himself. We'll be in Lódź by tomorrow morning.'

Father, in his mysterious way, had secured them places in a military truck. Lódź was not all that far away and in normal circumstances could be reached in a couple of hours by train, but the Germans had ripped up all the track before retreating. So they hefted their suitcases, Stephanie hugging Alice to her breast, and left the house, tramping through the snow to the assembly point. The younger children, having eaten and regained Father, were in a state of high excitement – only Beth paused at the corner to look back. There was smoke coming out of the house chimneys as more of Mother's beautiful furniture was consumed. She wondered if, when the last of the furniture was gone, the Russians would start burning the house itself.

Again she was surprised at her lack of grief. She had lived in that house for nearly all of the fourteen and a half years of her life, except for the occasional holiday. Now she was leaving it forever. She knew she was never going to come back, and indeed she did not want to. Over the past few years it had not been a happy home, and the last six months had been desperate. While today . . . she had been raped, by four men, again and again and again. She still did not know for sure what that meant. They had hurt her, and they had put their fingers and their members into her, and they had awakened sensations she had never suspected existed – and they had changed her, forever. She knew that instinctively. They might even have done her some irreparable damage, she thought, remembering the blood on her thigh. But her brain was still too clouded by the vodka she had drunk, and too distracted by wondering what was going to happen to them now, to arrive at any decisions as to her attitude, either to herself or to the men who had attacked her. When they had been doing it she would gladly have killed them all. Now she was just grateful to have escaped them.

But it was disturbing that none of them, not even Father, seemed distressed to be leaving their house.

They had to walk about a mile to the assembly point, and it was dark and freezing by the time they arrived. The truck engines were already running, filling the still air with exhaust fumes, and there were Russian soldiers everywhere, chasing civilian spectators, half-starved ghosts in tattered clothing, away. They began to chase the Janskis away as well, but Father stood his ground and showed his piece of paper, and after much muttering and consultation between various officers they were told to get into one of the trucks, where they sat huddled together with their suitcases, in the midst of some twenty Russian soldiers. One was Polish, a boy hardly older than Beth herself, who showed great interest in the family of refugees, and spoke to them with perfect fluency. But Father snubbed him, and he turned away.

'Are the Russians always going to be our friends, Father?' Stephanie asked, with that devastating way she had of dealing only in essentials.

'Of course,' Father said jovially, obviously suspecting some of the other soldiers might understand Polish. 'Now you settle down and try to sleep. When you wake up, you'll be in Lódź.' He squeezed Beth's hand. 'I am so grateful to you, and so proud of you, for taking care of them, Beth. I feel so guilty at not being able to get back to you, but . . .'

'You went to Praga, to the Russians, to ask for help,' she said.

'Why, yes. How did you guess?'

'It's obvious now, Father.' She didn't tell him that

she didn't understand why the Russians should wish to help him, an avowed Nazi. 'I thought you were dead.'

'I'm not that easy to kill,' Father said. 'But when I think what they did to you, my poor little girl . . .'

'They did nothing to me, Father,' Beth insisted. That secret she would carry to her grave.

The convoy rumbled off into the night, using their headlights. They knew there were no German planes left to strafe them, and even in the last twenty-four hours the sounds of battle had receded over the western horizon, so fast were the Germans retreating.

The same thoughts were apparently occurring to Tony. 'Have the Germans lost the war, Father?' he asked.

'Oh, yes,' Father said. 'Oh, yes.'

Tony fell silent again. Poor little mite, Beth thought, he must be even more confused than the rest of us.

Incredibly, she dozed, while the truck slithered and bounced and occasionally hit the one in front, or was hit by the one behind, while every half hour or so they had to stop at a checkpoint. Because, even more incredibly, she felt secure. No matter what had happened to her, and no matter how difficult she found it to understand Father's changes of direction, she still felt totally safe when in his company.

She awoke with a start when they rumbled through Lowicz, disturbed by the glare of the flames. Lowicz was a shambles, and no one was making any attempt to put out the fires. She wondered what Lódź, even farther to the south-west and therefore more recently evacuated by the Germans, would be like. And in fact, only an hour later, the convoy was stopped, and a Russian officer lifted the flap of their truck and issued orders. Immediately the soldiers started getting out, taking their equipment with them.

'Come along,' Father said. 'We have to get out here.'

'Are we in Lódź?' Anna asked, sleepily.

'No,' he said. 'The road is too bad. We have to walk the rest of the way. Just follow me.'

They stumbled behind him, carrying their suitcases, breath misting in front of their faces. They went to the side of the road, slid down into a ditch, and clambered up the other side, gasping and grunting. The Russian soldiers, busily forming a column on the road, paid them no attention at all.

'Hurry now,' Father said. 'We must be well away by dawn.'

Beth, too tired to wonder what he meant, followed him into the darkness across what appeared to be a ploughed field covered in snow. Now she was carrying Stephanie's suitcase as well as her own, as Stephanie could only manage Alice. Vaguely she wondered that they were walking towards the flickering lights on the horizon, and indeed the sounds of gunfire were much closer, but she didn't ask why, until they stopped for a rest, at four o'clock. By then they were so exhausted Stephanie fell down in the snow, and Father had to lift her up. And by then, too, all sounds of the Russian convoy had died.

Beth looked back, and saw flames on the horizon, to the south. 'Father,' she said. 'Isn't that Łódź?'

'That's right.'

'But . . . we are walking away from it.'

'Of course. We aren't really going to Łódź,' he explained. 'The Russians aren't really our friends. I had to hoodwink them, you see. Now we must get far away from them before they find out.'

'But what about Aunt Katerina?' Anna asked.

'I know nothing about Aunt Katerina,' Father said. 'I haven't heard from her in six months. She could well be dead.'

'But where *are* we going, then?' Tony asked.

'To Germany. To Dresden,' Father said. 'I have friends in Dresden.'

The next fortnight was the worst Beth had ever known, far worse than the six weeks in the cellar or the week leading up to the Russian invasion. It was a long, walking nightmare, which at times she doubted was ever going to end.

They abandoned the suitcases the next day, too heavy for their frozen fingers and tired muscles to sustain. Then they walked, at nights, and occasionally during the day, when the country seemed empty, following always father's compass to the west. The country was seldom empty, as they approached the new front line, and most days they spent sheltering in ditches or copses while Russian tanks manoeuvered about them. Certainly they were seen, often, but no one paid them any attention, as they were not the only refugees roaming about western Poland.

The other refugees were far more dangerous than any soldiers? Or were they the most dangerous of all the refugees. On the very first morning they halted at day-break, and ate some of the food Father had with him. Then the children remained hidden in a small wood while he went off to reconnoitre. They were exhausted and immediately fell asleep, even though it was very near freezing. Beth was already realising that there was no way they could possibly carry their suitcases any farther, but she was too tired to worry about it at the moment, and slept herself.

She awoke to find them surrounded by six people, four men and two women, civilians, wearing rags and obviously as cold and hungry as they were. 'Food,' said one of the men. 'You have food.'

'No,' Beth said. There was some food left, but not enough to share.

'You are lying,' the man said, and pointed at the suitcases. 'Open them up.'

'No,' she said again, while the others crouched around her.

'Don't argue with me, little girl,' the man snarled, and stepped forward, to give a gasp and crumple to his knees and then his face as a shot rang out.

Father stepped from the trees, a Luger automatic pistol in his hand. 'Clear off,' he said.

The people stared at him. So did his children, who had had no idea he was armed.

One of the women screamed and ran forward. 'You shot him,' she shrieked, dropping to her knees beside the man. 'Just like that, you shot him. You . . .'

'And I shall shoot you, too,' Father said, 'if you do not clear off this instant.'

There could be no doubt that he meant what he said. The woman rolled the man on to his back and stared at him. He was certainly dead, his chest a mass of blood. She began to cry.

'Leave him,' Father ordered.

Slowly she rose to her feet, still staring at Father, then backed towards her companions.

'You will rot in hell for this,' one of the men said.

'It's a long and uncertain journey,' Father told him. 'You take your way, and I'll take mine.'

The group edged away from them, and then turned and fled. Beth looked at Tony, Anna and Stephanie.

'That was wonderful, Father,' Tony said. 'I never knew you had a gun.'

'I have to protect you,' Father said.

'And you're such a good shot,' Anna said.

'I practice,' Father said modestly.

Stephanie said nothing. Perhaps she was too bemused. Beth didn't know what to say, either. The man, all the men, had been unarmed. Just to shoot one of them in cold blood . . . Yet she couldn't deny that she was glad Father had had the gun, and the resolution to use it . . .

'What shall we do with him?' she asked.

'Leave him,' Father said. 'When we have gone, those others will come back for him. They haven't gone far.'

That was the first of the horrors. By the next morning they had eaten the last of their food, and that night they came upon another group of refugees, sitting round a small fire. These seemed disposed to welcome them, when they realised they were mostly children, but to Beth's consternation, Father pulled out his gun and

74

made them all lie on their faces in the snow, then made her go amongst them and collect all the scraps of food they had.

'Now hurry,' he said, when she was finished. 'Run.'

He led them in a mad dash away from the group, but himself stopped at the next rise, turned, levelled his pistol, and fired. Beth looked back in time to see one of their pursuers fall; the rest stopped.

'Oh, Father,' she said. 'Did we have to shoot them as well as rob them?'

'They would have lynched us had they caught us,' he said. 'You must understand, Beth, that until we reach Germany, it is us against the world. We cannot afford any pity. My business is to protect you, always. That is what a father is for.'

She didn't dare argue with that reasoning, but she felt quite sick as they trudged on. Two days later they were definitely close to the front line, as they approached the Oder, on the far side of which the Germans were dug in and holding. Now they could only move very occasionally, as they were in the thick of battle, with shells bursting all around them, and men and tanks in every direction.

They soon ate all the food they had stolen, as well as some potatoes and carrots they dug up from the yard of a deserted and half destroyed farm house. But for coming across a dead Russian soldier, lying in a deep ditch, with his haversack full of rations, they would have starved. They dragged his body out of the water in which it lay, and crouched around him while they ate his biscuits; five savages, Beth thought. They even looked like savages, with their unkempt hair and tattered, filthy clothing, their dirty faces and yellow teeth, and Father's stubble of beard.

'But we are alive,' Father reminded them. 'Better than this poor fellow, eh?' And he nudged the dead Russian with his shoe. 'We are going to stay alive, too. All we have to do is cross the river.'

It was difficult to see how they were going to achieve

either of those objectives, with the Russian army all around them and the Germans waiting on the other side, but Father had apparently worked it out. He remembered this area very well from before the War, knew that the whole river bank was patrolled rather than held in strength, and also knew there were little boats, used by fishermen, concealed in various places along the bank.

He left them in the ditch with the dead Russian while he went to find one of the boats. Beth decided that was the worst experience so far. They sat on the frozen ground, as usual huddled against each other for warmth, and gazed at the stiff features of the dead man, jumping in terror every time a twig snapped for fear they would be discovered. Tony wanted to take the man's rifle and pretend he knew how to use it, but Beth wouldn't let him. Unarmed, they were refugees; armed, they were guerillas, and would be shot on sight.

But did it matter? she wondered. What could any of them possibly become now, after watching their house, their city, their country destroyed? After having watched their mother shot down, and having been raped? If those last two applied only to her, she knew she was by far the strongest of the four of them, and the others would be no less affected. They had certainly seen their father murder a man, and then rob several others at gunpoint, all in the name of survival. And now they sat in a ditch with a dead man for company.

So what were they surviving for? What could Stephanie, who had never known anything different, ever hope to become? And the poor little thing was not even aware of it, even if she understood that the Russian, like Mother, was gone for good.

Sound, close at hand. Beth scrambled to her knees and gazed at three young men. They were unshaven, dirty and dishevelled, and wore the haunted look of the starving. Despite her refusal to let Tony touch the dead Russian's gun, she instantly picked it up and tried to look serious about using it.

'We are Poles,' one of the men said. 'You wouldn't shoot a Pole?'

'The Russians would hear the shot,' said the second.

'We only want food,' said the third. 'Don't you kids have any food?'

'We have . . .' Anna began.

'We have nothing,' Beth interrupted. She was carrying out Father's instructions, because they did still have half of the Russian's rations. But if they gave it to these men, they would have nothing.

The men gazed at her, licking their lips. But they would not chance the rifle. They looked at the Russian instead. 'Then let us take him.'

Beth frowned at them. 'He has nothing. We have searched him.'

The first man grinned; he reminded Beth of a wolf. 'We will find something.'

She suddenly realised what they meant, and felt quite ill. But the only way she could stop them would be to shoot them, and she wasn't going to do that over a man who was already dead. 'Not here,' she said, her voice thick with saliva.

The man nodded, and seized one of the dead man's ankles. One of his companions grasped the other, and they dragged the corpse up the slope and away into the trees.

'Why did they want a dead man?' Stephanie asked.

'Probably . . . probably they want his clothes,' Beth said, and prayed for Father to return.

He did at dusk, and Anna told him about the men. Immediately he went into the trees, and came back ten minutes later. 'They have gone,' he said. But he too was looking sick, and he stared at Beth for several seconds. She shook her head, to indicate that the others had not understood what had happened.

He forced a grin. 'We'll move off at dusk,' he told them. 'So let's rest up. I hope there's some of that biscuit left.'

His confidence and good humour was as infectious as

it was irresistible. It was impossible to reconcile his loving protection of them with his callous attitude to everyone else. Was it really them against the world? But whatever the truth, she knew only he stood between them and death, and she was not prepared to argue.

They went down to the river at dusk, crouching in the bushes while the guns roared to either side, sounding terribly close at hand, and bright flashes lit the sky. Father knew exactly where to find the boat, and guided them to it, while they gazed at the swirling dark water, packed with floating ice.

'Can we cross that?' Anna asked.

'Of course,' Father assured her.

But Tony had thought of another danger. 'Won't the Germans shoot us?'

'No, no,' Father said. 'They won't even see us. Besides, the Germans are our friends.'

Beth could only hope he was right. They climbed on board the skiff, which had never been intended to take five people, and sank dangerously low in the water, which began to lap over the sides. But Father paddled them out into the stream, apparently unafraid. He gave Beth a paddle as well, but all she had to do was thrust it into the water every so often to keep them straight – he did all the work. She had never felt so exposed in her life as when they were in mid-stream, and there was an explosion very close at hand, turning the sky, for a few seconds, as bright as day.

Immediately there was a challenge from the west bank, followed by a shot. 'Don't shoot!' Father shouted in German, a language the children understood as they had learned it in the German school in Wrakinow. 'We are friends.'

Now there were shots from behind them as well, but the light had faded into utter darkness and they were not hit, although Beth wondered just how close the Russian patrol had been.

A moment later they were swept into the west bank,

and Beth's blood froze as she heard the click of weapons all around them.

'Children,' someone said in disgust.

'Girls!' pointed out another.

'Where is your commanding officer?' Father asked, helping them up the bank.

'Back there.'

'Well, take me to him.' Father spoke very brusquely.

'And who do you think you are?' asked one of the soldiers. 'Goddamned Polish shit bag.'

'Oh, take him to the captain,' said his companion. 'He may have information. You can leave the girls here, Pole.'

'They come with me,' Father insisted, and to Beth's amazement he sat down and began to take off his right boot. Yet, although she knew what the soldiers wanted, she wasn't the least afraid. It was impossible to be afraid with Father.

The soldiers were no less surprised. 'What are you doing?' one demanded suspiciously, obviously fearing Father had some kind of weapon hidden in his socks; yet they hadn't thought to search him and find the automatic pistol.

'I am going to show you something,' Father told them, and held out a piece of cardboard.

One of the men switched on his flashlight, and they both peered at the card for several seconds. Then, incredibly, they stood to attention.

'Your commanding officer,' Father said again.

'Right away, Herr Janski,' the first soldier said, and they were led through the trees.

'What was that you showed him, Father?' Beth whispered.

'My authority as an officer in the Gestapo,' Father said.

'Are you really an officer in the Gestapo?' Tony asked excitedly.

'No,' Father said. 'But I have a card which says that I am, and these front line troops don't know any different.'

Father was as usual right. The German captain was politeness itself, could not do enough for them, gave them food and hot ersatz coffee and a soft, warm bed to sleep on, before next morning allotting them places in a convoy of wounded going west, which would apparently pass quite close to Dresden. Not that he could understand why they wanted to go there. 'Dresden,' he said, 'it has been badly damaged.'

'My duty calls me there,' Father explained, and away they went. Having a full stomach and having had a full night's sleep, it was the first time in weeks that Beth had felt like a human being. She thought that if she could just have a hot bath and a change of clothing, she might even be able to forget the Russian soldiers. Perhaps such luxuries would be forthcoming in Dresden.

It took them three days to get there. The entire country seemed to be on the move: troops advancing up to the front line – most of them just boys younger than herself, Beth thought – and troops being withdrawn to rest because they were no longer combat worthy; troops and civilians digging ditches and throwing up fortifications in the vain hope of stopping the Russian tanks; and refugees. Everywhere there were refugees, sometimes in small groups, sometimes in bands of a hundred or more, carrying their pitiful bundles of clothing on their shoulders, plodding to the west, anxious only to escape the Russian advance.

Well, Beth thought, are we not also refugees, and do we not also have to escape the Russians? She certainly. If any Russian ever touched her again she would go mad. Or did she really mean, any man?

The difference between them and the other refugees was that they did not even have any pitiful bundles of clothing anymore – only Stephanie's doll, which she absolutely refused to abandon.

And always there were the Russian planes overhead, night and day, forcing the convoy to stop constantly and everyone to shelter in ditches as they roamed the skies at will, bombing and strafing. Although not only

Russian planes were involved now. During the day they could look up at huge masses of aircraft, flying wingtip to wingtip, bigger planes than they had ever seen before.

'American flying fortresses,' Father explained. 'On their way to blow the hell out of Berlin.'

The drone continued all the nights, as well, but these apparently were not Americans. 'The Royal Air Force,' Father told them. 'They are blowing the Reich apart.'

Then what are we doing here Beth wondered, seeking refuge in a country which is being blown apart? Presumably being blown apart was still better than the Russians.

On the third morning they reached Dresden. At least, the convoy stopped and the officer in command invited them to disembark. There was fresh snow on the ground, and Beth stretched and looked down the slope at the River Elbe, flowing lazily northward, and then at something which suggested a surrealist painting. It covered a huge area, on both sides of the river, and the two sides had once been connected by several bridges. The bridges were now represented by one or two stone pillars, while the water flowed through and around the line of rubble which had once been the spans. Similarly what had once been a great and famous city was also represented by one or two stone pillars, the remaining walls of what had once been elegant buildings.

'But what happened?' Father asked in amazement.

'The Royal Air Force sent a thousand bombers to blast it out of existence,' the lieutenant explained. 'And that is what they did.'

Father scratched his head.

'Over two hundred thousand people died in Dresden,' the lieutenant said. 'Most of them are still down there, buried in the rubble. It is a pestilential place, Mr Janski. Are you sure you wish to go there?'

'Yes,' Father said. 'I am sure. Come along, children.'

He held Stephanie's hand and led the way. The others followed slowly, and the convoy drove on.

'Are all the people down there really dead, Father?' Stephanie asked. Beth found it distressing the way an eight-year-old could speak like that, and wondered if she really understood the meaning of the word 'dead' – and what would happen when she found out.

'Of course not,' Father said. 'It is not possible to kill everyone in a city.'

'But suppose your friends are dead?' Tony asked.

'I will find them,' Father said with his usual confidence. 'But first I must find somewhere for you to wait safely until I have found them.'

Obviously it could not be in the city itself. Even from a distance they could see that while there were people down there, soldiers and some civilians, they were wearing masks and protective clothing as they sifted through the rubble. While now they were halted by armed guards.

'But we have family in the city,' Father protested. 'And I have business there.'

'You may enter, Herr Janski,' the soldier said, having examined his fake Gestapo pass. 'But not your children. The risk of disease is too great. There is a camp, only a mile away, where they can wait for you.'

It reminded Beth of a gypsy encampment. There were tents and rough wooden huts, and some army vehicles, and a great number of people, as tattered and half starved in appearance as they were themselves, staring at them.

'Your children are welcome,' said the tough looking woman who seemed to be in charge. 'What have they brought with them? Everything must to into the common pool.'

'We have brought nothing with us,' Father said. 'We have lost everything.'

'That's what they all say,' the woman remarked, but she could see that he was telling the truth, and sent them to a tent where there were already three girls.

82

'The boy will have to go somewhere else,' the commandant said.

'Oh, please,' Tony wailed. 'Don't separate me from my sisters.'

'We must stick together,' Beth explained. 'He is only a litle boy.'

'Oh, let them all come in,' said one of the girls in the tent. 'We don't mind a little boy.'

The commandant shrugged. 'There are two meals a day,' she said. 'Those who do not attend, do not get fed.'

Father took Beth aside. 'I am going to be as quick as I can,' he said. 'But I may be gone a few days. You can wait a few days, eh?'

'I have waited before,' Beth reminded him. 'But Father . . .' Suddenly she was afraid. 'You are going to come back?'

'Haven't I always come back before?' he asked, and gave her a squeeze and a kiss. 'I'll come back, Beth. Just look after the others. You are really all they've got, now.'

Then he was gone.

'You're Polish,' accused one of the girls when Beth entered the tent, becoming immediately aware that the initial welcome had vanished. Anna, Stephanie and Tony were sitting together, huddled up and looked beleaguered. 'We thought you were German, but your sister says you're Polish.'

'That's right,' Beth agreed, wishing Anna would learn to keep her mouth shut. 'But my father works for the Gestapo, and has done throughout the War.'

She realised that she also might have said too much; the other girls stared at her with even more hostility than before. Then one said, 'You stink.'

Indeed, in the warmth of the tent the atmosphere was quite foetid. But Beth was sure they hadn't brought it all in themselves. 'So do you,' she pointed out.

'My father always said all Poles were subhumans.'

'Do we look like subhumans to you?' Beth asked.

'Your father is a cretin.' She was also sure their best course lay in aggression.

The girl burst into tears.

'Her father is dead,' said the first girl.

'Oh, I'm sorry,' Beth said.

'So is my father,' the first girl said. 'All our fathers are dead. They died in the firebombing. Have you ever been firebombed?'

'I don't think so,' Beth said.

'Of course she hasn't been firebombed,' said the third girl. 'Or she'd be dead.' Her tone indicated that would have been a good thing.

'It doesn't matter whether we have been firebombed or not,' Beth said. 'We have suffered too. We have walked for two weeks through the snow with hardly anything to eat. Our mother is dead.' She almost added, shot by the Germans, but decided against it. 'We are all in the same boat, and it is stupid to quarrel about it.'

'It is a wall of flame,' the first girl said, reminiscently. 'It comes with a whoosh, because it creates its own wind. There is no escape. People jumped into the river, and they still died; the water simply boiled. There was no escape.'

It sounded too horrible to think about. Beth wondered if she should tell them about the Russian soldier, and decided against it. But what a crazy world this is, she thought, that we should be sitting here comparing horrors: I am better off than you because I still have a father, even if I have lost a mother – but I have suffered more than you because I have seen a man being eaten and you have just been firebombed.

To her relief, there was no further unpleasantness from the German girls. This was partly because they were all still suffering from shock and exhaustion and lack of food, but also because Beth was the biggest girl in the tent and obviously the toughest. With that matter settled, life in the camp was actually the best they had known since the day the Warsaw uprising had begun and their contented existence had fallen apart. They had a roof over their heads, even if it was only made of canvas, and they were given two meals a day, even if they had to line up in the snow for them. And if the meals themselves consisted of watery potato soup and pieces of cabbage, together with some bread so hard they had to tear it up into bite-size pieces for dipping in the soup, the soup was at least hot.

They were so exhausted, both emotionally and physically, after their escape from Warsaw and their experiences on the road, that they spent most of every day sleeping; the only other thing to do was to go to the edge of the camp and watch the bodies being taken out of Dresden to be burned. But always there was the grumble of guns, steadily moving towards them, and when another week had passed and Father had not returned, Beth once again began to worry.

'We are going to die,' one of the German girls announced, 'when the Russians get here. The Russians eat little girls alive, my father always said.' She was the one whose father Beth had earlier described as a cretin, and he certainly seemed to have been a prophet of doom. Anna promptly burst into tears.

'That was a horrible thing to say,' Beth snapped. 'And it's not true.'

'We were captured by the Russians,' Tony declared. 'And they didn't eat us alive. All they did was make Beth take off ...'

'Shut up,' Beth told him. She didn't want the German girls to know what the Russians had, done to her. They might just know what rape was, and tell Anna, and that would drive her into hysterics.

'Anyway,' Tony said proudly, 'We escaped. Father helped us to escape.' Then his eyes filled with tears. 'I do wish Father would come back.'

A few days later there was a fresh problem; now they could hear gunfire to the west of them as well.

'Those are the Americans and the British,' the commandant said. 'I hope they get here before the Russians do.'

'Are the Americans better than the Russians?' Beth asked her.

'Anybody is better than the Russians,' the commandant assured her. 'Just don't tell them your daddy worked for the Gestapo, when they get here.'

If they got here in time, Beth thought: the Russian guns were certainly closer. And there was no sign of Father. She obtained permission to leave the camp and ask the guards on the road into Dresden if they had any word of him. One told her that Father had been unable to find his 'relatives' and had left the city and gone north, perhaps to Berlin, he thought, several days before.

That was a blow to Beth. Father had gone without saying goodbye, and he had gone to where the Americans were bombing every day. And he had been gone a very long time. And every day the Russians were coming closer. Beth lay awake all night, and then made a decision. She knew that not even she could stand being captured by the Russians again. The thought of those brutes getting their hands on Anna, or even worse, Stephanie, could not be contemplated – and they would probably shoot Tony out of hand. Father would certainly think she had done the right thing, and Father had himself said, when they had left the road to Lódź, that their ultimate aim was to reach the Americans.

She kept her plan a secret until the following night, then she told the others. 'Father will know where to look for us,' she said when they objected to abandoning the relative security of the camp. 'Anyway, he left me in charge, and I have decided what we are going to do.'

As usual, they agreed. There was not one of them prepared to argue with Beth.

At midnight, they got up and crept out of the tent; none of the German girls woke up. Beth would have liked to steal some bread, but it was too risky. Instead they crawled out of the camp and then went down to the river. Although it was now March, it was still

86

bitterly cold, and the water was icy. By crawling along the bank they reached one of the collapsed bridges, and crossed by means of the half submerged span. There were no guards down here; now that the thaw had set in the stench of death and rotting flesh was everywhere.

It was a long slow crossing, and once Anna slipped into the water and uttered a scream, which Beth was sure had given them away, but they dragged her back out, wet to the waist and shivering, and gained the other side without anyone being prepared to notice them. The soldiers were too cold and too fed up to care who crossed the bridge.

On the west bank they entered the old city of Dresden, and this was even worse than the new city on the other side. But they got through it, clambering over rubble, sometimes stumbling over dead bodies already reduced to skeletons by the rats, driven onwards as if the devil himself was on their heels, as indeed he was, as far as Beth was concerned.

By dawn they had reached the park on the high ground above the city, and there they collapsed beneath some bushes in an exhausted sleep. Beth wasn't worried about being pursued; she guessed the commandant would be just as happy to have four less mouths to feed. Her only concern was to get somewhere before they starved to death. So she made them move again as soon as it got dark, although they were all moaning about the aches in their stomachs.

They walked all night, hiding whenever they heard anyone approaching, whether they sounded like German soldiers or other refugees, and sheltered again at dawn. By now Beth realised she had made a mistake. They were exhausted, and half frozen, and without food there was no way they could keep moving. For the first time she just lay on the ground with the others and sobbed in despair, and then raised her head as she heard voices, speaking a language she had never heard before.

THE FOURTH CHRONICLE

December 1984

It was snowing in Berlin, which made the drab city look even drabber than usual, although perhaps, Meyer thought, the blanket of white hid some of the scars. He had been to Berlin before, several times, as many of his leads had emanated from here, but as he had only come here for the first time in 1966, after the Wall had been built, he had always found it difficult to accept that this had once been the most exciting, attractive city in Europe. Now it was as if the long night of the Nazi tyranny had never ended, here.

It was also just before Christmas, and Meyer found this disturbingly reminiscent of his childhood when he had lived as a Roman Catholic, and had not known what he was. The visit to Warsaw had been equally reminiscent, and disturbing. Dan Sobieski had offered not a word of reproach, yet the reproach had been there. His father had saved Bob Meyer's life – at some risk to himself and his family – and then had arranged for him to emigrate to Israel the moment he could find a family to take him in. And Meyer had never been back. How to explain to a Communist that he hadn't returned simply because he had been afraid of what he would find?

Captain Linten was anxious to help. The East Germans, like the Poles and even the Russians, were always anxious to help, providing the Nazi being sought had escaped to the West. Where he had travelled east, or remained in East Germany and made his peace with the new regime, there was nothing but brick walls. But Janski . . .

'Yes, indeed,' Linten said. 'We remember Janski.'

He was neat and precise; his nails were manicured and he wore a little moustache. Meyer suspected there could well be a 'von' in the family background, prudently discarded for his Communist masters.

'But my dear Mr Meyer,' he went on, 'Janski is dead. He died in 1945, trying to escape from Warsaw.'

'You have proof of this?'

Linten shrugged. 'There is hardly any proof of anything that happened in 1945. It was destruction, collapse of civilisation, on a scale never witnessed since the Mongols rode across Poland in the thirteenth century. But it is reasonable to suppose that if he had survived he would have surfaced again by now.'

'We think he has,' Meyer told him. 'Or did, twelve years ago.' He told Linten about the diary entry.

'Well, it is certainly possible,' the German agreed when he had finished. 'But I would say that you are in the wrong continent, Mr Meyer. Should you not be in the United States?'

'I intend to be,' Meyer agreed. 'When I know what or who I am looking for. Right now, I have a name, which cannot be traced. My people have tried. I do have a photograph of Janski, taken in 1940. It was given to me by Colonel Dubrowski. But in forty-four years a man can change a great deal. As for the children ... Dubrowski apparently met them once, and recalls them as being very handsome. The girls, anyway. But they were teenagers, then, if that. Who can say what they look like now they are middle-aged? I have to find some thread, which I can use to trace their movements, and attempt to pick up some solid information about them. There are some two hundred and fifty million people in the United States. I can hardly interview each one.'

'Yes,' Linten said thoughtfully, perhaps speculating on the two hundred and fifty million Americans. 'Well, if ... and I think it is a big if ... if the Janskis got into Germany, which would have meant passing through the front line remember – and the records show that while thousands tried to do that, only a few succeeded – and then managed to get to the West, almost certainly they would have been sent to a displaced persons camp. The Americans, the British, and the French all had such

89

camps set up in West Germany to handle the various refugees who so mistakenly elected to flee from their Russian saviours.'

'Where are the records of those camps kept?' Meyer asked. He knew, of course. He had been through enough DP camp records in his time. But perhaps Linten might have something up his sleeve.

He didn't. 'If the records are still kept at all, they will presumably be in Bonn, or London, or Paris, or Brussels, perhaps. If they are still kept at all. If they are not ...' he gave another shrug, 'then you had better accept that your man is dead, or at least, untraceable.'

CHAPTER 4

The Camp 1945-47

The children stood in a huddle in front of a desk behind which sat a kindly looking man who wore a khaki uniform and a lot of medal ribbons. He kept talking to them, but they couldn't understand what he was saying. Other men kept coming into the tent and addressing them, and one finally spoke German.

'I can speak German,' Beth said.

'You are German,' the man suggested.

'No,' she said. 'We are Polish.'

'Polish? You came all the way from Poland? Just the four of you?'

'Our father was with us,' Beth explained. 'But . . . we got separated. Please, sir, do you have anything to eat?'

The sergeant translated to the officer, who opened his desk drawer and took out a bar of chocolate.

The children stared at it. They had not seen chocolate in a long time; Beth did not suppose Stephanie even knew what it was.

'The colonel says you may take it,' the sergeant said.

Beth licked her lips. One bar of chocolate wasn't going to do them much good. 'I . . . we need food, sir. Real food.'

Once again the sergeant reported, and the colonel grinned at them. 'The colonel says you shall have all the food you can eat. He also asks, when last did you have a hot bath?'

'A hot bath?' Beth asked.

'Last summer,' Anna said.

'Last summer?' The sergeant spoke to the colonel, whose smile faded for a moment, and then returned. 'Then you shall have a bath as well,' the sergeant said. 'And we shall see if we can't find something to do with you.'

The children could have stayed with the American

battalion for the rest of their lives. Not even Beth could actually remember so much food, and so much good cheer, not even at the Christmases before the War. The three girls were given a tent to themselves, and allowed to wallow in a huge tub of hot soapy water, while an MP stood guard over them with his back carefully turned. Beth was horrified to see lice floating away from their hair; if she had been aware of vague itchings she had not had the time during the walk from Lódź to give it much thought. And the soap was so sweet smelling. When they were finished bathing they washed their clothes as well, and then wrapped themselves in blankets while they hung them up to dry; the American soldiers gathered round to watch.

They were given toothbrushes and toothpaste. They hadn't seen either since leaving Warsaw. Then they were fed, and given warm sleeping bags in which to curl up and forget the world. Tony was being similarly looked after, although he was sharing a tent with three men. It was quite a blow, the next day, when a truck appeared.

'You have to leave,' the German-speaking sergeant said.

'Why?' Tony asked.

'Because we're going back up to the front line, that's why. That's no place for kids.'

Beth supposed they had spent more time in the front line than anyone else in the camp, but she knew it would be useless to point that out. 'But where are we going?' she asked.

'To a camp,' the sergeant explained.

'A camp?' Beth was horrified. She had been so sure the Americans didn't send people to camps.

'A place for you to wait until your family is traced and you can be reunited with them,' the sergeant said. 'Until your daddy can be found. You'll be well looked after.'

She didn't know whether to believe him or not, but there was nothing to do but obey. Before they left the colonel gave them each a bar of chocolate and patted Beth on the head. She hoped the camp commandant would be like this, and was sure he would, if it was an American camp.

They drove all day steadily west, passing more men and guns and trucks than she had ever seen in her life, all marching and driving east, while overhead the planes flew ceaselessly, but these were American planes, and there was no strafing. Then they saw the camp: barbed wire fencing, and inside, a collection of odd huts and tents and bare, snow-covered ground. It looked like a prison, save that the watch towers were unoccupied, and Beth's heart sank. It sank even further when she saw not the Stars and Stripes but the Tricolour flying from the flagpole, and it reached the pit of her stomach when the four of them stood in front of another desk and faced the commandant.

He stroked a little moustache while he inspected them through cold blue eyes. 'Filthy German ratbags,' he remarked in German.

'Please, sir, we are Polish,' Beth explained.

'Don't interrupt me, girl,' he snapped. 'That's what it says on this paper. But the Yanks don't know any different. Of course you would say you were Polish.'

'We are Polish,' Tony protested.

The commandant stared at him, then he stared at Anna and Stephanie. Stephanie clutched Alice against her chest. 'Where are your belongings?' he demanded.

'We have no belongings,' Beth said. 'Only these toothbrushes given us by the Americans.'

He snorted. 'And where are your parents?'

'Our mother is dead,' Beth said. 'And we were separated from our father during ... during a bombing attack. Will it be possible for you to find him?' Oh, if only someone would find Father, and get him to take them away from here.

'Me?' the commandant asked. 'I have better things to do.' He rang a bell, and a hard faced woman, much harder looking than the camp commandant at Dresden, appeared. 'Take these ... these Polish orphans, Madame Lesage,' he said. 'Have them bathed ...'

'We bathed yesterday,' Anna told him.

'How interesting. Well, you will be bathed again now, and you will be bathed every other day for as long as you are in my camp. I will have no typhus, you understand?'

'Typhus?' Beth asked

'It is a disease, carried by lice. Are you going to pretend you have no lice?'

Beth remembered the dead lice in their bath the previous day, and did not reply.

'Typhus kills,' the commandant went on. 'And it is my business to keep you alive.' His tone indicated that he could not understand why. 'So you will be housed and clothed and fed twice a day. Enjoy it. I think you are going to be here a long time. I have no doubt at all that your father is also dead. So I really have no idea what can possibly become of you. Now go with Madame Lesage.'

'I don't think he likes us,' Stephanie remarked as they left the commandant's hut. 'I know I don't like him.'

'Is Father really dead, Beth?' Anna asked, lip trembling, as they walked in the drizzling rain over the uneven, muddy ground behind Madame Lesage and towards a cluster of huts and tents some distance away from the administration centre.

'Of course not,' Beth said confidently. 'He'll find us.' Actually, she believed that he would; he had the most reassuring habit of always appearing just when she had given him up.

'What are you speaking?' Madame Lesage asked.

'We were speaking Polish,' Beth explained.

The woman shook her finger at her. 'You will speak no more Polish. There will be no secret conversations in this camp. You will speak German until you can learn French.'

'Beth,' Stephanie whispered. 'I don't like her, either. And I know she doesn't like us.'

Stephanie's judgement was as usual unerringly correct, but that was because Madame Lesage and the commandant didn't seem to like anyone. Their hatred for the Germans was quite pathological, which Beth supposed was not so difficult to understand, as the French had spent just about the entire century fighting the Germans, but it was bad luck for them to be lumped in with the defeated enemy. All the other inmates of the camp were German, all claiming to be staunchly anti-Nazi. They didn't like the Poles either – presumably, Beth thought, all their fathers had described the Poles as sub-humans – and the commandant recognised this by giving the four children a tent of their own and not forcing Tony to go off and sleep with a group of boys. 'You are responsible,' he told Beth. Well, she was used to being told that by now, although she had no idea what she was actually responsible for.

Despite the dislike with which they were surrounded, the feeling of total isolation, the jibes from the other children – and the camp consisted mainly of other children – and the occasional fights which broke out between Tony and the other boys, which had to be ended very quickly before the commandant found out, life in the DP camp was the best they had known for nine months, and in many ways was almost heavenly, compared to those nine months. They were warm and dry, most of the time – even their colds dried up. They had clean clothing, and a change of clothing as well, even if it consisted of hand-me-downs donated by the good mothers of England and the United States for the relief of the European refugees. They were indeed made to bathe every other day, – as was the whole camp – in water which stank of disinfectant, but presumably it was to protect them and Beth certainly didn't want them to accumulate any more lice. But they were also given two good meals every day, and with the coming of summer the sun shone, and it was almost possible to feel happy, and secure about tomorrow.

Most important of all, they were together. They were

so used to depending entirely upon each other for help and entertainment and affection that they found it relatively easy to ignore the hostility around them.

They also had a lot to occupy their minds, for the commandant made them work. They were allotted their own patch of ground on which to grow vegetables, and these they could either keep to supplement their own diets, or trade off to other inmates for something else. And when they were not tilling their vegetable garden, they were in class.

This was the least happy period of every day, and it occupied several hours of every day. None of them had been to school since the previous spring term, a year ago, and they found settling down to study difficult, which left their knuckles exposed to repeated raps of the ruler from Madame Lesage. The work itself was quite interesting, because in addition to actual school work the girls were taught needlework and cookery, having to take their turns at preparing the camp meals, and the boys were taught wood-working – and encouraged to make furniture for their tents and huts as well as keep them in repair – and also primitive engineering: the commandant had an old motor bike which did not work but which they were made to strip down and reassemble over and over again.

In class, while they were taught mathematics in a perfunctory fashion, the two main subjects were French and Recent Events. Madame Lesage was obviously under instruction to make them all fluent in French as rapidly as possible, as if this would counteract the fact that they were Germans and Poles. But she was a good teacher, and they rapidly picked up the language. Recent Events, however, was both confusing and at times, distressing. If Madame Lesage was even close to the truth in what she insisted on telling them every day then Father had been a sorely misled man during the past six years. Or a very wicked one.

Madame Lesage's catalogue of horrors, which began with the indiscriminate bombing of cities – and that

Beth knew was true, at least as regards Warsaw – extended through the equally indiscriminate shooting of hostages, to camps where, she said, hundreds of thousands of people, perhaps millions, had been murdered by the Nazis. She claimed several of these camps had been in Poland, and that when people had been sent away from places like Wrakinow they had all been going to such camps. It seemed impossible that Father had not known about that, but then Madame Lesage admitted that the Allies had not known about them either, until they had invaded Germany.

Tony was thunderstruck. 'Were the Germans really bad people?' he asked Beth in the privacy of their tent, instinctively allotting them to the past. The other children in the camp, however objectionable at times, could hardly be described as bad people.

Beth didn't know what to tell him, because to reply might have led to the question as to whether Father had been a bad person, too. But she couldn't help remembering that Mother had described Nanny as a very bad person just before the Home Army had taken her away – to be shot? She didn't doubt that now. But had Nanny been shot because she was a Nazi supporter? Father had certainly been that.

To make confusion worse, Madame Lesage also knew about the Home Army, and claimed that it had been composed of gallant patriots, who had died fighting in an attempt to free Warsaw from the oppressors. She said they had been betrayed by the Russians, who had indeed been in Praga Suburb, just across the Vistula, all the time, but had stopped their advance just to let the Germans and Poles kill each other off, in the hopes that few of the Home Army leaders – who were anti-Communists – would survive.

Madame Lesage appeared to hate the Russians every bit as much as she hated the Germans. When Stephanie piped up and said, 'Our mother was killed, fighting with the Home Army,' Madame Lesage actually smiled at her. 'Then your mummy was a heroine,' she declared, and from that moment some of the hostility dwindled.

97

But Father had said the Home Army people were criminals, and had hinted that Mother had been criminal even to allow herself to be forced to join them. Beth wished Father would come for them, and for a while during the summer remained quite optimistic. The War actually ended only a few days after they had reached the camp, and there seemed no reason for him not to be able to find them. But as summer faded into autumn, she once again knew the terrible fear that he was dead. And as usual it was tempered with a personal feeling of desolation. The other children in the camp, the Germans, were constantly leaving, as their parents were found, or some relatives willing to take them in. But there were no relatives available for the four Polish children, who could only stand outside their tent and listen to the joyous shrieks and watch the tears and hugs which accompanied each family reunion. As the commandant had said, they were going to stay here for an awfully long time – if Father didn't come.

The thought was chilling. But it also filled Beth with a fierce determination. When she thought of Father, so gallant and handsome and confident, and so successful, too – however terrible some of the things he might have had to do to protect them – he was still the finest man she had ever known. If he was dead, then it was up to her to protect and nurture the others, and somehow guide them to safety and happiness. As Father would have done, and as he had told her to do when he had said she was all they had left, in his absence.

There were increasing problems to be dealt with. By the spring of 1946, Beth was sixteen years old, and life seemed to be rushing by and leaving her on the sidelines. Even more to her concern, Anna was nearly fourteen, and looked eighteen, and was forced to disguise her growing beauty beneath worn out, ill fitting hand-me-downs. Tony was twelve, and a big, strong boy, who did nothing but hoe the vegetable patch. Only Stephanie continued on her happy way, able to find pleasure in almost everything she did, but she too was growing up every day.

Anna remained the main problem, however. How much of a problem Beth only began to grasp that summer's day in 1946 when her sister wandered off during their gardening session, and didn't appear when it was time to go in. Beth left Tony and Stephanie and went looking for her, and came upon her behind a clump of bushes, lying on the ground, with one of the German boys. They were kissing, Anna had her hand inside the boy's trousers and he had his hand inside Anna's blouse, and they were wriggling and gasping against each other.

Beth was horrorstruck. The idea that a woman could actually want a man to touch her like that was nauseating; the very thought of those Russian men in Wrakinow could turn her stomach, especially since she had listened to the German girls in the camp discussing their experiences. Going by what they had said, she *had* been raped, gang-raped, the German girls would have called it, had she ever told them about it instead of just listening and pretending total ignorance.

But apparently, however much the Russians had knocked her about, she had been enormously lucky. The girls said that having a man push his way into you was the way you had babies, thus she could easily have had a baby, which was an impossible thought. They also said that was the way you got diseased, and indeed, several of them had been diseased, and very ill for some weeks. Beth couldn't quite reconcile how you could get babies and disease from exactly the same thing, but the whole idea sounded too unpleasant ever to be contemplated voluntarily. And now, to see her own sister apparently enjoying it . . .

Beth flew into a rage, and attacked the boy, hitting him about the head and face with all her considerable strength so that he ran away in terror. Then she made Anna undress. The German girls had also told her that the blood did not necessarily mean that you had been hurt inside, but that you had lost your virginity, a very serious state of affairs, apparently, because you could never get it back, and no man would marry a girl who was not a virgin. Beth had been brought up to believe that marriage was essential for any happiness in life, and she had not yet worked out how you could be happy with a man, who might want to rape you. Now, although she was relieved to find that Anna was not bleeding, she was still so angry that she slapped her face as well, and made her cry.

The boy ran weeping to Madame Lesage, and that same afternoon Beth was summoned before the commandant.

To her surprise, he was quite pleasant. 'Sit down, Elizabeth,' he said.

Beth perched herself on the edge of the chair before his desk. She could not imagine what was going to happen next. She knew he had a cane which he often used on boys guilty of continued fighting, or stealing. If he attempted to use it on her she would scratch his eyes out . . . but what would happen then?

'You are very protective of your sisters,' the commandant observed. 'This is good. Very good.'

Beth waited. She couldn't believe he had called her in here just to compliment her.

'And young Schurer was very wrong, but then . . .' he shrugged. 'Boys will be boys, eh? And girls . . . will be girls.' He gave her what was intended to be a reassuring smile but was more like an ugly leer. 'Anyway,' he went on, 'I consider you were justified, and therefore the matter is closed. I do not intend to punish you for assaulting the boy.'

'Me?' Beth shouted. 'Punish me? What about what he was doing to my sister?'

'He does not appear to have forced her, and that is what matters,' the commandant said. 'But really, I called you in here to discuss a more important subject. Yourselves. Do you realise that you are now the oldest inhabitants of the camp? I mean in terms of time you have been here.'

'Yes,' Beth muttered. 'We would leave if we could.'

'Indeed. But where would you go? Three young girls and a little boy? The world out there is a cruel place, Elizabeth. You are better off here, for the time being.'

'For the rest of our lives?' she asked bitterly.

'Well . . . until perhaps I can find a home for you,' the commandant said.

'Home?'

'You must face facts, Elizabeth. Your father is never going to come for you now. It is a year and a half since last you saw him, is it not? There is no possibility that, had he been looking for you, he would not have found you by now. Undoubtedly he is dead.'

Beth's shoulders sagged. 'Yes,' she said. 'I have thought of that.'

'Believe me, I am sorry about it. But what is done is done. Now you want to think of yourself, and your sisters and brother.'

'And you can find us a home?' Beth raised her head.

'It is possible. But it will be difficult. It would be easier if I were to try to find four separate homes . . .'

'No,' Beth said. 'Never. We cannot be separated. I must look after them. Always. I promised my father this.

The commandant stroked his chin. 'As I have said, that will make it more difficult, and will certainly take some time. But I will try, and you are welcome to stay here for a while longer. It was this I wished to talk to you about. I would like to do more for you, and for your sisters. I would like to help you. I know that you have been very unfortunate. I would like to change that.'

Beth frowned at him. She couldn't believe what she was hearing.

The commandant smiled at her. 'So I thought we would begin by . . . well, how about dinner tonight. You and your sister Anna could come here and dine with me. We shall be tête-à-tête, eh? And we can discuss so many things, and consider the future. Consider how I may best be able to help you.' He winked. 'There is chocolate cake.'

101

Beth's frown cleared, even as she felt an enormous lump of lead forming in her stomach. She stood up. 'No,' she said.

'You refuse my invitation?'

'Yes, sir,' she said.

The commandant leaned back in his chair. 'You are an arrogant little bitch,' he remarked.

'I must protect my sisters,' she said. And added, 'And my brother.'

'You? A slip of a girl? You are going to make a very hard path for yourself, Pole. A path you will not be able to survive. Can't you see that I am offering to protect your sisters, and yourself, for you?'

'I understand what such protection means, sir.'

He snorted. 'Are you pretending to me that you and your sister are virgins? After weeks on the road, earning food where you could, how you could?'

'Our father was with us on the road, sir,' Beth said evenly. 'And both my sisters *are* virgins.'

'Aha. But you . . .'

'I have been raped,' Beth said, breaking her self-imposed vow of secrecy. 'Which is why I will not be raped again. And my sisters will not be raped, either.' She watched the commandant's knuckles whiten as he gripped the arms of his chair preparatory to getting up. 'And if you attempt to touch me, I will scratch both your eyes out.'

The commandant leaned back again. 'Do you really suppose that you, a sixteen-year-old girl, without a friend in the world, can defy me?'

'I am not defying you, sir,' Beth said. 'I am not going to let you take advantage of our situation, either, if we have to stay here for the rest of our lives.'

The commandant glared at her for several seconds, then he gave a short laugh. 'We shall see,' he said. 'Now get out, shit bag.'

The children were terrified. She had been gone so long they had supposed she had been locked up, or at least

102

beaten. Now when she came home with flushed cheeks and flashing eyes, Anna was afraid she was going to hit her again. Tony and Stephanie were mystified by the whole thing.

'They were playing,' Stephanie said. 'Weren't they?'

'Just playing,' Anna sobbed.

'It was not a nice game,' Beth said. 'And if I ever catch you playing like that, Stephanie, I am going to whip you with a belt.'

That brought Stephanie as near to tears as she ever came. But she immediately recovered. 'I don't really like playing with boys, anyway,' she said. 'Except Tony, of course.'

Tony obviously didn't have any idea what playing with girls apart from his sisters could entail. And Anna, after weeping and sulking for a good twenty-four hours, seemed to forget the whole incident.

But the hostility was back. Not only from the German children, but from the commandant, and even, Beth realised, from Madame Lesage. Because they were four friendless orphans, surviving only by charity, and she was causing trouble. She should have gone to dinner with the commandant, and let him tell her to take off all her clothes, and stretch her on a bed ... with Anna beside her. She shuddered. She would never do that again. Never. Not for any man. And neither would Anna. Nor Stephanie.

But how she wished she could see even the slightest ray of hope for their future. Even during this last summer, when the terrifying realisation began to dawn that Father was not coming for them, she had yet only contemplated a future with Father. They would go wherever Father went, whether it was back to Warsaw when the Russians left Poland, or wherever else in the world he chose. And Father, because he was Father, would be successful, and earn a lot of money, and they would have all the things, the fine clothes, the good food, the music, the horses, the total security, they had known as children.

But if Father wasn't ever coming for them, then the only person who could earn them those things was herself. And she had no idea at all how to go about it. She felt utterly damned, and had to use all her will-power to maintain a confident and optimistic air for the others.

But it was a bleak winter, with Christmas even less enjoyable than the previous year. Last year the commandant and Madame Lesage had been quite pleasant at Christmas. There had been extra food, and even a present for each of the children, even if the presents, which just like their clothes, had been donated by generous English and American children, and were mostly toys which no longer worked. This Christmas there was nothing.

It was also one of the coldest winters western Europe had ever endured, with even the daytime temperatures below freezing for weeks on end. There was a fuel shortage, and the children spent much of each day huddled in their tent, their arms round each other, while Beth told them stories. She tried to remember every book she had ever read, and relate it to them. But often she forgot. Anna and Tony were no great help, but Stephanie, to her surprise, was. Not that Stephanie remembered any stories. She made hers up as she went along, and some of them were bizarre in the extreme, all filled with dead bodies and blazing houses. But they were remarkably entertaining, and also comforting. Not so much the stories, but the way they had all come to depend on each other. Beth realised that they could never be separated again, no matter what happened, because without each other they would just wither and die. They were four branches of the same stem.

In February Beth was again summoned to the commandant's office. But this time they all were. Oh, Lord, she thought, what is he going to do now? Maybe he's just going to throw us out, because I wouldn't go to bed with him.

'I'm sure he's found Father,' Tony said confidently.

'Oh, I do hope he's found Father,' Stephanie said. 'It's so long since I've seen him.'

Beth made them brush their hair and look as presentable as they could in their ill-fitting clothes, and then led them to the hut, which had now been developed into a house, with chintz curtains and carpets and upholstered chairs. They filed through the doorway of the commandant's office, having carefully wiped the snow and slush off their shoes, and lined up, while Beth realised that the commandant was not alone.

Seated beside the desk was quite the most elegant woman she had ever seen since Mother had stopped wearing her ball gowns at the outbreak of the War. This woman was older than Mother, although not much. She wore a pale green tunic suit, the skirt of which came down to mid calf in the latest Paris fashion. Her shoes were brown crocodile skin, matching her handbag. She wore a pale green toque on her head, which effectively concealed her hair, but Beth guessed it was probably blonde, with her pale skin and green eyes. Her face was handsome rather than pretty, and she wore a great deal of makeup, while her fingers were a mass of rings. The gloves which lay carelessly in her lap were kid, and there was a fur coat draped over the back of the chair.

The others had now noticed her as well, and were blinking in astonishment.

'Here we are, Madame Suchet,' the commandant said. 'The Janski children. I told you about them.'

'Of course.' Madame Suchet's voice was soft, and like liquid; it seemed to flow over them. 'The so unfortunate Janski children. Let me see ... you will be Beth.'

'Say hello to Madame Suchet, Elizabeth,' the commandant ordered.

'Madame!' Beth gave a hasty bob. She was still taken aback by the presence of so much obvious wealth and sophistication ... but her instincts warned her that things weren't quite as they seemed.

'And Anna,' Madame Suchet said.

Anna also gave a brief curtsey. 'Madame.'

Madame Suchet looked at Tony, but said nothing, and turned to Stephanie. 'And Stephanie. What pretty children.'

Stephanie, embarked on a curtsey, lost her balance and Tony had to grab her arm to stop her from falling over.

'Commandant Jerome has told me of your misfortunes,' Madame Suchet said sympathetically. 'Both parents dead, home destroyed, oh, my God, what a catalogue of horrors.' She looked ready to weep, but there were no tears in her eyes. 'How would you like to come and live with me?'

'With you?' Anna's incredulous tone answered for the rest of them.

'Madame Suchet is offering you a home, out of the generosity of her heart,' the commandant said.

'Where?' Tony asked suspiciously.

Madame Suchet regarded him as if he were a beetle. 'I have a house in Paris,' she said.

'Paris!' Anna shouted. 'I've always wanted to go to Paris.'

'Then you, and your sisters,' Madame Suchet said pointedly, 'are welcome.' She grew enthusiastic. 'It is a big house, with lots of rooms, and large gardens, and there are ponies to ride ... and I have some other young ladies living with me who will be so happy to be sisters with you.'

'Oh, how wonderful,' Anna said. 'Oh, you are so kind, madame.'

'So kind,' Stephanie agreed, but she looked at Beth for guidance, a bewildered expression on her face.

'We can go nowhere without our brother,' Beth said.

Madame Suchet raised her eyebrows, but did not change her expression. 'Well, I am sure we can think of something to do with him.'

'Oh, gosh,' Tony said, 'I'm going to Paris. I'm leaving this camp.' He gave the commandant a guilty glance.

'Well?' the commandant asked. 'You must make the decision, Elizabeth. As the oldest child, you will have to sign the papers, releasing yourself and your sisters and your brother from my custody. I must warn you that you will never have such an opportunity again. Madame Suchet is really being most generous.'

Beth licked her lips, and looked from him to Madame Suchet, and discovered that Madame Suchet was looking at her, or rather, her body, with a speculative expression. She felt the lump of lead return to her stomach.

THE FIFTH CHRONICLE

January 1985

'Oh, it is so long ago,' remarked Mademoiselle Jardin. 'I do not know why the records have not all been destroyed.' She led the way down the steps into the vault, the walls of which were filled with dusty shelves, filled with even dustier files.

'Because, like me,' Meyer said, 'there must be other people around still looking for their relatives. What you should have done, mademoiselle, long ago, is transfer all this data to a computer.'

'A computer! Ha! We have no money for computers in this department.' Mademoiselle Jardin, who clearly had not been born in 1945, climbed the short ladder; she had very good legs. She began passing down folders. 'And why have you come here, monsieur? We French only maintained a few camps, compared with the British and the Americans.'

'Because I have already been through their records,' Meyer said wearily, 'and have found nothing.'

'Perhaps there is nothing to find,' Mademoiselle Jardin said darkly, dust clouding in the air as she dumped more files beside him. 'Now you see, Monsieur Meyer, it is very methodically put together. There is a master file, and then the subsidiary files, all numbered. So if you know which camp you wish to investigate, it is very easy.'

'I don't know which camp I am looking for,' Meyer confessed.

Mademoiselle Jardin removed her horn-rimmed spectacles to gaze at him; without them her face almost matched her legs. 'You mean to go through every name in all of those files?'

'I'm afraid so.'

'My God, but that will take ...'

'Several days. I am so grateful for your assistance.'

He took off his jacket. It was warm in the cellar, and yet felt cold. He cast a regretful glance up at the thick glass window let into the roof, which was the paved courtyard of the records office, and on which snow was clustering, and thought that he would like to be again lying on that beach in the Seychelles, possibly with Mademoiselle Jardin at his side. He got to work.

It took him three days to finish, and then he called Mademoiselle Jardin from her desk at the far end of the room; they had shared innumerable coffee breaks during the past seventy-two hours, and she had thawed to Meyer's genial personality.

Now she asked, 'You have found what you are looking for?'

He shook his head. 'I have found nothing I am looking for.'

She shrugged. He was getting used to people looking at him pityingly, and shrugging. Mademoiselle Jardin at least did it more attractively than Dubrowski or Linten or the women in Brussels or London. 'Well, there it is. After all but thirty-nine years, what did you expect?'

'There is one file missing,' Meyer told her.

She peered over his shoulder at the control. 'Oh, yes,' she said.

'Can you find it for me?'

'No,' she said.

'Why not?'

Another shrug. This girl was growing on him. 'It has been destroyed.'

Meyer frowned, his interest in Mademoiselle Jardin suddenly decreasing as the bloodhound took over. 'Why was just one file destroyed?'

'Because there was a scandal about that camp.'

'And so the file was destroyed?'

'Oh, no. We did not burn the file. It was the commandant who destroyed the file. I was told about it by the woman who was here before me. There was a trial.' She gave a delightful tinkle of laughter. 'I was not born then.'

'Tell me what you remember about it,' Meyer said, feeling like a man who is at last seeing light at the end of a very long tunnel.

'Well ... it was a children's camp, mainly. And when, after perhaps a year, maybe two, all the children with relatives living had been claimed by their relatives, there were still some left. Really quite a few. So the commandant, his name was Jerome, was told to start looking for foster homes for the children. The government wished to close down the camp as it was costing money. He did, and then there was a fire, and the records were destroyed. No one thought anything of it at the time. It wasn't until three years later that his assistant, Madame Lesage, told the truth. He had started the fire himself because in his haste to be rid of the children, and also to make money, he had actually sold some of them.'

'*Sold* them?'

'Yes, to people who wanted children but weren't qualified to adopt. The whole story only came out when one of the children, a German girl, for whom this Jerome had found a 'home', ran away and told her tale to a newspaper reporter. Then, as I say, there was a big scandal, and Jerome was arrested, and after Madame Lesage had given evidence against him, sent to prison.'

'Where is he now?'

'Oh, he is dead, monsieur.'

'Well, do you know where I can find Madame Lesage?'

'She is dead, too.'

'And the file is destroyed. Oh, damn and blast.'

'It was a sad business,' Mademoiselle Jardin remarked. 'But at the end of wars people behave strangely. Yet the facts of Jerome's crime were bad, much worse than had been suspected at first. This Madame Lesage actually claimed that Jerome had sold some children to Madame Suchet.' She took off her glasses to look at him. 'You have heard of Madame Suchet?'

Meyer pulled his ear. 'Do you know, I believe I have.'

Mademoiselle Jardin nodded. 'She ran the biggest
... what do you say, house?'

'House will do,' Meyer agreed.

'Well, it was the biggest house in Paris, just after
the war. Some say she ran it during the war, too, for
the Germans, but nothing was ever done about it.'
Mademoiselle Jardin tapped her nose. 'Maybe it was
used by the Maquis too, eh?'

'Maybe,' Meyer said. 'But what about the children
who were sold to her. Weren't they found?'

'Three years had passed, monsieur. The police did
interview Madame Suchet, I believe, and she admitted
having purchased some children from Jerome. But she
said they had already left her. Disappeared. Well ...
how could they be found? They were Polish, you
understand, orphans, and ...'

'Did you say they were Polish?' Meyer asked.

Mademoiselle Jardin nodded. 'Yes. Well ...'

'I love you,' Meyer said. 'Let's have dinner, and talk
some more.'

CHAPTER 5

Paris 1947–48

Beth stood up. 'We are grateful, of course, Madame Suchet, for your generous offer, but . . .'

'My God, she is going to refuse,' Commandant Jerome said. 'I do not believe it.'

'Oh, Beth,' Anna cried.

'I do so want to go to Paris,' Stephanie said.

'Please, Beth,' Tony begged.

Madame Suchet smiled. 'I think Elizabeth and I should have a little talk, in private,' she suggested.

Beth gazed at her.

'Of course,' Commandant Jerome said. 'That is a splendid idea. You will be able to explain . . . Yes, splendid. Off you go, children. Off you go.' He hurried round his desk and ushered them out. 'Do listen to what Madame Suchet has to say, Elizabeth,' he recommended, and closed the door behind him.

'Madame,' Beth said. 'I understand what you wish of us. So you must understand my refusal.'

'Sit down, Beth,' Madame Suchet said. 'Of course I understand your feelings. Monsieur Jerome has told me all about you, about your misfortune. Was it Germans, or Russians?'

'They were Russians, madame, but . . .'

'You are going to say that has not influenced your decision? My dear, it is most relevant. It has understandably had a profound effect upon you, upon your attitudes to life. Yet life is there, alas. It will not change. It is we who must change, adapt ourselves, to life, or perish. Let me talk to you very seriously. Have you considered the future? It can be a dark and dismal place, when one has no money, no relatives, not even any friends. In your case, not even any country. You do not wish to be sent back to Poland? To the Russians?'

Beth stared at her in horror. It had never occurred to her that that could possibly happen.

'It could happen,' Madame Suchet said, reading her thoughts. 'To all of you, if a place is not found for you, very soon. I happen to know that it is the intention of the French government to close this camp. Now let us consider what I am offering you. Security. Comfort. Constant care and companionship. The best food money can buy, and the best clothes, too. And wealth. You need fear nothing, and no one. I will take care of that. You will be a queen, and treated like a queen.

'And what is required of you in return? That you ... rent yourself from time to time. Believe me, however distasteful it may seem to you, you will be very fortunate to find yourself any job that will not be distasteful on occasions. But it helps if it is well paid, and you will be well paid. You will not earn less than a thousand francs a day. Often more. I guarantee it. With your body, and your obvious strength, and that strong face and that flowing hair, and your personality, so determined and yet so attractive, oh, you will be in great demand. And I will also guarantee that there will be no disease and no rape. I screen my clients very carefully. And some of them are the very cream. I have had princes in my house. Cabinet ministers, pouf, they are two a penny. Some of my girls have married very well, have become rich and famous. I am offering you a limitless future.'

She paused, and gazed at Beth, while Beth gazed back at her, although without actually seeing her. It had never occurred to her before that someone might actually pay her to rape her. Had that been what the commandant had been offering? Of course, at least in kind – better conditions, better food, better clothes ... and she had been too stupid to realise it.

Of course the concept of selling one's body was utterly wrong, and utterly distasteful. The thought of the fingers and the pain and the penis in her mouth ... as far as she was concerned what did she have to lose? She could stand anything if it would get them out of this dreadful camp and earn them money. And what Madame Suchet had just outlined was exactly the sort of future she had always dreamed of. Madame Suchet was suggesting that her way was the only possible one for someone in her position, if she really was going to achieve that dream. What was a little pain and disgust if such a goal could be reached?

Madame Suchet had been watching her closely. 'As for the men themselves,' she said, 'they are nothing. If you are afraid of being ill-treated again, forget it. Any man who attempts to harm one of my girls is thrown out on the street, be he a king. I will teach you how to deal with men. All men, my dear girl. Of course, there are men who want strange things from us, and these we are sometimes prepared to grant . . . for a fee. But that is a matter for negotiation. I do most earnestly entreat you to consider my offer.'

It was sounding better and better. Because, if she could achieve mastery over men, it would be revenge, of a sort, on all mankind for what those Russians had done to her. And perhaps marriage, to a rich man . . . That was the ideal, of course, especially once she had learned that mastery Madame Suchet was apparently promising to teach her.

'But it is wrong,' she muttered.

'Pouf,' Madame Suchet remarked. 'All women sell themselves. Most of them for next to nothing. They are fools. But even marriage is a bargain, between a woman and a man. And it is often a very bad bargain. I will make sure all your bargains are good.'

'But how could I ever go to confession?' Beth asked.

Madame Suchet smiled. 'I have my own confessor, and he will be yours as well. You will find him very indulgent.' She studied Beth's expression. 'Then you accept?' she asked winningly.

Beth gazed at her, and her face fell. 'I cannot, madame. I cannot ask my sisters to become . . .' She didn't know the word.

'I call my daughters "daughters of joy",' Madame Suchet said, even more winningly. 'Because that is

114

what they are. As for your sisters, your little sisters, listen, I am glad that you care about them, and wish to protect them. Commandant Jerome had told me about this, too. Nothing is more important that caring for one's family. I will make you a promise. It is you I wish, because of the qualities I can discern in your body, in your eyes, because of the glittering future I foresee for you. Your sisters are children. I can employ them about the house. They will be happy, and cared for as yourself. I will send them to school, and no one will lay a finger on them unless they wish it. You have my word.'

She was lying, of course, Beth knew. Or if she was not lying, she was confident that Anna and Stephanie would wish to become daughters of joy – it sounded beautiful in French, *filles de joie* – as she called them, in due course. She would see to that. But if it could be postponed for a while . . . because here was their opportunity, perhaps their only opportunity, to get out of this hateful camp, and a way to meet someone who might take her, take them all, to the happiness and prosperity she dreamed about. Why, if she could really earn a thousand francs a day, she might achieve it herself, without any outside help – it sounded like a great deal of money. Beth had no doubt that she could be quite as devious as Madame Suchet.

'Well, madame,' she said, 'if you promise . . . but there is my brother, too.'

'Oh, he may come as well,' Madame Suchet said. 'I am sure I can find a great deal for him to do.'

'Then I accept,' Beth told her.

'You are a dear, sweet girl,' Madame Suchet said, and kissed her. 'Now let us prepare to leave this dismal place.'

'But there are no bomb craters,' Stephanie exclaimed in wonder. 'And all the houses are standing. And that big thing . . .'

'The Eiffel Tower,' Madame Suchet explained. 'Of course there are no bomb craters. We have repaired them all.'

'Do you think they will ever repair Warsaw?' Tony asked.

'Not as long as the Russians are there,' Madame Suchet declared. 'We have arrived.'

It had been two days of utter wonder. Wonder first of all at leaving the camp, with Commandant Jerome and Madame Lesage beaming at them and saying what good children they had been, and then the long train journey – Stephanie could not remember ever travelling in a train before, although Beth assured her that she had. At the Franco-German border they had had to present their papers, and to Beth's amazement they actually had papers. When she had asked Madame Suchet, in a whisper, where they had come from, Madame Suchet ruffled her hair and told her not to worry. But by then Beth had been long past worrying.

They had to remain at the camp for a further four weeks, while certain formalities were gone through, the commandant said; that had certainly included obtaining those papers which Beth assumed were like Father's Gestapo pass. But the commandant had now become their friend; they had never suspected he could be so affable and helpful – although he winked at Beth and promised to come and see her in Paris, which took her aback. The men with whom she would be dealing had hitherto appeared as a faceless mass, but the thought that the commandant might be amongst them, or that any of them might resemble him was shattering. But then their new clothes had arrived, and all fears had disappeared.

Madame Suchet had measured them up before she had left the first time, but they had expected nothing like this. For Stephanie there was a smart little frock and a panama hat, white socks and patent leather shoes, and even little kid gloves; she had never looked so smart in her life. Anna had an even smarter frock, with a band for her hair. Tony had a grey suit, the first one he had ever owned, and leather shoes which fitted, and a tie which the commandant had to show him how

116

to knot. While for Beth there had been a dark blue dress – she thought of it more as a gown – with a peek-a-boo neckline and a hem fashionably midway down her calf, and high heeled shoes.

Even more delightful, there had also arrived a box of silk underwear, including a brassière. Beth had never worn a brassière before. Nor had she ever worn a suspender belt and silk stockings; the very feel of them gave her a sensation of great wickedness. And there was also a box of makeup, which Madame Lesage taught her how to apply, lipstick, rouge and powder, and the most heavenly scented perfume.

When she was dressed and made up she stared at herself in Madame Lesage's mirror, and didn't recognise herself at all. Next week she was going to be seventeen, but surely this immaculate creature beneath the matching dark blue slouch hat was past twenty.

That had been the start of the adventure. Now they were at the end, as the expensive chauffeur-driven car which had been waiting for them at the railway station drove between wrought-iron gates and up a driveway lined with tall elms to draw up before a three storied house in the heart of Paris.

And now they were surrounded by servants anxious to assist them, and by half a dozen other girls, only a year or two older than herself, Beth thought, but similarly dressed and made up, who hugged and kissed them, even Tony, called them darlings, and hurried them inside to be shown the most luxurious of bedrooms, one each, just as in Warsaw, and more clothes which Madame Suchet had bought for them.

'Oh, Beth,' Stephanie said, bursting into rare tears, 'I am so happy.'

Madame Suchet decided that the younger children could have the rest of the week off as a holiday, and made her chauffeur take them out riding every morning on her own ponies. The unfortunate Alain was also ordered to take them sightseeing and to the top of that

Eiffel Tower which had so fascinated Stephanie. 'But you understand, my dear Beth,' she said, 'that I must put you to work immediately. I have invested a great deal of money in you and your sisters. It must be earned back.'

'Of course,' Beth said. She did not like being beholden to anyone, and she intended to fulfill her side of the bargain. Besides, she was in a hurry. However unpleasant the prospect of what she had to do, if it was her way to wealth and security she wanted to get at it. She kept reminding herself that no man could ever do anything to her as terrible as the Russians in Wrakinow, and that she would be paid for anything she allowed.

Despite Madame Suchet's reassurances, and her own resolution to carry out her plan no matter what it entailed, she had spent much time during those last four weeks in the camp considering the moral aspects of the situation, wondering how she could ever confess what she was planning to do to Father Simon, for instance . . . or how she could ever face Father again, supposing he was still alive and would one day find them. But then she reflected that Father Simon was dead, that Father had killed and robbed for them, and that she could hardly do less, if she had to. And she was not being asked to do that.

Of course there would have to be a real confession one day, but she had not been inspired by the priest who had visited the camp every Sunday to hear their confessions and celebrate mass. She comforted herself with the thought that though the War might have ended, it was still going on for a lot of people, when she heard or read in French newspapers of what the Russians were doing in Poland, and that it was still going on for the Janskis more than anyone else. They were alone in the world, and it was up to her to use every means she possessed to earn them victory.

First of all there were lessons, which she found terribly embarrassing. She was taught the use of condoms, and how to put one on a customer. Madame Suchet had a lifesize wooden model of a male body with an erect penis on which Beth had to practise, being careful never to let her nails touch the wood. Madame Suchet warned her that it would not always be this easy as sometimes men were not quite as hard as her wooden specimen, even when wanting sex. Then she was taught a great deal about personal hygiene and the avoidance of pregnancies. 'Because it can happen,' Madame Suchet warned. 'Even through rubber. The quality is so poor, nowadays.'

Most embarrassing of all, however, was learning about men themselves. This was done by means of one way mirrors, in which the floor of Madame Suchet's mansion set aside for 'entertaining' abounded. It was possible for Madame to look into every room used by one of the other six girls and see exactly what was happening. During the busy hours, which were from ten in the evening to two the next morning, she paraded constantly up and down the secret corridor between the rooms, keeping an eye on her girls. Beth soon learned that it was less to be able to interfere in cases of possible harm to her protégées, than to make sure no money changed hands for services which had not previously been agreed. Madame Suchet looked after all financial arrangements, and she had no intention of being cheated by any of her young ladies. Beth could only hope that she was as scrupulous about giving them their shares. But the girls all seemed very happy and content.

There were other embarrassments. The house was visited every week by Madame Suchet's doctor as well as her confessor. And if Beth was afraid of her first confession, she was terrified of the doctor, who made the girls bend and stretch this way and that while he peered into them, almost as if he were raping them himself. Then there was learning to handle the various accessories which some men apparently wanted or needed. Tying a man up seemed a very good idea, but the thought of being tied up herself was horrifying, even if Madame Suchet assured her that it was actually rather enjoyable, so long as there was no violence involved, and she would make sure there wasn't.

'Besides,' she explained, 'the number of men who wish that sort of thing is very small. Most of our clients fall into one of two categories, those who cannot get enough sex at home, or whose home sex has become boring because the woman is afraid to experiment, and those who, even if happily married, like constant variety, and prefer to pay for it and thus forget about it once they are satisfied, rather than engage in a series of affairs, any one of which might become known and involve all sorts of scandals and even legal repercussions. We are actually providing a very valuable service in doing so much to maintain the fabric of society.'

As Madame Suchet was fond of talking like that, Beth was only partly reassured, especially when she saw the array of canes. She could not imagine why any man should wish to be caned, and asked Madame Suchet if the men ever wanted to cane the girls back; she didn't like the idea of that at all.

'Some do,' Madame Suchet agreed. 'But that is a very special service, and is very expensive, so not many men can afford it. Also, I insist upon being present, which not all men like. Do not worry, my dear girl, you will never have to do it, unless you genuinely wish to, and as I say, in my presence – I cannot have your skin broken, or even badly bruised.'

This was a contingency she apparently kept much in mind when it was necessary to punish someone – the only crimes that could be committed were not satisfying a client or attempting to do a private deal with him. Then Madame Suchet could be very angry indeed, and when Madame Suchet was angry she was quite terrifying. But she never lost control of herself to the extent where she would mark any of those bodies or faces on which she depended for her high standard of living. Punishments consisted of having to do all the other girls' laundry, run errands for them, and most serious of all, not being allowed to work for several days, and thus not earn. Every girl received a third of what Madame Suchet charged, and Beth soon discovered that she was meticulous about her payments, and that the thousand francs a day she had been guaranteed was the very bottom of the scale.

'She's a good sort, really,' Jeannette, the most senior of the girls, said. 'But you don't ever want to cross her. If she decides she can't employ you any more, either for incompetence or dishonesty, then she doesn't care what you look like when you leave here.'

A sinister threat, for Beth had every intention of leaving, taking the others with her, as soon as she had accumulated enough money. But she knew she would have to be careful. She also knew that her departure was a long time in the future. First she had to make her debut.

She was terrified, in the first place because while Madame Suchet gave her a stunning evening gown to wear, in deep red Lurex, the bodice was slashed in a deep V almost to her naval and she was forbidden to wear any underclothes at all, except for her suspender belt, stockings and very high heeled red shoes. Her hair was carefully dressed, to lie in dark brown ringlets on her shoulders, and Madame Suchet herself attended to her makeup and nail varnish, as well as rigorously inspecting her to make sure she was absolutely clean all over. But she remained in a state of nerves when she was escorted into the reception room at half past ten on that first night, thanking God that her brothers and sisters had long been sent to bed – they were packed off at nine sharp, before the evening had really begun.

There were several men already in the room, every one well dressed and clearly wealthy – only the rich could afford Madame Suchet's prices. The customers were talking with the other girls, laughing and smoking and drinking, some of them openly fondling their anticipated partners, but all eyes turned to Madame Suchet as she entered, Beth at her side. 'Voila!' Madame Suchet announced. 'My latest protégée.'

Beth wanted to turn and run, as almost every man immediately abandoned the girl he was with and came to stand around her, smiling and talking all together.

'Now, please,' Madame Suchet said, 'do not frighten her. She is a Polish young lady, from a very good family, and has only recently arrived in Paris.'

'Then I must have her first,' said one man. 'I adore the Poles.'

Madame Suchet tapped him on the chest with the fan she always carried. 'You are a spendthrift, Jacques. I doubt if you could afford her. She is very expensive.'

'Do you mean she is a virgin?' asked another man.

'She is very expensive,' Madame Suchet repeated pointedly. 'Raoul, I had her in mind for you, on her first night.'

Beth turned her head, and felt her heart go pop-pop-pop like a machine gun. This man was tall and dark, not handsome, but with strong features and pronounced lips. He was clearly old enough to be her father, and she found herself suddenly thinking of Father, and wanting to run even faster and farther. But then she realised that all the men in the room were old enough to be her father, and this man was smiling at her, and taking her hand.

'I should be charmed, madame,' he said. 'I too adore the Poles.'

'Then she is yours,' Madame Suchet said. She hissed at Beth, 'Do say something, child.'

Raoul drew her away from the other men and towards the bar in the corner of the room, where Alain, whose work never seemed finished, was dispensing drinks. 'I think, champagne,' he suggested.

'I should love some,' Beth agreed, delighted that her voice was not shaking, but the nearness of Alain gave her confidence, and she knew he would not really give her champagne – the girls were forbidden to touch alcohol. All drinks were poured under the counter, and although the two glasses looked identical and sparkled together, hers was slightly coloured soda water.

Raoul raised his glass. 'To your beauty, mademoiselle, may it never diminish.'

'You are too kind, monsieur,' she murmered, sipping her drink.

'It makes me impatient,' Raoul confessed. 'Shall we retire?'

'Oh! Shouldn't you speak with madame first?'

'Madame knows my requirements,' he said, and took her hand. She glanced over the room, but Madame Suchet appeared to be deep in conversation with one of the other men, although she knew that Madame Suchet always watched everything that was going on, and that if Raoul had not already paid or come to some prior arrangement, she would have stopped their departure. In fact, she realised, as they mounted the short flight of stairs to the mezzanine floor off which the rooms opened, Raoul apparently even knew to which room he was to take her. He was clearly a favourite client.

Thus it was time to concentrate. He opened the door for her, and she stepped inside. Madame Suchet believed that a bedroom should look like a bedroom, and this had sheets and pillowslips as well as an eiderdown, and clean, fluffy towels by the basin, but Beth couldn't help staring at the huge mirror which took up almost all of one wall. A tall, strongly built young woman stared back, face pale but determined, framed in the curling brown hair, breasts rising and falling half out of the red Lurex. A fascinating picture, she thought. But she knew that by now Madame Suchet would have excused herself from the conversation in the reception room to see to some detail about the house, and would be standing in the secret corridor behind the wall, gazing through this same mirror at her.

Raoul stood behind her, put his arms round her waist, and kissed her ear. 'I think you are beautiful too,' he said, and touched her breasts. She suppressed a shiver, but it was a very light touch, and was gone again a moment later.

Raoul sat down in the comfortable armchair. 'May I see some more of you?'

Beth turned to face him, took the straps from her shoulders, and let the gown slowly slide past her breasts and hips to the floor, as Madame Suchet had taught her.

Raoul nodded. 'Quite entrancing. How old are you, girl?'

Again as instructed, Beth replied, 'Twenty-two, sir.'

He smiled. 'Give or take five years, I imagine. And you are experienced?'

'Not experienced,' Beth said. 'I have been . . .' she paused.

He nodded. 'You have had some experience, at any rate. And I would say it was distasteful. Then why are you here?' He held up a finger before she could think of a reply; Madame Suchet had not anticipated such a question. 'Because a girl has to eat, eh? That excuses almost everything. Now come over here and kiss me.'

She stepped out of the dress, walked across the floor towards him, trembling on her high heels, and stooped.

'Not my mouth, silly girl,' he said. 'I can have my wife do that.'

Beth hesitated, but she had known she would almost certainly have to do this. She knelt between his legs, having to hide her disappointment. For a moment she had almost thought he might be different to the Russians.

In fact he was. In the first place, because he was clean and had to be encouraged . . . And then because he was so very gentle with her, and considerate. He adjusted the condom himself, to her great relief, and then wanted to stroke her flesh instead of hurting her; she found herself enjoying his caress. He entered her both from in front and behind, and each time she tensed herself for the thrusts of pain she remembered, and discovered there was none. He toyed with her breasts and nipples, instead of biting or pulling them. He kneaded her buttocks instead of slapping them. She was almost beginning to enjoy the sensation of him when he climaxed. Then she just wanted to lie there

124

and feel, but only ten minutes after he had left Madame Suchet came in.

'Come on, come on,' she said. 'You have done well. Raoul is pleased with you, and wishes you again tomorrow night. But it is only midnight. Get up and douche. We only really get busy after the opera.'

Not all men were as gentle or as easy to please, or as helpful, as Raoul, who, according to Madame Suchet, had the misfortune to be married to a woman who thought all sex was disgusting, and lay absolutely still with her eyes tight shut whenever he would mount her. 'She is very rich,' Madame Suchet added sadly, 'and her family is very powerful.'

But as she had promised, none of the other men in any way resembled the Russians, and some of them were the easiest customers in the world, as they didn't even want proper sex, but merely conversation with some masturbation thrown in. Others, of course, wanted a great deal more, and the ones she liked least were those who wanted her to swear at them during foreplay and toss and scream during intercourse. She was grateful that the two way mirrors were at least too solid for Madame to hear what was going on.

And after every night, her pile of francs grew.

Working for Madame Suchet could have become a way of life, as it had for the other six girls, at least on the surface. Beth realised that, for all their sweetness and charm, they were really very hard young women indeed, who regarded themselves as opposed to the entire world, and would take their profit wherever they could. Well, was she not also against the world? Father had told her that, and she had her sisters and brother to look after. They indeed were the spur which prevented her from ever just lying back and enjoying her job – which she was discovering would not be all that difficult to do – and accumulating money.

Madame Suchet was here again as good as her word, and it even seemed possible to feel that the youngsters had no idea where they actually were. They were put to work, at helping in the kitchen and laying the table and in the laundry and a host of other household tasks, while Tony helped the gardeners and Alain with the heavy work about the house and grounds, but they were always in bed by nine, and Madame Suchet did not permit male visitors during the day. Of course it was impossible to disguise the fact that they were living in an unusual society.

'Does Madame Suchet really entertain every night?' Anna asked, and when Beth said she did, she pouted and said, 'Then way aren't we ever allowed to come and meet the guests? Mother always made us come in and meet the guests before dinner.'

'Well,' Beth said, 'Madame Suchet isn't Mother.'

'She treats us like servants,' Anna grumbled.

'Oh, come now,' Beth protested. 'She is treating us like royalty. When have you eaten so well or been so well dressed or slept in such comfortable beds? Not since before the War. So what if you have to launder a few sheets? That is the least we can do.'

'You never launder any sheets, I notice,' Anna remarked. 'You never even get out of bed until lunch-time. And as for the sheets . . . she changes them every day. I have never seen so many sheets.'

'Madame Suchet is a very clean person,' Beth pointed out, which was no lie.

Tony and Stephanie were less querulous, more inclined to enjoy the good life which had suddenly been thrust upon them, probably, Beth thought, because they couldn't remember what it had been like before the War at all. Stephanie was as happy as a lark, even if Madame Suchet insisted that both she and Tony attended school, which kept them out of the way for most of the day.

Anna was the main problem, and she was a growing one, literally. In the spring of 1948 Beth realised that in August Anna would be sixteen, and had a figure every bit as good as her own, while her long blonde hair caused heads to turn on the street. Beth was disturbed by the fact that the other girls were also attracted by the beautiful Pole. It seemed that many daughters of joy, forced to treat all men as customers, found their only real emotional outlets in their own sex. One or two of the girls even made advances to Beth, but she was so obviously disinterested – however much she liked them all she certainly felt no affection for any of them, nor could she ever imagine doing so: all her softer feelings were reserved for her sisters and Tony – they soon abandoned her to be nice to Anna, who would respond to anyone.

But Madame Suchet frowned upon lesbianism, not on any moral grounds – she reminded Beth increasingly of Father in her pragmatic approach to life – but because she wanted her girls to reserve all their passionate feelings for the evenings. Madame Suchet liked her girls to 'come off', as she put it, with their clients.

'It so thrills a man,' she explained to Beth. 'And there is no risk to it in my establishment. Girls working alone now, they have to be careful, or they might get robbed or cheated if they let themselves go. No girl of mine is going to be cheated, I can promise you that. So they can really enjoy themselves, and it is good for business.' And she stared very hard at Beth, because it was obvious that Beth had never let herself go in her life. 'I know you have a lot of unpleasant memories,' Madame Suchet said sympathetically. 'But you must try to relax more. Men want you as it is. Think how much more they would want you if they felt they were exciting you.'

Beth mumbled something about trying, but while she could not avoid enjoying some of the things which were done to her, she could not imagine relaxing while in bed with a man, or with anyone. As Madame Suchet had first suggested, it was a lucrative job of work, and had to be endured for the sake of the money it brought in.

Her biggest cause for concern was that Madame

Suchet was beginning to take a special interest in Anna as an employee. She had always shown more interest in her than in Stephanie, but now she began to buy Anna more clothes and to teach her to use makeup, and the two of them spent long hours walking together in the garden.

When Beth asked Anna what they talked about, she replied, 'All sorts of things,' with a dreamy look in her eyes. Beth was handicapped by not wishing any of the others to know what really went on in the house, so she could not ask her sister outright if Madame Suchet had invited her to become one of the girls.

She asked Madame Suchet instead, reminding her of her promise, and Madame Suchet smiled and said, 'I never forget a promise, Beth. But I will admit that I have been talking to Anna about her future. After all, she is going to be sixteen in a few months, and can no longer be considered a little girl. Of course she will do whatever she wishes. But I would hope to be able to advise her and guide her.'

And sell her off, the first time, as a virgin worth a fortune, Beth thought angrily. She had no doubt that was what Madame Suchet had in mind – with Stephanie to follow, in the course of time.

Escape was imperative. But it was daily becoming more difficult to achieve. She was accumulating what seemed to be a large sum of money, but every time she went shopping the prices seemed to have gone up a few more francs due to the post war inflation. She realised it would take her years to accumulate sufficient capital to set herself up, or even to remove herself from the wrath of Madame Suchet, who would undoubtedly feel herself cheated if she lost the entire Janski family.

And just how terrible Madame's rage could be, she discovered that very summer, when one of the girls, Simone, privately accepted ten thousand francs to attend a stag party, perform a striptease, and generally entertain the guests. Simone asked for the evening off to visit a sick aunt, but Madame Suchet immediately guessed what she was up to. She said nothing, gave her the permission, but when she returned had her seized and searched by Alain. The money was found, and Madame Suchet lost her temper – or appeared to do so: Beth felt the whole thing was an act, and that Madame had actually decided to make an example of the unfortunate girl. She allowed Alain to beat Simone up, hitting her again and again in the face until it was cut to ribbons and her eyes were blackened and puffy. Then she was thrown into the street; Madame letting her take the money she had accumulated, but nothing else save the clothes she was wearing.

It was horrifying, but certainly salutary, made the more frightening by the way Madame smiled at the rest of them when it was done. 'Good riddance,' she said cheerfully. 'She was always dishonest. Not like you girls.' And she looked from face to face.

So escape and advancement, when it was attempted, would have to under the aegis of another protector. And that protector could only come from amongst the customers; she was allowed to meet no one else. Beth had been considering this possibility since the turn of the year. Obviously men like Raoul – who, however attractive was clearly at the mercy of his wife's family and was also a friend of Madame Suchet's – or any of the freaks, were out of the question. She had no intention of running off with a customer, to be discarded the moment he became bored or found someone else. And besides, when she ran, she had to take Anna, Tony and Stephanie with her. Her man had to be a very special kind, and in very special circumstances. He needed to be very rich, and powerful, or at least tough enough, to protect her from Madame Suchet – and he had to have fallen for her sufficiently to set her up in style as a mistress, with her own apartment, big enough to contain all four of them.

The trouble was that she had never encountered anyone who seemed capable of filling that large bill. She half picked more than one of her customers, and rapidly discarded each after sleeping with him, either because of his habits or his conversation or what she could discover about his position in life, and most important of all, his finances. By June she was in despair, as it was now certain that Madame intended to introduce Anna on her sixteenth birthday.

It was then that she met Georges Mathieu.

Beth had now been at Madame Suchet's for two years, and she had never seen Monsieur Mathieu before. Yet he was clearly not only an old customer, but an important one: Madame Suchet positively fawned over him. Beth found this difficult to understand, as he was shabbily dressed, sported no jewellery, and arrived by taxi instead of in his own car. He was also older than most of Madame Suchet's clients; she estimated him to be more than sixty, which seemed awfully old. With his paunch, and his jowly, if friendly, face, which made him look like a bloodhound gone to seed, his thinning hair and his Provençal accent, he was not even terribly attractive, and she was disappointed when she was presented to him as something he simply had to sample.

Her disappointment grew when he turned out to be close to impotent. She felt no pity for men who were impotent, but she was conscious that Madame would be watching, and that if he was important or an old friend, she would be angry were he not satisfied. So Beth worked harder than ever before, and when she finally got him aroused she even faked an orgasm herself for the first time; she had watched enough of the other girls doing it to be very convincing.

Certainly Monsieur Mathieu was convinced. 'You are a charmer and a devil,' he gasped when he lay beside her. 'My God, the most delicious devil I have ever known. I will come again tomorrow.'

Madame Suchet, who had indeed been watching, and appeared to have been taken in herself, was very pleased, and gave Beth an extra thousand francs for making Monsieur Matthieu so happy. Beth could

hardly wait for the following night, but this time nothing she could do would arouse him. He just wanted to
lie beside her on the bed, naked – he even made her
take off her suspender belt, which was unusual – hold
her in his arms, and talk. Beth was too alarmed at what
Madame Suchet's reaction to this total failure – the first
of her career – might be to listen very carefully to what
he was saying, at first. Then she began to realise that
she might have missed something important.

'There are several hundred of them,' Monsieur
Mathieu was saying. 'Running wild. My cowboys have
to round them up, every so often, for the market. Oh,
they are a magnificent sight. But not as magnificent as
my bulls. Do you know, I export semen all over the
world?'

Not his own, certainly. So he was a farmer. A *farmer*?

'Do you like horses?' he asked.

'Oh, yes,' she said.

'You would like the Carmague,' he told her. 'It is one
of the few untamed parts of Europe remaining. The
only untamed part of France. I have always been happy
there. But since my dear Mathilde died, it has been so
lonely.'

Beth wondered who Mathilde had been, and found
herself beginning to get excited. But he was a friend of
Madame Suchet's, that was obvious. Therefore she had
to be more careful than ever; this could be a trap.

'Do you know why I like you so much?' Monsieur
Mathieu asked. 'Not only because you are so big
and strong. I have always liked big strong women –
Mathilde was small. But because there is a quality
about you, a quality of sympathy, which I find especially attractive.'

Beth reflected that it was her business to be all things
to all men, however much she disliked them as a sex.

'I should enjoy showing you the Camargue,' he continued, his eyes shut. 'Do you ever have any time off?'

'You would have to ask Madame Suchet about that,'
Beth said cautiously, picturing Simone after Alain had

131

finished with her. This dear old soul was not the man to stand up to Madame.

'That ratbag,' he commented, still with his eyes closed, and speaking very quietly and without emotion. 'If I say you are coming down to visit with me, she will agree.'

'Madame Suchet?' Beth asked, in genuine surprise. She could not envisage Madame Suchet agreeing to anything not in her own interest.

Monsieur Mathieu opened his eyes. 'I know all about your precious madame,' he said. 'Oh, yes. Nazi officers have lain in this very bed. So she let me and my men use the house as well, and we gained information. But she was a collaborator who played both ends against the middle. If I had denounced her ... indeed, if I had not defended her, she would have had her head shaved, if she had not been shot.'

Beth began to understand a lot of things.

'So, if I wished you to come down to my château for a week, even a month, she would agree.' Georges said. 'But I would wish you to want to come.' He smiled at her. 'And make a lonely widower very happy.'

Beth was by this time propped on her elbow. Château? Widower? Men who owned châteaux, and farmed vast herds of wild horses and bulls, simply had to be very wealthy, no matter what they looked like or performed like. And a widower might indeed be lonely enough to set the right girl up as a mistress.

'Well?' he asked, watching her expression.

'Oh, monsieur,' she said. 'I should love to visit your château. But ... I cannot.'

'Because of Madame Suchet? I have told you, she will do as I wish.'

'Because of my sisters, monsieur. And my brother. I must be here to take care of them.'

Which was the truth. She had no doubt that the moment she was gone Madame Suchet would introduce Anna to the salon, even before her sixteenth birthday.

He frowned at her. 'You have sisters? And a brother? Tell me about them.'

Beth drew a long breath, and obeyed, in great detail. She also told him about herself, in great detail; she had learned a lot from Stephanie's stories. When she was finished, Monsieur Mathieu put his arm round her shoulders and hugged her against him. 'You poor child,' he said. 'To have seen the Countess shot before your eyes ... how that must have upset your poor father, the Count. It makes my blood boil. It makes my blood boil even more to think of your estate being sequestrated and broken up. Eight thousand acres. Why, do you know, I only have ten thousand, in the Camargue?'

Beth felt tears start to her eyes.

'And now, to find you in a place like this ...'

Beth recalled Raoul's words on her first night in the salon. 'It is necessary to eat, monsieur,' she pointed out. 'And I must provide for four.'

'You are a brave and noble girl,' he said. 'I should like to meet your family.'

'Madame Suchet would never permit it.'

'Bah,' he said, and sat up.

'They are in bed,' Beth said desperately, wondering if she had gone too far. Now Madame Suchet would know what she was about.

'Ah. Then, I will come to see them tomorrow.'

'Tomorrow? Madame does not permit visitors during the day. Besides ...' She didn't know what to say. This could just be her big opportunity ... but the risk.

'Tomorrow,' he said, and got out of bed.

'But monsieur ...' She caught his hand. 'You have not finished.'

'I cannot, tonight. It happens, sometimes. I am content to have held you in my arms.'

'But ...' she cast a glance at the wall mirror.

'Of course,' he said. 'She watches.'

Beth sat up in alarm. 'You know?'

'Of course,' he said again. 'I have stood out there with her, and watched the Nazis at play.' He smiled at the mirror, and beckoned. 'She will be here in a moment.'

Beth could not imagine what would happen then. She hugged her knees, and gazed at the door, watching it open. Madame Suchet was certainly not pleased. 'Wretched girl,' she declared. 'She has failed you, Georges. She has always been a disappointment. Well, I shall take a belt to her ass, and see if I cannot put some life into her cunt.'

Beth's blood seemed to freeze. She had never heard Madame speak so coarsely, not even to Simone.

But Monsieur Mathieu continued to smile. 'You will give her a bonus, you mean, Aimée. Why, this little girl has made me happier than at any moment since dear Mathilde passed away. Now, I wish to meet her sisters.'

'Sisters?' Madame Suchet glared at Beth, who opened her mouth and then closed it again.

'I wheedled her story out of her,' he explained. 'I know they are young, and asleep. I will come to lunch tomorrow.'

It was Madame Suchet's turn to open her mouth and then close it again.

M. Mathieu kissed her hand, and then did the same to Beth. 'Au revoir,' he said.

Madame Suchet watched the door close behind him. 'You are an unutterable little whore,' she remarked. 'I should take the skin from your back, anyway.'

Beth's courage was returning. 'I am sure Monsieur Mathieu will wish to see my back tomorrow, madame,' she said. 'Besides, what have I done that is wrong? I did make him happy, just lying here.'

'Ha,' Madame Suchet commented. 'You think he is an old fool. Well, he is, but not in the way you imagine. Georges Mathieu knows what he wants, and he usually gets what he wants. He wants your sisters, as he assumes they will be like you. Can you not see that?'

That could well be a problem, Beth realised, but also a weapon. She decided not to tell Madame Suchet what Georges really wanted of her, but let him do it himself.

Which he did, next day after luncheon. It was a great occasion, because the other girls were delighted to have a male guest on an off duty occasion, as it were, and Anna, Tony and Stephanie were delighted to have been invited to lunch. Madame Suchet had spared no expense, and there were lobsters, prawns and oysters followed by rack of lamb and a fabulous gâteau. There were also bottles of champagne with the fish course and of Château Latour with the meat.

The girls looked at Madame Suchet in concern, and Madame Suchet looked at Monsieur Mathieu. 'I do not like to drink alone,' he announced, and Madame Suchet sighed and raised her eyes to heaven.

After that, the afternoon became very merry indeed. Beth endeavoured to stay sober, but it was impossible, and eventually even Madame Suchet herself succumbed to the Calvados which followed the meal, and started telling interminable, obscene stories. The only person present who didn't get drunk was Monsieur Mathieu, although he drank more than the rest put together. But he was enjoying himself, had Anna on one side of him and Stephanie on the other, laughed and joked with them, patted their hands and knees, admired Anna's hair and Stephanie's enormous eyes, and spared the time to engage Tony in conversation as well. But he spent most of the meal staring at Beth, who sat opposite, and after the meal retired with her to one of the upstairs rooms, where, far from being impotent, he left her with nothing to do, which was just as well, because she was half asleep.

'I hope you are satisfied, Georges,' Madame Suchet said when he was preparing to leave. She had spent the afternoon sitting in a hot tub and drinking black coffee, and looked distinctly the worse for wear. 'I am sorry to have to charge you double, but you have rendered my entire staff all but incapable.'

'Think nothing of it,' he said. 'Now you will have to work out a new set of charges. I wish to take Beth and her sisters down to Château Lorges for a weekend.'

'And my brother,' Beth said sleepily from the depths of the bed.

'Oh, indeed. And the boy.'

'I don't know what this wretched child has been telling you, Georges, but that is quite impossible,' she declared. 'You know I never permit such things. And as for the two young girls, why, I never heard such a thing.'

'I adore young girls,' Monsieur Mathieu said candidly. 'But I will return them to you unharmed. You have my word. I merely wish to entertain them. My home has been empty of laughter for too long. You will not deny me this brief moment of happiness, Aimée. I would consider it most unkind of you.'

Madame Suchet snapped her pencil in two.

THE SIXTH CHRONICLE

February 1985

'You are asking me find three Polish girls, who thirty-five years ago were prostitutes in Paris?' Henri Lefèbre scratched his head. He was an old friend of Meyer's, and being a senior officer in the Sureté, had proved his value more than once in the past. But now he looked helpless. 'That is a very tall order, Bob.'

'I don't know for sure they were prostitutes,' Meyer pointed out.

Lefèbre grinned. 'It is unlikely that a woman like the Suchet would have bought them for any other purpose, my friend. But thirty-five years . . . that is a lifetime to a whore. Disease, drugs, who can say what might have killed them off.'

'I have a hunch that at least one survived,' Meyer said. That she married, and could now be living in America.'

'But you are looking for her in Paris.'

'I have to have a name,' Meyer said patiently. 'Or at least, a photograph. Something. Right now I have nothing, not even a description.'

'And you expect me to conjure up a name or a photograph? Thirty-five years! My God! I doubt even the Suchet herself remembers them. But then, I doubt the Suchet remembers anything.'

Meyer frowned at him, while his heart began to pound. 'The Suchet is still alive?'

'She was, when last I heard. Just.'

'But . . . good God. She must be . . .'

'In her eighties, yes. Retired, you might say. I said she was only just alive.'

'You have an address?'

'It is on file. But Bob, I doubt you will get anything out of her.'

'She seems to be the only lead I have,' Meyer pointed out.

Lefèbre nodded. 'I would say she is.' He picked up his intercom, spoke rapidly to his secretary. 'Well, go along and see her; Marie will give you the address. You will at least gain some insight into the hand of God.'

Meyer wasn't sure what his friend meant, until he found himself in the narrow, odiferous back alley on the Left Bank, looking at the tumbledown rooming house.

The concierge peered at him from beneath eyebrows which nearly met her moustache. 'She does not receive visitors.'

'This is a most important matter,' Meyer explained. 'I have news from an old friend. Perhaps an inheritance.'

He had been trained to lie convincingly. The concierge's eyes came alive. 'An inheritance! Ah. There is rent outstanding, you know, monsieur, and various other matters.'

'They will all be attended to,' Meyer promised, 'if I can see Madame Suchet.'

The concierge appeared to consider. 'I don't know,' she said doubtfully. 'She might agree to see you, for a bottle of wine.' She stroked her moustache. 'But then, I don't know. I don't know if I should admit you . . .'

'Does she like Cognac?' Meyer asked.

Once again the concierge's eyes gleamed. 'Everyone likes Cognac, monsieur.'

'I'll be right back,' Meyer promised, 'with two bottles.'

It took him fifteen minutes, and when he returned, the concierge was waiting, to hug her bottle hungrily to her chest. 'The top floor,' she said. 'She never comes down.'

Meyer climbed the creaking staircase, watched a rat scurrying away from his heavy footfalls, listened to odd unhappy noises from behind the various doors he passed, babies wailing hungrily, someone coughing wetly, people shouting at each other, the gurgle of a toilet being flushed. One of the doors opened and a young man came out and stared at him, fingers deep in the pockets of his jeans, one hand making a fist round the flicknife which was clearly outlined. Meyer stared back, gloved hands curled back into big fists, jaw stuck out aggressively. The young man went back inside again.

Meyer reached the top, slapping his freezing hands together as he took off his gloves. He knocked, and listened, and knocked again, and heard a rustling sound and a creak.

'Have you got it?' a quavering voice asked.

'Yes,' Meyer said.

He listened to more sound, a slow shuffling, and then the bolt was drawn and he stared at the woman. He had expected age, but not total decrepitude. The Madame Suchet described to him by those who had known her in her heyday had been tall and elegant; this woman was shrunken and bowed. Her fingers were like purple talons, clawing out from beneath the shawl she wore over her tattered dress. Her nose was a beak, her face a mottle of white and purple, her hair straggles of untidy grey peeping out from beneath her mob cap. And she smelt. The entire room smelt, of urine and dirt and rats and rotten food.

Madame Suchet did not even look at him, but only at the bottle, and stretched out one shivering hand.

Meyer reminded himself that she had a lot to answer for, and pulled the bottle away. Now she did raise her head. 'You said it was mine,' she protested. Her voice shook, and tears dribbled down her cheeks. 'I gave the money for it.'

'You gave the money for wine,' Meyer reminded her. 'This is Cognac. I will give it to you, when we have talked.'

Her faded eyes blinked at him, but she licked her lips. 'I have committed no crimes,' she said. 'You have hounded me enough.'

'I am not from the police,' Meyer said reassuringly. 'I am only looking for some information, about a girl. A girl you may have known, many years ago.'

139

Madame Suchet's face moved. It was difficult to decide whether it was a smile or merely a readjustment of her gums; she clearly had no teeth. 'I knew many girls, many years ago.' She turned away from him, and shuffled back to her rocking chair, set by a grimy window which gave her a view of another grimy window just across the alley. Meyer felt vaguely sick.

He inhaled sharply. 'This girl was a long time ago, Madame Suchet,' he said. 'More than thirty years.'

Madame Suchet commenced to rock gently, to and fro. 'More than thirty years,' she commented. 'Have you ever driven in a Rolls Royce, young man?' She snorted. 'I owned three, thirty years ago.'

'Thanks to the girls,' Meyer reminded her.

'They were nothing,' Madame Suchet said. 'I made them.'

'And you also destroyed them.'

'I have talked long enough.' Madame Suchet said.

Meyer went to the washstand, took the toothmug which had not been used in some time, he estimated, and poured a little of the brandy. When he took the cup to her, she wrapped her claws round it and drank greedily.

'I wish you to tell me about three of the girls,' he said.

Madame Suchet blinked at him sleepily.

'They were sisters, Poles,' Meyer said. 'You bought them from a refugee camp in Germany. Do you remember them? Their name was Janska.'

'Three girls,' Madame Suchet said, her eyes closing. 'Poles.' She almost spat the word. 'I remember the Poles.'

Meyer's breath escaped in a sigh of satisfaction. 'Tell me what you remember of them, Madame Suchet. Three pretty girls, were they not?'

Madame Suchet's mouth worked for a moment before she answered. 'Pretty girls,' she agreed. 'I remember the eldest. Beth was her name.'

'That's right,' Meyer said. 'Elizabeth. Can you tell me what became of her, and her sisters?'

140

Madame Suchet turned her head to look at him, and he gave her another mug of brandy. She drank, and made a curious whistling sound. 'I should think the big one is burning in hell,' she said.

Meyer sat on the bed, beside her chair. 'Tell me why she should be doing that,' he said.

CHAPTER 6

The Camargue, 1948–52

'Well? Madame Suchet demanded. 'Come in.'

The four of them filed into her office, rather like deliquent schoolchildren, Beth thought. But then, she supposed they had been playing truant.

'Was it as grand as you supposed?' Madame inquired.

'Oh, yes, madame,' Stephanie said. 'The château . . .'

'Was like a palace,' Anna said.

'So many rooms,' Tony said.

'So many servants,' Anna said.

'And you could see for miles, over the country,' Tony said.

'We rode horses, every day,' Stephanie told her.

'And we punted on the canal,' Tony said.

'And we watched the men rounding up the bulls,' Anna said.

'And riding them,' Tony added. 'I'm going to be a cowboy when I grow up, and ride the bulls.'

'Then you'd be a bull boy, stupid,' Anna pointed out.

'And Monsieur Mathieu took us in his motor car for a drive down to the coast, to St Cannes,' Stephanie said dreamily.

'She means, he took us to Cannes and St Tropez,' Anna said scornfully.

'We saw a film actress,' Tony said.

'More than one,' Anna corrected.

Madame Suchet looked unimpressed. 'I am sure you had a jolly time. I am so glad. Now, off you go. Not you, Beth.'

The others hurried from the office, while Beth waited. She had known this confrontation was inevitable, and yet had hoped it might not be. Now she must accept the consequences of her folly, she supposed. Of her dreams.

'You did not join in the paean of praise,' Madame

Suchet remarked. 'Was Lorges not as beautiful as they say?'

'Oh, yes, madame, it was beautiful.'

'And was Monsieur Mathieu everything you had hoped?'

'He was a perfect gentleman, madame. And a man of his word.'

'Ha. You mean he did not touch your sisters. But I am sure he touched you.'

'He touched me, madame, yes.'

'I'm sure he did. Well, hand over whatever he gave you. You know the rules.'

'He gave me nothing, madame.'

Madame Suchet's eyes narrowed. 'You spent a weekend with Georges Mathieu for nothing? Don't make me laugh. What is that you are wearing?'

Beth held out her wrist; the gold watch gleamed in the sunlight drifting through the office windows. 'It is a personal present, madame.'

'I do not permit personal presents, as you well know. Take it off.'

Beth bit her lip. 'He said he wanted me to wear it, always.'

'Well, I will return it to you the next time he comes to visit, and you can wear it when you are in bed with him. But it belongs to the house. Come along.'

Beth hesitated, then obeyed. She had known she would have to.

'Now the money,' Madame Suchet said.

'He gave me no money, madame.'

'For four days? How many tricks did he take?'

Again Beth hesitated. 'Seven, madame.'

'In four days. My God! He will kill himself, the silly old fool. And you gave seven tricks without asking payment?'

'I assumed he had settled with you in advance, madame.'

Madame Suchet stared at her for several seconds, then smiled. 'Why, so he did. But do you expect me to believe you sought no profit for yourself?'

Beth bit her lip. 'Yes, madame.'

Madame Suchet threw back her head and gave a peal of laughter. 'My God, but I see it all. You poor deluded girl. You hoped he would take you away from here and set you up as his mistress. Oh, you little fool.'

Beth said nothing. The ridicule was almost more than she could bear. Of course she hoped that, had set her entire store by that. She had put herself out as never before, and even risked Anna and Stephanie, had been sure that she had convinced him he was someone special to her, and that she could make him happy. Indeed, she had made him happy – and nothing had happened. He had made love to her, time and again; he had shown her his château and his immense estate with great pride, and basked in her admiration of it – and at the end of the four days he had sent her, sent them all, packing, with the present of a gold watch, which he must have known she would not be allowed to keep. She was just a whore, with whom he had amused himself.

Madame Suchet continued to smile. 'Well,' she said. 'It has all been valuable experience, I have no doubt. I suppose you think I am angry with you, and will punish you. My dear Beth, I can blame no girl for wishing to better herself. But since we are embarked upon the gaining of experience, I think it is time to expand yours even further. There is a man coming tonight who has asked for you several times. I have always refused to let him have you, but I think tonight I will say yes. Mind you please him; he is very important, and if he is pleased I will forgive you for everything. Run along now, and have a rest. You will need to be alert tonight.'

Beth was too crushed to consider what she meant, or to be aroused by the thought that she was to entertain a very important man; she did not think she could undergo the humiliation of making such a play and having no success. And now there was clearly no way to save Anna; she would just have to make the best of it. What was particularly galling was that she was sure

Anna had no desire to be saved. But she would be failing in her responsibility, breaking her vow to protect her siblings and look after them. Now it was important to look after herself, because she did not doubt that Madame Suchet, for all her smiles, was very angry indeed. She had to be placated, or they might all find themselves out in the street.

She dressed with her now instinctive care, and took her place in the salon, to find herself being introduced to a tall, thin man with a hatchet face who kissed her hand with great enthusiasm. 'The Pole,' he said. 'I have long awaited the pleasure of this moment,' he said. 'But you have always been so busy.'

'She is in great demand, Armand,' Madame Suchet said. 'But she is yours tonight, if you wish her.'

'Indeed I do,' he said. 'Is my room ready?'

'Of course,' Madame Suchet said. 'It is waiting for you.'

He held Beth's hand tightly, and led her along the corridor. To number six, Beth realised. She had never used number six before. It was where those men with unusual tastes were entertained, and she had never been required there; that was usually the province of Jeannette.

Before she could decide on her attitude, he had opened the door, ushered her inside, and closed the door again. It looked like any of the other rooms, and she was curious as to what this very masculine looking man did want. Mechanically she walked to the other side of the bed, and allowed her gown to slip from her shoulders as she turned, and then bit her lip in annoyance. Armand was not even watching her, but was opening a chest in the corner, from which he took a thin cane.

Beth caught her breath; of course, he wanted to be whipped. Something she had never done before. So this was what Madame Suchet had meant by further broadening her experience: the old bag had been afraid to tell her straight out what she would have to do. Well, she thought, if that was what she wanted – she actually felt like laying into a man, any man.

'Kneel on the bed,' Armand commanded. 'Put your head down, and get your backside as high as possible. You may scream if you wish. I like to hear women scream.'

Beth gazed at him in horror. That he might wish to beat her had never crossed her mind. Because it could not happen without her consent, and without Madame Suchet's presence. 'There has been a mistake,' she said quietly.

He shook his head. 'Madame Suchet said I could have you for as long as I wished. She said you enjoy being whipped. She even said I could mark you. She does not usually let me mark Jeanette.'

'Mark me?' Beth shouted, panic clawing at her. 'You must be crazy.' She reached for her gown, and he seized her arm and swung her round.

He was grinning at her. 'I do not mind if you fight me. I would like that. But you mustn't hurt me.'

Beth gazed at him, and then kicked him on the ankle with all her strength; she had not yet taken off her shoes. He gave a howl of pain and she leapt past him and reached the door, the gown bundled in her hands like a rugby football.

'Bitch!' he bellowed, and charged at her, swinging the cane. It caught her across the right shoulder with a sting which drove the breath from her lungs, the strength from her knees. She dropped the gown and almost fell, but clung to the door, pulled it open, and staggered into the corridor. Armand swung at her again, and she stumbled against the wall, regaining her balance beyond his reach. Now she kicked off the high heels and ran down the corridor, bursting into the salon, which was as crowded as ever. Every eye in the room turned to look at the startling apparition, wearing only garter belt and stockings, like some refugee from a strip show.

'Beth!' Madame Suchet's voce was like a knife edge. 'What are you doing?'

'He wants . . .' Beth drew several long breaths, increasingly aware of the burning pain in her shoulder.

'I know what Armand wants,' Madame Suchet said, more coldly than ever. 'Now get back to him.'

'You said . . .' Beth fought to keep her nerves under control. 'You said I would never be caned unless I wanted it. You said you would always be there. You said . . .'

'You are making a spectacle of yourself,' Madame Suchet said, getting up and advancing on her, face angrily flushed as a ripple of laughter spread round the room. 'As you have such a penchant for going off with men on their own, I supposed you would prefer to enjoy Armand on your own. As you do not wish to, very well, I will come in with you. And then we shall see.'

'You're punishing me,' Beth gasped. 'After saying you wouldn't. You lying . . .'

Madame Suchet slapped her face. The force of the blow sent Beth reeling backwards, and she clutched at the bar for support. Then she became angry. 'You cheating bitch,' she shouted, having learned the word from Armand. 'You . . .' she swept her hand over the bar counter, picked up a glass, and hurled it with all her strength. Madame Suchet ducked, and the glass struck one of the men behind her. He gasped and fell over a chair, taking another customer and one of the girls with him. The room exploded into pandemonium.

'Are you mad?' Madame Suchet demanded. 'Oh, you will suffer for this, you little hellion. Alain!'

Alain hurried round the bar. Beth looked left and right, realised she could expect no help from anyone present, and ran for the door to the private part of the house. But one of the girls, Jeannette, stepped in front of her and tried to catch her hands. She checked, understanding for the first time how much they must have always hated the upstart young foreigner who had taken so much of their share of the business. And Jeannette . . . Jeannette had always served Armand before.

147

She swung her fists to and fro, but Jeannette avoided them and grasped her round the waist. She seized the older girl's hair and pulled it, and Jeannette gave a scream of pain and rage. Beth grasped her shoulders and thrust her aside; she was bigger and stronger. But the delay had given Alain time to reach her. His fingers closed on her arms and he turned her round while she subsided, all the energy draining from her muscles. There was no point in attempting to fight Alain.

Madame Suchet was breathing heavily, her face positively vicious. 'Take her back into number six, Alain,' she said. 'I will come too. I am going to let Armand enjoy himself,' she told Beth, 'while Alain and I hold you down.' Her voice was almost a snarl. 'And when he is tired, I am going to beat you myself. When I am finished with you, Dr Buget will have to come. Oh, yes, you will not sleep on your back for a month.'

Beth didn't know what to do, was aware only of a consuming anger, increased by her helplessness. She felt exactly as she had done when she had been thrown on the bed by the Russian officers. If she had had a gun she would have shot everyone in the room. But she didn't have a gun, and she was going to be beaten insensible, and then ... She realised that the noise had died, that Alain was standing still rather than dragging her towards the steps to the mezzanine, and that the salon door had opened.

Madame Suchet was swallowing. 'Why, Georges,' she gasped. 'I did not expect you in Paris again so soon.'

'I understand that,' Monsieur Mathieu remarked. 'It was a whim, you understand. Now tell me what is happening to Elizabeth.'

Madame Suchet arranged her features into the facsimile of a smile. 'I ... she ... she is entertaining a customer, Georges.'

'She is going to have me whipped, monsieur,' Beth shouted. 'For spending the weekend with you. Oh, please help me.' Because he was back. She dared not think what that might mean; she only knew he was the only person in the whole world could help her at this moment.

Georges Mathieu pointed. 'Release that young woman, Alain,' he commanded.

Alain looked at the shorter man, so stout and old and seemingly soft, and then at his mistress. Madame Suchet nodded and Alain's fingers fell from Beth's arm.

'Go to your room, Elizabeth,' Monsieur Mathieu said. 'Get yourself dressed in street clothes, and pack whatever belongs to you. Wake up your sisters and your brother and tell them to do the same. I have a car waiting. You are all leaving here tonight.'

'Indeed?' Madame Suchet demanded, recovering some of her aplomb. 'And where do you think you are taking them?'

'To Lorges, Aimée. They are to live with me.'

Beth gasped. Her dream had come true.

'You suppose you can just walk in here and remove three of my girls like that?'

'Are you going to stop me?' Monsieur Mathieu walked to the telephone, picked it up and asked for a number.

It was Madame Suchet's turn to gasp.

He smiled at her. 'I happen to know that the Prefect is home, because I spoke to him earlier. He is waiting to hear from me.'

Madame Suchet ran to the telephone and pressed the circuit shut.

'There is no need to be upset,' he told her. 'I will not cheat you. Do you wish a price for Elizabeth? Then name it. The others are not yours yet.'

Madame Suchet glared at him. 'You silly old fool,' she snapped. 'What will you do, set her up in a house in Lorges? Do you not know that she will leave you the moment she finds someone better? She is as cold as ice. She does not know how to love, only to hate.'

'I do not think she has ever been taught how to love, Aimée,' Monsieur Mathieu said mildly. 'I intend to do

149

that. And I do not intend to set her up in a house in Lorges. I intend to set her up in the château at Lorges, as my wife.'

'Beth,' Stephanie whispered. 'I don't understand.'

Monsieur Mathieu had left the first class compartment to go in search of breakfast, and they were alone for the first time. Dawn was just breaking over the French countryside, but none of them had slept. It was all too exciting, and confusing.

'I don't understand why Madame Suchet was so angry,' Stephanie went on.

'And the girls,' Tony complained. 'They didn't even say goodbye. I thought they liked us.'

'Ha,' Anna commented.

'Madame Suchet practically threw us out,' Stephanie went on. 'I should have thought she'd be pleased about your marrying Monsieur Mathieu, Beth.'

'Ha,' Anna said again.

'Are you really going to marry him, Beth?' Tony asked. 'I didn't know you knew him at all, really.'

'She knows him very well,' Anna remarked. 'A decrepit old man. It's disgusting.'

Beth refused to lose her temper. 'He is very sweet and charming and I am very fond of him.'

'I thought you had to be in love with someone to marry them,' Stephanie said.

'That's what being very fond of someone means,' Beth said carefully.

'Ha,' Anna commented.

Beth didn't expect them to understand; she didn't understand herself – her brain was in a whirl. But at the moment it was a glorious, happy whirl. It centred about the scene in the salon, the exclamations of the customers and the girls, the expression on Madame Suchet's face. For a moment she had thought Madame Suchet was going to have a heart attack. She would have enjoyed that. But on reflection, she knew it was better for Madame to live, and remember, how

Beth Janska had escaped her clutches. That memory would last far longer than the burning sensation in her shoulder.

But marriage . . . to Georges Mathieu!

'I realised, after you left, that you were what I wanted,' Monsieur Mathieu had said, holding her hand as they had driven in the taxi through the darkened Paris streets to the Gare de Lyon. 'My house seemed so empty without you there. And my bed was even emptier. I knew then that I did not care what you had been forced to become, how many men you had been forced to know, that I wished to spend my last years with you.' He had smiled. 'With a ready made family. I have no children, no close relatives at all. Mathilde would never give me children. She could not. But you will give me sons, and I will have Anna and Stephanie and Tony around me, to laugh, and make me happy. I do not care what people will say. Why should I care about people any more? I shall care only about myself. And about you.'

She hadn't known how to reply to that. There were too many facets to the situation which had to be considered. Have children? That was an impossible thought. It was not an idea she would have entertained in any circumstances, but for a man who had just bought her, and was old enough to be her grandfather – because he *had* just bought her. He had not asked her to marry him. No matter that she would have said yes without hesitation. He still had not asked.

But he was taking her away from Madame Suchet's, and she would be his wife. There would be money, and position . . . and perhaps even an inheritance at the end of it. As he had himself said, these were his last years. He had bought her for those years, to play with, like a toy. That was fair enough. Or would he want something more from her?

She wondered if Madame Suchet had been right about her, that she was as cold as ice, because she felt no spark of warmth towards the man, not even true gratitude, just relief that she was away from Madame. Of course she did not love him. How could she love a customer? He must understand that. But she would give him what he wanted from her – except children – and make him happy, and let him die happy.

In only one thing was she determined to oppose him: he would never lay a finger on either Anna or Stephanie. If he was really dreaming about setting up a harem in his declining years, he would have to think again. But she doubted that was what he had in mind. It was impossible to believe of someone so basically kind, honest, and simple as Georges Mathieu. Madame Suchet had undoubtedly been slandering him when she had suggested it.

Ideas, plans, half forgotten dreams, were already filling her mind. She would need to be patient, and wait and see just what Monsieur Mathieu was prepared to offer his wife. But she had advanced another step, and achieved her goal, that of escaping Madame Suchet, just as Madame Suchet had been a means of escaping the DP camp, and the DP camp had been a means of escaping starvation. Now it was a matter of considering, carefully, what should come next. But she reminded herself that she had no reason to be dissatisfied; Father would certainly be proud of her.

'Anyway, even if you are going to marry Monsieur Mathieu,' Stephanie was saying, 'I don't see why we had to leave Paris as well. I did like it at Madame Suchet's.'

'Of course we didn't have to leave as well,' Anna grumbled. 'It is all Beth's idea. It's going to be so boring. Lorges is very nice for a visit, but to live there, in the middle of a big swamp. Ugh.' She stared at Beth as she spoke, and Beth again felt sure she knew exactly what Madame Suchet's had been, and had been looking forward to taking her place in the establishment.

'Well, I think the Camargue is going to be a lot of fun,' Tony said. 'I found Madame Suchet's boring. I'm going to be one of Monsieur Mathieu's cowboys. He told me I could.'

'When you have finished school,' Beth said. 'You are all going to go to school in Lorges. Even you, Anna.'

'Oh . . . anyone would think you were Mother,' Anna shouted. 'Always bossing us about, telling us what to do. We're not children any more. I'm not, anyway.'

'Then stop behaving like one,' Beth snapped. 'You are going to be much happier at Monsier Mathier's than you ever could be at Madame Suchet's. I will tell you all why, some day. Now just learn to show a proper gratitude to Monsieur Mathieu for being so kind as to have you in his house. And if I sound like Mother it's because I am Mother, and Father, too. They're dead, and I'm responsible for you all. Just don't ever forget that.'

She glared from face to face, and they all flushed and looked down, even Anna. Because Beth could look just as fierce as Madame Suchet, when she wanted to.

Elizabeth Janska and Georges Mathieu were married in a civil ceremony at Lorges hôtel de ville that very evening. The mayor himself officiated; he was an old friend of Monsieur Mathieu's. They wore the same clothes in which they had travelled, as Monsieur Mathieu had wanted the ceremony performed immediately, and Anna and Stephanie were the bridesmaids. The only other guests, apart from the mayor, a widower himself, were Tony and the château staff. But as there were some fifty of them, including the cowboys, it was a big gathering, and everyone had to kiss the bride, which left Beth breathless, while Monsieur Mathieu looked on and beamed.

Then she was escorted upstairs to the huge chamber overlooking the river, beneath the turreted roof, and Monsieur Mathieu showed her the nightgown he had bought for her. In satin and lace, it was the most exquisite thing Beth had ever seen. She didn't want to wear it to bed, and was horrified when Monsieur Mathieu didn't let her take it off to make love, but instead gathered it round her waist, regardless of how the material crushed. But then he wanted other things, too, and used his lips and tongue on her. This had never happened to her before, however often she had had to do it to customers, and she was scandalised as well as alarmed, and then astonished by the depths of feeling which followed. She almost did not have to fake her orgasm, and made love to him with the most passionate abandon, which delighted him and left him exhausted.

Only when they were finished did she remember that they had not used a condom. He was asleep. She hurried into the bathroom and used the bidet for half an hour until she felt secure again. Then she returned to bed and propped herself on her elbow to look down on his sleeping face and listen to his stertorous breathing. She wondered what would happen if he were to die of a heart attack on his wedding night. He would hardly have had time to make a will in her favour yet. Of course, he might not mean to at all. But surely he would leave her a legacy; he had to stay alive long enough to do that.

She lay down herself and gazed at the huge tent which formed the arch of the fourposter; it had folds of mosquito netting which could be let down during the rainy season, when the mosquitoes were at their busiest. Madame Suchet was right, she thought. She was a cold hearted wanton. This man was trying to love her, and she was waiting for him to drop dead, providing he left her something in his will. But he had bought her, as a whore, and no doubt when he was tired of her he would sell her again, or just throw her out. There was no feeling for her involved. She would not, for instance, be lying here had she a wooden leg or a squint or a bad complexion. She had always to remember that it was her alone against the world, with her brains and her good looks, and on behalf of her sisters and brother. That was what she must always keep at the forefront of her mind, no matter how kind people pretended to be to her. They were only interested in what they could get out of her, therefore she could only afford to be interested in what she could get out of them.

She slept heavily, and was awakened by Georges shaking her arm. She sat up in alarm, supposing that her dream was ended, and he was about to put them all on a train back to Paris, and Madame Suchet, then gazed at the thick gold band he had placed on her finger the previous evening. The fears of last night vanished. That ring had to mean something. No one would ever send her anywhere again, unless she wanted to go.

'My darling,' Georges said, kissing her. 'Come with me.'

She was pulled out of bed before she knew what was happening, and looked down at the crumpled satin nightdress. 'Like this?'

'Just like that. You are more beautiful than ever like that, with your hair tousled and your eyes filled with sleep. Come.' He led her into the next room. 'I would like this to be yours. It was Mathilde's. You will not mind this?' He looked at her anxiously.

Beth looked at the panelled walls, the huge wardrobe, the three-mirrored dressing table, through the opened door to the bathroom suite, and through the windows at the view down the valley. 'I shall not mind,' she said.

Georges went to the great built-in wardrobes and threw the doors open; they were empty, except for hangers.

'I wish you to fill these. I do not want you to return to Paris for a while. But Toulouse is not far. Neither is Bordeaux nor Marseilles. And if you do not find what you want there, why, we will go to Rome.'

'Rome?!' Her head was spinning. 'But what shall I buy?' Madame Suchet had always bought all their clothes.

'Whatever takes your fancy. Just fill these wardrobes.'

Beth chewed her lip, and tried to order her thoughts. 'I shall not know how much to spend.'

'Spend anything you choose. I wish you to buy your-

155

self a mink coat to begin with. I give you unlimited credit.'

She stared at him. A mink coat! Mother had always wanted a mink, and Father had always said they couldn't afford it; she had had to settle for squirrel. This had to be a dream after such a long nightmare. She had to pull herself together and remember that she was not alone.

'I cannot buy for myself, monsieur, and not my sisters.'

'Take them with you, and buy for them as well. I want you to be happy. And I want you to call me Georges, not monsieur. I am your husband, now, not your client. I also want you to be happy, as I said. Be happy, and make love to me always as you did last night.'

He held her hand again and led her down the stairs. The maids were already up and about, with their mops and brushes and brooms. They curtsied to their new madame, and avoided looking at the déshabille. Georges led her into the downstairs reception room, where they had entertained their guests the previous night. It was a huge room, with high ceilings and massive, overstuffed furniture.

'I have given orders for this room to be emptied, and all the furniture burned.'

Beth thrust her fingers into her hair. 'But why?'

'Because it is Mathilde's room, not yours. I want it to be your room, Elizabeth. I want it to be filled with your personality. I want you to be the lady of this house, in every way. Forget the kitchens. Antoinette has always been in charge there, and she and Emile make a good team. But refurnish my house, as you would wish it to be.'

Beth licked her lips and looked around her. She thought the room was rather charming. But the idea of being given carte blanche . . .

Georges looked at her. 'Money is no object, my darling girl. You know I have never had any children.

156

Mathilde and I never had anything or anyone on which to spend our money. And since she has died, I have not even had a woman to spend it on. It has just accumulated. Now it should be spent, by the woman I love.' Beth burst into tears and continued to weep as he took her back upstairs and made love to her again. If he goes on like this, she thought, he will have a heart attack. And suddenly she didn't want that to happen. Not for a while. There was too much to be done.

It was as if she had stumbled on a secret chamber and found in it a chest containing all the riches of a Monte Cristo. She had no idea of how wealthy Georges was, but he was as good as his word, and put no limits on her spending. She took Anna and Stephanie in the big, chauffeur-driven Citroën into Toulouse, and bought every article of clothing which caught her and her sisters' fancy, beginning with the mink coat. It was the most gorgeous feeling to walk to and fro in front of the mirror, smoothing the silky fur with her hands.

Even Anna's grumblings were silenced as the boxes piled up and up, although Beth refused to buy her a mink, making her settle for a beaver, while Stephanie's mouth became a vast O.

'Uncle Georges must be very rich,' she commented. 'Very,' Beth assured her.

Then it was time to buy furniture. This took longer, and could be lingered over, week after week, with long, leisurely drives into the city to look out various choice articles. It took her more than a year, but by then she had virtually redecorated the entire house.

Her days were filled from dawn until midnight. She had every intention of obeying Georges and keeping aloof from the kitchens and the management of the house. She would have had no idea how to begin, in any event, and both Antoinette the cook and Emile the butler were rather awesome people, as well as very efficient. But she would never have had the time. Georges wanted her constantly at his side, except when

157

she was shopping. He worked as hard as he played, and took her with him when he went out to inspect his horses or his prize bulls.

It was an enormous pleasure to ride at his side across the fields, with the water always flowing a few feet away, and inspect the bulls, horses and pigs, for he was also a large scale pig farmer. Once their mounts waded through a shallow swamp and he showed her a flock of stately pink flamingoes, resting on one leg as they contemplated the morning, not the least disturbed by their intruders. Beth was entranced.

Then Georges wanted to entertain. He had done little entertaining since Mathilde's death, several years before, but now he threw lavish parties. The guests were invariably middle-aged local magnates and dignitaries, – many of whom had fought with him in the Maquis during the War – grave, paunchy men in starched collars and old fashioned suits and ties which never seemed to be properly knotted, while their wives had obviously come only to stare at the new châtelaine of the castle and her sisters, and gossip about them afterwards.

But despite the dull company, Beth, after an initial nervousness that no one might come at all the first time, enjoyed herself enormously, dressing both Anna and herself in daring décolletages and the highest of heels, sparkling with the jewellery which Georges lavished on them all, and which she knew must have cost a fortune – jewellery was the one item which she was not allowed to purchase for herself. Some of it had belonged to Mathilde, who had had a weakness for emeralds, but Beth did not mind. She thought she could easily cultivate a weakness for emeralds herself. As for the gossips, she reflected that no one in Lorges had any idea what she had done in Paris, Georges not being prepared to discuss her background with anyone other than to say they were the children of a Polish friend of his who had been killed in the War. And, apart from the word 'friend' that was the absolute truth.

She studied to make her husband happy, in every way she could, even if it was necessary to practise a continuing subterfuge to prevent herself from having to give him what he clearly considered the ultimate in happiness – a child. She did make love to him with all the abandon she could display, whenever he was able. His sexual abilities seemed to come in spurts, when he would perform like a young man, and then dwindle for days, perhaps weeks on end. But when he was in the mood she had to exhaust him, so that the moment he was asleep she could hurry to the bathroom and rid herself of his sperm.

Her failure to conceive disappointed him, she knew, but he took the blame upon himself. 'I am too old,' he told her. 'But we can still enjoy ourselves. And I have your sisters and Tony to be my children.'

She gratified him by having all their names changed to Mathieu, and by taking out French citizenship for them. She no longer suspected that he had the slightest designs upon her sisters, but remained watchfully anxious about them, happy to see them so fit and healthy and well dressed, and hopefully beginning to forget the nightmare of the end of the War. She couldn't help worrying about their futures. As usual, the problem was centred on Anna. Stephanie and Tony accepted that they had to continue with their schooling, and fitted into the Lorges Church School quite happily. Anna did not, and was rebellious and rude to the priests and even to Georges. Where Tony found his leisure working with the men and the bulls, and Stephanie would ride her pony through the marshes by herself and dream, and no doubt, Beth supposed, work out her fantastic stories – she was becoming a very private person who seemed to spend more and more time in her dream world – Anna merely sulked about the house, and wore the most outrageous clothes.

One day in 1950, soon after Beth and Georges had returned from a glorious holiday in Rome, where they had stayed at the Hassler and pretended they were on

159

their honeymoon, Beth found her sister sunbathing on the upstairs porch without a brassière.

'The actresses all do it,' Anna snapped when Beth told her to get dressed. 'In St Tropez. I've read about it.'

'This is Lorges, not St Tropez,' Beth reminded her. 'Suppose Georges were to come upon you like that.'

Anna smiled, almost dreamily as Stephanie. 'Why, then, he might buy me a mink coat as well. My tits are bigger than yours.'

'Your ...' Beth was scandalised, but also angry and alarmed. 'You are a little whore,' she said.

'Ha ha,' Anna sneered. 'Look who's talking, the big whore herself. Do you think I don't know what you and all the others were doing at Madame Suchet's? You were in a brothel. We were in a brothel. You had us living in a brothel.'

It was all Beth could do to stop herself from hitting her sister, even if she had always known in her heart that Anna had been aware of the situation. 'I suppose you've told that to Tony and Stephanie?' she said, with deceptive quietness.

'No, I haven't,' Anna said. 'But I will, if you keep me cooped up like this much longer.'

'I see,' Beth said. She was more than ever tempted to slap Anna's face. But she had to keep her temper under control. The thought of Tony, or even more, of Stephanie, ever knowing the truth about her ... 'You let men play with you,' Anna said. 'You let them put their dingdongs into you for money. That's disgusting.'

'How else do you suppose we lived?' Beth asked. 'It was that, or starvation, or being sent back to the Russians to be put in prision. Do you remember starving, Anna? Do you remember how cold it got? How our bellies rumbled? How we had only old clothes to wear and how dirty we were? Or how we were treated like animals in that camp, and made to bathe in Lysol? Do you remember?'

'Stop it,' Anna shouted. 'Of course I remember.

That doesn't alter the fact that you were a whore, or that you ran off with a customer. My God, a man that old! That's disgusting if you like. So don't try to come over all moral to me.'

'I'll come over any way I like,' Beth told her evenly. 'I married Georges because he agreed to take us all away from Madame Suchet's, so there'd be no necessity for you, or for Stephanie, to undergo what I had to. Besides, he is a really nice man. And now I have fallen in love with him.' She thought she had better add that in case Anna got any foolish ideas about blackmailing her by telling Georges she didn't love him. 'But I suppose what you really want to do,' she went on, loading her voice with all the contempt she could, 'is go crawling back to Madame and ask to be allowed to lie on your back for the rest of your life with a man between your legs. That would be preferable to being cooped up here, would it?'

'I could do it,' Anna claimed. 'If you could do it, so could I. I've never had a man between my legs. You wouldn't let me, remember? But I think it might be nice. Madame Suchet let me look through one of her mirrors once, and . . .'

'You didn't,' Beth shouted. 'At me?'

'No.' Anna pouted. 'Madame wouldn't let me look at you. It was Jeannette. But it looked awfully exciting. And who's to say I wouldn't wind up marrying some rich old bird as well?'

'The odds are against it,' Beth told her, mentally swearing to strangle Madame Suchet if she ever met her again. 'And you just saw the nice side of it. What when they want to whip you, or bugger you, or make you suck them?'

Anna's brows drew together. 'Do they really want you to do that?

'All the time.'

'Have you done that?'

'Sometimes,' Beth said.

'Good lord!' Anna looked vaguely sick. 'Anyway, I

161

don't really want to go back to Madame Suchet. I just don't want to be bullied all the time, and made to live in this deadly hole, where there are no boys, and . . . oh, Beth . . .' She caught her sister's hand. 'I'm beautiful. I know I am. I want to be a lady, and wear a mink coat and lovely rings, like you. I want to live. I want to be married and have lots of children. And how can I hope to do that when I'm buried alive in a place like Lorges?'

Beth considered her for some seconds, but she realised she was on the way to a considerable victory. 'All right,' she decided at last. 'I will make you into a lady, and I will see that you get all of those things you want, if you will promise to do as I say for the next two years.'

'Two years? Doing what?' Anna asked suspiciously.

'You will be eighteen in August. In September I will have Georges send you to a finishing school in Switzerland,' Beth said.

'A finishing school?'

'Where girls are made into proper ladies,' Both told her. 'They'll teach you how to walk and how to dress and how to cook and everything that goes with being a lady. And a wife, eventually.'

'Will there be boys there?'

'Of course not.'

'It sounds terrible.'

'It's necessary. And if you can stick it out, after the two years are finished, you can do what you like with yourself. I will have Georges give you an allowance, and you can take yourself off. You can even go topless on the beach at St Tropez, if you really want to.'

'Oh, Beth, can I? And you won't be angry?'

'I promise,' Beth said. 'But you must promise me you'll stick out the two years.'

'Oh, I will,' Anna cried. 'I will.'

'Then, as your graduation present, I'll give you a mink coat,' Beth said.

'Oh, Beth.' Anna threw both arms round her sister and hugged her. 'And you'll really give me an allowance? A proper allowance?'

'I promise. But you must also promise me that you will never, until the day you die, breathe a word of what I was doing at Madame Suchet's to Stephanie or Tony. Swear it. Swear it by Mother's memory.'

'I swear it,' Anna said. 'Oh, I swear it.'

The following September, Beth accompanied Anna to Lucerne, and saw her into the best establishment she had been able to find. Georges had not been in favour of sending Anna away, had complained that Beth was breaking up the family, but Beth had pointed out that they all had to go away some time – they couldn't spend all of their lives in Lorges, even if, she hastily added, she was going to. He had hummed and hawed, but had finally agreed that a finishing school was really a very good idea, and Anna would be home for every vacation.

When they got to Switzerland, Anna took one look at the rules and regulations governing the behaviour of the young ladies and nearly turned and fled, but the thought of the allowance and the freedom which would go with it steeled her resolution.

'I want her taught to speak English like a native,' Beth told her headmistress, who was English herself and named Mrs Golightly.

'She will do that when she leaves here, Madame Mathieu,' the headmistress promised, obviously uncertain what to make of this very young but so sophisticated woman – even she could not conceive that Beth herself was only twenty – setting out so carefully the things she wanted her sister to learn. 'And presumably you will wish her to be taught to ride?'

'Anna has been riding all her life,' Beth said.

'I meant, properly,' Mrs Golightly said stiffly. 'Like a lady.'

'Ah. Oh, yes,' Beth agreed. 'Like a lady.'

'And to play tennis?'

'Tennis?'

'All young ladies should play tennis,' the headmistress pointed out. 'Tennis parties are the ideal places to meet eligible young men.'

'Oh, then she must learn to play tennis,' Beth said. Clearly there was more to being a young lady than deportment and grammar. She spent a week on her own in Lucerne after Anna was settled in, thinking, and making various inquiries. It was the first time she had been alone in her entire life, and she enjoyed herself thoroughly, lying in bed as long as she chose, eating and drinking whatever she chose, and above all, thinking whatever she chose with no lurking feelings of resonsibility for anyone else. With her expensive clothes and jewellery and her handsome looks and obvious youth she caused quite a stir, but she was not interested in any flirtations, much less any of the affairs which were suggested to her. Men were only tools to be used on her upwards climb, never for pleasure, and none of the gigolos she met beside the lake could in any way offer her what Georges possessed.

But she was more than ever determined to prepare for life after Georges, which surely could not be long delayed. When she returned to Lorges she persuaded him to install a tennis court, and then hired a young woman who had once played at Wimbledon to stay with them for the next summer and coach Stephanie and herself, as well as Tony. Georges had been opposed to the court as a waste of time and money; he had indeed been rather disgruntled when she returned from Lucerne, because she had stayed away on her own, and grew quite angry when she told him she had been living in an hotel entirely by herself. This in turn alarmed her. It had never crossed her mind that he might be jealous, and the one thing in life she was afraid of was making him angry. But to her great relief he now enjoyed the tennis, or at least, the players, sitting on the terrace to watch the short skirts flying and the long white legs flashing to and fro, and applauding contentedly.

Beth also hired an English teacher of her own, again

for the three of them at home. Once again Georges grumbled. 'English, bah,' he remarked. 'It is a barbaric language.'

'It is the lingua franca of the world,' she argued.

'Once that was French,' he said sadly, but as usual he let her have her way. He was in a pessimistic frame of mind that summer of 1951, because the war in Korea had developed into a full scale international crisis, and even if France was not involved, what with that and the continuing struggle in Indo-China – which he said was bankrupting the country – he felt that there might be a third world war at any moment, and he was too old to take part in it. 'Besides,' he would say to Beth, 'I do not want there to be another war. I want us all to enjoy all of this forever and ever, until I die.'

'But I do not want you to die, Georges,' she protested, only half lying. She was not yet ready to face the world on her own, mainly because she had not yet discovered what, if anything, she would be left in his will.

As usual, he might have been able to read her mind. He hugged her and laughed. 'You shall never want,' he promised her. 'I swear it. And when I am dead, you will be able to find some handsome young man and fall in love. Someone to take you dancing, and play tennis with, and go swimming with. Someone to love.'

'I shall never do that,' she promised in turn. And this time she was not lying at all.

It was a great relief to have Anna out of the way and off her mind most of the time. When she returned to Lorges for the long vacation, Anna was already showing signs of being a lady, speaking quietly, sitting decorously, and eschewing the peek-a-boo clothes of which she had earlier been fond. And with every holiday she improved. The following year at Easter she brought home two girlfriends with her, pretty young things who delighted Georges by flirting with him and making him laugh. It was at last possible for Beth to

165

begin to feel that the Anna problem might have been solved.

Tony was next in line. In 1951 he was seventeen. Now that he was a French citizen, he would, the following year, be called up for national service, and Beth had no intention of allowing that to happen. The thought of his being sent off to Indo-China to fight the Vietnamese curdled her blood, however much he might want to go. But Tony appeared to have become less warlike with maturity, and was more interested in horses and bulls than in guns, for which she thanked God. Yet it was necessary to act now, and so she made him study harder than he had ever before, to get good grades at school, while she talked to Georges into helping as well, by seeing the right people, or writing to them – a large number of the senior civil servants in France had known him in the Maquis.

Beth's plan was that it was possible to have national service deferred for a few years if one was exceptionally able scholastically, and could secure a place at university. The university she wanted had to be in England, because England, and eventually America, was her aim, for all of them. America was the land of opportunity. But she had no intention of going there as a penniless immigrant. And Tony would have to be fully qualified at something, to make the best of himself in that highly competitive society.

But the immediate aim was to get him safely out of France, after which the authorities could whistle for their chances to put him in uniform.

She had no fears for Stephanie, who was in any event just fifteen, and appeared to be getting along very nicely. She, too, would go to Switzerland in due course, and be prepared to make an advantageous marriage.

While she ... Georges took her to Vienna for her twenty-first birthday, and endured a season of opera for her sake, although he was clearly bored. She was bored herself, but regarded it as an important part of attaining that culture she sought. Her dreams were taking on the vague fantasy of bursting on to the world after Georges' death, like Athena from the head of Zeus, fulled armed in every direction – to what end she had no idea. Everything depended upon Georges.

As usual on the Vienna trip they made love with tremendous abandon, but to no purpose. He did not seem to be getting any older. She was, in fact, appearing to rejuvenate him, day by day. She wasn't sure she wanted to do that. She was torn several different ways about Georges. He was such a nice man, so generous and undemanding – except in bed – and so very passionately in love with her, that she could not help but respond to him. That he did not attract her sexually was irrelevant, because she could not imagine any man ever doing that. But he, or rather, his demise, also represented her future – as opposed to dwindling away here into a second Mathilde, beloved by the villagers and doing absolutely nothing with her life.

She kept getting moods of almost irrational impatience. Irrational because, when she really sat back to think about it, she knew she could hardly live better, anywhere in the world, than as Madame Mathieu of Château Lorges, in the Camargue, with unlimited credit, with total comfort and security. And yet, she wanted to be up and doing, something. She was twenty-one years of age. Her life was only just beginning. And she didn't know what direction it should take. Especially if any direction away from Lorges meant wishing Georges to die.

Sometimes, when she gave her imagination full rein, she would suppose that it might be possible to put the problem frankly to him. She wanted to be his wife, but she wanted to be free as well. She had never enjoyed herself so much as during that week in Lucerne. Surely, if he loved her so much, he would let her live away from Lorges for a few months in every year, have her own apartment in London and New York, travel and do all the things she had ever dreamed of.

But then she would remember how upset he had

been about Lucerne, how jealous. She understood why. He had himself to leave Lorges from time to time, on business trips to do with the selling of his bulls or his horses. He never invited her along on these trips, and she never asked to go. But she had no doubt that, knowing Georges, he visited brothels on those occasions, even if she doubted he ever returned to Madame Suchet's. She didn't mind him doing that, or being away, in the least; it gave her a welcome rest. But of course if she asked for the same priviledge he might think she wanted other men as he seemed to want other women, and even if that was the last thing she would ever consider, she didn't dare have him suspect it. If he invariably let her have her own way, that had always been in relatively minor matters, to do with the house or the other three – never anything to do with their own relationship.

He was not as simple as she supposed, however. One night, soon after her twenty-second birthday, as they lay together in the huge bed high in the tower room of the château, he sighed and said, 'You make me so happy, my darling girl. I only wish I could do the same for you.'

'Oh, Georges,' she protested. 'Can there ever have been a happier woman than I?'

'Yes,' he said. 'I see you, staring into space with a most pensive expression in your eyes. What do you think of when you look like that?'

A possible cue? 'Oh,' she said. 'Faraway places. I would so like to travel.'

'We do travel,' he pointed out.

'Once a year.'

'Well, I have the farm and the ranch to look after. Anyway, I do not really enjoy travelling. I have to do enough of it on business. I only travel for pleasure to oblige you.'

She took a long breath. 'Then would you object if I did some travelling on my own? Just occasionally,' she hastily added as she saw his expression and realised she had made a mistake.

But he wasn't angry, and squeezed her hand. 'You will have plenty of time to travel when I am dead and gone.'

'Oh, Georges,' she protested again. 'Don't talk like that, as if you were about to drop dead.'

He kissed her. 'Don't worry, I am not going to die for a long time yet. I have never felt so healthy in my entire life. I think I may live to be a hundred. My father lived to be ninety-seven. We have lots of time together, my darling.'

So that was that. And he was sixty-four. If he were going to live to be a hundred that would be thirty-six more years. She would be fifty-eight. For the first time she began to feel a sense of imprisonment. Yet there was nothing she could do about it. And suddenly the future became the present with full force.

Everything had been going so well, until in July of 1952 Anna finished with her school. She was now twenty, alarmingly beautiful in her softly blonde way, but almost equally alarmingly groomed and soignée. Mrs Golightly was very pleased with her. So was Beth, and she was even more pleased when Anna announced that she was not returning to Lorges for the summer, but was spending it with a Scandinavian girl she had met at school. Beth knew the girl, who had visited Lorges previously, and had liked her enormously, partly because her father was a millionaire. She could think of nothing better than for Anna to get in with that sort of society.

Anna came home at the beginning of September in a pensive mood. This Beth found a pleasant change, although she couldn't understand why Anna didn't immediately broach the subject of her mink coat and her allowance – that freedom to take off her bikini top on the beach at St Tropez which had so seemed to attract her.

Stephanie was amused. 'I think she's in love,' she said, watching her sister sitting moodily on the verandah, gazing out over the valley. 'Anna! Isn't it a scream?'

'It's the best thing that could happen to her,' Beth said. Oh, she thought, what a blessing it would be for Anna to be married, perhaps to the son of a Swedish millinaire, someone she could really love and with whom she could be happy – and who would take care of her and absolve her of part of her responsibilities.

She determined not to press the matter, waiting for Anna to confide in her. But Anna never did. And at last, three weeks before Christmas, Beth could contain herself no longer. 'Why don't you tell me about him, Anna?' she asked, entering her sister's bedroom one morning while Anna was still in bed.

'About who?' Anna asked in a dull voice.

'You're obviously thinking about someone,' Beth pointed out.

Anna gazed at her for several seconds, her eyes enormous and almost beseeching, a most un-Anna-like expression, then she scrambled from the bed and ran into the bathroom to vomit.

THE SEVENTH CHRONICLE

March 1985

The Camargue in March was at its worst. It had been raining for several days, and the ground was a soggy mess. There were mosquitoes everywhere. It was difficult to believe that this country could ever be liveable in, much less beautiful.

Lorges huddled damply beside the flooding river, a village of half a dozen streets walled with small houses and populated, it seemed, by as many dogs as human beings. Meyer had taken the train from Paris, intending to hire a car at the station. But there were none on offer, so he had to take the local taxi.

'The Château Lorges,' the driver remarked. 'Of course, monsieur. You are staying there?'

'Should I be?' Meyer asked.

The driver shrugged. 'There is nowhere else in Lorges, monsieur.'

'Ah,' Meyer remarked, and watched the turret appearing over the mist-shrouded trees. Not for the first time on this quest he felt a sense of running into a brick wall. But he had surmounted many brick walls in the past. 'When did it become an hotel?'

'Oh, many years ago,' the taxi driver said. 'I was not living here then.'

Meyer walked beneath the arched doorway into the reception hall, wondering how those three young girls felt, thirty-five years ago, as they did the same.

'A room, monsieur? But of course.' This was also a relatively young girl, white shirted and efficient.

'It is many years since I was in Lorges,' Meyer lied chattily. 'Then there was no hotel. This castle belonged to a man named Mathieu.'

The girl was writing busily. 'That must have been a long time ago, monsieur.'

That evening in the bar he managed to have a word

171

with the manager. 'Mathieu,' the Frenchman said thoughtfully. 'Yes, indeed, the château used to be owned by a family of that name. I did not know it then, of course. I am from Paris. I think it was sold, oh, about a dozen years ago.'

'Only a dozen years?' Meyer queried, hope returning. 'Was that when Monsieur Mathieu died, 1973?'

The manager shrugged. 'I really cannot say. It lay empty for a couple of years before this chain bought it and refurbished it and turned it into an hotel. We are quite busy in the summer,' he added, as if feeling obliged to give reason for having an hotel in a place like Lorges.

'Quite,' Meyer acknowledged. 'Is there anyone here who might know about the Mathieu family? If there are any of them still around?'

'Why not try the hôtel de ville,' the manager suggested.

Next morning Meyer squelched through the mud to the village cemetery. Georges Mathieu's grave was not difficult to find, for it was surmounted by a large and elaborate headstone. If not neglected, for it was a well kept cemetery, it showed no signs of having been visited recently by anyone with a personal interest in the man.

He stooped to read the inscription. There was a small one to one side, 'In loving memory of my dear wife, Mathilde, 1900–1943.'

In the centre there was a much larger piece of carving, which read, 'To the memory of Georges Matthieu, 1888–1968, hero of the Resistance, and much beloved husband. This stone was erected by his wife, in respectful memory.'

Meyer stroked his chin as he gazed at it, then he walked along to the hôtel de ville, and after various obstructions found himself in the office of the mayor himself, who was also the village postman.

'Monsieur Mathieu,' the mayor remarked thoughtfully. 'Oh, yes, monsieur, I remember him well. He was the patriarch of the village in his time, eh? Some patriarch. He was a funny old bird. Very odd. And very standoffish, except amongst his cronies. He was a war hero, you understand, a commandant in the Maquis and one of its most daring leaders. His deeds were legendary in this area after the Germans came here in 1944, but before then he operated in the German-held territory, even as far away as Paris. But I suppose, like all war heroes, he felt he wasn't sufficiently rewarded when the shooting stopped, although they gave him the Legion of Honour. And then, he didn't like the way the country was going. I am a socialist, monsieur, and proud of it. Monsieur Mathieu had no time for socialism.'

'Oh, quite,' Meyer agreed. 'I too am a socialist, when it suits me to be one. How many times did Monsieur Mathieu marry?'

'Oh, twice, monsieur. And the second one was his real downfall. His first wife, she died during the War. I did not know her, but from all accounts she was a quiet, pleasant woman, a woman of the country, monsieur. And a sensible woman. She knew enough to put up with her husband's peccadilloes, eh? Every man has his peccadillo, monsieur.' He paused, but as Meyer made no comment he continued. 'Monsieur Mathieu perhaps had more than most. One must suppose it was the War, having been in a position of authority when one lived on a knife edge.' His eyes gleamed, and Meyer realised that he would hardly have to ask a question of this man. The mayor wanted to talk about his famous predecessor, and his downfall. The reasons would be various, he estimated – jealousy, both of the man and the period and the authority, criticism of a political opponent, a desire to gossip. To a total stranger? There was hatred here, as well.

'Oh, indeed,' he agreed.

'You knew the Mathieu family, perhaps, monsieur?' the mayor asked.

'I knew of them,' Meyer said. 'Did Monsieur Mathieu have any children?' He could afford, and would probably do best, to approach his goal by a circuitous route.

'Ah ...' the mayor pulled his nose. 'By Madame Mathieu, none. I believe it was some physical matter. But Monsieur Mathieu adored children. It was sad.'

'Tell me about the second wife, if you would,' Meyer suggested.

'You are interested in Monsieur Mathieu, monsieur? You are from the newspapers?'

'Heavens, no,' Meyer protested. 'I am writing a book on the exploits of the Maquis, and of course Monsieur Mathieu figures prominently in it. But to round it off, I must say what became of him. I did not even know he was dead ...'

'Haha,' the mayor remarked. 'He would have been all but a hundred, were he still alive. He used to boast that he would live to be a hundred. But that woman, the second wife ... oh, that was the end of him. He brought it on himself, of course. You know the saying, monsieur, that there is no fool like an old fool. You will not believe this, monsieur, but when the War was ended, the first Madame Mathieu having died in 1943, Monsieur Mathieu went up to Paris and came back with a girl young enough to be his daughter. His grand-daughter, in fact. Well, what do you expect?'

'I don't know,' Meyer said. 'What do you expect?'

'Why, she was out for what she could get. A girl from Paris, indeed. And he did not only marry her, he married her whole family, they say. There was a brother and two sisters. No better than herself. There were those who said they were not even French. Here, I will show you.' He opened his desk drawer.

Meyer was suddenly so excited he nearly lost his cool. 'You mean there is a photograph?'

'Taken on their wedding day, right here in this office,' the mayor explained. 'The mayor at that time, this is back in 1948, you understand ...' clearly he accepted no responsibility for anything that might have happened in 1948, 'was a friend of Monsieur Mathieu's. They had fought together in the Maquis. He had this photograph framed and hung it on the wall over there.

174

Would you believe that it hung there for more than thirty years, monsieur? Long after anyone knew who or what it was. But I . . . I took it down.'

But did not destroy it, Meyer thought. He could hardly contain himself as he gazed at the dog-eared piece of stiff paper, the figures turned sepia. His heart pounded as he looked first of all at a middle-aged man, not very tall and stout, with receding grey-black hair and a jowly chin, totally unhandsome or romantic in appearance, but at the moment the photograph was taken the proudest and happiest man in the world. With reason. Standing beside him and holding his hand was a remarkably attractive young woman. It was difficult to judge her age, but she was taller than her husband, with curling dark brown hair on her shoulders, and a splendidly full figure beneath the crushed dress she was wearing. Her face with its perfectly carved features, and its expression, half defiant, half apprehensive, both halves overlaid with uncertainty, was entrancing.

To either side of the couple were two other girls. One was blonde and quite startlingly lovely with the crisp features of her sister, spoiled only by a petulant mouth. The other was quite young, and Meyer had an idea that with her softer contours, her smiling mouth, and her huge eyes, she would probably have been the loveliest of them all in a few years time. But any one of them would have stopped traffic. Handsome children, Dubrowski had said. Handsome children. And then, beautiful women. The Janska girls. At last he felt he had made contact, and almost wished he could have done so thirty years ago.

But however lovely her siblings, he had eyes only for Beth. He had no doubt that she was the key he sought.

'They are beautiful, eh?' the mayor asked. 'But wanton. What could you expect of Paris girls?'

'In what way were they wanton?' Meyer asked. 'Did not Elizabeth Mathieu remain with her husband until his death?'

'Elizabeth,' the mayor repeated. 'Yes, that was her name, Elizabeth. Oh, no, monsieur, she did not remain with Monsieur Mathieu until his death. There was the scandal, you see. It shook the village. And ruined Monsieur Mathieu. Some said he was lucky not to go to gaol. I do not know the truth of the matter. But I am more inclined to think that he was, how do you say?'

'Conned?' Meyer suggested. 'It sounds intensely interesting. Just what I need for my book.'

'You will give credit?'

'Of course. Providing it is not libellous.'

'Ah,' the mayor said. 'We will have to think about that. There is no proof, you understand.'

'Why not tell me first,' Meyer said. 'In confidence. Then we can decide together, perhaps over a glass of cognac, whether I can use it or not.'

CHAPTER 7

The Camargue, 1952

Stephanie heard the noise and ran into Anna's bedroom, where she found Beth slapping Anna's face, time and again. Anna was shrieking and vomiting at the same time, and Beth's face was harder than Stephanie could ever recall it, even on the walk from Warsaw to the refugee camp.

'Beth,' she screamed, catching her sister's arm. 'Please! You'll hurt her.'

'I wish I could,' Beth snapped. 'Oh, you wretched, disgusting girl. Who was it? One of those Swedish boys? Oh, you wanton whore.'

Stephanie continued to hold on to her arm, and Anna was regaining her breath. She left the bathroom and fell across the bed. 'I don't know what you're talking about,' she gasped. 'I don't.'

'Beth, please,' Stephanie begged. 'Why are you so angry? Whatever has Anna done? She has an upset stomach. It must be something she ate. Beth . . .'

Beth glared at her, then her expression softened. 'You poor, innocent little child,' she said. 'I suppose it's my fault for trying to protect you. But you . . .' she turned back to Anna again, and Anna moaned and huddled herself against the bedclothes. 'I suppose you will pretend you didn't know what you were doing.'

'You . . . I . . .' Anna's cheeks were flushed, and she was rolling from side to side.

'Please tell me, Beth,' Stephanie begged.

'She's pregnant,' Beth said.

'Pregnant?' Stephanie's eyes were huge. 'But how? I mean . . .'

She was sixteen, Beth thought. And she had kept her totally innocent. As for Anna . . . perhaps the fault was partly hers.

'Pregnant?' Anna stopped moaning and sat up. 'Oh,

my God, I can't be. Beth . . .' She clutched her sister's hand.

'But how?' Stephanie asked again.

Beth sighed. 'Haven't you seen the horses mounting one another? The dogs?'

Stephanie's eyes grew even larger and rounder. Her imagination was working overtime.

'Well,' Beth said, 'a man and a woman do the same thing. Only they usually get married first. But Anna has clearly not bothered with that little formality.'

Anna seemed to recover herself, and her flush reached her eyes in anger. 'Get married? Why, you . . .'

Beth slapped her face again, very hard. Anna gave a shriek and fell back across the bed, weeping.

'Beth!' Stephanie shouted, unable to understand her sister's behaviour.

'You had better remember our agreement,' Beth said to Anna, speaking evenly but harshly. 'Or you will get nothing. I will have you thrown out into the street. I swear it.'

'You . . .' Anna sat up again and stared at her sister as if she would defy her, then thought better of it.

'So tell me the name of the man,' Beth demanded.

Anna continued to gaze at her sister for some seconds, while Stephanie looked from one to the other in amazement. Her lively imagination was still filled with the image of Anna kneeling before some man . . . It just didn't seem possible. Did Beth kneel like that before Monsieur Mathieu? And Monsieur Mathieu . . . Uncle Georges . . . even her imagination couldn't cope with that idea.

'It's my business,' Anna said.

'You think so? It's my business, too, now. And suppose I tell Georges about it? What do you think will happen then?'

A peculiar expression crossed Anna's face. 'Go right ahead,' she suggested.

'Oh, yes,' Beth said. 'You imagine he has always wanted to have a family of whores about the place.

178

Well, I can tell you that he would be very angry. He'd probably throw you out himself.'

Anna's expression had changed, as if she had suddenly remembered something. Now she chewed her lip. 'We have to tell him,' she muttered.

'So he can approach the man, you suppose? Have you thought of the scandal? Georges has a position to uphold, a reputation in the community. Have you thought how much gossip he's had to withstand these last few years, all because he's taken us in and is looking after us? And now you would prove all the gossips to be right? Oh, no, that is not going to happen.'

Anna was looking frightened. 'You don't understand,' she muttered.

'Oh, yes I do,' Beth declared. 'You fell for some handsome Swedish lout. All right. Tell me his name?'

A look of stubborn determination replaced the earlier fear on Anna's face. 'No. I will not tell you. I dare not.'

Beth studied her. 'If his father is very rich, it will be easier.'

'No,' Anna said. 'No.'

Beth looked at her, then at Stephanie, who was watching the pair of them, open-mouthed. Beth shrugged. 'Very well. If that is how you wish to behave. It alters nothing, anyway. You cannot have the child, and we are not going to tell Georges a word. You and I are going to take a trip together, and have it all cleaned up. Do you understand me?'

Anna's fear was horrible to behold. 'You mean ... oh, Beth. I couldn't.'

'You must,' Beth told her.

'But ... it's a mortal sin.'

'How many mortal sins do you suppose Father had to commit to save our lives? How many mortal sins do you think I have had to commit to get us where we are now? That's all that matters,' Beth said fiercely. 'Us. The family. You and Stephanie and Tony and me. We're all any of us have, the four of us. It's us against the world,

179

remember? Father said so just before he ... before he went to Berlin. And any one of us who lets the others down is the worst kind of traitor. All right, so maybe you didn't know enough to understand what would happen if you let a man get between your legs and didn't take the proper precautions. I accept that may have been my fault. And maybe you are fond of him, and don't want to let him down. I suppose that's honourable, in a way. But now you have to help me save us all. You must understand that.'

Again Anna looked as if she wanted to argue, but it was difficult to argue with Beth when she was in one of her aggressive moods. Anna's shoulders sagged. 'If you're sure that's the best thing. I don't want to be a traitor to the family, Beth. You know I don't.'

Beth's expression softened, and she rumpled Anna's hair. 'Of course you don't. Just leave it all to me. It really is a very simple matter, believe me. I'll arrange everything. And you, miss ...' she turned on Stephanie so suddenly Stephanie jumped backwards. 'If you breathe a word of this to a soul, even to Tony, I'll break your neck.'

Stephanie was utterly bewildered and distressed by the whole thing. If she had always been aware of the recurrent friction between Beth and Anna, it had never come out into the open since the business with the boy Schurer in the DP camp, and over the past couple of years, since Anna had gone away to school, they had seemed almost friends. Besides, the suddenness of it distressed her. Suddenness was something she hated. Suddenness had to do with those terrible nightmares she still suffered from time to time: of Warsaw in flames, of Mother, appearing like a Valkyrie, carrying a rifle and shouting orders, of Nanny being dragged away, of walking through the snow ... and of dead bodies. Life had only seemed to begin properly when the suddenness had ceased to happen so regularly. She hated the memory of the refugee camp, but there had been little suddenness there, and what she had liked best about Madame Suchet's had been the even tenor of every day, the way each had been the same. She had liked that better even than the clothes and the food and the comfort.

Monsieur Mathieu had been sudden, and thus at first she had hated the whole idea of him. Being awakened and told to get up and get dressed and packed because they were going away with Monsieur Mathieu had been an upheaval horribly reminiscent of Father appearing and saying Mother was dead, or that they must leave Warsaw. She had been terrified, and even more alarmed by the obvious anger of Madame Suchet, the disgust of the older girls. That had been the most difficult thing of all to accept. Madame Suchet had rescued them from the camp, had looked after them and cared for them ... and they had simply walked away from her, at Beth's command. It had never crossed her mind then, it would not cross her mind now, to disobey Beth, but she felt her sister had behaved very badly about that.

Thus she had arrived in Lorges in a state of total confusion and fright. But Lorges had turned out to be a heaven. Even less happened here, day in and day out, than at Madame Suchet's, and at the village school she was mysteriously one of the brightest of the pupils, whereas at the school in Paris she had been regarded as a dunce. Best of all, Georges Mathieu had turned out to be far kinder than Madame Suchet. Madame had given her, given them all, lots of clothes and presents and treats, and yet managed to make them very aware all the time that her 'gifts' were really loans, which might one day have to be repaid; you never had that feeling with Uncle Georges.

Yet life at Lorges, at least for her, had been a very lonely business. She had never been able to make friends easily; indeed, she had never made any friends of her own age at all. In Warsaw the only girls of her age she had known had been Germans, and in Paris she had been a foreigner. She had never minded this. Her companionship had always been sought within the family – and she had never known anything else, or wanted it. In Paris she and Tony had done everything together, and had such fun. But in Lorges, even they had drifted apart. Tony was in a different form at school, and was a very grown up young man now. Even out of school he spent most of his time studying, while what leisure he did have he would use in rounding up the bulls or the horses, too muscular a business for a girl, even had the cowboys allowed her to try. But the cowboys were Tony's real friends, now.

Then Anna had been away at school, but she had never been very close to Anna anyway – she feared Anna's biting tongue, And Beth of course always seemed to have so much to do. Yet it hadn't mattered, up to now; they had always been there.

She had also become very involved, privately, in the business of growing up. She had first menstruated at Madame Suchet's, and Madame herself had explained the whole business; in such detail, especially about what would afterwards be involved, that Stephanie had been consumed with embarrassment. It was not something she had ever wanted to think about. Nor had she had to, up to about a year ago, because she had always been so thin and slight that for all her height, and she was already taller than Anna, she had looked younger than her age. But Beth, who said it was a result of the malnutrition she had suffered in the camps and during those last terrible months in Warsaw, had concentrated on building her up, insisting that she drink milk with every meal, and eat meat regularly, with the result that over the past year she had suddenly put on weight and blossomed from a scrawny little runt, as Tony had lovingly called her, into a young woman.

She had hardly been aware of the change herself, until at school boys, as well as girls, had wanted to make friends. That had been most flattering, and as Tony had already drifted away, she had slipped into a relationship with a boy in her form, named Jacques,

182

had let him walk her home almost to the door of the château, and carry her books. Most of the other girls in her form had beaux, and there had seemed nothing wrong or strange about Jacques, although she had never told Beth about him – remembering Beth's reaction to Willy Schurer – or allowed him to come right up to the house.

But then had come the day, only a couple of months ago, when he had suddenly kissed her, and put his hand on her breast, and then tried to insert it in into her gym slip. That had frightened her, after all of Beth's strictures, and she had pulled away and run all the way home, nor had she ever walked with Jacques again, which had caused a good deal of comment amongst her schoolmates, and left her lonelier than ever.

Now, after what was happening with Anna, she was even more frightened at what she might have so narrowly escaped. She didn't understand how Anna could have done anything like that. Since that day she had never stopped to chat with even the other girls, had hurried home as fast as she could, and got out her books or gone riding on her pony, or sat up on the verandah and looked out over the valley and dreamed of Huguenot followers of Henri of Navarre galloping over those cobbled streets on their way to do battle with the Catholic League. Why she, a devout Catholic, should imagine settings with Huguenot knights she had no idea, but she had never attempted to control her imagination; it was such fun to let it run wild.

The important thing about Lorges – Jacques apart – had always been its atmosphere of total security, based on the happiness of her sisters and brother. Beth was married to Uncle Georges. Stephanie had never attempted to consider what might be involved between man and wife, or what sort of happiness a girl of twenty might find with a man over sixty. She accepted that that was what Beth wanted. And Anna had seemed happy and secure at her Swiss school, to which Beth had always said she would be going in the course of time,

183

while Tony, however hard he was working, had also seemed perfectly happy. So how could she not be happy, too, even if Beth sometimes remarked that she did not bubble any more, the way she had as a little girl. But she had been happy, even if she still slept with Alice clutched tightly in her arms to comfort her if she woke up with a nightmare.

Now it appeared that all of that happiness had been nothing but a sham. Anna was miserable, and it had suddenly occurred to Stephanie that Beth was miserable, too. Therefore was Tony also miserable? Certainly she felt miserable.

And confused. But everyone seemed to be confused. Tony had no idea what was happening, but then, neither did Uncle Georges. He had gazed at Beth in amazement when she had announced that she was taking Tony to England for an interview about his university place – this had been expected although not three weeks before Christmas – and also to do some shopping, and that Anna would be accompanying them. Uncle Georges had scratched his head and hummed and hawed, and then said he would accompany them.

'Of course you can't,' Beth said, speaking more forcefully to her husband than Stephanie had ever heard before. 'You'll be awfully bored. Besides, I wish to buy your Christmas present, and walk up and down Oxford Street. I've always wanted to do that. Imagine how that would bore you.'

'You know I do not wish you to travel on your own,' Uncle Georges grumbled, embarrassed at having such a discussion before the children, as he still called them; but Beth, had carefully engineered this.

'I won't be alone, my dear,' she pointed out. 'I'll have Tony and Anna with me. I also want to see what I can find for Anna to do. That would bore you as well.'

'Anna wants to live in England?' Georges asked with increasing bewilderment.

'That's what she wants to do,' Beth insisted. 'Isn't it, Anna?'

Anna mumbled yes. Anyone could have told she was lying, but Uncle Georges apparently didn't realise it.

'And anyway,' Beth concluded irrefutably, 'someone has to stay and look after Stephanie.'

Stephanie was tempted to ask why she couldn't go, too, but school hadn't broken up yet. To her surprise, however, Uncle Georges seemed more impressed by that final argument than by any of the others, and gave his permission.

Stephanie went with them to the station, where they would catch the train to Dieppe, and there board the ferry for England.

'Beth,' she asked, 'what's going to happen to Anna?'

Beth hugged her. 'Nothing,' she said. 'We are going to see someone who will terminate the pregnancy, that's all. He'll take away the baby, and she'll be right as rain again, and no one will ever know.'

'But . . . can you do that?' Stephanie wondered. 'Is it legal?'

'Of course it isn't legal,' Beth said. 'That's why we couldn't tell Georges about it, and why we have to have it done secretly. And mind you remember not to say a word to a soul, especially Georges.'

'I promised,' Stephanie said, with dignity.

'Of course you did,' Beth said, hugging her again. 'Laws just don't understand personal problems like this. But it would be terrible for Anna to have an illegitimate baby, now wouldn't it?'

'Why?' Stephanie asked, with genuine interest. She thought it was terrible for Anna to have let a man push himself into her, but as it had been done, she thought she might as well have the baby and gain something worthwhile out of it.

'Oh . . . here's our train,' Beth said in relief. 'I'll explain it all when I get back. We'll only be away a week. Mind you're a good girl, and don't annoy Uncle Georges.'

Stephanie waved them out of sight, then returned to the château. Suddenly it seemed empty. The servants

185

were all still there, but it was the presence of Beth and Anna and Tony, all doing their own things, which had always filled the house in the past. Knowing they weren't there made her feel totally isolated.

At lunch she took her normal place on the side at the far end of the long table from Uncle Georges, close by the other head of the table, where Beth always sat.

'You're a very long way away,' Uncle Georges said. 'I can hardly see you down there. Come on up and sit by me.'

She obeyed, cautiously. She had never felt totally at ease with Uncle Georges. He had always been kindness itself, and she knew how much he adored Beth, that was obvious. Most of the time he paid very little attention to either her or Tony, but every so often she would discover him staring at her in a most abstract fashion, as if she were a total stranger and he did not know what she was doing there.

But today he was smiling at her. 'Now tell me,' he said. 'What are Beth and Anna really up to?'

'I have no idea,' Stephanie replied loyally.

'You don't expect me to believe that Anna really wants to live and work in England?' Uncle Georges demanded.

'I think she probably does,' Stephanie said.

'Hm,' Georges commented, looking thoughtful. But to her relief he didn't raise the subject again.

She went riding that Saturday afternoon, then up to the top verandah to enjoy the sun. It was distinctly cold even for early December, far too cold to sunbathe, so she only sat there for a short while before going inside. That evening she spent with Uncle Georges, reading in front of the fire in the big withdrawing room. But once, when she put down the book, he was staring at her. Hastily she gave him a bright smile.

'How old are you now, Stephanie?' he asked.

She raised her eyebrows, because surely he knew. 'I was sixteen last month,' she reminded him.

'Of course you were. How time flies. And a very

186

beautiful young lady you have become,' he remarked. 'You have, you know,' he insisted as she blushed. 'Would you like a drink?'

'A drink?'

'Pernod,' he said, getting up and pouring two. 'It is good for you on a cold evening like this.'

It smelt dreadful, and tasted worse; she had never cared for liquorice, but she sipped it to please him, and certainly it filled her body with warmth, even if it also made her head spin.

Next morning Uncle Georges accompanied her to mass, which was a surprise, because Uncle Georges seldom went to church nowadays. He complimented her on how smart she looked in her new coat and medium heeled shoes, with her hair in a fetching pony tail. He really was going out of his way to be nice to her, she thought, no doubt to make up for the absence of Beth – who had not been away by herself since she had taken Anna to school in Lucerne, more than two years ago – and Stephanie could not help warming to him.

That evening she again accepted a glass of Pernod, and he began to tell her stories of the days during the War, in the Maquis, which were both interesting and exciting.

'Those were the days,' he continued to reminisce over dinner. 'We lived, then. We killed Germans, and we stole from them, oh, those were the days.'

'Weren't you ever afraid of being caught?' Stephanie asked.

'Oh, yes. One is always afraid of being caught,' Uncle Georges agreed. 'And to be caught by the Nazis was a terrible thing. Why, do you know what they did to the girls of our company whom they caught?'

'No,' Stephanie said. She didn't really want to know because she was sure it would be something horrible, and yet she was fascinated as well.

'They raped them for a start,' Uncle Georges said. 'Do you know what that is?'

Stephanie shook her head. She did, of course, from talking with the other girls at school. And now it seemed that something like that had happened to Anna. But she didn't want to let Uncle Georges know that.

'It means they took off all of a girl's clothes and interfered with her body,' Uncle Georges explained, filling her glass with wine. 'And then they put their tools into her. Do you know what a tool is? You must do, you must have seen Tony's.'

Stephanie buried her face in her glass and drank heavily to hide her embarrassment. Now she wished he'd stop, but he wasn't going to.

'Then they would torture her,' Uncle Georges said happily. 'They'd strip her naked and tie her to a post and flog her, and then they would strap her down and give her electric shocks, you know, clipping the electrodes to her nipples or her slit ...' He refilled her glass. 'Have you ever played with your slit? Of course you have. That's fun, eh? Imagine having an electric shot put through that and up your ass as well.'

Stephanie wished the floor would open and swallow her up. Even her fevered imagination had never considered such horrors. She had never suspected people even talked about those things. As for being asked if she had ever played with herself .. !

'And often,' Uncle Georges went on, 'when they had finished with a girl and decided they weren't going to get anything out of her, they would cut off her breasts. Terrible.' To Stephanie's total consternation, he leaned across the table and stroked the bodice of her dress, giving the flesh beneath a gentle squeeze. Jacques had done that, and it had frightened her, and Jacques had been a boy hardly older than herself. Uncle Georges ...

He continued to smile at her. 'Aren't you glad you never had to experience anything like that? You have such lovely breasts.'

Stephanie swallowed and finished her third glass of

wine; coming on top of the Pernod she had drunk before dinner, it made the room rise and fall.

'And yet, it was a good time, too,' Uncle Georges said. 'For the girls as well. They lived, as we all did. They took what they wanted, because they never knew what the next day might bring. Why, a girl like you, with your looks and your big breasts and nice bottom would have lost her virginity long ago.'

Stephanie could feel her cheeks burning. She had never heard anyone talk like that before. She wondered if he was drunk. Anyway, she couldn't listen to any more of it, and she felt pretty drunk herself.

She pushed back her chair and stood up. 'It sounds terribly exciting, Uncle Georges, but if you'll excuse me, I'll go to bed now.'

He caught her hand as she tried to pass his chair. 'I've offended you.'

'Oh, no, Uncle Georges,' she lied. 'I'm just very tired. I think I've had too much to drink.'

'I'm sure you haven't,' he argued. 'You're offended. One should never be offended by words, Stephanie. Words can never harm you.'

'I'm not offended, really, Uncle Georges,' she protested.

'Then stay down with me a while longer. It is very lonely for me with Elizabeth not here. Stay down with me.'

She hesitated. But he was Beth's husband, and even if his talk had shocked her, he had always been so very kind to her. She really didn't want to offend him or hurt him. So she nodded, and he escorted her back into the drawing room and poured two glasses of cognac.

'I've had enough, really, Uncle Georges,' she said.

'Cognac rounds off a meal,' he said. 'And you'll be going to bed soon. It cannot harm you.'

'Beth doesn't like me to drink cognac,' she attempted.

'Ah, but when the cat's away, the mice will play, eh?'

She wasn't sure she liked Beth being referred to as the cat, but she pretended to smile and sat on the sofa with the glass held between both hands as she had seen him do, wishing the room would settle down. To her consternation he sat beside her, and put his arm round her shoulders. 'Haven't you ever wanted to have a good time, Stephanie?'

'I don't know what you mean,' she told him. And she didn't, but she had a terrible feeling that it was to do with his horrible dinnertime conversation.

'Haven't you always wanted to know what life is all about?' Uncle Georges asked, and to her utter horror took his arm from round her shoulders and placed his hand on her knee. Her dress covered the flesh, but he immediately began to slide it up.

'Uncle Georges!' she protested unhappily.

'I'm not going to hurt you,' he promised. 'Really I'm not, Stephanie. I just want to look at your legs. You have lovely legs, you know.'

She gulped. As it was warm in the house and there had been no guests, she had not put on any stockings this evening.

'And then I'm going to try to make you feel really happy,' Uncle Georges went on. 'I'm going to kiss you. Will you mind that? Or will you enjoy it? I know you'll enjoy it.'

Stephanie goggled at him, trying to keep her nerves under control. She supposed no harm could come of a kiss, although she was sure Beth wouldn't like it. 'Well,' she said. 'I suppose ...' she would agree to anything to enable her to escape and reach the safety of her bedroom.

'You will like it,' Uncle Georges promised her. 'I adore kissing girls. And afterwards, if you wish, you can kiss me back.'

Stephanie nodded, and closed her eyes. She waited for a moment, holding her breath, but nothing happened, and the room became giddy again, so she opened her eyes and saw him raising her skirt all the way to her hips, exposing her thighs, at the same moment as his hands touched her knickers, to draw them down her legs. She stared at him in horror, for he had slipped from the couch and was kneeling in front of her as he stroked her.

'Uncle Georges!' she screamed, leaping to her feet with such violence that he fell over.

The taxi drew to a halt outside the huge front door of the Château Lorges, and Beth got out, followed more slowly by Anna. The two women looked up at the grey walls rising above them, and Anna shuddered. 'There's going to be so much trouble,' she muttered.

'There is going to be no trouble at all,' Beth promised her, and Anna shivered again. She had never seen her sister in such a mood, was only happy that her anger had been directed away from herself. Now she looked positively demonic. Anna knew that Beth was actually prepared to enjoy the coming half an hour, while all she wanted to do was get as far away from the crisis as possible. She wanted to creep into her bed, and she didn't care if she never got up again.

The door was opened for them by Emile, who looked suitably surprised, but also alarmed. 'Why, madame,' he said. 'Welcome home. But you were not expected until Saturday.'

'We changed our minds,' Beth informed him. 'Bring in our cases, if you please.' She swept past him into the house, and stood in the great hall, looking to left and right. 'You will go to your room, Anna, and remain there until I send for you,' she commanded.

'Yes, Beth,' Anna gasped, and hurried for the stairs.

'Madame!' Antoinette the cook emerged from the pantry. 'But we did not expect you until Saturday.'

'So there will be two extra places for dinner,' Beth told her. 'Where is Mademoiselle Stephanie?'

'Oh, madame . . .' Antoinette appeared to wring her hands.

'Oh, my God!' Beth gathered her skirts and ran up the stairs.

'Elizabeth!' Georges came out of the library. 'My

dear,' he said, attempting to arrange his features into a smile. 'Thank God you are back. We did not expect you until Saturday.'

'The next person who says that to me is going to have his or her head broken,' Beth declared, looking from her husband to Antoinette to Emile, reappearing in the doorway with a suitcase under each arm and looking more alarmed than ever. 'And can you think of no reason why I should have come home early, my dear Georges?'

'I have been so worried,' he said, preferring not to answer the question. 'And there was no address at which I could reach you. You did not give me an address,' he accused.

'I, too, have been worried, Georges,' she told him, 'which is why I am home. Now tell me what you have done with my little sister before I call the police.'

'The police?' Georges goggled at her.

'The police!' Antoinette exclaimed. 'What a catastrophe.'

Emile dropped one of the suitcases.

'You are being hysterical,' Georges protested. 'Stephanie is in her room. She has locked herself in. We have tried everything we can think of to get her out, but with no success. These doors were built to withstand a siege. If you can persuade her to come out I shall be the happiest man alive, but . . .'

'Persuade her to come out?' Beth threw her mink coat on the floor and ran along the corridor, heels slipping on the parquet floor. 'Stephanie!' she shouted, banging on the door. 'Stephanie, open up.'

'Beth?' She listened to the bolt being drawn, and a moment later Stephanie was in her arms. 'Oh, Beth.'

'My poor darling,' Beth said. 'Oh, my dearest girl. I had no idea, until twenty-four hours ago. Oh, my dear, what has he done to you?'

'I . . .' Stephanie bit her lip and looked past her sister as Georges, standing at the head of the stairs, his face a picture of misery. 'Nothing.'

192

'Nothing?' Beth shouted. 'How long have you been locked in there?'

Again Stephanie looked at her brother-in-law. 'Since ... since Sunday night.'

'You have not been to school? My God! You have spent the last four days in your room with him trying to break down the door. ...' She could see the marks now, scours on the stout oak. 'And you say he has done nothing to you? When did you last eat?'

'Elizabeth, really,' Monsieur Mathieu protested, coming slowly along the corridor. 'We must talk.'

'When?' Beth thundered.

'Oh, they ... they have put food outside my door,' Stephanie said. 'And I took it when they were all asleep. Really, Beth, I don't want to cause any trouble.'

'You,' Beth said, turning and pointing at Antoinette, who with Emile had come up the stairs behind their master. 'Prepare a meal, immediately. I want fresh vegetables, whatever you can find, beans and carrots and spinach and cabbage, as well as pork. And fruit. Lots of fruit. Understood? Now.'

They looked at Monsieur Mathieu, who nodded. 'Prepare it,' he said.

'While your dinner is being prepared, Stephanie, take a warm bath and then get dressed. I will speak with you later. Nothing, indeed.'

'But, Beth ...' Stephanie attempted.

'Elizabeth, you are being hysterical,' Georges said again.

'You think so?' Beth inquired. 'Well, you wanted a word with me, I believe. Shall we go into the study?'

She marched ahead of him, past Antoinette and Emile, who exchanged glances before hurrying back to the pantry. Georges almost ran behind her and closed the study door on them. He looked so bewildered, guilty and pitiful that Beth almost felt sorry for him. But she reminded herself that he was guilty, and that this was the moment she had been waiting for, subconsciously, for three years. It had dawned on her in Paris, where she had taken Anna to procure the abortion, as she knew that Dr Buget had done that sort of thing in the past for Madame Suchet's girls who had made a mistake, and she also knew that Dr Buget, although employed on a regular basis by Madame, and therefore certain to know about her desertion, would do anything for money.

He had in fact been very quick and efficient, but it had been horrible to watch, and had terrified Anna as much as it had sickened her, so much so that Anna had tearfully confessed the truth. Then Beth had known a moment of weakness, even of fear, but then, too, she had known a sense of shock as she thought of what she might have exposed Stephanie to. Hence her decision to return the moment Anna had been pronounced fit to travel.

But gradually, too, other thoughts had entered her brain. Georges had played into her hands. Now she could do whatever she wanted, with right entirely on her side. She could be what she wanted. It was not a question any longer of being grateful to him or being fond of him. He had behaved like a sex maniac. She wasn't sure that he could not be *classified* as a sex maniac. But more important, if she missed this golden opportunity she might never have another.

So now there could be no weakness. Madame Suchet had described her as being as cold as ice. Well, she did not think she was, really. But she was prepared to be as cold as ice to achieve her goals. Another stepping stone to success lay before her, waiting to be taken.

Georges walked past her to poke the wood fire. 'You are such a violent person,' he remarked, and smiled at her. 'But that is one of the things I love about you. Has Tony not come back with you? Anna?'

'Tony has remained in England,' Beth said frigidly. He had gone to England on his own, for his interview. 'It seemed the best thing.'

'Indeed?' He faced her, raising his eyebrows, attempting to regain some authority, restore some sanity to the evening. 'And Anna?'

'Anna has gone to her room. She is not feeling very strong. Nor would you be feeling very strong if you had just had an abortion.'

'An abortion?' He stared at her as he slowly lowered himself into his chair. 'Anna has had an abortion?'

'Of course.' Beth also sat down, opposite him. 'So you may as well tell me the truth. About everything. She has.'

'An abortion?' Georges was looking distraught. 'You mean you have destroyed my child? My child? My God!'

'Do you know,' Beth remarked. 'I almost thought you might try to deny it?'

'You have destroyed my child,' Georges said again. 'My child. My first and only child. Oh, my God.'

'So tell me the truth,' Beth said relentlessly. 'When you went on those business trips you always included a visit to Lucerne, didn't you? She has told me everything. She has told me how you saw her sunbathing up on the roof and approached her. How you seduced her.'

'My God, my God,' Georges repeated.

'You . . . you ogre,' Beth said. 'You went to Switzerland, playing the part of the loving stepfather, persuaded Mrs Golightly to let you take Anna out to lunch, and then took her up to your hotel room and raped her, time and again, swearing her to secrecy. She has confessed all of that. You are a horror, Georges.'

Georges raised his head. 'It was hardly rape, Elizabeth. She seduced me as much as I seduced her. I think she even dreamed of replacing you in my affections.'

'Oh, yes,' Beth remarked, making a mental note that that was worth remembering. 'And Stephanie? I suppose she seduced you as well?'

Georges sighed, and his shoulders slumped. 'I am entirely guilty there. She is such a lovely child. They are both lovely children. I am sorry, Beth, but I have my faults. Every man has his faults. Mine is women. Girls. I have always adored girls, wanted to touch them, wanted to feel them ... never to harm them.' He raised his head again. 'I meant her no harm, I swear it. Neither of them. I swear it to you that Anna was not a virgin when I took her to bed, or I would not have done so. As for Stephanie ... I would never harm Stephanie. I love that girl, almost as much as I love you. I just wanted to kiss her.'

'Kiss her?' Beth demanded.

'You know. Well ...'

'Between her legs? My God, but you are an ogre.' Now she was genuinely angry, and shocked. 'A totally innocent sixteen-year-old girl?'

'How was I to know she was innocent? Anna wasn't. And a girl like Stephanie ...'

'You mean a girl like my sister,' Beth observed coldly. 'Is that not the truth? The sister of a whore.'

He sighed again and repeated, 'I love her. I love you all. Although I love you best, Beth. Cannot you understand .. ?'

'I understand entirely,' Beth said. 'You had this planned from the beginning. You did not just want me. You wanted all of us. Madame Suchet said as much, and I was stupid enough not to believe her. My God, talk about innocence. I was stupid enought to believe that you were an honourable man ...'

Georges threw back his head. 'Honour? I am a hero of the Maquis. I never turned my back on an enemy, or let down a comrade.'

'And that is your total concept of honour,' Beth said. 'Well, it is not mine. I have given my entire life to protecting Anna and Stephanie, and now what do I find? I feel sick.'

His shoulders slumped again. 'I know. I am sorry. Sorrier than I can tell you. But my child ... you should not have destroyed my child. That was a crime and a mortal sin. And for me ... I have wanted a child all of my life. My child. You could never give me a child, Elizabeth. I would have made Anna's child my heir. I would have given him everything I possessed. Or her,' he added miserably.

'You would, would you,' Beth remarked, more than ever certain that she had done the right thing in forcing Anna to have an abortion.

'And you have destroyed him,' Georges said, holding his head. Then he stared at her. 'You have taken an innocent human life. Do you not realise that? You have committed murder, of a helpless child. It is you who are the ogre. If I were to take you to court . . .'

'I would be condemned for having procured an abortion,' Beth told him, refusing to weaken. 'I might even be sent to prison for a month or two. But even if I were to be condemned, what do you suppose they would say of you, hero of the Maquis? A seducer of young girls? Of his own sisters-in-law? A rapist?' She pointed as he would have spoken. 'Oh, Anna will accuse you of rape. And Stephanie of attempted rape. They are my sisters. They will do as I tell them.'

He frowned at her. 'You are mad. You will take this to court? The scandal . . .'

'Will ruin you, Georges. It cannot harm me. I am a whore, remember? What else can I return to, lower than that?'

He opened his mouth, and closed it again. 'Then let us attempt to forget what has happened, and resume our lives.'

'Never,' Beth declared.

'Are you determined to ruin me? Elizabeth, I love you. I have given you everything I possessed. A home, my love, my money . . . but that is not enough for you.'

'I cannot expose my sisters to your lust,' Beth insisted.

'I will swear never to touch them again.'

She shook her head. 'I am sorry. I cannot accept such a promise.'

'Then what do you want?'

Beth drew a long breath. 'I intend to leave you, with my sisters, and Tony. I will do so quietly, unless you force me to do otherwise, and will tell no one what happened here. When I am gone, you may give out whatever reason you please to the local people. If you oppose me, I will go to the police.'

'Leave me?' Georges was bewildered. 'But how will you live? Madame Suchet will never take you back again. She never forgives or forgets an injury.'

'I would not go back to Madame Suchet for ten thousand pounds,' Beth said. 'But you will support me, Georges, with ten thousand English pounds, every year. I wish a written contract drawn up.'

'Ten thousand pounds?' He stared at her. 'More than a million francs? That is blackmail.'

She shrugged. 'Call it what you will. Ten thousand pounds a year, Georges, and neither I nor my sisters will ever trouble you again. If you refuse, I shall take Anna and Stephanie with me to the police station, now.'

THE EIGHTH CHRONICLE

April 1985

Meyer caught the train from London's Victoria Station down to Virginia Water in Surrey.

He was aware of a tremendous sense of exhilaration, partly caused by the sight of the English countryside in early spring. There could be nothing lovelier, more indicative of the regenerative process, than that. But he was also quite absurdly excited, far more excited than an experienced pursuer like himself should ever be, even when nearing the end of his quest. And he did not doubt that, now. With a name, all doors were opened to him, and it had taken very little time to trace the Madame Mathieu who had arrived in England at the beginning of 1953 with her sisters and brother, down to a house in Virginia Water. Of course she would no longer be there. But from here on it was simply a matter of following her movements.

The excitement was caused by the thought that he might be close to meeting Elizabeth Janska. He took the photograph from his pocket, and studied it for the hundredth time. The mayor of Lorges had been reluctant to let it go, but had had no sound reason for keeping it, once Meyer had reminded him that it was a memory of a political enemy from a bygone era. Now he again was fascinated by that defiant, beautiful, almost guilty, eager, determined face. Perhaps he would even find out what had really happened at the château, that fateful week before Christmas.

The mayor's story had been sketchy to say the least. The servants had gossiped, as servants will, of how Monsieur Mathieu had assaulted the younger girl and then locked her in her room. Or had she locked herself in her room? Of how there was a rumour that the middle girl had gone to Paris to have an abortion. Of whose baby? No one knew. Of how Madame Mathieu

199

had returned to Lorges like an avenging angel. All gossip, all uncertainty. Monsieur Mathieu had apparently never spoken of it at all, never given any reason for the abrupt ending of his marriage. The only fact Meyer possessed was that after living with Monsieur Mathieu as his wife for more than two years in seeming contentment, Beth Janska had found some reason for leaving him, very suddenly – and taking with her not only her family, but a good deal more. Virgina Water, where he had discovered she had leased a house, was in London's stockbroker belt, and not a place for the penniless.

And yet, someone claiming to be Monsieur Mathieu's wife had erected that elaborate headstone, nearly twenty years later!

He had the strangest feeling that he was pursuing Beth Janska, and not her father. Indeed he was, for his own satisfaction. He had no proof that she had ever committed a crime, but the vision of her, established by Madame Suchet and corroborated by what had happened in Lorges, building upon what he knew conditions had been like in Poland at the end of the War, and in any displaced persons camp, out of which she had not only arisen like a phoenix but carried her sisters and brother with her, added to the photograph, was giving him a picture of a woman, so strong, so determined to protect her siblings and see them prosper . . . even if she had to bend a few rules to do it.

She would be a worthy opponent; he had bent a few rules in his time himself, had always prided himself on his ruthlessness.

Then he wondered what he would feel like if he found out – or perhaps, when he found out would be the more appropriate phrase – that she had bent a few rules, and had been prepared to be as ruthless as himself, to protect her father?

And might still be doing so?

CHAPTER 8

London 1953–59

Stephanie was more confused than ever by Beth's determination to leave the château, and even more, she was guilty. She could not escape the feeling that she had caused all of the trouble. 'But Beth,' she protested, 'we don't want to leave Lorges, do we? It is so pleasant here. And Uncle Georges is so kind, really.'

'I am leaving Georges Mathieu,' Beth told her. 'More than Lorges. After what has happened, it is impossible for me to live with him any longer.'

'I'm sure he didn't mean to harm me,' Stephanie said. She wasn't prepared to offer an opinion on Anna's situation.

'Of course he meant to harm you. To rape you at the very least, if you hadn't got away from him and locked yourself in your room,' Beth insisted. 'He is a horrible man. I am only sorry that I inflicted him upon you for all of these years. Bitterly sorry.'

Stephanie hadn't known what to make of that. She was sure Uncle Georges wasn't a horrible man, even if he might have some frightening desires. She felt guiltier than ever whenever she saw him during the month before all the papers were drawn up and they left the château. He looked so miserable, and at the same time so stiff and proud, that she almost wanted to throw her arms round his neck and tell him that she forgave him and that she would come back to see him whenever she could ... but she didn't dare. She had no idea what Beth would say to that.

And moving was sufficiently exciting, on this occasion, to bury her conscience for the moment. Everything Beth did was exciting, and when she got the bit between her teeth, as she did now, and had sufficient money, as she seemed to have now, she carried everyone and everything along with her.

She sailed down the gangplank from the ferry boat in Folkestone, wearing her mink coat and hat, her jewellery and her expensive clothes, with her sisters and brother trailing behind her like a gaggle of geese. She had done her homework, knew how not to excite the British Customs and Immigration, announced that she had come for a holiday while her brother was settled into university, and took them to an hotel, called the Savoy, which was the very best hotel Stephanie had ever seen – and then commenced finding them a place to live. She had obtained passports for them all the moment they had got their French citizenship, and as they were aliens these had to be presented at the police station every week, but as Beth was so well off and so brilliant and beautiful and forceful and well dressed, no one seemed to take it too seriously when the four of them stayed and stayed.

Tony would have stayed anyway, because, remarkably, he had obtained a university place at a Cambridge college, and Stephanie was immediately packed off to school, too, a very expensive girl's school down in Kent called Benenden. 'Just for your last two years,' Beth explained. This, too, was exciting, even if the prospect of speaking English all the time was daunting; as it turned out she was the centre of attention during her first term, as a rich French girl. Rich! She had no idea how much money Beth had, but there seemed a great deal of it.

Most exciting of all was the house that Beth rented, in a village called Virginia Water. The name presumably had something to do with the small lake near the house, which itself was set back from the road at the end of a long drive of dripping willow trees which ended in a gravel parking place before the front door. In many ways it reminded Stephanie of Madame Suchet's mansion in Paris, although it was smaller. It was still big enough to contain four bedrooms, so that they could have one each – as well as a fifth little room which Tony remarked would make a good nursery and

202

reduced Anna to tears – with a lounge, dining room, kitchen and utility room on the ground floor, and a neat little lawn at the back on which they played croquet, just as in the old days in Warsaw.

The house was fully furnished, though not very attractively. It belonged to a British colonial official and his wife who were renting it until they retired, when they would occupy it themselves. It was also very cold when they first arrived. Although there was central heating the previous tenants had not used it much because of the expense, but Beth immediately turned it on twenty-four hours a day and it warmed up very rapidly. She also bought them personal things for their rooms, individual counterpanes and rugs and pictures, to make them feel at home.

'Oh, Beth,' Stephanie said worriedly. 'Can we afford it?'

'We are never going to want again,' Beth told her.

Then she set about making them known in the vicinity, put down all four of their names for hacks from the local stables, and called on all her neighbours, leaving them each a visiting card which said 'Madame Elizabeth Mathieu, Château Lorges'. Soon there were ladies coming to tea, and, when Stephanie was home for the Easter holidays, jolly girls also coming to tea, with her. Then there were dinner parties, and by the summer they had all been elected members of the tennis club, where she would go with her new friends and play almost every day during the long vacation.

There were always lots of boys around as well, as most of their neighbours had sons as well as daughters, and there were also Cambridge friends of Tony's, who sometimes visited during the holidays, but Stephanie paid them as little attention as possible, however anxious some of them were to flirt with her. She had a pretty good idea of what boys wanted – all boys, from Jacques to Uncle Georges, with the exception of Tony himself, of course – and the thought continued to horrify and disgust her. She was far more interested in the Labrador puppy Beth brought home one day, who was to be named Prince, and who became her favourite companion when she was home from school. He was a constantly happy fellow, even if she suspected she was the only member of the family who gave him any loving; Beth had only bought him because every other family in the neighbourhood had a dog.

This almost visible, and daily, hardening of Beth's character was deeply disturbing to Stephanie. Of course she worshipped the ground her sister walked on. When she remembered how Beth had looked after them in Warsaw, and stood between them and the Russians, and led them away from Dresden ... Beth had to be the bravest girl she would ever know. And she had always cared deeply for them. Yet the way she was practically buying her way into English society, just as the way she had walked away from Madame Suchet, and most of all, the way she had turned her back on Lorges without apparently a moment's regret or even hesitation, abandoning a man with whom she had slept virtually every night for three years ... That behaviour worried Stephanie.

One summer's day, when she and Beth were knocking croquet balls about on the lawn with just Prince for company, she plucked up the courage to ask Beth, 'Didn't you ever really love Uncle Georges, Beth?'

'Love Georges? Good heavens, no,' Beth replied. 'He was a cus ... an old man.'

'But you married him.'

'Well, I had to find some way of getting us away from Madame Suchet's clutches. She was a terrible woman. You have no idea how terrible.'

'You said you'd tell me about her one day.' Stephanie could not accept that Madame Suchet had been a terrible woman.

'Yes,' Beth said, stooping to line up a shot through the next hoop. 'Well, one day isn't yet, my darling girl. You're too young.'

Obviously there was nothing sufficiently convincing

to tell, Stephanie decided. But she still couldn't understand how Beth could have done what she had with Uncle Georges. 'To marry a man you didn't love, to let him, well ... touch you. And then ...' she licked her lips as she remembered Uncle Georges' stories of what the Germans had done to the French girls they captured, and what he obviously enjoyed doing as well, except for the torture and mutilation, of course. 'It must have been terrible.'

'It was,' Beth agreed, bringing off the shot with perfect ease. 'But sometimes it is necessary to do unpleasant things. Maybe if you're lucky you'll never find that out. I do hope so, my darling.'

'Don't you miss Lorges at all?' Stephanie persisted, seeking some spark of softness or sentimentality.

'I used to miss things,' Beth said thoughtfully. 'I was terribly upset at leaving Warsaw. More than you ever were.'

'I don't remember too much about it,' Stephanie confessed.

'Well, you were very young,' Beth said magnanimously. 'Anyway, I got over it. And then I learned not to get upset about things like that. Never look back, Stephanie. Only forward. Only tomorrow counts.'

'But if we don't look back, we'll forget Father,' Stephanie objected.

'We must never forget Father,' Beth told her. 'Or Mother. But they're dead, and that is the end of the matter. Looking back isn't going to bring them back to life again. We must remember them, but we must resolve to do better than they did, so that they can always be proud of us, wherever they are.'

When Beth exhorted like that, it was impossible not feel a swelling in the chest, a determination to get on and succeed, no matter what had to be done. . . . But it also raised another question, which Stephanie had always been afraid to ask. But as they were sharing this intensely intimate moment, she decided to chance it. 'Beth ... did you really marry Uncle Georges just for his money?'

Beth gazed at her for several seconds. Then she made a face. 'I suppose I did, Stephanie. Don't look so shocked. We had to have money, to get away from Madame Suchet, and to live in a place like this, and enjoy all the good things we now have. One simply has to have money in this world, and Georges was prepared to give it to me. It was a bargain, my body for his wealth. He got what he wanted, and in the end I got what I wanted. What we all wanted.'

Stephanie opened her mouth, and then closed it again. What Beth had just admitted was shocking. But it was even more disturbing to reflect that Uncle Georges had not really got what he wanted at all. He had had Beth for only three years, and it had cost him, was still costing him, a fortune. That made Beth some sort of a cheat, she was sure. But she knew that was a subject she had better not broach, even in a moment like this.

Besides, it had all been done for them. For her. She must never forget that.

Meanwhile there was the future to be considered. Stephanie enjoyed her two years at Benenden, and made a lot of friends, but she didn't do very well at her examinations. 'You really are a dummy,' Beth remarked. 'When I think of Tony doing so well at university . . . you don't have a hope of getting a place with those results.' She sighed. 'I suppose it's all part of your being moved about so much, and having to go to a strange school with a strange language . . .' She ruffled Stephanie's hair. 'Oh, don't look so upset. It's not vital. You can go and work with Anna.'

Now that was an exciting prospect. Stephanie had no desire to go to university, even had she been examination-minded, and she had long accepted that the plan to send her to Mrs Golightly's finishing school in Switzerland had been abandoned. Beth wanted her close at hand after everything that had happened to Anna, and she wanted to stay close at hand. Now Anna had been found a job in London by one of Beth's new friends, as a counter assistant in a very big and expensive jewellery store called Preytier's, from the name of the family which had founded it some two hundred years before.

Preytier's was the very top of the market, and on one of their visits to town Beth had paused to look in the window, while Stephanie had held her breath, as the cheapest item cost over a thousand pounds. Naturally in such a place it was impossible to describe any of the shop assistants as shop assistants, and indeed only the best people worked there; Anna's colleagues were all the daughters of well to do bankers or stockbrokers or captains of industry; Stephanie suspected that Anna would never have been accepted but for that 'Château Lorges' on Beth's visiting cards.

The girls were paid very little, as it was assumed by the management that they would be receiving substantial allowances from their wealthy parents, but it was a fabulous place to be, Anna claimed, where one had to dress very well, and be perfectly mannered, and where one met the very best in clientele. It helped to have a French background, too, as the Preytier family had originally been French; Beth warned them both never to reveal their Polish origin, as although the British were supposed to be friendly to the Poles the Russians had installed a Communist government in Warsaw and Poland was now very much a member of the Communist Bloc, as the very words Warsaw Pact indicated. So to all intents and purposes they were French born and bred.

The only drawback to working in London was having to rise very early in the morning to catch the train from Virginia Water to Victoria, so as to be at the shop by eight-thirty. Anna found this a terrible drag, especially as they never got home again until about seven in the evening, and she kept agitating for Beth to allow her to take an apartment, a flat, the English called it, in London itself. There were other reasons for this than merely avoiding early rising, of course. Anna had remained very emotionally upset and indeed crushed by what had happened at Lorges and by her abortion, and it had been more than a year before she would consent to go out to work at all. But after Beth threw a huge party for her twenty-first birthday in the late summer of 1953, she came back to life, so to speak, agreed to work at Preytier's, and was soon her old self again.

Now she wanted to go to parties in London, which would mean staying over night, with a girlfriend, she claimed – or having one's own apartment. But Beth refused to consider it. She said it was because of the cost – her income, although considerable, would only stretch so far – but Stephanie was sure it was because she did not trust Anna sufficiently to let her live on her own. After she had worked at Preytier's for a year herself, though, and was nineteen, she raised the matter. 'I'd keep an eye on her,' she promised.

'You?' Beth smiled and kissed her cheek. 'On Anna? You don't know her the way I do.'

'I do know she's very unhappy,' Stephanie persisted. 'And after all, Beth, she's twenty-three. You can't treat her like a child forever.'

Beth frowned at her, as if just realising the truth of what she had said, but said nothing. And you, Stephanie thought, you're twenty-five, and utterly beautiful and desirable and attractive and rich . . . and doing absolutely nothing with your life. Beth had given out that she was a widow, and as she was clearly well off there was no lack of bachelors or other widowers to take her out. She had a busy social calendar and at every dinner party – and she either gave one or attended one every week – there was an unmarried man to make up the numbers, to whom Beth would give an affectionate squeeze and ask to look after the drinks, which pleased them no end . . . but every week there was a different man. Stephanie understood that Beth could never get married, as she was still married herself, but it puzzled her that she never even seemed to want a steady boyfriend. The fact was that Beth did not like men; presumably her experiences with Uncle Georges must have been even more unpleasant than she had admitted. But if that were the case, why bother to pretend that she did at her parties? And why not find something else to do with her life, rather than moving from one social circle to another, from coffee mornings to hacking to tennis parties to bridge parties to church bazaars to cocktail parties to dinner parties. . . . It was as if she were searching for something, but as it couldn't be a man, what could it be?

Stephanie didn't like men herself, or at any rate, she could not bring herself to trust them. On the other hand, she was sure there must be men like Tony around in the world, so handsome and dashing and kind, and it was so romantic to serve the newly engaged couples who came into the Preytier showrooms looking for rings, holding hands and gazing at each other with the most rapt adoration.

Stephanie thought it must be marvellous to be able to love someone so utterly and completely, because that would mean trusting them as well, and knowing that you could. She had never done that with anyone, except within the family of course. She had trusted Father like that, and he had never let her down. And since Father's death – because he had to be dead as they had not heard from him since he had gone off to Berlin ten years ago – she had loved Beth like that as well, and of course, Tony. She wasn't sure about Anna, with her sarcasm and her black moods.

Anna worried her just as much as she worried Beth, although for different reasons. Beth worried about Anna getting pregnant again. Stephanie worried about her sly ways, which included slipping out of the shop whenever she could find and excuse, and being away for ages, and taking an extra ten minutes over her lunch hour, and disappearing into the Ladies Room for far longer than she was supposed to, and complaining about how the showroom was either too hot or too cold, and how her feet hurt ... Stephanie was sure these things were being noticed by the management and would eventually get Anna the sack, and that would have to rub off on her sister.

But Tony was a dream. Beth had set to work immediately they were settled in at Virginia Water to have them nationalised as British citizens. This had not proved as simple in England as it had been in France, as she was not married to an Englishman, but she had not given up, had used her new friends with that ruthlessness Stephanie was now coming to notice and to fear, and by the summer of 1956 their nationalisation papers came through. It was a great occasion, as it coincided with Tony's completion of his time at Cambridge, and to celebrate the four of them had gone out to dinner at the Dorchester.

Tony was now meaning to qualify as a lawyer, which meant being apprenticed to a firm until he was called to the Bar, such was the quaint British terminology. But first, as a new Englishman, he had to do his national service. Beth seemed quite happy about this, as Tony wanted to go into the Royal Navy, and Britain was not fighting any serious colonial wars at the moment, or at least, none in which the Navy were actively involved, while the fighting in Korea had ended in a stalemate.

When he came home for his first furlough, he was so handsome and dashing in his uniform that Stephanie nearly fell in love with him. 'Of course,' he told her, 'I'll only be in the Navy for two years, you know. Still, it's going to be great fun.'

She was thrilled for him, and wished she could do national service as well. That November she was going to be twenty, and suddenly she was bored with the life she was leading, which in essence was just as futile and meaningless as Beth's. Because of Beth's caution about Anna she could go to no parties in London, and those at Virginia Water were very stereotyped and dull, even if the young sparks considered themselves to be the most daring generation on earth as they smoked cigar-

210

ettes and drank vodka and played silly games such as finding out how many of them could cram into one of the very small British cars called Minis, which involved a lot of intimate shoving and pushing and grasping, or sat for hours strumming washboards, and singing mournful dirges which predicted the imminent end of the world in an atomic holocaust.

Beth was utterly contemptuous of the young people they met. 'They've experienced nothing,' she said. 'A few bombs, that's all. Yet they think they know all about war. They're so afraid. There'll never be another war, I can tell you that. It's the people like you and me, Stephanie, who have seen what war can really be like, who'll make sure of that.'

But she was wrong. The people like herself and Stephanie who really knew what war was like had no influence on events at all. Only a few days before Stephanie's twentieth birthday, England was at war again.

It was a very brief, and muddled affair; Stephanie could not make head nor tail of it. The Egyptians had nationalised the Suez Canal, and the British and French were determined to regain control of it, with the help of the Israelis, who were at war with Egypt anyway. So they bombarded Port Said and landed troops and beat the Egyptians all over the place. But the Americans didn't want it to happen, and withdrew support, and apparently both Britain and France would be bankrupt without American aid, and had to abandon their adventure and put the best face they could on things. Within a week, on Stephanie's birthday, 6 November, the fighting had stopped.

But it was a traumatic period for Beth, quite apart from spoiling Stephanie's birthday party, which had been cancelled: Tony was at sea on his first ship. At Christmas, when he came home on furlough, he told them that he had never been anywhere near the Suez Canal or Port Said and had neither seen nor heard a shot fired in anger throughout the entire crisis. Beth hadn't known that at the time, and had been frantic with worry.

The Suez war had a nuisance quality as well, such as petrol rationing, and Beth had just bought herself a car, a Standard Ten, having been taking driving lessons. She was furious at not being able to drive as much and as far as she felt like, and denounced Mr Eden, the British prime minister, as an aggressor. But the upshot of the whole business was a happy one, although Stephanie was never sure whether the war actually had anything to do with it, or whether Beth had at last found a reason of her own for wanting her sisters out of the house except on weekends. In the new year of 1957 she agreed that the two girls could find themselves a flat in London.

This was enormously exciting. It would be the first place either of them had ever had of their very own, and it would be theirs, because they were now between them earning just enough to be able to share the rent and the outgoings. Anna found the flat in Fulham just a few hundred yards from the river. It was only when they went to move in that Stephanie discovered that Anna seemed to have an awful lot of male friends, for a girl who lived in the country, all whom turned up to help them. Not that there was that much to do, apart from cleaning the place up – the previous tenants had been three boys – as it was fully if cheaply and unimaginatively furnished. 'We must throw all of this junk out, as soon as we can afford to,' Anna announced. 'Beginning with that carpet. It's horrible.'

They were sitting on it at the time, eating baked beans out of a can in front of the fire. 'Heaven alone knows when we'll have the money for that,' Stephanie pointed out. 'A new carpet will probably cost a hundred pounds.'

'Four hundred,' Anna said. 'I priced them. But I can't live with this. We'll get a new one next week.'

Stephanie stared at her with her mouth open, and

Anna chucked her under the chin. 'Stop worrying. I know how it can be done.'

They had alternate Saturdays off work, and the following Saturday Anna went off by herself, and returned at lunchtime with four hundred pounds in cash. Stephanie gazed at the money in suspicious wonder. 'Where did you get it?'

'I earned it,' Anna said. 'Easy as pie. I let a man take photographs of me.'

'A man paid you four hundred pounds to take a photograph of you?' Stephanie's incredulity grew.

'Not just one photograph,' Anna explained. 'Hundreds. I spent the whole morning with him. He's going to sell what he calls a layout to a magazine. It's a man's magazine, you know. I'm going to have a big double page spread, and lots of other ones. Mick says I could become a famous pin-up. He doesn't usually pay as much as four hundred, but I insisted, and he finally agreed. He says I'm the most beautiful girl he has ever seen.' She winked. 'I told him you'd probably want to be photographed too, and he got quite excited. I told him you're as pretty as I am, well, almost. I'm sure we can get two hundred and fifty out of him for you.'

'But ...' Stephanie drove her hands into her hair; she had never opened a man's magazine in her life, could imagine nothing more boring. 'I still don't understand. Four hundred pounds ... just for a bunch of photographs?'

'Well ...' Anna lit a cigarette; she had taken up the habit although she knew Beth didn't approve of it. 'You have to take off your clothes, of course.'

'Do what?' Stephanie shouted.

'Well,' Anna said, a trifle sulkily, 'that's what men want to see. Your tits and bottom and legs and things. They can't show your front, you know. Mick photographed me there, of course, but that was for his private collection. His perks, he said. It felt really strange, lying there with my legs apart, and him do

213

nothing but snap away. I thought we were bound to. . . . Well, he's a queer, I suppose.'

'You must be mad,' Stephanie declared. 'My god, if Beth were to find out . . .'

'There'd be nothing she can do. I can tell you some things about Beth which would make your hair stand on end.'

Stephanie frowned. Things to do with Madame Suchet? she wondered. 'Tell me.'

Anna hesitated, then shook her head. 'No. I won't. So don't try to wheedle it out of me. The important thing is that Beth isn't going to find out, is she?' Her voice was menacing.

Stephanie sighed. 'No, I won't tell her. But you won't catch me doing a thing like that. Just to take off my clothes before a man . . . I'd die with embarrassment. As for letting him photograph me and putting it in a magazine . . .'

'You get used to the idea,' Anna said. 'I was a bit embarrassed at first, but I got used to it. And the studio is quite warm,' she added practically.

'Never.'

Anna shrugged. 'Suit yourself. Just remember that our new carpet belongs to me, then.'

Stephanie was shocked that Anna could have done a thing like that. On the other hand, she could not deny that the new carpet made the flat, or that Anna was happier and more vivacious than she had ever known her. Of course it was necessary to lie to Beth when she came to see them, and explain that the carpet had been bought on the never-never, as the English called it. Beth wasn't pleased about that, and lectured them about the folly of getting into debt, but she also seemed pleased by their determination to make the flat into a real home. After that, lying to Beth became a habit. A very necessary habit, because Anna now began doing a great number of things which Stephanie knew Beth would not approve of.

214

She began to throw parties, almost every Friday night. . . . It had to be Friday because Beth liked them to come home on the weekends they were off, and every Sunday. Anna's parties would sometimes go on until nearly dawn, and the loud music – the latest pop songs played on gramophone records – often aroused complaints from the other tenants in the building. But when the landlord's agent came to call, Anna, who usually contrived to have just come out of the bath at that moment and be wrapped in a dressing gown or towel, merely fluttered her eyelashes and allowed either a leg or half a breast to peep out from behind the towel at the bemused – and at the moment totally happy – man, and the complaint was dismissed.

More disturbing were the parties themselves. The place was littered with young men and women Stephanie hardly knew, drinking vodka and Coca Cola and smoking cigarettes or something they called pot, more properly known as marijuana. Stephanie tried both varieties and got no kick out of either at all, neither did she very much care for imbibing too much vodka, which gave her a hangover. As for the necking that went on in every corner, with partners often being changed halfway through an evening, and a good deal of groping and heavy breathing, it as all too reminiscent of Jacques and Uncle Georges.

Soon even Anna put her down as a square, but when she attempted to opt out and remain in her room she was kept awake by the noise and the constant invasion of young men and women, looking for a bed or the toilet, and always eager to get into bed beside her. She didn't dare take off her clothes, while if she locked the door they banged on it until she thought they were going to break it down. So she accepted the position of permanent waitress, passing drinks and sandwiches, which pleased her just as well, as she was thus able to observe human nature in some of its most grotesque moods and behavioural patterns.

These freaks could in turn be incorporated into her

dream world, which was beginning to take on a more substantial form as time went by. She was even writing down one or two things, composing little cameos, in which she placed various of her acquaintances and often herself, in extreme situations, some dangerous, some comical, some sexual, but out of which she invariably emerged unscathed, however close to the brink she might sometimes be forced. She knew she could not live in such continually sensual an atmosphere, and Anna was the most sensual of people, and not feel sensual herself; the scenes she composed were a useful outlet for her emotions. She longed for a sexual adventure herself, but was afraid of it, and felt a total distaste for indulging in public, in a corner of a crowded sitting room. Besides, none of the boys, who were nowadays growing their hair and affecting outlandish modes of dress which they fondly imagined were reincarnating the richness and elegance of Edwardian England – and which earned them the nicknames of teddy boys – were the slightest bit attractive. Rather they seemed to her to be overgrown children, for all of their wildly expressed freedom to behave exactly as they chose.

But above all was the recurring fear of what would happen when Beth found out about the life they were leading in London, as Stephanie knew she had to, eventually. She declined Beth's offer to co-hostess a party at the flat for her twenty-first birthday, claiming that she would far rather just the four of them – Tony was home on furlough – went out to dinner. It was a great occasion, especially as opportunities for them to get together were becoming increasingly rare, and Beth gave her a pearl necklace with a matching bracelet which was the most expensive piece of jewellery she had ever owned. Even Anna did not appear to be as bored as Stephanie had feared she might, while at least she had prevented the chance of Beth meeting some of Anna's friends, and being horrified.

In fact, Beth never did find out what went on in the

flat by herself. It was Stephanie who eventually told her.

She and Anna had lived in the flat for more than two years, when the parties started to diminish. At first Stephanie thought Anna might be getting as bored with her shallow circle as she always had been, which was a great relief. Then she thought her sister might be being careful because Tony had now come out of the Navy and was in chambers in London, and had a flat of his own, which he shared with two other young men. But Tony seemed to throw just as many parties as Anna had ever done, and when Stephanie allowed herself to be persuaded to go to one, she found they consisted of entirely the same goings on, which didn't fit in with her idea of a budding lawyer at all.

So there had to be another reason for Anna's new and quieter image, and suddenly she realised what it was. She first saw the man in Preytier's, when he came in to look at some rings. He was short, and inclined to stoutness, with jet black hair which he wore smoothed straight back from his forehead, and the most perfectly cut suit Stephanie had ever seen. He seemed in every way to be very wealthy and confident ... but he was also quite old, at least to Stephanie's eyes. Not as old as Uncle Georges, to be sure, but certainly about forty, which seemed too old for Anna. And he was certainly fond of Anna. That could be seen in a moment, in the way he waited for her to be free to serve him, and then stroked her hand, while she positively fawned.

Stephanie tried to forget the whole thing, but when a few mornings later Anna, who had taken to spending a lot of time out of the flat, had stayed out the whole night and staggered in just before dawn, looking like something the cat had dragged out of a dustbin but wearing a four thousand pound diamond solitaire ring which Stephanie had seen the dark man buying in Preytier's the previous week, she was terrified. Anna was having an affair! With a man old enough to be her father, and unpleasant as well, Stephanie was sure. Suppose she got pregnant again?

217

She didn't know what to do, as she knew that Anna would never take any advice, or even any adverse criticism, from her. So, after several sleepless nights, she felt she had to tell Beth. She did so the next weekend, in such a state of nerves that she twisted Prince's ears and made him howl. To her enormous relief, however, Beth did not explode, but listened quietly, and nodded from time to time. 'I'd better come up to town next week, and have a word with her,' she decided, when Stephanie had finished.

'You don't think I'm sneaking or something?' Stephanie asked anxiously, having learned the rights and wrongs of sisterly conduct at Benenden. 'It's just that I'm so worried about her. I'm sure he's a wide boy.'

Beth raised her eyebrows. She could never understand British slang.

'A crook,' Stephanie explained.

'I'm sure he is, too,' Beth agreed. 'From your description of him. And you did exactly the right thing in telling me about it. That's what being sisters is all about; we have to look out for each other. Don't worry, I'll sort it out.'

She duly came to dinner the following week, having informed Anna that she had to spend the night in London and begging a bed. Anna was quite happy about that, and even laid on a candlelight supper party for just the three of them, which was very jolly as there was a bottle of Beaujolais as well as vodkas and orange juice. But of course alcohol had no effect on Beth because she hardly drank any of it, merely watched while both Anna and Stephanie got tight, Stephanie through nerves, Anna through habit.

'Now, Anna,' Beth said conversationally while they were having coffee after the meal. 'I want you to tell me all about this wog who's dating you.'

Stephanie caught her breath. She hadn't expected Beth to come out with anything like that. But she should have, she knew; Beth was getting more and more arrogant and uncaring of other people's opinions with every day.

Anna also caught her breath, but her gasp was in anger, and she glanced at Stephanie as if to indicate that she knew who was responsible for this happening. 'I have no idea what you are talking about,' she said.

'Oh, come now,' Beth said. 'Aren't you going to show me your ring?'

Now Anna glared at Stephanie. 'You disgusting little rat,' she remarked.

Stephanie flushed scarlet. 'I didn't know what to do. I'm sure he's a crook.'

'You think he's a crook? You didn't know what to do?' Anna shouted. 'Don't you think I know what to do? For Christ's sake, I am twenty-seven years old. Twenty-seven, God damn it, and you all persist in treating me like a child.'

'Well, what else can we do?' Beth asked quietly, 'when you persist in behaving like a half wit. I want to meet this man.'

'Oh, yes?' Anna asked. 'So you can be rude to him? No way. Istvan is my friend.'

'Istvan? What kind of a name is that?' Beth demanded.

'His name is Istvan Szabo, and he is Hungarian,' Anna said, stopping her shouting and speaking with dignity. 'He came to England two years ago, after the revolution in Hungary, because he's an anti-Communist, just like us, and he had to get out of the country or he'd have been shot. Just like us in 1945, remember? He's had a very hard time of it. He's lost all his money and all his family, he doesn't even know where his wife is . . .'

Up to that moment Beth had been very calm about the whole thing. Now she exploded. 'His wife? You are having an affair with a married man?!'

'I told you, he doesn't know where she is,' Anna said. 'She could be dead. She probably is.'

'Or she could arrive in London tomorrow and scratch out both your eyes,' Beth snapped. 'You really are a

219

half wit. Hard time he's had? Lost all his money, has he? So now he's shopping at Preytier's and buying expensive rings for his girlfriends. My God! If you see him again you need your head examined. In fact, I absolutely forbid it.'

Anna stood up. For a moment Stephanie thought she was going to throw something, she was so angry. 'I am not going to be bossed about by you any longer. It's my life and I'll live it as I choose. I love Istvan . . .'

Beth snorted.

'And I'm going to go on loving him,' Anna shouted. 'No matter what you say. And if you don't like it, you can jolly well lump it.' She stormed out of the room.

THE NINTH CHRONICLE

April 1985

'Here we are, Mr Meyer,' said the young man, having delved deeply into his filing cabinet. 'That was going back a bit. But we did lease the house called Dunroamin to a Mrs Elizabeth Mathieu in January 1953, for a period of ten years. However, she seems only to have occupied the premises for seven; the lease was terminated, I see by mutual agreement, in 1960.'

'Can you tell me why? Or anything about Mrs Mathieu?' Meyer asked.

'Heavens, sir, I wasn't working here thirty-one years ago. As a matter of fact . . .'

'You weren't even born then,' Meyer said wearily. He glanced over the estate agents' office. 'Is there anyone here now who was here then?'

'I'm afraid not, sir, Old Mr Prentice – he's the boss, you know – might remember something about her, but he's on holiday in Spain, right now. He was here then, though, in the days when his father ran the firm. If you'd are to call back in about ten days time . . .'

Meyer nodded and got up. 'I may just do that.'

The woman seated at the next desk smiled at him. 'Is that the Mathieu woman you're talking about?' she asked. 'Wasn't there some kind of a scandal involving her? It had something to do with her giving up the lease.'

'Scandal?' Meyer asked. Definitely Beth Janska. 'But surely you weren't here then?'

She gave a little simper. 'Oh, no, sir. But I think Mrs Mathieu had something to do with the trial of that man Szabo. There was a TV documentary on him, a couple of years ago. I don't remember much of the details.'

'Szabo?' Meyer queried. The name was vaguely familiar, but then, it was a very common Hungarian name, meaning 'tailor'.

221

'You know,' the woman said. 'The London gangster of the sixties. According to the documentary he virtually ruled London for a few years. King of the underworld, they called him before the police finally caught up with him. I'm sure Mrs Mathieu was involved.'

'And he's still in prison?' Meyer asked.

'Oh, no, sir. He only served a few years. Then he was released because of ill health.'

'Would you have any idea where he is, now?'

'That was the point of the documentary,' the woman explained. 'Nobody knows what happened to him. He was sent to hospital after being released on parole, discharged from there in due course, and soon afterwards disappeared. He never reported to his parole board or anything. The police tried to find him, but never did. The documentary suggested that he might have been murdered by some previous criminal associate, but they couldn't indicate who it might have been, or even why, although a man like Istvan Szabo obviously had a lot of enemies. No trace of him has ever been found.'

Meyer caught the next train back to London.

CHAPTER 9

London 1959–63

Stephanie expected another explosion from Beth, but Beth took it all very calmly, even when Anna moved her things out of the flat a few days later, and quit her job at Preytier's. Beth merely shrugged at the news.

'She's always been difficult,' she remarked. 'I suppose she's the cross God sent me to bear. Not like you, my darling girl,' and she gave Stephanie one of those affectionate hugs which Stephanie so loved to receive. 'She'll come crawling back when this Hungarian lout throws her out, or when she discovers he doesn't really have any money. For God's sake, how can a Hungarian refugee have any money? But what can I do? Anna is twenty-seven years old. I can't chain her to the bed post as much as I'd like to.'

'But suppose . . .' Stephanie bit her lip.

'That she gets pregnant again? I imagine that is highly likely. Oh, well, I suppose I'll have to take her back to Dr Buget again. Knowing Paris well does have some advantages. Maybe after having had two abortions she'll learn her lesson. They really are the most disgusting things.'

Stephanie was as usual mystified. She remembered Dr Buget very well; he had come to examine her at Madame Suchet's when she had had the flu. But she had no idea he had performed the abortion on Anna, or that he engaged in anything illegal at all. Equally this was the first time Beth had admitted that an abortion could be an unpleasant thing; in the past she had always suggested it was simply a matter of taking a pill or something. She dearly wished Beth would tell her everything about Madame Suchet, because she was beginning to suspect more and more that there was something shady about her, which Beth had found out. That would account for their abrupt departure and

Madame Suchet's anger . . . but Beth absolutely refused to talk about it.

Meanwhile, Anna's departure left her with problems of her own. 'What do I do about the flat?' she asked. 'I can't possiby maintain it on my own.'

'You advertise for someone to share it with you,' Beth told her. 'London is full of people looking for a place to live. Just make sure she's a nice girl.'

In fact, Stephanie didn't have to advertise at all, as one of the other girls at Preytier's, who was Stephanie's age and had just started working there, was looking for a flat, and she willingly moved in to share expenses. Beth was delighted. If her first name was rather exotic, Astral, her second name was commonplace, Smith, but her father was an executive in one of the big motor companies. She was also a very quiet girl who liked nothing better than to curl up in front of the television in the evenings after work with a good book, and as she wore horn-rimmed spectacles and suffered from a poor complexion, she was not overly troubled by men. There were no more loud parties at Stephanie's apartment, to the relief of the landlord's agent.

There were still parties at Tony's, to which she was constantly invited, and to which she occasionally went. To her consternation, at one of these in the autumn of 1959 she met Anna. 'Well, look what the cat dragged in,' Anna remarked, loudly. 'Little Miss Goody Two Shoes.'

Stephanie was relieved to see that Istvan Szabo was not there, and Tony apologised for Anna's remarks. 'I didn't want the rift to become permanent,' he explained. 'Even Beth says she's going to want to come back some time. And right now, you can't blame her for being bitter.'

Stephanie thought she had every reason to blame her for being that bitter, but she was too overwhelmed by Anna's appearance to make an issue of it. She had now lived in London for long enough to be able to evaluate clothes, and Anna's dress had come from Harvey

Nichols or Harrods, as had her shoes and handbag. In addition to the diamond ring on her finger she wore a ruby brooch which Stephanie estimated was worth as much as her yearly Preytier's salary, and her hair had been dressed by somebody like Randolph.

She was also the centre of attention. Stephanie decided to forget about the remark, and settled into her usual routine of passing drinks and canapes, and observing. ... She was surprised to be accosted by a young man who remarked, 'I have just heard an absolutely scurrilous rumour.'

'Oh?' Stephanie asked. 'What was that?'

'That you're the only virgin in this room.'

Stephanie looked at him properly for the first time. She was tempted to slap his face, or upend the tray she was carrying over him – but his suit was so very well cut, and he was so very handsome in a splendidly clean-cut fashion, with dark hair and a thin, clean shaven face, and broad shoulders to match his six feet plus of height, and looked so tremendously fit, she wondered if he mightn't be a film actor in between roles. She also realised that he was older than she had thought, perhaps even thirty, which probably meant he wasn't quite as callow as most of Tony's friends.

'Is that a crime?' she asked.

'I think it is just magnificent,' he told her. 'If I could understand why, in this day and age.'

'I suppose I've never met a man worth having on top of me,' she said boldly. 'Or underneath me.' She knew all about sex, now, from listening to Anna talk, and if this fugitive from a male beauty competition wanted to mix it then she was quite ready to co-operate – verbally.

'Now that is a challenge,' he said. 'My name is Geoffrey Trene, by the way. And you're Tony's sister Stephanie, right? Sister also to the gorgeous Anna.'

'Yes,' she said.

They both looked across the smoke-filled room to where Anna was holding court in the midst of several young men. 'Only, compared with you, she's not so gorgeous, is she?' Geoffrey Trene remarked. 'Unless you happen to like blondes.'

Stephanie couldn't make up her mind what to reply to that one; if Anna had just been beastly to her she was still imbued with her sense of family loyalty. So she murmured, 'Most men do.'

'This is a great party,' Geoffrey Trene went on. 'But I happen to hate parties. Why don't you and I sneak out for a bite of supper? I know a lovely little trat just around the corner.'

Stephanie considered, and then nodded. Because this man she wouldn't mind in the least having on top of her, at least in her dreams – she had no intention of allowing him any such liberty in the flesh. He was far too cocky and there was something about him she didn't quite like, which made her uneasy, but which was still fascinating. A sort of underlying menace, she thought it was, as if he might not be a film actor at all, but perhaps a special branch man or a motor racing driver or a contender for the world light heavyweight title in between bouts. She could fit him into the current cameo she was writing for her own amusement.

He fetched her coat and took her round the corner as he had promised, where to her surprise and gratification, he was very well known to the proprietor of the trattoria, who positively fawned as he escorted them to the best table and produced a most delicious meal, standing round and rubbing his hands together as Geoffrey tasted each dish. Stephanie found herself introduced to the delights of Frascati wine and was taught the proper way to eat spaghetti. She would have thought it one of the very best evenings of her life had she not become more and more convinced that the proprietor was afraid of her companion, and when, just as they were leaving, Geoffrey remarked casually, 'By the way, Alberto, I thought you'd like to know that Thompson will be calling next Monday morning,' the Italian turned quite pale.

'Do not worry, Mr Trene,' he said. 'Do not worry. I have promised, and I am a man of my word.'

'I knew you were,' Geoffrey agreed with one of his flashing smiles, and escorted Stephanie out.

'You seem to know him very well,' she ventured.

'Well, we do business together, now and then.'

'Oh? What line of business are you in?'

He shrugged. 'I'm what you could call an agent.'

'You mean you sell property?'

He smiled. 'There are several different kinds of agent, Stephanie. My business is getting things people want, which they can't obtain through normal channels.'

It seemed an odd, and precarious, line of work, but before she could pursue the matter her breath was taken away by the car to which she was being shown, a Lagonda. 'Oh, how beautiful!' she exclaimed.

'Beautiful cars are my hobby,' he explained. 'And beautiful women, of course.'

After that, she braced herself for a struggle, but he didn't even ask to come into the flat, merely kissed her knuckles in a very French fashion, and drove off. Almost she felt cheated. But he did fit so perfectly into her dreams.

She had hoped to hear from him again the following week, but didn't, to her disappointment. Instead, unexpectedly, Tony came to see her. 'I'm thinking of giving up chambers,' he told her.

'You can't set up on your own,' she protested. 'No one can do that in England.'

'I don't mean to try. The fact is, sis, I've been offered a job.'

'Outside the law?'

He grinned. 'I wouldn't put it like that, exactly.'

'Oh, I meant outside the legal profession.'

He nodded. 'Do you think Beth will mind? The fact is, being an articled clerk is a terrible bind. The pay is dreadful, and there's no hope of a partnership for at least a dozen years, as far as I can see. It really isn't for me. The job I've been offered carries three times the salary I'm now earning. I'll be quite well off. And that's for starters. The only way is up.'

'It sounds tremendous. What is it?'

'That's the tricky bit. Istvan Szabo wants me to go and work for him.'

'Istvan Szabo? You can't be serious.'

'I am very serious.'

'That Hungarian refugee wants to employ you? And pay you some vast salary? Has he got a company or something?'

'He has several companies, as a matter of fact,' Tony told her. 'He's a very wealthy man. Didn't you know? Haven't you seen what Anna is wearing nowadays? And my God, you should see his house.'

'Where?'

'In Hertfordshire. It is the most splendid place I've ever seen. It makes Madame Suchet's look like a slum, and the Château Lorges like a toy castle.'

'And you've been there?'

'Of course. I've had dinner with them.'

'Them? You mean Anna lives there, too?'

'Well, of course she does, stupid. She's his mistress.'

'Yes,' Stephanie said sadly. Somehow she had supposed he would have set Anna up in a flat somewhere. To have her living in his house seemed so flagrant.

'Gosh, I wish I knew what to say. Istvan Szabo! I can't believe Beth is going to be happy about it. But I suppose she can't stop you.'

'I don't want to upset her.' Tony said. 'I thought perhaps that if you had a word with her ...'

'Me?' Stephanie cried in alarm.

'Well, you're her favourite. You always have been. Baby sister and all that.'

'But I don't really like Mr Szabo.'

'How well do you know him?'

'I've never met him. But I've seen him.'

'There's a brilliant way to form judgements on people. What you mean is that you don't like his looks, but you don't really know anything about him. Did you know that Geoffrey Trene works for him?'

'Geoffrey? Mr Trene?'

Tony grinned. 'Geoffrey. I heard you. And I saw you sneaking off with him the other night. Yes, he's a director of several of Istvan's companies. So they can't be all that bad. What do you think of that car of his, eh? I could wind up having one of those. Come on, be a sport and have a word with Beth, please.'

Stephanie considered the matter and said she would think about it. But before she returned for the weekend, Geoffrey telephoned and asked her out to dinner again. She felt she shouldn't accept, now that she knew he worked for Szabo, until she had spoken with Beth, and yet she desperately wanted to see him again, Besides, she thought, perhaps she could do some investigating of her own about Szabo's business, and thus have more to tell Beth when she saw her. So she accepted, and waited in some anxiety for him to arrive.

'Where are we going?' she asked. 'Back to that delicious little Italian place?'

He sighed. 'I'd like that. But we can't.'

'Oh? Why not?'

'There's been an accident there. It's closed.'

'What kind of an accident?'

'God knows. I don't have any details. But I believe one of the stoves in the kitchen caught fire and just about burnt the place out. Terribly tragic. Alberto cooked good food, too. But you know what Italians are like, so careless, always waving their arms about. He must have knocked something over. Now he's in hospital.'

'In hospital?' she cried.

'He broke his arm or something trying to put out the fire.'

'Oh, I'm so terribly sorry,' Stephanie said.

'So am I,' Geoffrey agreed. 'I was very fond of Alberto.'

It seemed a strange comment. He took her to a Greek restaurant instead, where he was met with the same anxious desire to please on the part of the owner, and where again the food was superb. Stephanie could not, however, appreciate the retsina wine, and Geoffrey grinned and ordered some ordinary white.

'I so wanted to talk with you,' she confided after her second glass had given her confidence. 'Did you know that Mr Szabo has asked Tony to go to work for him?'

'Bertie?'

'Bertie?'

'That's what we call Mr Szabo, as you put it,' he explained.

'Oh.' Somehow the nickname ruined Stephanie's idea of a bigtime crook. 'Well ... you work for him, don't you?'

'In a manner of speaking. I'm a director of some of his companies.'

'Yes. That's what Tony says. What sort of companies are they? If you don't think I'm being nosy.'

'I don't think so at all. What sort of companies are there? They're a tax dodge, really, I suppose. You know, with a company you can write off things like cars and suits and other things against expense accounts.' He gave one of his devastating winks. 'I'll probably put tonight down as an expense, entertaining a visiting client or something like that. Who's to know?'

'Oh,' she said, feeling more relaxed every moment. If he could speak in such a careless fashion about breaking the tax laws ... because everyone broke the tax laws, didn't they? She was keenly aware of having done so herself in her last return, very slightly. 'But what do your companies do?'

'I told you, we're agents. We supply requirements to people.'

'And people always need you?'

He gazed into her huge eyes. 'People always need good agents, Stephanie.'

She bit her lip. 'I just ... well, Tony could be a barrister, one day.'

'Of course he could. But I don't think he really wants to be. And let's face it, only the top ten barristers in the

230

country earn what I would call good money. Bertie is offering Tony a place in our organisation at executive level. Of course, he's only doing it because Tony is Anna's brother. I won't deny that, or argue with it. Bertie is very much in love with Anna. He'd marry her tomorrow, if he could. But both he and I also recognise that Tony is a very bright boy. So we'd like to have him working with us. And if all goes well, and he has what it takes, he could be a director like me in a year or so.'

It sounded very positive and exciting. It was next morning before Stephanie remembered that what she had meant to ask was how a Hungarian refugee, presumably penniless, had built up such a vast business in two or three years. Because by the next morning a great deal had happened.

They drove back to Fulham in the Lagonda, as before, and as before Geoffrey double parked outside the apartment house front door, but this time he turned off the lights and the engine. Stephanie found she was holding her breath. 'Would you like to come up?' she asked.

'I don't think I had better,' he said.

'Oh, don't bother about Astral. My flatmate,' she explained. 'She's almost certainly in bed by now.' She bit her lip; it had sounded awfully like an open invitation, and she hadn't really meant it that way.

'That's the problem,' he said. 'If I were to come up with you, I'd probably want to go to bed as well, with you.'

She caught her breath, and was grateful for the darkness. He had such a direct way of speaking, and she could never tell if he was serious or not, just as now she had no idea what she could possibly reply.

'But you're not that sort of a girl, are you?' he asked quietly. 'Unlike Anna.'

She had a sudden wonder if he'd ever been to bed with Anna herself; if perhaps 'Bertie' shared her around? But that was an impossible, disgusting thought about her own sister. Or was it, for a girl who could

231

pose for nude photographs? She wondered if Istvan Szabo knew about that.

'No,' she replied, as calmly as she could. 'Anna and I have always been different.'

'Even when someone is very fond of you? Is falling in love with you?'

She stared into the darkness, and saw his face coming nearer. She didn't know what to do, so she did nothing, but when he kissed her she put both arms round his shoulders to hold him close. At that moment she didn't care what he did to her, which was just as well, because his hands came between them and unbuttoned her blouse while he held her mouth with his. He even found his way through her brassière, and stroked her with such gentle care she could almost feel the passion flowing from his finger tips. When one of his hands left her breasts and slid under her skirt she sighed, but when he reached her briefs she clamped her legs together.

By then they had run out of breath anyway. He took his mouth away and stared into her eyes in the gloom. 'I am falling in love with you,' he said.

'Oh, Geoffrey,' she said, wondering if she could possibly have chosen anything more inane. 'Would you . . . would you care to come up?'

He kissed her again, lightly this time, and kept his hands on her arms. 'I would, but I'm not going to. I don't like one-night stands, either. Besides, there's this virginity business. When I have you, I want all of you, and for always. Would you like that?'

Oh, yes, she thought. But she said, 'I don't know what you mean.'

'We'll talk about it,' he decided. 'Let's see . . . how about Tuesday? Dinner?'

'Oh, yes,' she said. And he kissed her again.

So there was a lot more to think about next morning than where Bertie had got so much money so very fast. And now she had to go and see Beth on Sunday. To tell her about herself? Without actually telling her anything, of course. She didn't know what she could possibly tell. She couldn't possibly be in love with a man she had met only twice – although he was claiming to be in love with her on no longer acquaintance. And she had let him touch her breasts and her bottom as if they had been the oldest of lovers. She was already regretting that instinctive leg clamping movement. If she hadn't, and he had touched her there . . . she had no idea what might have happened then. Save that she was sure it would have been beautiful. He was the most exciting person she had ever met, and she knew she could trust him absolutely. But Beth had to know.

She repeated as best she could everything Tony had told her about Anna's new set up, while Beth drank coffee and gazed out of the French windows at the garden where Prince, now something of a senior citizen, was rolling on the grass beneath the apple tree.

When Stephanie had finished, she remarked, 'You almost sound as if you approve of this Hungarian.'

Stephanie wished Beth wouldn't say things like that. Because, if the truth about them were known, might there not be people who might disapprove of 'those Poles'? However, she was here to get Beth on her side, not to argue with her. Besides, she had never argued with Beth.

'Well,' she said, 'I've met some of the people who work for him, and they all seem very nice.'

'Some of the people?' Beth quizzed.

Stephanie knew she was flushing. 'Well . . .'

'You have found yourself a boyfriend,' Beth observed, not unkindly.

'Well . . . he found me, sort of.'

'I'm glad of that; it's the way things usually happen. And I am relieved. I was beginning to worry about you. But I don't like the idea that he works for this Szabo. What kind of work does he do?'

'He's a director of one of Mr Szabo's companies,' Stephanie explained. 'They run some kind of supply agency. I don't understand it, really. But Geoffrey . . .

Mr Trene, is very rich, and he's so, oh, Beth, he's the most handsome man I have ever met. As well as the nicest.'

Beth frowned at her. 'You do seem to have fallen. You haven't by any chance let him . . ?'

'No, I have not,' Stephanie interrupted. There was no point in telling Beth that she had almost made up her mind to, though. Not right now. 'The point is that Geoffrey and Bertie . . .'

'Bertie?'

'That's the nickname everyone, even his employees, call Mr Szabo.'

'Oh?' Beth looked speculative.

'Which makes him sound rather a jolly fellow, don't you think?' Stephanie hurried on. 'But what I was going to say is that they want Tony to work for them, too.'

'Tony? He's going to be a barrister.'

'He doesn't really want to be, Beth. And he's being paid a pittance. Bertie will make him a director of one of his companies and he'll be as rich as Geoffrey. He's very keen. But he wanted to know how you'd feel about it, in view of your quarrel with Anna.'

'And he didn't have the courage to come and face me himself?' Beth snorted. 'Silly boy.'

'Do you approve, Beth?'

'How can I possibly approve of something I know nothing about?' Beth inquired. 'So I suppose I will have to find out about it. I think I had better pay your friend Bertie a call.'

It would mean admitting that her instincts had been wrong, for the first time in her life, Beth reflected, and it might also mean eating humble pie to Anna – and yet, it could all be a blessing in disguise. Almost she considered discussing the matter with Harry, but then decided against it. This was a Janska affair, pure and simple, and she had always dealt with Janska affairs by herself, and perfectly successfully. She must rely on her own judgement when she met this Szabo. But if he turned out to be the paragon that Stephanie and Anna – and Tony – seemed to consider he was, and as rich as they supposed, it would solve an enormous number of problems.

Because it was time to let them stand on their own two feet. Beth would never admit to them, she knew, just how exhausting and tense had been the past seven or eight years. She had stuck out her chin and led from the front, but she had not been sure it would work, had never known from one month to the next if Georges would suddenly stop paying her alimony – as she privately considered it – and if she would have to fight him in the courts. Although she had a signed contract with him, with every month her case against him became progressively weakened. Even if she could force Anna and Stephanie to testify against him, she had condoned what he had done in return for a monetary settlement, and the courts might take a sceptical view of that. Especially the French courts. While since her quarrel with Anna, she had felt she might be living on borrowed time.

In fact, and to her unceasing surprise and relief, Georges never failed to pay her allowance, every month. A hero of the resistance, she would think contemptuously when she was in one of her arrogant moods, who collapsed completely before the blackmail of a young girl. But then she would think, perhaps he is old and tired and perhaps he really had loved her as well, and was ashamed of what he had done. But equally he had never sought to get in touch with her. Sometimes she felt elated, sometimes downcast about that. Sometimes she remembered the warm feeling of security she had had at Lorges, and wondered if Georges, having seen so much more of life than she, would know that she could never be as happy again, and that her life would have to be all downhill from then on. Presumably he was sufficiently wealthy not to miss ten thousand pounds a year, and it might seem to him a reasonable sum to pay her to go to hell in her own way.

Feelings such as these had been growing on her over the years. In the beginning, she had not been sure what she wanted, except to escape Georges and even France, and all the memories of those hateful, shameful years at Madame Suchet's. She had never lost sight of her dreams, her goals. Georges had been a stepping stone to higher things, she had reminded herself when her conscience had threatened to get out of hand, nothing more. It had been such a treat to be independently rich, and yet on her own, that she had just sat back and enjoyed it. Ten thousand pounds a year put her into the same class as top directors of big companies, and even after paying the exorbitant English income tax she had been very well off. Of course inflation had been gnawing away at it, and where she had begun by having a considerable surplus, last year she had only just about broken even, nor could she possibly consider going back to Georges and asking for more.

But in the beginning, too, she had had so many plans for if the money suddenly dried up. She would get a job, and by that time the others, or at least Anna and Tony, would also have jobs, and things would work out, as they always had in the past. Then she had been an optimist. Nowadays her mood was changing. If they all had jobs, because presumably what Anna was doing could be called a job, none of them was earning more than peanuts, or had any real security. If this man Szabo was as rich and in love with Anna as they all seemed to think, and if he could establish Tony, then her immediate goal would have been reached, and she need never worry about Georges again.

And then, perhaps, she could think about Harry. She had not intended to marry again. She had never intended to be beholden to another man again, as long as she lived. Or another woman. But Harry did promise that security she suddenly felt she lacked. She had met him three years before, one of those tall, quiet

236

and distinguished looking pipe smoking Englishmen, director of a big company. He was much older than she, somewhere about forty-five where she was only coming up to thirty, but that was a comfort; she had a hearty dislike for very young men, and older men reminded her too much of Georges. Harry was passionately in love with her, bombarded her with flowers and invitations to dinner and cocktail parties at his house with monotonous regularity.

Over the past year he had invited her to act as his hostess – he was a widower. She had early confessed to him that she wasn't really a widow, but a divorcée, keeping her Roman Catholicism under wraps. Thus he had, only a few months before, asked her to marry him. She had promised to consider it, and had done so, in a mostly negative sense at first. Apart from her responsibilities for the children there had, initially, been the nauseating thought of having to submit to the caresses of a man once again. But over the months she had begun to reconsider the situation. Harry Paine was so kind and well mannered, so thoughtful, so quiet. . . .

She had experimented by allowing him to kiss her, and even on occasion to become quite emotional. But when he had accidentally touched her breast he had pulled his hand away as if scalded, and been hopelessly apologetic. Yet she had enjoyed the touch. Physically hers had been a very lonely existence since leaving Georges. Could it be that she might enjoy love making now? She was sensible enough to know that without it she was missing a large part of what made life enjoyable to ordinary men and women. And she knew she would enjoy his company.

Yet she had still hung back, worrying about Anna, worrying about Stephanie, whose refusal to discover a boyfriend had begun to appear almost abnormal, worrying about Tony, who was now nearly twenty-six and was hardly earning as much as Stephanie was, even with a university degree to his name. He would hardly have done worse to have stayed in the Navy and made a career of it, she sometimes thought, except that you could never tell when those silly people would go to war again.

The final obstacle which had lain between herself and Harry Paine had been that marriage to Harry might mean the final abandonment of her dream of getting them all to America. But again, over the years, she had been coming to realise that she was not yet properly equipped for life in America as she gathered it should be lived. She lacked the money. Ten thousand pounds, one million francs a year – since de Gaulle's revaluation of the French currency it only amounted to about a hundred thousand francs a year. But whichever currency she thought of, it remained peanuts to what she would require to live in style in New York. And there was no possible way of obtaining any more.

Save by marriage to the right man. Of course England was about the most heavily taxed nation in the world, after perhaps the Swedes – but there still seemed to be a lot of millionaires about. She didn't know if Harry Paine was a millionaire or not, but he drove a Rolls Royce, and he owned his house, which was considerably larger than Dunroamin. So far as she knew he had absolutely no intention of ever emigrating to the States, but suppose history were to repeat itself, a case of Château Lorges on a much larger scale? It was certainly possible, even if the exact circumstances would have to be different – she no longer had two innocent young sisters.

As cold as ice, Madame Suchet had called her. Well, she thought, it was events and people like Madame Suchet herself that had made her so.

But the biggest restraint of all on marrying Harry, up to now, had been the necessity of supporting the children. She had never doubted that Anna would one day come crawling home with a swollen belly without revealing any of their tangled background, something she knew would be impossible in a marriage. But if that problem, too, could be solved, she thought she could settle very comfortably into being Mrs Harry Paine, and let the future take care of itself. And would mean the end of her worries over Georges. Of course, legally, so far as she knew, she was still married to him. But who was to know? Certainly not Georges, as long as she didn't make the mistake of having her marriage reported in the international press. As for the red tape in England, she had applied for British nationality as a widow, and if there had been some talk of a death certificate, she had explained that her husband had gone missing in Indo-China several years before and was presumed dead, and they had accepted her story.

If only this remarkable Bertie could be everything Stephanie claimed he was. And his aide, Geoffrey Trene, as well. She picked up the telephone.

'Madame Mathieu. I am so glad, so very glad, that you have come to see me. Do you know how often I have almost made up my mind to come and see you, but have lacked the courage?' Istvan Szabo smiled as he talked, and held Beth's hand, and kissed it. He had a distinct accent, and wore a rather sickly aftershave, but Beth, like Stephanie, could not help but be impressed by the cut and quality of his clothes, while she was still trying to recover from the overwhelming effect of seeing the house for the first time. Set well back from the road in an enormous acreage of rolling fields and clustering trees, and rising five stories up to gabled roofs with tall Elizabethan chimney pots, the house possessed bay windows, and a terrace, and a butler to open the door for her . . . while outside were parked not only a Rolls, but also an Alfa Romeo sports and a Rover, beside which her three-year-old Standard looked like a battered child's toy.

Inside matched the exterior, with heavily carved wainscoting on the lower walls, massive Persian carpets, glass-fronted cases enclosing exquisite sets of china and crystal, huge mirrors, silent, smiling, uniformed housemaids, and in the study to which she was being shown, a world of leather, and good brandy and cigars.

'I thought I would not ask Anna to join us just yet,' Szabo went on, as Beth was temporarily speechless. 'As I supposed you would wish a private chat.' He walked her to an overstuffed armchair. 'Won't you please sit down?'

She did so, crossed her knees, and made a violent attempt to pull herself together. She could only thank God that she had thought to wear her mink, although she hated driving in it.

'Will you have a cigarette?' Szabo asked.

'I don't, thank you,' she said in a low voice. 'But please do go ahead.'

'Thank you. But I am sure you could stand an aperitif.' He pressed the bell, and the butler appeared as if by magic. 'Two bloody Marys, James,' Szabo said. 'Good and spicy, eh?'

Beth opened her mouth and then closed it again. She had expected to be offered sherry.

'Now ...' Szabo sat in the chair beside her, lit a Balkan Sobraine, rapidly filling the room with the delightful, sensuous aroma. 'You have come to see me because you are worried about Anna. I understand. Anna has told me how you have been virtually a mother to them all since the tragic deaths of your own parents. I salute you. Let me say that I count it a great privilege to meet you. Now I must tell you how much I love your sister. How I wish her to be my wife. But ...' he gave a tragic sigh. 'My situation is an unfortunate one. My wife and I escaped from Hungary together, in 1956. What shall I say to you about that, Madame Mathieu? You are a woman of the world. My marriage was long over. Indeed, my wife and I hated each other. But she was my wife, and in my own way I have always tried to be an honourable man. We were separated as we made our escape. When I got to Austria, I sought news of her. I have been seeking news of her ever since. I have employed private detectives and even govern-

240

ment agencies. And there has been not a word. I have been advised that according to English law after seven years I may consider her to be dead, and then legally remarry. Seven years. It is not so long a time when you are young. Anna is prepared to wait. I am less prepared to wait, but then bigamy is a serious crime, is it not? And I want only the best for my Anna. Your Anna. Our Anna.'

Beth had opened her mouth several times during the speech, and then closed it again as he was not about to be interrupted. And now the butler arrived with the bloody Marys, so heavily spiced that after a sip she was again forced into silence for several seconds while she tried to avoid choking. She was also choked by his remark about bigamy, for wasn't that what she was contemplating?

Szabo sipped his own drink thoughtfully. 'I give her the best now,' he said, half to himself. 'She has un-limited credit, her own car, everything a girl can want in this day and age.' He glanced at Beth. 'I do so want her to be happy.'

Shades of Georges Mathieu, Beth thought.

'And we are engaged,' he went on.

'I didn't know. I must have missed the announcement.'

He smiled. 'There was no official announcement, Madame Mathieu. Or may I call you Beth? Anna has told me so much about you I feel I have known you all my life. No, there was no announcement, because I am a man with many enemies. I have the knack of being more successful than other men, and this is resented by my rivals in business. I did not wish to publicise my relationship with so fragile a flower as Anna. But we are engaged.'

His arrogance was almost attractive. 'Exactly what line of business are you in?' Beth asked.

He shrugged. 'My business is making money. I have no inheritance, nothing, when I came here, so I thought to myself, how can I make money? For someone in my position, there was only one answer. I went to see

241

people, and I asked them what they wanted but could not get. And I got those things for them.'

'It doesn't sound a very easy way to get rich,' Beth commented.

'Oh, people will pay a great deal to get what they want. What they need.' He smiled. 'And one line of business leads to another.'

'I suppose it must. And now I believe you wish my brother to work for you. In what capacity?'

'With me, Beth. Not for me. Yes. Tony is a young man of considerable talent. I like talented men. They can go far. Tony will go far, working with me. I do not yet know what capacity will best suit him. That we will have to find out. But I have every confidence in his ability.'

'As you have every confidence in Geoffrey Trene?'

Szabo's eyes played over her lazily. 'Why yes. Have you met Geoffrey?'

Beth shook her head. 'I have heard of him.'

'Of course, your other beautiful sister, Stephanie, will have told you of him. Geoffrey was one of my first partners, and he is now my closest associate. I might add that he is desperately in love with Stephanie.'

'But he also has a long lost wife.' She was determined to be aggressive.

Szabo did not take offence, but gave one of his quiet smiles. 'I do not think so. I know he wishes to accumulate one.'

'Stephanie is still very young,' Beth pointed out.

Szabo raised his eyebrows. 'I had thought she was twenty-three?'

'I consider that very young.'

'But you were married at nineteen. I know it is a common fault to forget our own foibles. I promise you that Geoffrey will make Stephanie an admirable husband.'

'I am sure he will, Mr Szabo. But the decision will be Stephanie's.'

'As it should be. But please, you must call me Bertie.

All my friends call me Bertie.' He pressed the bell and ordered another bloody Mary. 'And James,' he said. 'Please ask Miss Anna to join us, and tell cook there will be a guest for lunch.'

'Pheasant, and Château Latour,' Beth confided to Stephanie. 'I don't know whether I've been conned or not.'

'Was there anything phoney about what you saw?'

'Not unless the house is mortgaged, or something like that.'

'So you agreed to Anna staying there, and to Tony working for him?'

Beth sighed. 'Unfortunately, I have no right to stop either of them doing what they want. I agreed to kiss and make up with Anna, if that's what you mean, and to give Tony my blessing. But there was another matter on which he sought my agreement.' She gazed at her sister.

Stephanie flushed. 'Yes. I . . . Geoffrey has asked me to marry him.'

'And you said?'

'That I'd think about it.'

'Have you slept with him yet?'

Stephanie raised her eyebrows.

And Beth smiled. 'I'm not quite the old square you think I am, you know. I'm well aware of modern morals. I'd just like to know.'

'Well, I haven't,' Stephanie said, and stuck out her chin. 'I want to. I would have. But he won't let me. He says he wants me a virgin on my wedding night. I didn't know men wanted things like that any more.'

'I don't suppose they can often get it,' Beth agreed. 'But it's nice to meet one who does. And even nicer to suppose he might possibly mean it. So marry him. But before then . . . be my bridesmaid.'

Stephanie stared at her with her mouth open. 'Your what?'

'I think I'm going to get married again, as it seems to

243

be in the air. A registry office. Very quiet. No publicity at all. Obviously not a word of it must get back to France.'

'But ... my God,' Stephanie said. 'Suppose it did? You could be locked up for bigamy. I mean ... why?' She didn't dare ask the real question, did Beth love this man or was she on the hunt for more money? It was a hateful thing to suppose of a sister she loved so dearly, but Beth did seem to feel justified in fleecing anyone if it furthered her ambitions.

'Well, why not? You're getting married. Anna is going to get married the moment Bertie can legally claim his wife is dead. Life is going to be pretty lonely for me down here now that all of you are flying the coop. As to anyone finding out, who can, supposing neither you nor Anna nor Tony tell anyone.'

'But can you trust ... I mean ...' Stephanie bit her lip and flushed scarlet.

'I've already discussed it with Anna,' Beth said. 'In return for my blessing on her relationship with Bertie, she's given me her absolute word she will never breathe a word to a soul. I think she's delighted that I am going to. Tony is pleased, too. We're still a family, you know, Stephanie. It's still us against the world. Only now the world seems to want to accept us. I really think we've come home at last.'

Where Beth Janska and Harry Paine were married quietly at a registry office in Guildford, Stephanie Janska and Geoffrey Trene were married in Westminster – Geoffrey, although a Protestant, willingly agreeing to being married in a Catholic church – and the reception, held in one of the private rooms at the Café Royal, was the biggest party Stephanie had ever attended.

She had never been so happy in her life. Always in the past there had been a shadow hanging over the family, the shadow first of all of those terrible days in Warsaw and on the road, and more recently the shadow under which they had left Lorges. But now, as Beth said over and over again, everything was working out.

Anna was happy, and even contented to be Stephanie's bridesmaid, while Bertie himself, who was turning out more and more to be an absolute dear, like a cuddly teddy bear, gave her away, as she lacked a father.

Tony was apparently doing very well, and if she saw much less of him nowadays, she gathered that it was a question of pecking orders, as Geoffrey was much the senior in the business and therefore felt he should only occasionally attend Tony's parties – it had been different before Tony had actually gone to work for Bertie. Stephanie understood also that if her brother seemed a trifle embarrassed and tongue-tied whenever they met, this was clearly for the same reason. But Geoffrey had asked him to be his best man, which she thought was rather sweet of her husband.

But then, Geoffrey was sweet in every way, as well as handsome and dashing and so kind and generous. He had bought her a new flat in London, but this, situated just off Sloane Square, could hardly be called a flat. It was a very large house situated on the top two floors of an even larger house; there was a roof garden where she could sunbathe in the nude on hot summer days. He had helped her decorate it and furnish it, or at least give the necessary instructions as to what she wanted done; there was to be both a maid and a butler and apparently she was never to lift a finger again except to raise a drink. That sounded rather pleasant after the long hours on her feet at Preytier's, although she knew she would never be able to live that idly. And even when they were alone together in the flat, before their marriage, he never did more than kiss her.

His wedding present was the flat and the furniture and the cutlery – Roberts and Belk – and crockery – Wedgewood – as well as an Austin Healey sports car of her very own. But he had also previously given her an engagement ring of a huge ruby set between two diamonds, which was her most treasured possession.

This came from Preytier's, obviously, as did most of the staff to attend her wedding, while Astral Smith was

245

the second bridesmaid. The staff even gave Stephanie a retirement present, as she was never going to work again.

Geoffrey also insisted upon paying for her trousseau, which offer Beth, after some hesitation, graciously accepted. The white satin gown came from Harrods, as did all the accessories, but he also bought her a complete set of nightgowns and lingerie in silk and satin.

When the priest said, 'You may kiss the bride,' and she looked up into Geoffrey's eyes, she knew she was the happiest girl in the world.

They honeymooned in Barbados, after spending the first night at the Savoy, where he finally held her naked in his arms. It was the most memorable experience of her life, because he was everything she had hoped and dreamed he would be, so gentle and yet so firm, so eager to teach her things, as she was so eager to be taught. She had waited all the twenty-three and a half years of her life for this moment, and she savoured every second of it, the more thrilled because he genuinely seemed to adore her body, and there, with her equally full breasts and much longer legs, she felt she did indeed match Anna.

For the next fortnight they did nothing but lie on the sand and swim in the warm sea and drink rum punches and make love. By the time they got back to London she was as brown as a berry.

There was only one blot on her horizon. Geoffrey's diabetes. It was astounding that a man so big and strong and powerful and confident could have such a dread ailment, and she knew he was ashamed of it because he had never told her, only confessed the day she walked into the bathroom and found him with the needle in his hand. She had noticed the spots on the skin of his arm and had assumed they were a blemish.

She was terrified, but he reassured her, holding her hands to explain that diabetes was no longer a killer, and could be kept under control by regular doses of insulin. 'But should you be drinking rum?' she asked. 'It's pure liquid sugar. And those chocolates we had yesterday. Oh, Geoffrey you bought them because I wanted them.'

Once again he smiled his reassuring smile. 'Sugar has nothing to do with diabetes, my darling girl, except as a symptom. It's the other way around, in fact. Lack of insulin, which converts the sugar to the body's use, creates a desire for more sugar. Don't worry, I've coped with this problem for years.' And as he could see she was still worried, he added, 'And I am going to go on coping with it for years.'

She was only partly reassured, but as he seemed to be as fit as she had always presumed him, her fears gradually dwindled. Once they were back in England they vanished altogether, in the joys of being mistress of so beautiful a flat, of having all the money she wanted for whatever she wanted, and of having all the time in the world, as well. She could not believe she deserved to be so lucky, and this time it was Beth who reassured her.

'Don't you suppose that you, we all, deserve a little luck after what we've been through?' she asked. 'It all works out in the end, for princes and for paupers.'

Which was a very reassuring philosophy, if un-Beth-like. Beth had always tried to make things work out; she herself had sat back and waited for them to fall into her lap. Determined not to be idle, she resumed her writing, far more seriously, and at Geoffrey's sugges-tion strung a lot of her cameos together into a novel, and, again at his suggestion, offered it to a publisher. It came back two months later with a polite note to say that the material was not quite what they were looking for at the moment.

'Silly bastards,' Geoffrey remarked. 'I've a good mind to go round there and knock some sense into their heads.'

'You'll do no such thing,' Stephanie insisted. 'It's only a hobby, anyway.'

Life continued to be absolutely wonderful. Geoffrey took her to plays and the opera and ballet, to dinner at the most expensive restaurants, while every so often they went out to Hertfordshire for dinner with Istvan and Anna. Strangely, they seldom entertained in the flat; apparently Geoffrey's friends were nearly all business acquaintances and he was not interested in socialising with them. This was a disappointment, because Stephanie so wanted to show off her exquisite silver and crockery and her crystal glasses; but the only real girlfriend she had made outside the family was Astral, whom Geoffrey found boring.

She entertained Beth and Harry from time to time, so proud to see the approval in Beth's eyes, and so happy to see that Beth at last appeared completely contented, so much so that it was possible to believe that she had married Harry for at least affection and not money. But it seemed that Harry did not altogether take to Geoffrey – jealousy, she supposed, as Geoffrey was ten years the younger man and apparently ten times the more successful man – and even these exchanges gradually dwindled. Instead she kept up her old habit of going down to see Beth once a week, only now she did it on Wednesdays instead of Sundays, when Harry was home.

Her real happiness was found entirely in her husband, and when at the beginning of 1963 she missed two periods, she was over the moon. She did not immediately tell anyone, not even Geoffrey, as she wanted to be absolutely sure, but it made 1963 promise to be the most important year of her life, the more so as by the end of this year Bertie's wife would have been missing for more than seven years, and therefore could legally be presumed dead, leaving him free to marry Anna. She knew Anna was counting the days, and she was, too. It would mean the whole family was settled – or would be the moment Tony found himself a wife.

It was just a month later when there was a frantic telephone call from Anna one afternoon. She was all but incoherent, but her gabbled message slowly got through: Istvan had been arrested by the police.

Geoffrey, who had just come in, was as amazed as she when he heard the news, and predictably, was also very angry. 'I must get him out of there at once,' he said, and left immediately, presumably to obtain a lawyer. Stephanie hastily got into the Austin Healey and drove out to Hertfordshire. It was dark when she got there, to find the servants in a highly excited state and Anna sprawled across her magnificent heart-shaped double bed wearing a pink shortie nightie, drinking neat vodka, and weeping. 'They just came,' she wailed. 'Suddenly appeared at the door, a whole mob of big men with big feet. And there were others out the back. It was horrible. And Stephanie . . . one of them was armed. I'm sure of it. I could see the outline of the pistol under his jacket. Oh, my God . . .' She burst into tears again.

Stephanie poured herself a vodka as well. She had given up drinking since her first missed period, as she was both desperate to be pregnant and not to harm the baby, but she felt that she needed something now. 'But what have they charged him with?' she asked.

'How should I know?' Anna wailed. 'They used a lot of stupid words. Oh, my *God*!' She heaved herself off the bed and staggered into the bathroom. Stephanie thought she was going to be sick, and followed her, paused in consternation as she saw her sister injecting herself, just like Geoffrey.

'Oh, Lord,' she said. 'I didn't know you had diabetes, too.'

Anna finished injecting herself, shook golden hair away from her face, and carefully put the needle away. She seemed calmer. 'What on earth are you drivelling about?' she snapped. 'Diabetes? Of course I haven't got diabetes, you silly cow. I just had to have a fix. My God, but I felt as if I were about to vomit.'

'A fix?' Stephanie asked.

'Heroin, you dim wit. Everybody uses it.'

'Do they?' Stephanie felt sick herself. She excused herself as soon as she could, Anna having clearly recovered her nerves after her 'fix', and went home. It was past ten by the time she got there, and Geoffrey was still out. She had a sandwich and a glass of milk, and then sat up all night, afraid even to watch television. Even at dawn he hadn't come in, while her brain swam round and round in circles. A fix? Heroin? She couldn't believe it. She didn't believe it. She would far rather believe Geoffrey than Anna.

She dosed off about five, and was awakened by the telephone. She leapt at it, and gasped as she heard Beth's voice. 'Stephanie! My God, have you seen the newspapers?'

'No,' Stephanie said. 'But I know what's in them.'

'That Bertie has been arrested? Christ, the charges!'

'What are they?'

'Oh, you name it. Extortion, assault and battery, blackmail, currency offences ... and murder. God Almighty, suppose Tony is involved?'

Stephanie hadn't thought of that one yet. But she knew she had to reassure Beth and above all not let her go chasing off to see Anna. If Beth were to find out that Anna was taking heroin ... 'Of course he can't be involved,' she said. 'He only works for Bertie. Anyway, he hasn't been arrested.'

'I think I am about to have a nervous breakdown,' Beth announced. 'The paper talks of 'Istvan Szabo, the acknowledged king of the London protection racket.' Holy Christ! I've tried to ring Anna, but the phone seems to be out of order or something.'

'She's taken it off the hook,' Stephanie explained.

'Have you seen her?'

'Yes.'

'How is she taking it?'

'She ... she's all right,' Stephanie lied. 'I persuaded her to take a sedative and go to bed. Naturally she was upset.' She heard the door opening. 'Listen, Beth,' she said. 'I'll call you back.'

She hung up, ran down the stairs, checked herself as she saw that Geoffrey had Bertie with him. Bertie looked untidy, unheard of for him, but he grinned at her, and came up the stairs to give her a hug and a kiss. 'Quite a to-do, eh?' he said in his guttural voice. 'The swine.'

'But . . .' she stared past him at Geoffrey.

He also grinned. 'He's out on bail. I saw to that.'

'But the charges?'

'Oh, it wasn't easy. But the fact is, the police were uneasy about the murder charge. They only have the one witness. The didn't raise all that much objection, although bail isn't usually given in murder cases. And it was steep. Five hundred thousand pounds.'

'Good Lord,' Stephanie said. 'But . . .'

'I am sure it is all too complicated for you, my dear,' Szabo's voice sounded like a steel bar being drawn along iron railings. 'Geoffrey, dear boy, I really would not discuss the situation, even with Stephanie, more than you have to. Of course the newspapers have had a field day, my dear, but equally of course the whole thing has been trumped up, as the police well know. The English are jealous of any alien who comes here and makes money. The police have been very foolish to have allowed themselves to be taken in by the complaints of one jealous man. Don't worry, I shall sue them for false arrest. Oh, yes, this is going to cost the Government plenty. Now, Stephanie, darling, I simply must have a wash and brush up. Do you mind if I use your bathroom?'

'Of course not. But Anna . . .'

'I shall go out there as soon as you have cooked me a decent breakfast. I am very hungry.'

Neither the maid nor the butler had come in as yet, so Stephanie herself went into the kitchen and broke eggs. Geoffrey joined her. 'I'm sorry about this. But he is quite right, he does have a lot of enemies who are trying to bring him down, and they have put this fellow Whiting up to making these absurd accusations. That's

251

the penalty for being successful in this day and age, if you don't happen to have gone to Eton and Oxford.'

He was her old Geoffrey. But he had never been anything else. She was so afraid for him. 'You're not involved, are you? Or Tony?'

'Good God, no. Bertie isn't involved. That's what I'm trying to tell you. I promise you, this case will never come to court.'

'Geoff . . .' she held his hands. 'Do you use heroin?'

He frowned at her. 'What on earth makes you say that?'

She told him about Anna.

'The silly little twit,' he commented when she had finished. 'I've had my suspicions of her several times in the past, but didn't dare believe it. I wonder if Bertie knows?'

'You mustn't tell him,' she begged. 'But Geoff . . . she was doing exactly what you do, every day.'

'So one injection is much like another,' he pointed out. 'Now come, my darling doll, do you really believe I would use heroin? Me?'

She hesitated, then was in his arms. 'Of course I don't. It's just that I'm so worried about this whole business.'

'Don't be,' he murmured into her hair. 'This case will never come to court.'

As he could see that she was still agitated, he drove down to Virginia Water with her to reassure both Beth and Harry, who were also very concerned.

'What are we going to do about Anna?' Stephanie asked him before they got there. 'Do you think we should tell Beth?'

'Not on your life,' Geoffrey insisted. 'We'll wait until this whole thing is over, then we'll have a chat with Bertie. Together,' he hastened to add as he saw her doubtful expression. 'It has to be done, Stephanie, and it's a husband's job to do it. Believe me, Anna can be cured, simply by going to a clinic, but it's Bertie who has to send her there. Don't worry, we'll sort everything out.'

He was so reassuring that she almost relaxed. But he was clearly worried, and doing everything he could to help make sure Bertie was not brought to trial, she was sure, because he spent so much time out over the next few days. She tried to contact Tony to get his version of what had happened, but although she telephoned several times and once called in person, he never appeared to be home. She didn't really want to see Anna again, not until she and Geoffrey had spoken to Bertie, which as Geoffrey had said, had to wait until at least after the preliminary hearing. The newspapers continued to be full of the case, but she wouldn't read any of them, although the maid, without comment, left them in a pile in a corner in the kitchen, and she almost refused to leave the house, because the other tenants and the people living in the neighbourhood who knew her by sight couldn't stop staring at her.

Three days later, the night before Bertie was supposed to appear at the preliminary hearing at Bow Street Magistrate's Court, at which time Geoffrey had told her their lawyer would seek a summary dismissal of the whole case for lack of evidence, she remembered that she hadn't told him of her pregnancy. Because now she was quite sure – she had just missed her third period. Presumably she could not go along and have some conclusive tests, but she wanted him to be the first to know.

She sat up waiting for him, as he was out as usual, ran to the door to greet him when she heard his latchkey, well after midnight, and recoiled in horror as she saw the blood on his face and covering his jacket, his shirt, and his tie. There was blood on his hands, as well.

'My God!' she screamed. 'Geoffrey! What has happened to you?'

'Nothing,' he said irritably. 'And for God's sake keep your voice down. I had an accident. The Lagonda is a write-off.'

'But you ...' He was unsteady on his feet and she had to help him across the room.

'A cut on the forehead. Just let me have a couple of aspirins and a wash. I'll be all right tomorrow.'

She stood in the bathroom doorway while he threw his clothes on the floor and washed the blood from his face. The cut on his forehead was still oozing, but he placed a strip of plaster over it himself. 'Shall I call the doctor?' she asked.

'God, no. We don't want to make a song and dance over this.'

She hesitated, then picked up his suit. 'These clothes will have to go to the dry cleaners.'

'Burn them.' He went into the bedroom and threw himself on the bed.

'But Geoff . . .' This suit, like all his suits, had come from Savile Row and cost some three hundred pounds.

'I don't want to wear it again,' he said. 'It's unlucky. Burn it.'

She rolled it up into a ball and stuffed it into the dirty linen hamper, just in case he changed his mind. When she returned to the bedroom he was already fast asleep. She didn't know what to do. Perhaps he was concussed: certainly he was acting very strangely. Perhaps she should call the doctor anyway. But she didn't want to upset him, and surely the best thing for him was a good night's sleep. Eventually she slept herself.

When she awoke he was still unconscious. He must have taken more than a couple of aspirins, she thought. But he was breathing evenly, and did not seem to have a temperature. She got up, poured herself a cup of coffee, took in the paper, and left it on the table while she returned to the bedroom to look at him. He hadn't told her so, but she presumed he would wish to attend court to be with Bertie, even if he was not personally involved. She would have to wake him some time soon. She returned to the kitchen, sat at the table, and opened the newspaper. Her heart seemed to slow.

'STAR WITNESS KILLED,' blared the headlines. 'SUPER-GRASS BITES THE DUST.'

The story beneath told of how the crown's chief

witness, and indeed, only witness, in its case against the well known 'mobster' Istvan Szabo, while being transferred from a secret police hideaway in the country to London in order to appear at this morning's preliminary hearing against Szabo, had been involved in an accident with another car. The police car, containing two detectives as well as the witness, had been forced off the road and into a ditch. One of the policemen had been killed in the collision, and the other knocked unconscious and badly hurt. The witness was found to be dead when other policemen arrived on the scene. The newspaper cryptically observed that he had had a broken neck, leaving it to their readers' judgements to decide whether that could have happened in the accident, or might not have occurred afterwards.

The driver of the other car, together with his vehicle, had disappeared, as well as any others who might have been with him. The injured policeman could only remember them being overtaken by a big, fast car, perhaps an Aston Martin, which had suddenly swerved in front of them. He had then been knocked unconscious and had not had the time to read the other car's number plate.

Stephanie stared at the words and had an overwhelming urge to be sick. But it couldn't be true. It just could not be true. Geoffrey? It just could not be true. Yet she could not stop herself from going into the kitchen and sifting through the papers which had been accumulating there over the past week. Istvan Szabo was accused of running a protection racket. Apparently his lucrative business had been built on demanding money from various small shopkeepers and restauranteurs in London, and if they did not pay up as required, he had his people use strong arm tactics to 'persuade' them. There were other alleged crimes as well, such as masterminding several well known but hitherto unsolved robberies, and various cases of blackmail. There was even a suggestion that he had once ordered the 'execution' of a colleague he had thought betrayed him and who had disappeared in mysterious circumstances, but it was the extortion Stephanie was interested in, because of something she remembered.

With a trembling finger she read down the list of premises allegedly 'done over' by Szabo's bully boys, and came to Alberto's Trattoria, where it seemed the proprietor had resisted the setting of his kitchen on fire and been beaten so badly that both arms had been broken. No names were mentioned of course; none of the injured men had dared identify any of their assailants ... but she could not help remembering Geoffrey's parting words to Alberto, on their very first night together, three and a half years before. Geoffrey had said, so casually, 'Thompson will call on Monday,' and Alberto had promised to keep his word at that time. And hadn't.

'Oh, my God,' she whispered, and looked up to see Geoffrey standing in the doorway.

'Exciting reading, isn't it,' he remarked. 'Every so often Hollywood comes to life.'

'Geoffrey,' she said. 'Please. Tell me it wasn't you.'

'There comes a time, my darling doll,' he said, 'every so often, when it is a case of all hands to the pump. There is no way we can let Bertie be brought to trial. Once that fellow Whiting started to sing in court it would have meant all of us going down with him. All of us. So now you are going to have to rally round the pump as well. Just in case. And I don't even think it is going to be necessary to do very much. I don't think they can trace the Lagonda; she's a lump of scrap metal by now. But the police are certainly going to come here, soon enough; they know I am one of Bertie's associates. They are going to be very unpleasant, and rely on us cracking and giving them what we want. But if we keep our heads and our nerves, they can't do anything. they can't prove I haven't sold the car for cash. So they'll start to harp on last night. That's where you come in. I want you to burn that suit and shirt, and I want you to swear that I was here with you all last night, and that this cut was caused when I fell here in this kitchen. Right?'

Stephanie found her head shaking from side to side. 'You killed a man,' she said. 'You have committed murder. My God, two murders!'

'The policeman died in the crash,' he said. 'As for Whiting, okay, we broke his neck. But he deserved to die. He was a rat.'

'You have committed murder,' she shouted.

He stepped towards her and swung his hand at her face. She reared away from him and threw her coffee cup in his face. He gave an exclamation of pain and stepped backwards, falling over a chair to hit the floor.

Stephanie stared at him for several seconds, breasts heaving. I loved you, she thought. I think I still love you. But you are a murderer. And, oh God, you are the father of my child.

Slowly Geoffrey got to his feet, wiping hot coffee from his face. 'I ought to push your face in,' he said. 'And I will, if you muck me about. But I accept that you're an innocent little bitch. You have got to be the most innocent little bitch I have ever met. I suppose it's your sister's doing, protecting you as if you were a china doll. Where do you suppose the money for all this came from? You certainly have enjoyed spending it, haven't you?'

Stephanie backed against the wall. 'You mean all those things in the newspaper are true?' she gasped. 'You broke that nice man Alberto's arms?'

'It is my business to make people pay,' he said. 'That's my job in the firm.'

'Oh, my God!' She thrust her hands into her hair as another horrible thought surged into her mind. Because if he had lied about all that, then ... 'Those injections! They *are* heroin.'

He shrugged. 'So what? It doesn't interfere with my performance, does it?'

'And that charade about Anna? You knew she was an addict. My God, I suppose Bertie knows, too.'

257

'Bertie uses the stuff himself, darling doll. And if you don't stop being hysterical I'm going to shoot some into you as well.'

'You lied to me. You've been lying to me all of these years.'

'I didn't think you'd be capable of understanding what makes the world go round. I can tell you that it isn't love. And I was right. Well, angel face, here is where you have to grow up, fast. You are my wife. You can't testify against me, even if you want to. Rather you have to help me, any way you can. You want to remember that without me, should I be sent up, just for example, you are nothing. Absolutely sweet bloody nothing. Don't ever forget that. So just be a good girl and do as you are told. I am going to shower now and then go along to meet Bertie and attend court. You sit tight until I come home, but build up a nice fire in that grate; even with the heating on its a chilly day. When I get back we'll burn those clothes. And remember, as far as the maid and John know, I was here all night.'

She sat at the kitchen table, absent-mindedly stirring coffee, but not drinking it. She felt she was in the middle of a long, unending nightmare. But where, and when, had it begun?

Geoffrey reappeared, fully dressed, and looking as immaculately handsome as ever; he had contrived to brush his hair so that the strip of plaster on his forehead hardly showed. 'There's just one thing,' he said. 'The police may come round for a chat. I don't expect they will until they've had a forensic report to suggest that Whiting's neck couldn't have been broken in the accident. On the other hand, they both know I work with Bertie and that I have a big Aston Martin Lagonda. So some bright young detective sergeant may just try to jump the gun. Now listen very carefully. You have no idea what he is talking about. I was here in bed with you all night, and this morning I've gone off to court with Bertie; if they want to talk to me, they can find me there. You know nothing about the car, save that I sold

258

it last week. You don't know who to, or how it was financed. And if he asks, politely, if he can take a look around, say no. He won't have a warrant with him the first time. He'll tell you he can get a warrant; that's a standard ploy. And I'm sure he can, in this case, but should that happen, the moment he leaves you'll burn that suit. Just don't panic about it. As I say, it's not likely to happen. If he doesn't come, then we'll do it together as soon as I get back. Right?

He bent over the table to kiss her. She never moved, although she wanted to. But which way? This was her old Geoffrey, confident and reassuring, outlining what they were going to do with masterful certainty. He hadn't changed. But he had just murdered two men. Didn't that mean he had probably murdered men before, as well as breaking their arms? She shuddered. And he had been lying to her since their first meeting.

She listened to the front door slam, then got up and put it on the chain, just in case he came back; she didn't want to have to face him again. Then she showered herself, and dressed, took the bloodstained clothes from the hamper and placed them in a carrier bag. She had no intention of waiting for the police and having to involve herself by telling a pack of lies.

She went downstairs, and found that he had taken the Austin Healey. So she caught a tube train instead, to Victoria, then a mainline train out to Virginia Water. She was running, to the only safe haven she knew. She called Beth from the station, and a few minutes later Beth had picked her up.

'You look like death,' she remarked.

'I feel like death,' Stephanie confessed.

'Well, have you heard the news?'

'Yes,' Stephanie said.

'That should cheer you up. It's certainly cheered me up. It appears as if Istvan is off the hook. This man Whiting seems to have had a lot of enemies himself. Talk about the luck of the devil.'

259

'Oh, Beth,' Stephanie said, tears welling out from her eyes. 'He only has one enemy.'

Beth glanced at her, then pulled off the road and down a lane leading to a field, stopped the car and switched off the engine. 'What's happened?' she asked.

Stephanie told her, bursting into tears.

'Oh, God,' Beth commented. 'Oh, my God! Why didn't I believe my instincts about those people?' She answered her own question. 'I suppose because I didn't want to. I was too anxious to get on with my own plans. Oh, my *God*!'

'And I'm pregnant,' Stephanie said.

Slowly Beth turned her head. 'How long?'

'I think . . . just three months.'

'Does Geoffrey know?'

Stephanie shook her head. 'I didn't want to tell him until I was sure. Now I don't want to tell him at all.'

'Thank God for that. Well, don't worry about it. I'll sort that one out just as soon as I get back. Did Geoffrey say anything about Tony being involved?'

Stephanie shook her head again.

'There's a blessing, anyway. Right! You leave everything to me. I'm going to take you home . . . no, I won't. Geoffrey might come looking for you. I'll take you to an hotel, where you can stay, not telephoning anybody, and not opening the door to anybody, until I get back. I'll be with you for dinner. Lie down and try to get some sleep.'

'But where are you going?'

'To Hertfordshire. To see Szabo, of course. I want Anna out of there, and I want Tony released from working for him, now.'

'Oh, Beth, do you really suppose Bertie is going to do anything you want? He's in the clear.'

'In the clear? He's up to his neck in it. We know he had the witness against him murdered.'

'We may know it. But nobody else does.'

'Yes, my darling. But the evidence you can supply will sink the whole lot of them if they don't co-operate.'

260

'That's just it,' Stephanie moaned. 'I can't testify against my own husband. Geoffrey did remind me of that. I don't think I could testify against Geoffrey even if he wasn't my husband.'

'Have you any objection if I do? Or at least threaten to? Oh, I won't actually do it if you don't want me to. Although I should. The man has to be locked up, Stephanie. You must realise that.'

'Oh, God . . . I suppose you're right. But . . .'

'You don't still love him, do you?'

'I don't know what I feel.' Because suddenly she was wondering if she had ever loved him, or had not just been swept off her feet by his looks and his generosity and his confidence. She recalled disliking him on their first meeting.

'Well, believe me,' Beth said, 'you won't when you've had a chance to think about it.'

'But you have no evidence of your own,' Stephanie said. 'Only secondhand from me. The police won't accept that.'

'There must be something concrete you can tell me or give me,' Beth said. 'Something to throw in their faces, to make them listen to me.'

Stephanie gazed at her for several seconds, then she reached into the back of the car and drew out the carrier bag. Why else had she brought it?

The traffic was heavy, and in addition there was a diversion because of a burst water-main. The delays gave Beth too much time to think, and she didn't want to think at all. Commonsense dictated that she should drive into London and go to Harry's office, and with him decide what was best to be done. But Harry didn't understand; he was too civilised. He had never had to fight for his existence. If he had been a serving officer in the War he had always been surrounded by his men, and backed by all the power and determination of Great Britain and its people. He had no idea what it was like to be absolutely alone, and defenceless, surrounded by one's enemies, with only one's wits and guts on which to depend.

She had known that feeling too often. Out of it had grown her code, that the only things which mattered in life was the four Janskis, their health and safety and well being. Now that was being threatened. She only knew one way to react, to fight the threat with all the fury and courage and determination and viciousness at her disposal. To involve Harry would be to let him have a glimpse of a woman he did not know to exist – and might not like.

It was nearly lunchtime when she finally reached the Szabo mansion. She parked the car, and was welcomed by a smiling James. 'Good afternoon, Mrs Paine. It is a good afternoon, isn't it?'

'We still have to find that out, James. Is Miss Anna in?'

'Of course, madam. This way.' He showed her into the second lounge, where Anna lay on a day bed, wearing see-through pyjamas, eating chocolates, and turning the pages of a magazine.

'Beth!' she cried, springing up. James averted his eyes and left the room. But Anna might not have noticed his presence at all. 'Isn't it splendid? I'm expecting Bertie home any moment. He telephoned from Bow Street just after ten to say the whole thing had taken only fifteen minutes. The charges against him have been dropped for lack of evidence.'

'Yes,' Beth said grimly. 'Well, come on. You go upstairs and get dressed and packed. We're leaving here.'

'Leaving?' Anna sat down again. 'To go where?'

'Anywhere. Just away from here.'

'I don't understand,' Anna said.

'Yes, it's obvious that you have never understood,' Beth said. 'Listen to me. Your Bertie is a cold blooded murderer, a blackmailer, a thief and an extortionist. Everything that's said of him in the papers is true.'

Anna gazed at her, eyes huge. 'He's only trying to make money, Beth. That is all you ever tried to do.'

Beth felt she had been kicked in the stomach. 'You mean you knew? Oh, my God! Don't you realise . . .'

'That that makes your sister an accessory before the fact, were the charges ever to be proved,' Szabo said.

Beth turned, to look at him and Geoffrey; she hadn't heard the car arrive from inside the double glazing. For a moment she felt a spasm of fear, but she was far too angry. And anyway, was she going to be afraid of two lying, conniving thugs? Not Beth Janska. 'Yes,' she said. 'But the charges are never going to be proved now, are they, Bertie?'

He smiled, and came forward to kiss her hands. 'It seems not. I did tell you there was nothing to worry about. Geoffrey, ask James to mix us up some nice spicy bloody Marys, will you? And tell cook there will be four for lunch.'

'Don't bother,' Beth said. 'I'm not staying. I have come for Anna, and as soon as she is ready, we'll leave. I also want Tony. Will you kindly tell me where he is?'

Szabo raised his eyebrows; Geoffrey remained poised just inside the door. 'I was about to ask you the same question.'

'Me?'

'I'm afraid Tony has proved something of a disappointment to me,' Szabo said. 'The moment this thing broke, instead of rallying round as all my people did, and knew they had to, the little . . . ah, he took himself off. He has quite disappeared. That would in any event be very annoying, but unfortunately, he has also removed quite a large sum of money from my safe before doing so. As my future brother-in-law, I had so stupidly taken him into my confidence as to trust him with the combination. But of course, you know all of this?'

'Why should I?' Beth asked.

'Because you will know what he has done and where he has gone. I want him back, Beth. I want my money back.' Szabo could sound quite menacing. But not as menacing as Madame Suchet.

'I don't have the slightest idea what you are talking about,' Beth said.

'Listen, don't mess me about,' Szabo snapped, abandoning his usual careful English. 'Or I'll . . .'

'I think she's probably telling the truth about Tony, Bertie,' Geoffrey said, coming into the room and closing the door.

'Of course I am telling the truth,' Beth said coldly. 'I am not accustomed to lie,' she lied. 'And that Tony has had the sense to cut and run is the only good news I've had this morning.'

'You think so?' Szabo inquired. 'He is the weak link that could put us all back on the spot. When the police discover he has disappeared, they are going to wonder why, and . . .'

'That is your problem,' Beth said. 'Tony has decided you are not the person he wishes to work for, and I entirely agree with him. Nor do I consider that you are a fit person for Anna to be associated with. She is going to come with me now, and from that moment you will get out of our lives and stay out of them, now and always. I want you to be very clear about that.'

Szabo stared at her in genuine amazement.

'I think you want to remember who you're speaking to, Mrs Paine,' Geoffrey suggested. Clearly he was realising that he could no longer think of her as a sister-in-law. 'And you want to think about your own position, as well.'

'No, Mr Trene,' she said. 'You are the one who has to think. I know everything about you. Stephanie has told me.'

'Stephanie?' He looked left and right as if expecting her to be in the room. 'That little bitch. I'll . . .'

'You'll do nothing, Mr Trene. Absolutely nothing. For one thing, she is where you cannot find her, and for another, if you attempt to harm her, or Tony, or Anna, I will destroy you. Both of you.' She pointed. 'Because if you go to gaol for murder, and I can send you there, then your boss will come down, too. The police will find the link.'

The men stared at her.

'You horror,' Anna shouted. 'You absolute horror. You can't do it. Bertie and I are getting married this year. I've waited so long for that.'

'Leave her with me,' Geoffrey said.

Beth's lip curled. 'So you can break both my arms? I wouldn't try that. My husband knows where I am and what I am about, and the evidence I possess is to be delivered to the police if I am not home for dinner.'

Geoffrey took a step towards her, but Szabo, deciding on this occasion that she might just be telling the truth, caught his arm. 'Let her prattle on. She has nothing. Only what that little bitch may have told her. That's not evidence; the cunt can't even testify against you.'

Beth smiled at him pityingly. 'Your true origins are showing, Bertie. Shall I tell you what I have? I have one suit, and one shirt, and one tie, all covered in blood, and I have a witness that you were out at the time of the attack on the police car. Stephanie may not be able to testify against you, but there is no law that says she has to lie for you. And if necessary, when Tony contacts me I'll persuade him to testify against you too. Who knows . . .' she glanced at Anna, contemptuously. 'When I've had a chance to talk some sense into this brainwashed dummy, she'll probably testify against you, too.'

Geoffrey looked at Szabo, biting his lip.

'So, you let your wife walk away with your suit,' Szabo remarked.

'I told her to wait at home for me,' Geoffrey explained. 'It never crossed my mind that she wouldn't. She's always done exactly what I told her to, in the past.'

'You really are a brainless wonder, Geoffrey,' Szabo observed. 'God knows how I ever got where I am with aides like you.'

'We have to get that suit,' Geoffrey said.

Szabo shrugged. 'I suggest that Beth goes home and burns it. Then we'll all be in the clear.'

265

'You really do exist on cloud seven,' Beth remarked. 'You really do believe that all you have to do is say that you want something done and everyone will click his heels and hurry off. Just as you believe you can just kill people when they become inconvenient to you. Well, Bertie, you have reached the end of that line.'

'I think you want to be very sure of what you are doing,' Szabo suggested. 'If I go to gaol, so does Anna. So does Tony.'

'Tony will turn Queen's evidence and get off,' Beth said. 'As for Anna . . .' Once again she looked at her sister. 'Perhaps gaol is what she deserves. But the choice is hers, not yours. At least you cannot touch Stephanie.'

'But I can touch you,' Szabo said gently.

'Me? Oh, drop dead.'

'You,' Szabo repeated. 'Do you think I don't know all about you, Elizabeth Janska, Elizabeth Mathieu, Elizabeth Paine, Paris's biggest whore, who is now bigamously married? Don't you think Anna has told me all about you? Anna has no secrets from me. If I give that information to the police, you'll wind up in a gaol cell, too. So, you destroy me, and I will destroy you. That hardly seems to make sense.' He smiled. 'I would say we have a stand-off.'

Beth looked at Anna again. 'Yes,' she said. 'You do deserve to go to gaol.' She left the room.

THE TENTH CHRONICLE

April 1985

'You mean you have never heard of the Szabo case?' Clive Carter, Editor in Chief of the *London Courier*, scratched his head, and looked around the crowded dining room of the Savoy Grill. 'It was quite a cause célèbre at the time.'

Meyer shrugged. 'I guess I had other things on my mind in 1963. I was just starting out on my line of business then.'

The newspaper editor nodded. 'By Jove, yes, I remember that well. You were something of a cause célèbre yourself, that year, Bob. So what makes you want to rake up the file on an old villain like Szabo? I can't believe he was a Nazi, as well as everything else.'

'I'm actually looking for the woman, Elizabeth Mathieu.'

'Ah, you mean Elizabeth Paine.'

'Paine?'

'Yes, she married again, bigamously.'

'Good Lord,' Meyer said.

'Oh, quite. That case had everything. But she certainly couldn't have been a Nazi. She must have been just a child during the War.'

'I think she may be able to give me some information I vitally require,' Meyer said carefully.

'I see. Hm. You may have a problem, there. When we've finished lunch I'll look out the files and the photos. Oh, there is no question that this Paine woman, or Mathieu, or whatever her real name was, was the centre-piece of the Szabo case; she attracted more publicity than Szabo himself. It was she who laid evidence against Szabo's strong-arm boy, a chap named Trene, on the very day after, as it turned out, he had murdered the chief witness against his boss in an endeavour to have the proceedings quashed. Well, they would have been quashed, but for the woman. Somehow she had got hold of the suit he had worn the night he had committed the murder, and it was bloodstained. She handed this over to the police, together with some other information, and he was arrested. Trene was taken into custody and broke down under interrogation. I suppose he wasn't as tough as he thought he was. Anyway, he pointed the finger in every direction he could think of, including, I may say, at this Mathieu woman's own brother, Anthony Mathieu. But he also pointed the finger at his boss, Szabo, and at Szabo's mistress, Anna Mathieu, a sister of the Mathieu woman. It was all rather incestuous, and as you can imagine, the press had a field day. But so did the police and the courts, with so many accusations flying thick and fast.'

'What happened to them all?'

'Well, let me see ... As I remember, Szabo was sentenced to life imprisonment for murder, as he had commanded the killing of the witness. So was the man who had been with Trene on the night in question, a real heavy named Thompson. We'd been stupid enough to abolish the death penalty by then, of course. Trene, having turned Queen's evidence, got seven years or something like that. Tony Mathieu was never found. He has never come to light, I believe. I supposed they bumped him off, before the police got to them. Anna Mathieu, as an accessory, also got seven years.'

'Someone told me Szabo got an early parole because of ill health, and then just disappeared,' Meyer said.

'Quite true. I don't think he served more than eight years, if that. The BBC raked it up a few years ago, but without much luck. Everyone connected with the case had either died or disappeared by then.'

Meyer caught his breath. 'Including Elizabeth Mathieu?'

'I'm afraid so. Now there was the real sensation in the case, as I said. In an effort to discredit her, Szabo's lawyers established that she had never been divorced from her first husband, a Frenchman named Georges Mathieu, who was still living. They brought out the fact as she was a Roman Catholic, something which her second 'husband' was apparently unaware of, she had never even sought a divorce, but after being separated from her real husband, had continued to collect an allowance from him for something like the ten years up to the trial. Well, you can imagine the fun the press had with that. And the silly woman hadn't even troubled to negotiate for immunity from prosecution by the police. Apparently she just acted out of wild anger, a Samsonish fury. She had discovered that both her brother and her sister were rotten to the core, and just brought the whole edifice crashing down, not bothering to consider that she was standing underneath.' He shrugged, and finished his wine. 'That was damned good. Seventy-six, was it?'

Meyer showed him the bottle. 'Eighty-one. It's just coming in very well, I think. So what happened to her?'

'Well, as soon as the Szabo gang had been put away, she was charged with bigamy.'

'And?'

'Oh, she got something like two years.'

Breath slowly escaped from Meyer's lungs. Then she would have been released in 1964.'

'I suppose that's right. I'll have to find out for you. She was no longer big news then. And by the time the BBC started putting their programme together, she wasn't to be found.'

'There was another sister, wasn't there?'

'Oh, yes. I remember her. A strikingly lovely girl. Well, they all were, but she was the only one who seemed completely innocent. She was Trene's wife, believe it or not, but the police seemed certain she had no involvement in the crimes or prior knowledge of them. So no charges were ever brought against her. I remember seeing her in court one day towards the end of the trial. She was then eight months pregnant, would you believe it? Pale and obviously under stress, and yet still looked stunning.'

'Pregnant? Was there a child?'

'Now that I can't say, although I suppose one could find out.'

'Well, what happened to Mrs Trene?'

'As far as I know she just disappeared too, just like her sister and Szabo.' Another shrug. 'Well, I suppose it was the best thing for them all to do, don't you?'

'And Trene?' Meyer asked.

'Ah, Trene. Now that rings a bell,' Carter said. 'Let's go on back to the office, and I'll look it all up for you.'

CHAPTER 10

London, 1963–65

'You may go in now, Mrs Trene,' the wardess said. She did not look unkind, rather sympathetic, Stephanie thought. How she wanted someone to look sympathetic.

She was extremely nervous; this would be the first time she had seen her sister since their quarrel, several months before. She had not been able to attend the whole bigamy trial, because of the baby, but she had felt she had to come on the last day, in time to hear Beth being sent to prison. Beth!

Beth sat in a straight chair before a plain table. She was neatly dressed, not yet, Stephanie was relieved to see, in any prison uniform, but in the dark blue suit she had worn in court, with her hair brushed and clean – but no makeup. She looked like a ghost of the forceful woman Stephanie remembered and loved. But her gaze was as steady and powerful as ever.

'Well, darling girl,' she remarked. 'Quite a foul-up.'

Stephanie glanced at the wardress, standing beside a woman police constable just inside the door. 'No physical contact, please, Mrs Trene,' the woman said.

Stephanie sat on the far side of the table, hands together. 'Is everything all right?'

Beth's mouth twisted. 'Is everything ever all right?'

'Oh, Beth,' Stephanie said. 'If only . . .'

'I didn't think they would do it,' Beth said, almost tonelessly. 'I gave them the crook they seem to have wanted for over a year. I gave them his entire organisation. For God's sake, I even gave them my own sister . . .' her tone hardened. 'But they wanted me as well.'

Stephanie sighed. Beth had, not for the first time, she thought, charged ahead, determined to destroy her enemies, without a thought for the possible repercussions. But this time she had also determined to destroy

271

Anna, she realised, or at least to punish her. 'Have you seen her?' she asked. 'Anna?'

'No,' Beth said. 'I didn't want to see her, and I gather the feeling was mutual. You heard what she shouted in court when they were all sentenced?'

Stephanie nodded. She would never forget Anna shouting, 'You bitch, you should rot in hell', as she was led away.'Have you seen Harry?' she asked.

'Oh, no,' Beth said. 'Again, I think, a mutual decision. I've seen his solicitor. The marriage will be annulled, of course. Dear Mr Paine is quite shocked that he could have been led into such an embarrassing situation.' She half smiled. 'I have also seen Georges' lawyer.'

'Oh, my God,' Stephanie said.

'Yes,' Beth agreed. 'I seem to have made rather a mess of things, haven't I? It was all rather unpleasant. Obviously, the good fellow said, my allowance will stop; Monsieur Mathieu is quite shocked at my deception. But, he told me magnanimously, Georges will not press charges, even of fraud – apparently he is entitled to reclaim all the money I received from him since my marriage to Harry. Dear old Georges. My God, I suppose he must be seventy-five. You'd think he'd be dead by now. I wonder if he still goes to Madam Suchet's?'

'Beth,' Stephanie said. 'Don't you feel anything at all?'

For a moment Beth stared at her. Then she said, 'Of course I do, Stephanie. I feel angry, and bitter, and vicious, and hateful. But if I allowed myself to really feel those things I would go mad. Or hurt somebody and be put away for longer than two years. Oh, Stephanie . . . I had such dreams. For us all. And now they're gone, shattered by Anna's falling in love with the biggest crook in England. And Tony! I haven't heard a word. Have you heard from him?'

Stephanie shook her head. 'I sometimes wonder if he isn't dead. If those beasts . . . God, how could it happen?'

'I don't think he's dead,' Beth said. 'I think Szabo was right about him, and the little rat just ran off with everything he could lay his hands on, and left us to face the music. I hope *he* rots in hell.'

Stephanie didn't know what to say. She had known Beth to be angry in the past, but never had she seen such concentrated venom. 'They tell me you could be out of here in a year,' she ventured

Beth gave a savage smile. 'Just over a year – if I behave. Then I'll be an ex-convict. And I won't have two pennies to rub together.'

Stephanie bit her lip.

'But you ...' Beth gazed at her, seeming to see her present shape for the first time. 'So you did have it?'

Stephanie sighed. Having the baby was the first time she had ever opposed Beth in anything. Beth had wanted her to go to Paris, to Dr Buget, and have an abortion. She had refused. Even if she had been able to consider such a horrible thing, she had wanted to have the baby. Beth had been unable to understand why, had pointed out that he would be a murderer's son, and much else besides. But she had stuck to her guns, and they had quarrelled.

She forced a smile. 'He's a boy. Seven pounds ten ounces at birth. It was a bit of a struggle.' She drew a long breath. 'I've called him George.'

'George? My God! You still have a conscience about that dirty old man?'

'Yes,' Stephanie said. 'I still think we'd have been better off had we stayed in Lorges. Anyway, I like the name. Would you like to see him?'

'God forbid. Does Trene know?'

'I suppose so.'

'You mean you haven't been to see him?'

'I never want to see him again.'

'He'll want to see you, when he knows you've had a son.'

'George is my child,' Stephanie said. 'Not Geoffrey's.'

273

'You think so? What happens when he gets out of gaol?'

'He's gone in for seven years.'

'That's not a very long time, you know. He'll probably only serve about five, anyway. Maybe less.'

'Five years.' Stephanie's shoulders drooped. 'I don't want to think that far ahead.'

'Well, try thinking what it's going to be like living with a child but no husband in this day and age,' Beth said brutally. 'Oh, I suppose you have lots of money. And you can always sell the flat. But I'm afraid I can't help you any more. I don't have a penny.'

Stephanie started to say something, then stopped. She hadn't come looking for help, however much she needed it. But she couldn't help Beth either, right now. 'I'll manage,' she said. 'See that you do, too.'

There would have been no point in telling Beth that she was not a wealthy woman. Quite the reverse. That point had been established the day Geoffrey had been convicted, when she had returned to the flat to find it full of people. She had been in a state of suppressed shock, added to the exhaustion of being eight months pregnant, and this was just too much. She had screamed at them and endeavoured to push them out of the door. They had had to send for the police, and for Geoffrey's solicitor, who had made her sit down, and poured her a drink, and tried to soothe her. But what he had had to say had been cataclysmic. 'I'm afraid the fact is that you have no title to the flat, Stephanie,' he had said. 'And no right to live here any longer.'

'But it's mine,' she had said, unbelievingly.

'I'm afraid Geoffrey deceived you there. It wasn't bought in your name. It wasn't bought at all. It was leased on a monthly basis in his name, and the past four months, with his being in gaol awaiting trial, no rent has been paid. I only became aware of this situation a couple of days ago, and I approached the landlord, asking if you would be allowed to make some new arrangement, but he refused to consider it. I suspect he

274

has been under pressure from the other tenants, who don't want the family of a convicted murderer living in the same building. And, even if he had agreed to let you stay on, I don't quite see how you would have managed to pay the rent, having had a look at the overall financial situation. But in any event, he has secured an eviction order, and that we have to accept.'

She had stared at him, almost uncomprehending; the one thing she had not worried about, throughout the strain of the trial, and her pregnancy, Anna's hysterics, and Tony's disappearance, and then Beth's arest, had been money – she only had to look around her at all the things she owned, and reflect that the flat had to be worth six figures. Now she did look around her, and the solicitor gave a gentle cough.

'Nor do you actually own any of the furniture. Geoffrey bought it all on hire purchase, and here again the payments have not been kept up.'

'The cutlery . . .'

'The same. And the crockery, I'm afraid. Of course, in most cases of this kind the courts are very lenient, and try to bend over backwards to try to help the parties about to be, ah, dispossessed, give them time to pay, or at least find accommodation . . . but in the case of a convicted murderer, well, I don't think we can expect any sympathy there.'

'I am about to have a baby,' she said, feeling as if it might happen at any moment. 'Where do you suppose I should drop it, on the street?'

'My dear Stephanie, you can move into slightly less expensive accommodation, surely. As for having your baby, you'll go to hospital. That won't cost you a penny.'

'What do I pay for this rented accommodation with?' she asked, trying to stop herself from screaming.

'Well, there is about two thousand pounds in a bank account which I have salvaged for your use. There was more, but after the fees of the barrister and my associates, and, well . . .' He gazed at her nervously.

275

'I wouldn't expect you to forego your fee, Mr Garnham,' she said, trying unsuccessfully not to sound sarcastic.

He ignored it. 'There is also your jewellery. Well, some of it.'

'Some of it?' She looked down at her engagement ring.

'Oh, that certainly, if you can bring yourself to part with it. And one or two other items have been fully paid for.'

'Do I own a car?'

'Ah, no.' He patted her hand. 'But you are really not a pauper. And once you are well ...' He looked at her stomach. 'Fit again, why don't you take a job? I know it's not something you are used to, and I know that you will have to accept a fall in your standard of living, but perhaps that may be only temporary. And frankly, Stephanie ... I don't know what else to suggest.'

Because, she had realised, as she was the wife of a convicted murderer, who had lived like a queen, however unknowingly, for three years on the proceeds of her husband's various crimes, she couldn't expect any sympathy either, even from her own solicitor.

As he didn't offer to help her, it had taken her a very long day, climbing on and off buses, walking up and down streets, each movement more exhausting than the last but she didn't feel she could afford to spend any of her suddenly frighteningly limited capital on taxis or agents – to find a furnished room in which she could wait for the birth of her baby, and at which the landlady hadn't been actively hostile.

During the wait she had refused to see Geoffrey at all, although he had asked for her. She wasn't sure of her emotions towards him. They were a compound of shock and revulsion and disgust, partly at herself for having been so taken in by a smiling, handsome face, and of a mixture of despair and determination that he should have nothing to do with the child she was carrying. He knew she was pregnant, of course; by the time he had come to trial it had been obvious to everyone. But yet she had felt that if he did not see her, somehow the child would be her own.

And while she was in labour, Beth had been charged and arraigned. If little George was not born with a complex she did not know what else he could be born with. But he had proved to be a happy, bouncing boy. She had fallen in love with her own baby at first sight. And the people in the hospital had at least been kind. That had been the last kindness she had known. Even in hospital she had been pestered by representatives of various Sunday newspapers asking for her story. She had not even been tempted. The thought of George growing up to know what his mother had been, and even more, what his father had been, was too ghastly to contemplate. She had told them she had no story to tell, even though she had been offered ridiculous sums, on one occasion as much as twenty five thousand pounds, for her 'revelations'. Eventually they had gone away in disgust. And soon after that, on her release, she had to face the facts of life.

'I know it's 'ard, dearie,' her landlady said, 'but no children. If I let you stay, I'll 'ave to let all sorts of kids about the place. Can't be done. Anyway,' she added, 'you'd 'ave to go anyway. The neighbours are talking.'

Stephanie had found accommodation farther out of town and lower down the social scale, but only by taking a false name. She had been contemplating that for some time, and chose Johnson, an anglicisation of Janski. Fortunately, she had only been photographed once or twice during the trial – the reporters had been far more intersted in Beth and Anna – and looked vastly different now to then, having lost weight and wearing her hair up instead of loose as she had always done; no one had given the slightest indication of suspecting who she really might be. She also gave out that she was a widow, and the good people of Surbiton were quite sympathetic.

By then her two thousand pounds had all but disappeared. Try as she might, she could not resist instinctively buying the most expensive items of food, or toiletry, and such matters as whether or not she was using too much electricity or gas never crossed her mind until the accounts arrived. She could do nothing for six months anyway, as she was feeding George, but in the spring of 1964 it became obvious that she would either have to get a job or sell the jewellery, or both. The obvious thing to do was to go back to Preytier's, where she was known and liked; there she could both ask for her old job back, and ask them to take the ring back. If both were going to be embarrassing, at least she would get it over in one fell swoop.

She asked her landlady to look after George for the morning, and then packed a valise with great care, leaving the house as she always appeared, her hair in a bun, and wearing a dowdy skirt and blouse and sensible shoes. At the tube station she darted into the Ladies and changed into one of her best dresses, added high heels and make-up, and her fur coat, and set off looking like a million dollars.

It was so good to walk through those doors again, smile at the uniformed doorman as he touched his cap, and then at all the familiar faces who had once been such good friends. And realised that the operative word here was 'once'. Even Astral Smith look embarrassed to see her. Mr Manley himself showed her into his office. She had only been in this holy of holies once before in her life, on the day he had wanted to congratulate her on her engagement.

'Do sit down, Stephanie,' he said. 'It is so good to see you looking so ... well, good.' She knew he really meant prosperous. 'Now let me see, to what do we owe the pleasure of this visit?'

Clearly, as she had asked for him, he supposed she had found herself another wealthy protector. There seemed no point in beating around the bush. 'Well,' she said. 'As a matter of fact ... I thought I would like to come back to work here.'

278

There was an awkward silence, while they both flushed.

'Oh,' he said at last. 'That does surprise me. Indeed it does. Ah ... I'm afraid we're fully staffed at the moment.'

'You mean you don't employ the wives of convicted murderers,' Stephanie snapped before she could stop herself.

'My dear girl,' he protested. 'Well ... we have our clientele to think of. The reputation of the firm for the highest integrity. The ...'

'I quite understand,' she said. She didn't even feel able to be properly withering, because she still had the other, even more distasteful, task to undertake. 'Well, then, perhaps you'll permit me to be one of your clientele, for a last time.' She slipped the ruby ring from her finger and placed it on his desk. 'Will you trade that in for me?'

Mr Manley picked up the ring with the expression of a man handling a suspected bomb, twisted it this way and that, and finally took out his eye glass.

'You sold it to me,' she reminded him. 'At least, you sold it to my husband. I don't think it actually has blood on it.'

He ignored the sarcasm. 'It is a fine piece of work,' he said. 'Good stones. Oh, yes, good stones. I imagine we can exchange it, yes. What other piece did you have in mind?'

'I have cash in mind,' she said.

'Cash?' He almost dropped the ring. 'My dear Mrs Trene, we are not in the business of buying secondhand jewellery.'

'Not even if it is yours?'

'We do not deal in secondhand jewellery,' he repeated firmly. 'You need to go to one of the ah ... Hatton Garden merchants.'

Stephanie had resisted the temptation to be rude, and had gone to Hatton Garden. Geoffrey had boasted that he had paid six thousand pounds for the ring, and she had never seen any reason to disbelieve him; she knew the value of the jewellery at Preytier's as well as anyone. In Hatton Garden she got fifteen hundred, after some haggling, and another five hundred for the smaller pieces. She had meant to sell her fur as well, but decided against it. Instead she went home and took a hot bath, as well as she was able in the small and rusty tub which was all she now possessed. She felt quite filthy. But there it was. As Beth had told her, she was now alone in the world, with no one to depend on but herself. But she had two thousand pounds, which was surely enough. Now her only duty was to keep George and herself together until Beth came out of prison. Only a year, she kept reminding herself. Only a year.

'Visitors,' said the wardress jovially. 'Come along, Elizabeth.'

'Always Elizabeth,' Janine remarked. 'You have to be the most popular girl here.'

That was an inside joke. But it contained no rancour, now. Beth would never forget when there had been rancour, and more than that. She remembered her first day here, when Janine, a husky washed out blonde, had stared at her and said, 'High and mighty. Mrs High and Mighty. Bigamy! Lord above, why didn't you just shack up with the man?'

'Because she's high and mighty,' the black girl, Esther, suggested. 'Hey, High and Mighty, have you got any fags?'

Beth surveyed the two women, with whom she was to spend much of the next fifteen months, at the very least, in a cell not larger than nine foot by six. She was already feeling distinctly out of sorts. The last time she has been treated as if she had been a piece of meat had been when the Russian soldiers had come into the house in Wrakinow. And somehow men at war had been understandable, if not forgiveable; the monolithic apparatus of a state to punish someone was both unforgiveable and nauseating. She had been forced to undress and abandon her silk dress and her Janet Reger underwear, and submit to a search, and then been made to stand beneath a cold shower, following which she had been given a medical which had been truly disgusting; not even Dr Buget had been quite so thorough and inquisitive.

'What are you actually looking for?' she had asked the doctor, both in an attempt to keep her temper, and because after the first five minutes she felt she had known him all her life.

'Anything you might have,' he had replied chattily; he came from Pakistan. 'But most of the women who come in here have some sort of venereal disease.'

'Well, I haven't,' she had snapped.

'Indeed you do not appear to,' he had agreed. 'But if you wish to prosper here, you will have to learn to be civil.'

Beth hadn't felt in the least like being civil, and felt even less so after being issued with the ghastly rough cotton drawers and dress and what almost amounted to a liberty bodice, which she was to wear from then on. So now, as she gazed at her cellmates, she said, 'Drop dead!'

'You know what I don't like?' the blonde woman remarked to her friend. 'I've got nothing against bigamy. That's a mug's game. But squealing now, putting the finger on friends and turning them over to the police, that really gives me the shits.'

'Me too,' Esther agreed. 'Let's teach her a thing or two.'

'Yeah,' Janine said enthusiastically. 'Let's tan her ass.'

She stood up, and Beth, who had been sitting on the narrow bed which was her sole possession in the world at that moment, got up also. She was only slightly taller than the blonde woman, but when Beth got aggressive she seemed to grow in size. Janine checked.

'You come near me,' Beth had said in a low voice, 'and I am going to break you Goddamned neck.'

281

Janine blinked at her. Perhaps she sensed that she was out of her class here, but having made the play she could not afford to back down, either. She glanced at Esther, gave a grunt, and charged. Beth had to make a very hasty decision not, after all, to break her neck, which might leave her in here for the rest of her life. Instead she evaded the rush, caught Janine's right arm as she passed, and with a single gigantic heave and twist, tore her shoulder right out of its socket.

Beth actually enjoyed being in solitary. As she hated all humanity for the moment, it was a great relief not to have anything to do with it at all. All she wanted to do, in any event, was sleep. And when she was taken out of the tiny cell, she found that no one else in the prison wanted to mix it with her. Even the wardresses seemed to have cultivated a healthy respect for her, and the governor, a kindly, grey-haired woman, was almost sympathetic.

'I am quite sure the fight was forced upon you, Elizabeth,' she had said. 'But you really cannot take the law into your own hands. I'm afraid it will go down on your record and may affect your remission.'

Beth had said nothing. She had virtually given up talking. She had nothing to say to anyone, and a great deal to think about. She was thirty-three years of age, and her life, which had bounded from plateau to plateau for the past twenty years, had suddenly come to a full stop. It was less the awareness that she had lost everything, that when she did finally emerge from this hell she would be a homeless pauper. It had almost nothing to do with the disgrace and publicity of her trial, the grinning faces, the flashing camera bulbs, the humiliation.

The cause of her despair was the realisation that the family, for whom she had fought so hard and so long, for whom she had taken such enormous risks and suffered such enormous pain, had exploded into nothing. More than anything else it had been anger at

Anna's betrayal of trust that had determined her to bring them all down, regardless of what had happened to herself. That and Tony. For all Stephanie's fears she was positive that if Tony were dead she would have known about it, because only Szabo or Trene could have killed him. No, he was alive, and as Szabo had said, the little rat had run off and left his sisters in the lurch. If he had only sent her a message explaining what he had done, she would have forgiven him. But just silence . . .

Only Stephanie remained, true to the Janskis. But Stephanie had revealed a streak of stubborn self will that had surprised and dismayed her. And now, having that absurd child, which would be hung round her neck like a millstone for the rest of her life. Yet she looked forward to her sister's weekly Sunday visit, because she had nothing else to look forward to. Stephanie never told her how things were going, but she could see, as the once beautiful clothes and the equally beautifully manicured hands began to grow shabby and unkempt, that things were not going well. And she could do nothing to help her. That rankled. But just to see her face was a treat.

So now she winked at Janine, and hurried along the corridor into the visiting room, and gazed, not at Stephanie, but at a man. For a moment she stood quite still, unable to go forward and take her seat. Her heart seemed to have stopped.

'He is waiting for you,' the wardress said anxiously.

Beth stumbled forward and sat down, watched the tears welling from the tired eyes. 'Father?' she whispered. 'Oh, my God! Father?'

THE ELEVENTH CHRONICLE

April 1985

'Oh, thank you, Helen.' Clive Carter surveyed the enormous file which had been placed on his desk, opened it, and began to sift through the papers. 'Yes, here we are. Geoffrey Trene was released from prison in June 1969, and was found dead three weeks later. He had been shot through the head.' He peered at Meyer over the tops of his spectacles. 'A just retribution, I would say.'

'Who did it?' Meyer asked.

'Ah, they never caught the man, but I would surmise that it was a member of the Szabo faction, wouldn't you? Now let's see ... Elizabeth Mathieu was not actually released from prison until the late spring of 1965. In fact, she served almost her entire sentence. It seems she early got black marks for fighting, but a more important reason for not granting her remission was that the prison doctor considered her not to have the requisite 'temperament', whatever that may mean. Would you like to see a photograph of her, taken at Szabo's trial, just before hers.'

'I would indeed,' Meyer said, heart pounding; the photo taken in Lorges was still in his briefcase. He took the newspaper cutting. The photo was blurred, but it was the same girl, become a woman. She had changed. The face was tighter and angrier than in his photo, the lips in particular had flattened and begun a downward turn. But it remained a beautiful face, and still, in its half defiant, half apprehensive expression as it stared at the camera, the most exciting face he had ever seen. Oh, Beth Janska, he thought, where are you now? Because it was pointless any longer to pretend, to himself, that he was still seeking the father above all else. He sought the woman, the face and the idea, who had fought so hard, and prostituted herself and cheated and

284

lied and even, betrayed, perhaps, to maintain herself and her family in a world which was totally hostile to them.

And who had failed in the end?

He didn't know that yet. It would not be possible to say until he found her, and discovered her present circumstances. And he knew that if he never found her, and spoke with her, his life would have been a failure, at least in his eyes.

And held her in his arms? He wondered what Isaac Stein would say to that romantic dream, or to the concept that his chief avenger had fallen in love with a photograph. But a photograph with a gradually filling frame of flesh and blood.

'Ah,' Carter was saying. 'Anna Mathieu. Yes, she was released in 1968, and like everyone else connected with case, promptly dropped out of sight. But only for a while. Helen, who does such a marvellous job of keeping these files up to date – she does, you know, until she is absolutely positive that the people in them are all dead – has added a note that Anna Mathieu married, in 1972, a neurosurgeon named Lionel Hunt. Good heavens! I remember Hunt. He was very well known in his field.'

'Where?' Meyer almost snapped.

'Well, here, at that time. Although they seem to have been married in France. Cannes. I wonder why? I did know that Hunt had emigrated to the States in 1972. I had no idea that his wife was the former Anna Mathieu. Well, well, well, what an odd world it is, to be sure.'

'Where in the States did the Hunts emigrate to?' Meyer asked patiently.

'I shall have to find out for you. Shouldn't be too difficult. But you know how it is, these chaps are big fish in a little pond over here, then they get lured across the water by promises of vast increases in pay and far better facilities, all of which may well be true, but then they vanish into some obscure hospital down in Missouri or Kansas and are never heard of again. I imagine that's what's happened to Hunt.' He stroked his chin. 'Mind you, there must have been some string pulling or some massive deception; the Americans aren't usually very keen on accepting immigrants with prison records. I'm talking about Mrs Hunt, of course.'

'Yes,' Meyer agreed. Massive deception obviously, he supposed – that was the Janski trademark. 'Well, I'd be most grateful if you could find out where the Hunts might be now.'

'Will do. It'll take a day or two I'm afraid.'

Meyer nodded. 'I'm flying back to Jerusalem tomorrow. My boss likes to get a progress report every so often. I'll give you a ring from there . . . say Thursday.'

He hadn't been looking foward to seeing Stein, because he had made very little concrete progress up to now, and he had been concerned that Stein might have decided the trail was too cold and call off the hunt.

But now at last he had a Janska who was in the States, however illegally. Could she be the daughter to whose security Josef Janski had been going in 1972? Anna? She was the least likely of them all to have taken in her old man, going on what he had learned about her. Equally, of the three sisters, she was the one he was least interested in finding alive and well. He had an almost real feeling of deprivation.

And he still had not a single idea of what Josef Janski looked like.

And then Carter said, 'Here's another photograph of the eldest Mathieu woman, if you'd like to have it.'

Meyer took the photo. This was an actual print, not a clipping from a newspaper page. It was a very good, clear print, too; the best he had seen of Beth Janska. As he stared at it, his heart seemed to slow.

'That was the day she was released from prison,' Carter explained. 'One of our enterprising young reporters had got wind of it, and was there to snap her as she came out. But as I said, she was no longer really news value, and the editor decided against using it. I think I would have done the same. So that photo has lain in the file for damn near twenty years. You can have it, if you like.'

Meyer was still staring at the woman, handsome and tall, proud and erect ... and at the man, perhaps even taller, once, and certainly as handsome, once, but now bow–shouldered and old, and afraid, Meyer thought, as he had looked into the camera lens.

'If you're interested,' Carter said. 'the caption suggested by the reporter was: 'Bigamist Elizabeth Mathieu leaves prison accompanied by her father.'

'Halleluja!' Meyer commented.

CHAPTER 11

London and New York, 1965–68

'Father!?' Yet Stephanie almost instinctively began to close the door in the man's face.

'Don't be afraid,' Josef Janski said. 'Beth told me where to find you.'

Stephanie hesitated, then stepped backwards, almost pulling him inside, closing and locking the door. 'Who did you ask for?'

'I told you not to be afraid, Stephanie. I asked for Mrs Johnson. Beth told me what to do.'

She gazed at him. It was certainly Father, although any resemblance between this battered and frightened looking creature and the confident, handsome man she so dimly remembered had to be coincidental. 'You've seen Beth? How did you know where she was?'

He had been looking at her with equal interest, and then at the small lounge, which opened into an even smaller bedroom, the tatty furniture, the threadbare drapes. 'I read about you all in the newspapers,' he explained. 'Up to then I thought you had all died, in 1945. Now . . .

'Now you know we are all criminals,' Stephanie said.

'When I learned that you were alive,' Josef Janski told her, 'I sat down and wept.'

Stephanie bit her lip. Perhaps she should be weeping now, at discovering that he was alive. But the baby was crying. She hurried into the bedroom and scooped him into her arms, returning to the lounge. 'Your grandson.'

Josef Janski peered at the babe, and then sat down without comment.

'So what have you been doing with yourself all of these years?' Stephanie asked chattily. She felt she had to keep their relationship on a very shallow level. Because, to her surprise, there was no feeling of amazement that Father should, after all, be alive. Perhaps she

288

had always known that he was, subconsciously; Father had always been a great survivor. Nor was there any real resentment that he should never have made any serious attempt to find them until now; she had no doubt he could have done so had he wanted to, but seeing what he had become she could only suppose he would have made a worse hash of their lives than Beth had done. More disturbing, there was no feeling of joy that he should have returned to them, at such a time. The instinct that had made her want to shut the door was warning her that he had not come to help his children in their hour of need, but to seek *their* help in his hour of need – and she had nothing to give anyone, save George. She felt as if she were sitting in a dentist's chair, waiting to have all her teeth pulled.

'I have been running,' Josef Janski told her. 'Escaping the Russians. They hate me, you know. I got to England about ten years ago. I have suffered, Stephanie. God, how I have suffered. And now ... I clean a men's lavatory.'

'Life is being pretty hard for all of us right now,' Stephanie said.

'For you?' He sounded disbelieving.

'Look around you.'

'But you ... the newspapers described you as a wealthy woman.'

'Well, the papers were wrong, Father.'

'My God, have you no money at all?'

'Very little. And now what I have is for the baby.' She had cuddled George back to sleep, and carefully laid him in the cot again.

'Stephanie, I have to have money. I am so poor, I can barely feed myself.'

'It is not possible to starve in England nowadays,' Stephanie pointed out. 'There's the dole. I receive the dole, and an allowance for the baby, and milk and orange juice at reduced prices, and all sorts of other benefits. All you have to do is register. But you say you have a job.'

'It pays me nothing,' Josef Janski grumbled. 'As for the dole, I am here illegally. How can I register? I have no papers. Without papers . . .'

'Oh, come now, Father, this isn't Poland or Russia. You've been here ten years? They'll hardly deport you now. And how did you get a job without papers? You must have a social security number. You must pay to the National Health. They must have you on file somewhere.'

'You don't know,' he said, ignoring her logic. 'You don't know. I cannot have any publicity. If there is publicity, the Russians will find out where I am, and they hate me. They want me, Stephanie.'

She realised that he was terrified, and it was horrible to watch. But if she could believe that the Russians might have wanted him once, when she remembered how he had hoodwinked them over leaving Poland, she could not accept that such a fraud was sufficient to leave him still a wanted man after all but twenty years, or that any government could be interested in this tired old man. 'Of course they do not, Father,' she said, trying to mix severity and reassurance. 'The War ended nearly twenty years ago.'

'They never forget, Stephanie. Stephanie . . . you have grown into a beautiful woman. Such a beautiful woman. But one could always see the beauty in you. Beauty, and generosity, and compassion . . .'

'I have no money to spare, Father,' Stephanie said, her face stony. 'Not a penny.'

Did that make her as hard as Beth? She didn't ever want to be that. But despite the dole, which was really only meant to prevent starvation, she was down to her last few hundred pounds, and she had nothing left to sell. In the beginning, there had been that simple goal, of keeping alive until Beth was released. But then had come the news that Beth was not going to get out after a year, after all. Because of the fight she had had with some other prisoners, and because of her unwillingness

290

to co–operate with any of the prison people, she would be in gaol until the spring of 1965, still several months away. Even more, she was realising, when Beth came out, she would be the one needing help. It had become absolutely imperative for her to get a job.

In fact, when she tried she discovered that there were a great many people willing to employ a young woman as handsome as Stephanie Johnson, and the employment office itself was happy to help. But there was a catch. Apart from having to get a job to which she could take George, or with hours during which she could obtain a baby sitter, too many of the jobs carried with them a subtle nuance; that the employers was less interested in the brains or hands of Stephanie Johnson than in her breasts and bottom. When she complained to the woman at the employment agency, there had been a shrug and a smile. 'Men! They're all like that. But what's in a fumble and a tickle, dear, if they pay you your wage?'

'I don't like being either fumbled or tickled,' Stephanie replied. 'And, I am not going to be. By anyone.'

Her determined prudery had cost her some sympathy. 'Well, dear,' the woman said. 'Perhaps the area around here isn't upmarket enough for you. Perhaps you should try the West End. Although you will find that men are always men.'

Of course Stephanie would have liked to try the West End once more, but there was always the risk that she might bump into someone from Preytier's, or anyone who might remember that she was really Stephanie Trene, and she couldn't bear the thought of that happening. If only, she thought, there was a job she could do, from home, where she need never be seen by anyone . . . and where she need not be separated from George.

'I think the woman at the office was trying to tell you something,' Beth remarked on one of her Sunday visits to the gaol. 'And for God's sake, I don't know why you don't go the whole hog. If your employer, or anyone else, wants a bit of sex on the side, let them have it. But make the bastards pay. Believe me, men will always pay to get their hands on a pretty girl. I can tell you that from experience.'

'You mean with Georges? That was different. You married him.'

Beth gave a hard little laugh. 'How do you suppose I met him in the first place? He came to Madame Suchet's remember, to lunch. But that wasn't the first time. He'd been there before, paying Madame Suchet ten thousand francs for the privilege of taking me to bed. That was two hundred pounds in those days. My God!' She looked at Stephanie's incredulous expression, and said 'Do you mean you never knew it was a brothel? Good Lord. Well, I was one of the whores. We called ourselves daughters of joy. And we spread a little of it around.'

Stephanie was too horrified to speak.

Beth shrugged, looking defensive. 'What the hell? It earned money. And through it, I met Georges.'

'And wound up in gaol,' Stephanie reminded her, determined not to approve.

'I made a mistake,' Beth agreed, 'in marrying Paine. But you made a mistake in marrying Trene. No one ever gets through life without making the odd mistake, my darling girl; it just happens that some are more disastrous than others. So I whored. I don't think that was a mistake. It was necessary, for you, as well as the others. I knew what I was doing. And I would do it again, if I had to.' Another brittle smile. 'God knows, I may have to.'

'You won't,' Stephanie said. 'Never again. The whole idea is too ghastly for words.'

'Well,' Beth said. 'Tell me how you propose to feed me when I get out? Or Father?'

Stephanie shivered. 'Father! I . . . I know it's a horrible thing to say, Beth, but I don't like him. He gives me the creeps, with his hand twisting and his whining, and his smell.'

'Maybe you'll be old and frightened one day, too,' Beth warned her.

'What's he so frightened of?' Stephanie wanted to know. 'It can't be true that the Russians are really after him. He was just a lawyer. All he ever did was trick them into letting him escape from Warsaw. And that was twenty years ago.'

'Maybe he'd done something really bad,' Beth said thoughtfully. 'Maybe he *was* a Gestapo officer, and that card he had was real. Or maybe he'd done something to the Jews. We saw a programme on TV here, a few nights ago, about how the Israeli government has special investigators on the track of all the Nazis who killed Jews during the War. You remember that man Eichmann a couple of years ago. The Israelis tracked him down. And they're doing it all the time. There was a man ... I can't remember his name. But he was awfully good looking. Yet he was called the Mountie, because he always got his man. It think his name began with an M, too. Anyway, that's not important, What's important is that maybe Father is on their list, and he knows it.'

'Good Lord!' Stephanie exclaimed. 'But if he was then he's a war criminal.'

'Never say that,' Beth snapped.

'But if he ...'

'It doesn't matter what he did,' Beth told her. 'He's Father. But for him none of us would be alive today. Okay, maybe he's not the man I remember, either. He's had it even harder than us, Stephanie. And he's still our father. I'm not going to see him starve.'

Which meant, presumably, Stephanie thought, that she couldn't let him starve either. Because even Beth, who hated all mankind, was prepared to protect her own family, no matter what their crimes. That was her only virtue, Stephanie supposed, but it was a virtue which had also played a part in keeping them alive ... and landed them where they were now? That was too harsh a judgement. They were where they were now

293

simply because Beth had for the first time in her life lowered her guard and given them their heads. Beth had every right to be bitter.

So she dutifully had Father to supper one evening a week. But it was strictly duty. They had little to say to each other, and he ate so hungrily he embarrassed her, quite apart from the fact that every time he came he asked her for money, which she refused to give him. In the strangest and most repugnant of ways, his visits made her increasingly aware of her aloneness. She had never felt that way in the past, because there had always been Anna, and Tony . . . and Beth – and it was quite a different sensation to being alone, or lonely. Now she was clinging to the thought of Beth as a drowning woman might cling to an oar. Knowing all the time that Beth had changed too much ever to be a haven again. Oh, undoubtedly Beth would be happy to look after her again, the moment she could – that was in her nature. But Stephanie knew she would never be able to trust her sister again, would never know what laws, legal or moral, Beth might be breaking just to get what she wanted.

In any event, Beth's being in a position to help anyone again had to be a long time in the future. She was the family breadwinner at the moment – and she was doing nothing to justify her role. Sometimes she thought she was on the point of having a breakdown with worry, and could only sustain her sanity by taking refuge in writing her little cameos, recalling events from the past, creating events for the future. If only that publisher had liked her work, four years ago, she thought sadly. And then wondered, why should he, or anyone, like her work? It was the purest sentimental, over-happy drivel, with a strong current of unreality. Yet she could write; she became sure of it every time she read what was currently being published. The difference was that those people seemed to have so much to recall, to have suffered so much, and be able to translate their suffering through the mediums of their pens into compelling reading . . .

294

She found herself staring at the wall, listening to George breathing in the next room. Hadn't she suffered? All of them? But to tell her own story would mean not only endeavouring to recall scenes from her past, things her mind had always instinctively rejected, like the hunger and the cold and the fear and the dead Russian soldier, and the smell around Dresden and the humiliation of wearing the hand-me-downs in the refugee camp; it would also mean bringing herself back into the limelight. If the newspapers had not been interested in that story, simply because they had not known it existed, they had still wanted to pay her twenty-five thousand pounds for the story of her marriage. And she had refused! My God, she had been foolish. If Beth were ever to find that out ... but she knew she could no more tell that story than she could prostitute herself. She had slept with only one man in her entire life, and she was resolved never to sleep with another, or to tell any of the secrets of her marriage bed.

She had not even troubled to get a divorce from Geoffrey, however much she loathed, despised and feared him, and however easy it would be to do; she did not believe in divorce any more than she believed in abortion – or prostitution.

But twenty-five thousand pounds. ... Perhaps they would pay as much for that earlier story. And why should anyone suspect it was written by Stephanie Trene? She wasn't going to write her own story. She was going to write *a* story. Suddenly she was excited. Surely she could do it, write a story with all the pathos and excitement and anger and adventure that she had experienced?

The next morning she bought herself six large spiral notebooks, and set to work. It was enthralling, and quite took, her mind off her problems; she even begrudged the time she had to spend with George. In a fortnight she had filled them all, and so far had only told the story of two children, a boy and a girl, escaping

295

from Germany after the War. Then she stopped, and read it through, and realised that she already had a complete book. So she bought another six spiral note-books, and sat down and wrote it all out again in her best hand, and with all the grammatical mistakes she could discover corrected, before taking it to a profes-sional typing agency and spending twenty five precious pounds to have it properly typed up. Then she del-ivered it by hand to Huyton and Lines, the publishers. To do so she not only put her hair into the severest bun, but bought herself a pair of horn-rimmed spectacles, and wore not even a trace of lipstick.

She could do no more, but need not have bothered so much; she never even got past the receptionist on the ground floor, who hardly looked at her as she remarked, 'I'm afraid we take no responsibility for unsolicited manuscripts,' and threw the parcel into a corner.

Stephanie had supposed she would never hear of it again, and was trying to make up her mind to spend another twenty-five pounds – she had only the single carbon – when a letter arrived in the post. This was exciting in itself, as since Geoffrey had stopped writing, she had received no letters at all, only bills.

It was from a Mr Jonathan Price, Editor at Huyton and Lines, inviting her to call and discuss her work. Her work! That night she bought a bottle of South African sherry and had a drink, smiling at George, who smiled back without the slightest idea why his mother should be so unusually happy.

'Mrs Johnson?' Jonathan Price was of medium height, undistinguished in a careless sort of fashion, for his pinstripe suit was flecked with scattered cigar ash and his shoes badly needed polishing. The corridors through which Stephanie had been guided on her way to this inner sanctum had not been any tidier, and women she had encountered had all worn heavy sweaters and horn-rimmed spectacles and low heeled shoes. The only difference between them and her was that their hair was universally untidy.

'Do sit down,' Price invited. 'Would you care for a glass of sherry?'

'Why, thank you,' Stephanie murmured, despite having had her fill the previous evening. 'That would be very nice.'

His secretary poured.

'Do you know,' Price said, 'my receptionist offered the opinion that you might be a schoolmistress. Are you a schoolmistress, Mrs Johnson?'

'Good Lord, no,' Stephanie said, without thinking.

'Ah. And you are not, by any chance, German or Polish, like your characters? Of course you're not. Forgive me. I mean, with a name like Johnson . . . ?'

'I am English,' Stephanie told him positively. She was not Beth's sister for nothing.

'Oh, quite. Do forgive me. It's just that some of this . . .' he tapped the folder in front of him, sounds almost autobiographical. As if you had been present.'

'I have spoken with many refugees,' Stephanie explained, having prepared herself for this sort of question. 'I was once briefly engaged in refugee work.'

'I see,' he said, obviously not seeing at all as he tried to reconcile her statement with her age. 'And of course,' he added brightly, 'there is a quality of true imagination in the book. An almost surrealist brilliance, from time to time.' He sipped sherry and smiled at her. 'From which you will gather that I find what you have written intensely interesting. Yes, indeed. It needs work, of course. What book doesn't? Would you be prepared to accept some editorial assistance? You know, a book nowadays, to be successful, needs to be more than just a straightforward story, however imaginatively told. It has to have punch, and . . . punch, yes, that's it. And a more identifiable central character. I wonder if the girl could actually be English? Perhaps we could work that into the story. What do you think?'

'Perhaps,' Stephanie said, slightly amused; the central character was herself.

'Would you be prepared to do this?'

'I am prepared to do anything that isn't illegal or immoral, Mr Price, to sell the book,' Stephanie said, gazing at him.

'That is a very professional attitude,' Price said. 'Then why don't you start calling me Jonathan, and we'll go out to lunch together.'

Despite her attempted warning, Stephanie braced herself for a possible assault, having by now as big an inbuilt distrust of the male sex as did Beth. But Jonathan Price was interested strictly in business, although he gave her a very good lunch in an expensive Soho restaurant. And she had something on her mind, anyway. 'Do you mean you may actually buy the book?' she ventured over coffee.

'Oh, indeed. I am most enthusiastic about it. I think it has great possibilities.'

'And . . .' she held her breath. 'May I ask what you are going to pay for it?'

'Oh, my dear,' he smiled. 'Of course, the vital question. Well, I do like the book. So much so that . . . well . . . I think we could take a flyer on this one. How about two hundred and fifty pounds advance?'

'Two hundred and fifty pounds?' Stephanie asked in a strangled voice, watching zeros dropping away from her mental vision like autumnal leaves.

'I know it's a bit over the odds,' Jonathan said. 'But as I say, it has distinct possibilities. That would be against a royalty of ten per cent on the first five thousand copies, and twelve and a half thereafter. Six per cent on Commonwealth sales, of course. Is that all right?'

Stephanie was speechless.

'Of course we would pay a hundred on signature, and the other hundred and fifty on publication,' Price went on, still assuming she was overcome by his generosity.

'Publication would be when?' she asked.

'Ah, I think we would aim for next spring. Yes, it will make a good spring book.'

'Spring?' she asked. 'You mean, the spring of 1966? That's a year away.'

'Oh, quite. But we really get a move on at Huyton and Lines when we get our teeth into something. We should, of course require fifty per cent of any reprints; I should think it has a chance, once it has . . . well, been spiced up a little. And ten per cent of any overseas sales, or any film sales. That's standard, you know. And of course, fifty per cent of any serialisation.'

Stephanie didn't know what to say. On the one hand, bitter disappointment that the advance should have fallen so far short of what she had dreamed, on the other, all the sudden talk about serialisation and film sales, left her totally confused.

'I hope all of that sounds satisfactory?' Jonathan Price asked.

He had given her a nice lunch, and she did so want to see her book in print. 'Oh, yes,' she said faintly. 'perfectly satisfactory.'

She had been anxious to impress Beth, who was due out in a week. Now she became a bundle of nerves. But as it happened, Beth was too relieved to be out of gaol at last immmediately to be scathing. Yet she brought with her immediate problems. She was accompanied by Father, who had met her at the prison gate; Stephanie had been unable to go as she hadn't been able to find a baby sitter for that morning. Beth swept into the tiny flat, looking right and left with dilated nostrils.

'This is George,' Stephanie said proudly, holding him up. At eighteen months he was a very sturdy young man.

'At least he doesn't look like his father,' Beth commented, and went into the bedroom. Stephanie followed, still carrying George, and kicked the door shut behind her.

'He can't stay here,' she said urgently. 'Father, I mean. There's only the one bedroom.'

'I understand that, at the moment,' Beth said. 'We share a bed, is that it?'

'I'm sorry,' Stephanie said. 'There really isn't room for another.' Even if I could afford it, she thought.

'Even in prison one didn't have to share a bed,' Beth pointed out. 'Still, beggars can't be choosers. Tell me about your job. Have you started yet?'

Stephanie had told her she had high hopes of employment. Now she drew a long breath. 'Yes.'

'Obviously it doesn't pay you much,' Beth remarked. 'What do you do?'

Stephanie told her, rocking George to and fro, and Beth listened. Then she laughed. Stephanie was relieved that she found it amusing; she had expected far worse. 'Two hundred and fifty pounds a year?' Beth observed. 'I used to make more than that in one night, sometimes, at Madame Suchet's.'

'I do wish you wouldn't keep going on about Madame Suchet,' Stephanie admonished. 'I should have thought that was an aspect of your life you'd be very happy to forget.'

'Well, you and I certainly cannot live on two hundred and fifty pounds a year,' Beth pointed out. 'Much less support Father and your baby.'

'You have the wrong order of precedence,' Stephanie said coldly. 'Anyway, now you are out you can also apply for the dole.'

'Me?' Beth said contemptuously. 'I'd sooner starve.'

'Then you go and do it somewhere else,' Stephanie told her, amazed at herself for standing up to Beth, of all people.

Beth gazed at her for several seconds, then took her in her arms and hugged her. 'My darling girl, you and I only have each other. We are never going to quarrel again. I swear it. I would like you to swear it too.'

Stephanie moved back her head to look at her. 'As long as you remember that George comes first. And I mean, first.'

Beth kissed her on the nose. 'As I said, he doesn't look like his father, which has to be a big plus. He could even grow on me, if he's good. All together, now. You and me and George. And,' she added thoughtfully, 'Father.'

Stephanie had been terrified that Beth, with her amoral view of life and her anxiety to make money as rapidly as possible, might go back to prostitution – she just wouldn't have known what to do about that. But to her enormous relief, the very next week Beth got a job, as a bus conductress. She was even given a uniform, and a large brown satchel in which to carry her change. The idea of Beth, so elegant, so regal when she wanted to be, wearing a uniform and being called dearie and being described as a 'clippie', would have been ludicrously funny had it not made Stephanie want to weep. The job didn't pay very much, but Beth gave Father half of everything she earned. This troubled Stephanie's conscience, the more so as suddenly, towards the end of the year, things started to happen. Jonathan asked her out to lunch again. By then she and a charming if slightly supercilious young woman named Bonnie had sat down and completely rehashed her novel, and Jonathan had had this new version professionally typed, and had seemed very satisfied.

But Stephanie was still surprised when he remarked, 'I have some good news for you. An American publisher with whom we do quite a lot of business has seen the book and wants it. He's offering two thousand dollars advance, payable on signature.'

Stephanie needed time to breathe, as he watched her anxiously. Thanks to the Labour Party's recent devaluation, two thousand dollars was around eight hundred pounds.

'I think you should accept it,' Jonathan recommended. 'America is a much bigger market than England. If you can get your foot in that door, you could do very well.'

'Then I do accept it,' she agreed.

It had suddenly become a most exciting year. Before English publication, Jonathan managed to sell paperback rights for five hundred pounds, which meant another two hundred and fifty for her, supposing the hardcover earned out – and he seemed confident of that – and then, at Christmas, came the big news that the Americans were going to launch the book, and would like her over there for publication.

'Between you and me,' Jonathan said, 'there's film interest. Now, Stephanie,' he warned, as her face lit up, 'only one in four of all books which attract film interest actually translate that interest into money. Still, it's a step in the right direction. Now, are you going to go, or aren't you? I most strongly recommend that you do.'

'I'd love to,' she said. 'But I can't afford it.'

'Oh, that's not a problem. They'll pay your passage and expenses.'

'Will they? Oh! That sounds tremendous.' New York, she thought. My God, America! Beth's dream! 'But there's . . .' Oh, my God, she thought.

'A husband?' he asked gently.

She stared at him.

'I did find that publicity questionnaire we sent you a little sketchy,' he remarked. 'I gained the impression you were keeping something in the background. Is it a husband? Surely he'd be happy for you to have a success?'

She gulped. 'It's a baby, actually.' He was a man who could so easily make her want to tell the truth. She had to remind herself to watch her step.

He nodded, without changing a single expression. 'I see. I didn't suppose anyone could write with as much feeling as you, at your tender age, if you will permit me to say that, without having lived a bit. Well . . . the Americans being what they are, it might not be a good idea to project the unmarried mother image, for openers. So I suppose . . .'

'Oh, but I am married,' she said without thinking.

'Are you? Of course you are. You're Mrs Johnson. Then .. ?'

'I mean, I was married,' she added hastily. 'I'm a widow.'

'Oh, my dear girl,' he said. 'I had no idea. I am most terribly sorry. But the Americans will lap that up. Oh, indeed. Young widow and mother writes successful book and all that sort of thing. Oh, certainly, you must take your child. A son, is it?'

'Yes.'

'Quite. Now, there'll be visas and things . . . would you like my secretary to look after that for you?'

Stephanie had to draw breath and remember that she had gone in quite deep enough. 'No, no,' she said. 'I'll do it.'

Stephanie was afraid Beth might be upset, but Beth was delighted, and almost as excited as Stephanie herself. It seemed that all of a sudden her life was moving on to a higher plateau. Her only worry was about the visa and passport business, but that was needless. She went along to Grosvenor Square herself, and saw a very nice young man. As she intended to tell him the truth she loosed her hair and wore makeup and one of her good dresses and high heeled shoes, and he obviously felt he was having a good day.

He checked up on what she had to tell him, had it confirmed that she had never even appeared at the trial as a witness, and was regarded as being entirely in the clear by the police, and was so estranged from her husband that she had never even visited him prison. 'Quite right, too,' he commented. 'I wonder why you have never divorced him?'

'I am a Roman Catholic,' Stephanie said, looking him in the eye.

'So am I,' he agreed enthusiastically. 'I quite take your point.'

Her other worry was that the publisher might want to see her passport and visa before arranging her passage, but that also proved needless. The money was sent to Huyton and Lines, who purchased the ticket. The girl at the Pan American check-in desk was only interested in making sure she did have a visa, but was a sharp-eyed young woman, and spotted that the ticket was in a different name to the passport.

303

'That's because I am a novelist,' Stephanie told her, 'using a pseudonym.'

Immediately the girl was very interested, and promised to buy the book. Certainly she asked no more questions.

Then she was on a jumbo bound for Kennedy airport, the first time in her life she had ever flown, with a special cot for George, and eager attention from the stewardesses. As it was August, she arrived in the middle of a heat wave, and the air conditioning in her hotel had broken down. 'Have it fixed in no time,' the bell hop assured her, but for the time being it was necessary to open all the windows. She enjoyed that, allowing the sounds and smells of the great city to drift in, but she found the hotel to be rather modest ... and the attention she received from her publishers even more so. They had arranged for a bottle of champagne to be waiting in her room, and the next day she went to the office and was introduced to the Chief Editor, a tall, languid woman, who told her how much everyone liked the book and then seemed rather anxious to be rid of her. She was taken over by a junior editor, who explained that she had copy-edited the book, and discussed various points in a vague fashion, but as they had offset the English edition she didn't really have much to do or say.

They lunched together, and that evening Stephanie, having arranged a baby sitter with the hotel, attended a cocktail party in honour of some other much more highpowered visiting author and was introduced to a lot of people whose names she couldn't remember and who obviously had never heard of her. Her already dented ego was the more battered by the constant chat about money which surrounded her, with so and so declaiming because he had only received fifteen grand for his last novel and someone else telling her that she needed to sell twelve thousand copies in hardback to get anywhere. That seemed an awful amount, and she kept very quiet.

The evening ended with the guest of honour, now rather the worse for gins and tonic – he was English also – remarking, 'You're a hot looking bird. How about dinner, and then a bit of the old heave-ho?'

Thoroughly out of sorts by then, Stephanie replied, 'Then off you go and heave yourself ho, you obnoxious little man,' and caught a cab home. If the hotel could possibly be regarded as home.

The following day was her publication day, but she didn't even receive a phone call of congratulations. Her sub-editor had said they were trying to arrange a television appearance for her – not an interview because no one had heard of her, but on a game show, 'So people can get to know your face,' she explained – and had asked her to be sure she was available at short notice.

Stephanie stayed in the hotel room all morning, waiting for a call which never came, and trying to cope with an increasingly restless George. After lunch she took him out for a walk, to the various book stores in the vicinity of the hotel. But there were no copies to be seen, and she was too shy to ask for any. So she took George to the top of the Empire State Building, and contemplated throwing herself off which should certainly sell a few copies – but as it would have meant leaving George lost on the 85th floor she abandoned the idea and returned to the hotel. There had been no calls for her, so she went out for a bottle of champagne, put George in front of the television, and sat down to get drunk on her own. Then the phone rang. She dropped the bottle and ran to it.

'Hi,' said the sub-editor. 'Sorry about today. I guess the networks just weren't interested. Ah, well, you win some and you lose some. Say, you all have a nice flight back home tomorrow.'

The phone went dead. So that was that. And although Stephanie had been a little anxious about the possible publicity of a television appearance, afraid that some eager American gossip columnist might find out that she was the wife of Geoffrey Trene – as if anyone in

America had ever heard of Geoffrey Trene – it was the last humiliation to drive her to tears, especially when she looked at the champagne soaking the carpet.

She had recovered by the time she and George got to Kennedy the next day, but she remained amazed at the pointlessness of the whole exercise, after they had spent very nearly as much as they paid her for the book in flying her across the Atlantic and putting her up for three days. It had been perhaps the most crushing disappointment of her life, even more traumatic than the realisation that the man to whom she was married was a thug and a murderer.

Nor did she hear anything more about the film deal, and she was never sure whether she had been swept under the carpet because that had fallen through, or if that had fallen through because no attempt had been made to introduce her to the film people or to have any publicity about her whatsoever.

Jonathan endeavoured to reassure her when she got back to London. 'I know the Americans are casual about these things,' he agreed. 'They are inclined to think on a much larger scale than us, and let's face it, a first novel never does attract all that much attention, unless it is written about an exceptional event, or by a well known personality. If the film deal had gone through, now, that would have made a lot of difference.' He patted her hand. 'Don't be upset, my dear. You've made a start, and a mark, however small. There'll be other film deals, and other books, I hope,' he said pointedly, watching her closely.

'Oh, yes,' she promised, because she had just about finished her second novel, in which she had relied on her imagination rather more than her memory. To her delight, only a few weeks later he managed to sell the first novel to France and Sweden, while the Americans placed a paperback sale for four thousand dollars. She actually got less than her half share of that, as the hardcover didn't earn out, but all in all she reckoned she had earned, with the European money, a little over

306

two thousand pounds for the book. If she could do that every nine months or so, she would be very comfortably off, and she even gave Father a gift of fifty pounds, which she regretted bitterly when he arrived for dinner two days later absolutely drunk, and with a bottle of the cheapest possible whiskey in his coat pocket.

'I know,' Beth said. 'He does drink. I suppose he has no other pleasure, the poor fellow.'

Stephanie didn't agree with that point of view at all. 'Well, he's not getting any more from me,' she declared. 'All surplus from here on goes into an account for George.' Besides, she wasn't quite as well off as she had first thought; once she told the employment office she had sold a book, her benefit promptly stopped.

To make matters worse, Jonathan was disappointed in her second. He tried to be encouraging, but he didn't feel he could publish it. 'It's too lightweight for our list,' he said. 'But I am sure you will find a publisher.'

'How?' she asked. It had never crossed her mind that he could turn it down, after being so pleased with the first one, and she dreaded the thought of having to begin a relationship with someone else.

'What you need is a good agent,' he told her, and sent her along to see a friend of his named Peter Brynne. Brynne turned out to be a tall, languid man who reminded her of her American editor, but who, to her surprise, had read both of her books and had some very pertinent criticisms to make. Like Jonathan, he took her out to lunch and asked some rather impertinent questions, she thought, about her private life which she parried as well as she was able. He also criticised her arrangements with Jonathan, who might have been his friend, but, as he explained, had to be on the other side of the table when it came to negotiating contracts.

'Ten per cent of any film deals, indeed. They all try that one. Well, there is no way we'll let him get away with that again.'

'Presuming there are ever any film deals,' Stephanie pointed out, feeling rather pessimistic on that front.

'Oh, there will be,' Brynne assured her. 'Your career is only just beginning. Now, let's talk about what we can do with this second book of yours.'

'I know it's not as grim as the first,' she acknowledged. 'I felt I needed some relief from it.'

'A writer should stick to what he, or she, does best,' Brynne told her. 'If the book is going to lack the intensity of the first, you have to make it up somewhere else, like sex, or drama, or even humour. I don't really recommend too much humour though. It isn't an exportable commodity. What makes us laugh doesn't necessarily amuse the Americans, for example. Now, I want you to go away and rewrite this, bearing in mind my comments, and we'll see what we can do.'

'What will be your fee?' she asked.

He smiled at her. 'Ten per cent of all sales in England, and double that for all overseas sales, including America. That's because I will be using other agents in those countries to market your book, and they will also want their ten per cent.'

She understood that, as the foreign sales Jonathan had negotiated for her had all had a ten per cent deduction. But twenty per cent of her meagre cake seemed a very big slice.

'You want to consider,' Brynne told her, 'firstly, that I don't get a penny unless I actually sell something; it's not a flat fee. And secondly, that if you set out to market a book on your own you would probably spend at least as much as that on travelling and telephone calls, and much more, because all of that will eat into the time when you could be earning money by writing your next book. Nor would you have my contacts. Of course, if you're content just to be a writer for the English domestic market, with perhaps an occasional spin-off into Europe or America, and settle at that very modest level for the rest of your life, then you don't need me. But if you want to become internationally known, and that means internationally successful, then your books need to be marketed, and pushed. That takes time, and money. But I think you write well enough to make it worth while. Isn't that what you want?'

'I want to become an international bestseller,' she said.

He grinned. 'Even I can't do that for you. Bestsellers aren't written, Stephanie. They just happen. You will have a bestseller, one of these days, and you will probably rank it way below most of your other books, as a work of art. Of course, lightning attracts lightning, at least for a while. But let's settle for international recognition. You'll find that just as stimulating, and a good deal less wearing. Now, how are you off financially? You have a job, I suppose? Success, I'm afraid, doesn't usually arrive overnight.'

Stephanie shook her head.

'I see. Then you have private income?' he asked hopefully. 'Your late husband's pension?'

'There isn't one.'

'My God!' he commented. 'Do you mean you just plunged in at the deep end, assuming you could make a living as a novelist? Not many people do, you know.'

'Well,' she said, and didn't know what else to say.

He obviously didn't know what to say either, and seemed dumbfounded, even after she had assured him that she would survive. When he asked how, she told him, as politely as she could, to mind his own business. He knew her as Mrs Johnson, a widow, and nothing more – as did Jonathan Price and the Americans – and she was determined that none of them was ever going to know anything more. She had already started putting together a fictional background for herself, and had applied for permission to change her name from Trene to Johnson, which seemed entirely reasonable to the solicitor she approached. Once that was done she could obtain a new passport and begin a new life.

Despite the disappointment over the first book

and the setback with the other, life had become more meaningful and exciting than ever before, and Brynne managed to place the rewritten version of the second book, although not with Jonathan and not with the States, so that in all it earned less than half of the first. But he skilfully avoided breaking the option clause with either Jonathan or the Americans, with the result that Huyton and Lines were delighted with her third novel, in which she managed for the first time to combine both the tragedies she had experienced with the natural good humour of her personality, and even to write in some sexual passages, although she was terribly embarrassed when she read them over, and was tongue-tied when Jonathan congratulated her on their realism. The Americans also bought this one, and it became apparent, even to Peter, that she could actually earn a modest living as a full-time author. Which was all she wanted to do, with sufficient spare to give George a decent start in life.

By now her change of name had been legalised, and she had obtained her new passport, so that by the end of 1967 she was beginning to be strongly tempted in the direction of emigrating to the States. The paperback of her first book was selling quite well there, and although Peter warned her that she would not be as well off, relatively, as in England, it would mean the complete severance of all the hateful reminders of the first twenty-five years of her life. She was sure that could she become at least an American resident, there would not only be no chance of anyone finding out about her past, but perhaps even more important, no risk of Geoffrey finding her once he came out of prison, which probability was beginning to loom very close as 1968 drew closer. He would then have served five years and might be eligible for parole.

This was her overwhelming fear. She had been terrified when, back in 1965, Jonathan had sent her off to a photographer to obtain a portrait for the dust jacket. Although she had consoled herself with the thought

310

that a prisoner in Pentonville was unlikely to be given a copy of a woman's book to read, and that her present appearance, at least in public, with her bun and her horn-rimmed spectacles and her total absence of make-up, bore no resemblance whatsoever to the long, dark brown hair, the daring, expensive dresses, the jewellery and the furs, the heavy lipstick and rouge and eye shadow, which he would remember, she had still been tempted to refuse. Of course it had been all right; she had hardly recognised herself. But when he got out and came looking for her . . .

It was George she principally worried about. He was now four, and a very lively and intelligent child. What sort of impact would the sudden appearance of a father he had always been told had died at sea have on him . . . and besides, in another year she hoped to start him at nursery school, and she wanted to be permanently settled by then.

The problem was Beth. She was entirely sympathetic to Stephanie's situation and plans, and advised her to go ahead. 'I can manage here,' she assured her. 'We're due for a rise this month.'

'I can't leave you,' Stephanie insisted. 'You have to come with me.'

Beth gave one of those lip-twisted smiles. 'Don't you think I've thought about that? Even a clippie in the States must earn about three times as much as here. The trouble is, my darling, that I have a criminal record. So, no visa. I've checked that out.'

'My God! But you mean, never?'

'I don't know. Anyway, I don't really have the money. And I have to remain here, don't you see, at least for a few years yet. I certainly can't afford to take Father with me, even if they'd have him, and I can't abandon him. Then I have to be here in case Tony ever contacts me . . .'

'Oh, Beth!' Stephanie exclaimed. 'That's a dream.'

'Isn't all life? I know he's alive, Stephanie.'

'But after the way he ran out on us.'

'He was lonely and afraid,' Beth said. 'And he never did have all that much resolution. I've forgiven him for running away. He'll come home one day, and I have to be here to make it home. There's Anna, too.'

'Anna?' Stephanie shouted. 'You can't be serious. After what she did?'

'She's our sister,' Beth said firmly. 'It doesn't matter what she's done in the past, she's still our sister. Would you throw George out, no matter what he'd done?'

There was no answer to that. But Anna . . . Beth was such a paradoxical person, Stephanie thought. She could be so hard, and brutal, and amoral, and ruthless . . . yet she would forgive her own sister and brother anything once she had got over her initial anger, simply because they were her family. And there was nothing she could do but admire such a point of view.

But it was disappointing. Because she couldn't go off to America and leave Beth all on her own, abandon her when she was so poor, supporting Father out of her meagre wage, and never complaining. Worst of all, Beth was so entirely lacking in a future. She had built a house of cards, and it had collapsed, and was now left scattered about her life, an aimless collection of stiff paper which could not even provide her with adequate shelter.

But she was wrong. It was she who spotted the advertisement in *The Times*, which read, 'If Madam Elizabeth Mathieu, sometime of Château Lorges, Lorges, Camargue, France, will contact this office, she may learn something of interest to her.'

She showed it to Beth over breakfast. 'What do you think? Some kind of a trap?'

Beth studied it. There was a telephone number to call. She checked with Directory Inquiries, and was told it belonged to the firm of Lawson, Lawson and Peat, solicitors.

'I'm sure it's a trap,' Stephanie said. 'Georges is trying to find out where you are. Maybe they want to prosecute you in France.'

'Nothing ventured,' Beth pointed out. She put on her uniform, but as she was not due to report for duty until ten, at nine-thirty she went downstairs to the telephone booth on the corner of the street. The flat did not have a phone, but by using a public call box there was no chance of her being traced to any exact address. Although commonsense told her that as she had not changed her name, and that her address was known to her parole officer, anyone who really wanted to do so could track her down without too much trouble. These people were just being lazy.

She was more excited than Stephanie had supposed. Something of interest! She knew instinctively what it had to be. Georges was dead! And he must have left her something in his will. There was no need for him to have done so; indeed, logic told her that there was every reason for him not to have done so, after the way she had treated him. But she was always prepared to dream, for at least five minutes at a time.

'You will have to come in, Madame Mathieu,' said the voice on the telephone. 'And bring adequate identification. Mr Lawson isn't in yet, but if you were to call in about an hour he may be able to see you.'

'You must think I'm a half wit,' Beth told him. 'I want to know what it's all about before I come traipsing into the City.'

'I cannot divulge the nature of the information we have for Madame Mathieu, madame,' the voice said, 'until I am certain I am speaking with Madame Mathieu. Why, yesterday, which was the first day we ran that advertisement, no fewer than three women telephoned claiming to be Madame Mathieu. None of them would come in, either.'

'They were claiming to be me,' Beth said. 'Because I am Madame Mathieu. Why don't you ask me something which only Madame Mathieu could possibly know?'

'I'm afraid that would be . . . ah, hold on. Mr Lawson is just coming in.' The man went away, and came back five minutes later. 'Are you there?'

313

'I'm not going anywhere' Beth told him.

'Well, madame, Mr Lawson suggest that perhaps you may be able to tell us the name of Monsieur Mathieu's cook and butler in 1948?'

'Of course I can,' Beth said. 'Their names where Antoinette and Emile. I can describe them for you, if you wish.'

'Excuse me, madame,' he said again, and left her holding on for another five minutes.

Then a new voice came on the telephone. 'Good morning, Madame Mathieu,' said this older man. 'There is just one more question I would like to ask you. Can you recall the exact date of the first meeting with Monsieur Mathieu?'

'I supppose so,' Beth said, beginning to get even more excited; this seemed an awful lot of rigmarole for a small legacy. 'It was in 1948, and it would have been May the fifteenth. No, it was the sixteenth, because we went down to Lorges three days later, and that was definitely the nineteenth.'

'Oh, very good, madame,' the man said, as if he were conducting a quiz show. 'And can you tell me where this meeting took place?'

'At Madame Suchet's in Paris,' Beth said. 'I was working there at the time.'

'Ah,' the man said. 'Yes. My name is Macdonald Lawson, by the way. I say, Madame, could you possibly come round to see me, right away?'

'You'll have to make it worth my while,' Beth told him.

'Ah,' he remarked again. 'Well, the fact is, I'm afraid I have some rather sad news for you.'

'My husband is dead,' Beth said.

'However did you know?'

'Clairvoyance,' Beth said.

'Ah. He was very . . . ah, he had attained a considerable age, of course. Eighty. But still, you have my deepest sympathy.'

'Thank you,' Beth said. 'If that is all you want to see me about, I'll take a rain check.'

'Oh, well, no, it isn't, Madame Mathieu. I would be grateful if you could come in to see me at your earliest convenience. We are acting for Monsieur Mathieu's French advocates, and they are naturally anxious to complete the formalities for probate etc and wind up Monsieur Mathieu's estate.'

'And what exactly has that got to do with me?' Beth asked.

'Why, Madame, by the terms of Monsieur Mathieu's will, you are named sole beneficiary.'

For a moment Beth went dizzy, and the telephone box began to spin in space.

'Did you say sole beneficiary?' she whispered at last.

'Yes, indeed. The will was drawn up in March 1952. A very long time ago. But it remains entirely valid. But of course there is a lot of legal work to be gone through, and . . .'

'How much?' Beth asked, getting her voice back under control.

'Well, as I say, a great deal, on which your French advocates feel they must have your instructions. There are documents relating to the unfulfilled orders for bulls, and for horses, and regarding the gymkhana that was to be held this year, and . . .'

'I meant,' Beth said, 'How much money is involved?'

'Oh, my dear Madame Mathieu, I couldn't possibly say, I have no idea exactly,' Lawson said.

'Be a devil, and be inexact,' Beth told him. 'Try an estimate. I won't hold you to it.'

'Oh, well . . . I suppose conservatively we are talking of something in the nature of thirty million francs,' Mr Lawson said.

THE TWELFTH CHRONICLE

May 1985

Isaac Stein read through Meyer's report, giving an occasional grunt. When he was finished, he raised his head. 'You really have all the admirable qualities of a bloodhound, Bob,' he said. 'The principal one being patient determination. What a trail you have had to follow. But now, at last, success. I do congratulate you.' He studied the photograph of Beth Janska leaving prison. But Meyer knew he was not looking at the woman; Isaac was a dedicated professional.

'The face of the enemy, eh?' he remarked. 'One can see that he must have been quite a formidable figure once upon a time. And now you have a definitive lead?'

'Well,' Meyer said carefully, 'I think that I should continue on the trail, as it were, instead of jumping too far at one time. I know that Anna Mathieu and Lionel Hunt were married on the Riviera in 1972. I'm sure I can locate the details of that without difficulty. Perhaps some more photos, as well. After all, once Janski regained contact with his family, he would certainly have kept in touch. In fact, we know he did.'

And he had a hunch, which had nothing whatsoever to do with Josef Janski. But he didn't dare let his boss know that.

'Yes we know he kept in touch with them, or one of them,' Stein agreed. 'And we know that he emigrated to the States the same year this daughter Anna married, so we can make a reasonable assumption where he went: to her, the moment she was reasonably established there. There is no necessity for you to go to Cannes. While you have the patience of a bloodhound, Bob, you are not a bloodhound. They have to go from scent to scent. We are more fortunate. We can spot when it is possible to step across a lot of country, because we can see our goal. Now, have you an address for this Hunt woman?'

Meyer sighed. 'I know where her husband went to work, fourteen years ago.'

'Then there is the place for you to jump to. Even if he has moved on, you will be able to trace him, and his wife. Prominent neurosurgeons don't just disappear. And where his wife is, there you will find Josef Janski, if he is still alive. If not, you will obtain proof of his death. Where did they go?'

'Miami,' Meyer said miserably.

'Well, that sounds very nice. Miami's weather in May is just as good as the Riviera's, I promise you. Get over there, Bob. Go to see Marineworld and ride on a dolphin. And find the Hunts. I'll expect to hear from you in a week. I'll have my people standing by. But if Janski is alive and has been living illegally in the States for the past thirteen years, I don't anticipate any problem with the State Department over an extradition order. Not when they hear why we want him.'

CHAPTER 12

London, the Riviera and New York 1968-72

When Beth didn't come home for over an hour, Stephanie wrapped George up and took him downstairs to the telephone booth, and found it empty. To her alarm she found Beth's change satchel, lying on the pavement outside, where it had obviously been thrown. Miraculously, it hadn't been touched, but it was still sufficiently disturbing to make her call the police. Something had happened. It almost seemed as if Beth might have been kidnapped. In broad daylight? And who on earth would want to kidnap a bus conductress, when she wasn't even on her bus?

Yet something odd must have happened but to involve the police in the life of an ex-criminal ... Beth no longer had to report to her parole officer as the six month's remission she had finally been granted had long expired, but Stephanie knew she hated the very thought of anything to do with the 'beastly fuzz', as she called them.

She didn't know what to do, went back upstairs and resolved to be patient, pacing the room, while George asked incessant and unanswerable questions. The situation was worsened just after eleven by the arrival of an aggressive inspector from the bus station to find out why Beth hadn't reported for duty. Stephanie said she wasn't well, apologised for not having called to tell him earlier, and stood guard on the bedroom door, beyond which he obviously wanted to look for himself.

Eventually he left and the waiting began again. At twelve-thirty she fed George, but was too anxious to take more than a glass of milk herself. By two o'clock she could stand it no longer, and determined that she would, after all, call the police. She left George in the flat, ran down the stairs to the telephone ... and met Beth just opening the street door.

318

If it was Beth. Her sister wore high heeled shoes instead of the stout brogues which usually protruded from beneath her blue uniform trousers, while the trousers themselves were invisible beneath a full length mink coat.

'Beth?' she whispered, wondering if she had been murdered, and this was a ghost from her past, come back to haunt her. Because definitely this was from the past.

To make it even more unreal, Stephanie caught a glimpse, through the open street door of a taxi pulling away; it was a long time since Beth had been able to afford a taxi.

Beth also carried a large carrier bag, which clinked in a most interesting fashion, and with the mink she wore kid gloves and had a most expensive leather handbag slung over her arm. 'You darling girl,' she said. 'You missed me.'

Stephanie ran behind her as she climbed the stairs. 'I was worried stiff. I thought you'd been robbed or something. Do you know you left your satchel on the pavement?'

'Did I? I meant to throw it in the gutter.'

'Beth! Where did you get that coat? Beth ... you haven't ...' Although she did not see how even Beth could have obtained a mink coat in payment from a man for letting him have her for two hours at the most.

'I bought it,' Beth said. She sailed into the flat, and picked George up from the floor to give him a kiss. 'Now,' she said importantly, taking the bottles of Bollinger form her carry-all. 'We shall drink these, and then you will dress yourself properly, and the boy, and we shall pack up and leave this place. I have reserved a suite at the Savoy for the time being. They are arranging an adjoining bedroom for George.'

'Beth,' Stephanie begged, because as far as she could see her sister had gone mad. 'Oh, Beth ...' then she lost her voice, for Beth was taking off her mink, and instead of a bus conductress's uniform, she was wearing absolutely nothing underneath, not even any under-clothes. 'My God!' she screamed.

'Oh, don't carry on,' Beth said. 'George has seen me naked before.'

'But . . . you went through the streets of London like that?'

'It's a warm afternoon,' Beth pointed out, and let the first cork fly. 'Wheeee. I'm never going to drink anything else from now on.'

'Oh, Beth . . . where are your clothes?'

'I left them on the floor of the changing room at Harrods,' Beth explained, fetching two mugs from the kitchen cupboard and pouring. 'I want to drink a toast. To Georges Mathieu, the only man I ever loved.'

'To . . .' Stephanie could not believe her ears.

'Georges is dead,' Beth told her, drinking heavily, and refilling her glass. 'The least you can do is drink a toast to his memory.'

'Dead? Georges? Oh, poor Georges.'

'He was eighty,' Beth pointed out, 'and I think we may say that he lived a pretty full life. Eighty is not an unreasonable age to die. Although the old sod once told me he was going to live to be a hundred. If I'd stayed with him he probably would have.'

'It really isn't very nice to drink to someone's death,' Stephanie told her, and kept to her single-minded determination to get to the bottom of this problem; as far as she could decide it probably involved shoplifting on a grand scale. 'Now, Beth, this coat . . .'

'He died without apparently altering the will he had made back in 1952,' Beth said. 'Or perhaps he didn't want to alter it. Perhaps he still felt guilty about what he had done. Perhaps he was just too old and tired to bother. We shall never know. But also, perhaps, he did love me, after all. I shall think that, anyway.'

'You mean he left you something in his will?'

'He left me everything,' Beth said, discarding the mug and drinking champagne from the neck of the bottle, allowing it to dribble over her chin and down her neck and between her breasts.

'Everything?' Stephanie's voice had gone up an octave.

'Every Goddamned, sodding, fucking thing,' Beth told her. 'All the bulls, and all of their semen, all the horses, all the pigs, and all the land. All the pink flamingoes. And Château Lorges, of course. I'm not sure if he actually owned the village. I shall have to find out.'

Stephanie sat down. Her legs would no longer support her. Now she did drink her champagne, entirely without meaning to.

Beth refilled her glass. 'Lawson, the solicitor, was a bit vague. He estimated that it might all add up to thirty million francs.'

'Thirty . . .' There were too many zeros involved.

Beth made an airy gesture and emptied champagne over the rug. Stephanie suspected that she might have left Harrods with three bottles rather than two, and consumed one in the taxi. 'Lawson was vague about the conversion rate, too. Apparently it is liable to change or something, as the French are in financial difficulties. Or maybe it's the British. I shall have to find out about that, too. But it works out approximately something between two and a half and three million pounds.'

Stepanie stared at her with her mouth open. George started to clap. He didn't even know what one pound would buy, but he could tell that both his mother and his aunt were ecstatic.

'The income, my dear, the income, is presently something like two hundred thousand pounds a year,' Beth said. 'That again is an estimate, but it must be pretty near the truth, because when I explained to Lawson how poor we were, he immediately gave me what he called a float, of twenty-five thousand. Pounds.'

Stephanie's mouth slowly closed. If these were the wages of Beth's sins, then her morality had to be all wrong.

'So come along,' Beth said, and rumpled George's

hair. 'Both of you. We are dining in the Riverside Restaurant. I've booked a table.'

George actually went to bed, with a maid detailed to listen for him. Stephanie wanted to concentrate as much as Beth was trying to do, no easy task after a bottle of champagne each and while drinking Latour with the meal.

'You'll have to go back to France,' Stephanie said. 'At least for a while.'

'Oh, I mean to go back to France for good,' Beth said. 'Bugger England is what I say. At least they never locked me up in France.'

'Will you go to Lorges?'

'Oh, yes. I'm looking forward to that.'

'Will you live at the château?'

Beth considered. 'I may, until the estate is wound up. But I don't think I'll stay there permanently. I'll put the château on the market. But I do want to remember Georges. Give him a nice big headstone and that sort of thing. The people of Lorges will appreciate that, don't you think?'

Stephanie couldn't imagine the people of Lorges appreciating anything Beth might do, if Georges had said a word about the way she had left him.

'But France, yes,' Beth went on. 'I think I shall buy a house on the Riviera. A villa outside Cannes, perhaps. Yes. That's where I've always wanted to live. And I'm going to buy a yacht. I've always wanted a yacht.'

'You don't know how to sail a yacht,' Stephanie objected.

'I'll have a crew, silly. And who said anything about sailing? It's going to be a motor yacht.'

'But what about all the bulls and the horses and the pigs?'

'With chrome all over the place,' Beth said dreamily. 'And a chef in a white hat to cook the most exquisite meals, and a barman in a red jacket, and a captain in a white cap and an engineer who will say, yes, ma'am, whenever I want to put to sea.'

Beth, Stephanie recalled, had always been an avid reader of her fellow countryman, Conrad.

'But the horses, and the . . .'

'And the semen,' Beth said, giggling. 'Oh, they'll be sold as well.' Then she grew serious, leaning across the dining table while the orchestra provided them with some privacy. 'Now I want to talk about you. How much do you want?'

'Me? I don't want anything.'

'Don't be absurd. What did your last book earn you?'

'Well, Peter says it could amount to five thousand pounds, this time. So . . .'

'Five thousand pounds,' Beth said contemptuously. 'I will settle . . . twenty thousand a year on you.'

'I don't want Georges' money,' Stephanie protested.

'It isn't Georges' money any more,' Beth reminded her. 'It's my money. And you are my sister. I don't intend to argue about it. I'll settle the same on Anna when she gets out of gaol, if she's prepared to behave, and on Tony, whenever he turns up.'

'Whenever,' Stephanie muttered.

'Oh, I'll be able to find him now. I'll hire a detective. As long as he has got himself out of England there'll be no problem.'

'You do realise that he was one of Szabo's strong arm boys himself?' Stephanie asked. 'Or at least engaged in defrauding and threatening people?'

'He happens to be our brother,' Beth said crushingly.

Stephanie decided it would be pointless to pursue the matter. 'What about Father?' she asked.

Beth scratched her chin. 'He'll come with me, of course. He needs looking after, and a bit of real luxury will do him good.'

'Aren't you going to give him any money?'

'No,' Beth said. 'He'd only waste it on cheap booze. No, I'll look after him for the rest of his life. After all, he's nearly sixty-eight. He needs looking after.'

Stephanie suspected that Beth was going to enjoy looking after Father far more than Father was going to enjoy being looked after, by Beth; Beth only appreciated men when they were forced to be her absolute slaves.

She was certainly getting set to resume her old life style, but on an even more arrogant level than ever. Stephanie didn't think she could stand that. She loved Beth dearly, more than anyone else in the whole world, save George, and she knew just how much she owed her, beginning with her very life during the walk from Poland, she was sure. But she just didn't want to live in that fashion, and she certainly didn't want to live in the same house as Anna and Tony again – she was not even sure she wanted to see them again. She didn't see how she could, anyway, without being revealed to be truly Stephanie Trene, and that she was determined would never happen.

'You could at least look happy about the situation,' Beth suggested. 'I am never going to be unhappy again.'

Stephanie took a long breath. 'And you're going to be all set up, with Anna and Tony and Father . . . Beth, would you be very angry if I did emigrate to the States?'

'Angry? My darling girl, you must do anything you want to. But are you sure that is what you want to do?' She frowned. 'I may have some difficulty in paying you your money, what with these stupid exchange control regulations, or don't they have them in France?'

'It doesn't matter,' Stephanie said. 'If you really want to pay me something, it can be done as soon as I'm officially regarded as being a British non-resident. There are things like blocked sterling accounts, which are legal, and from which funds can be freely transferred overseas after a few years.'

'How do you know all of these things?' Beth wondered. 'I suppose it comes from researching your books. And of course you're going to give up your British citizenship in any event,' she added thoughtfully. 'Aren't you? I'm certainly going to give up mine. We still have French citizenship, you know. At least, I think so. I must check into that.' She took a gold plated ballpoint pen from her handbag and started making notes on her linen napkin.

'I don't know,' Stephanie mused. 'I haven't quite made up my mind about that, although I suppose I shall. I certainly want George to become an American citizen. And I'm sure that's where my future as a writer lies.'

'Of course it does, my darling,' Beth agreed sceptically. 'And in America you'll be able to meet some nice man and get yourself set up. The first thing you must do is divorce Trene, or have the marriage annulled. I should think even the Pope would give you a dispensation for that. After all, the man's a murderer.'

Beth wouldn't care if she got a dispensation or not, so far as Stephanie was aware, her sister hadn't attended a single mass or been to confession once since coming out of prison. Stephanie herself had been to church every Sunday morning since the birth of George, just to give thanks for that huge chunk of happiness, the only thing she had salvaged, or wanted to salvage, from her marriage. Nowadays, George went with her. But the idea of considering a divorce, dispensation or not, of having to go through a court appearance and have all the muck of Geoffrey's trial raked up again, was appalling. She would need the hide of a rhinoceros, or of a Beth, to survive that.

Anyway, where was the point? She was never going to marry again. She couldn't pretend she didn't miss sex, didn't sometime wake up at night hugging her pillow and thinking she was back in Geoffrey's arms. But she knew should would never again be able to trust herself in the all embracing love and confidence of a marriage.

So she gave a mock shudder. 'Never.' And then gave a real shudder as she thought of something. 'But Beth, I want you to promise me something.'

Beth raised an eyebrow.

'I want you to promise me on your word of honour

325

that you will never tell anyone, not even Anna, or Tony, especially not Anna or Tony, who I really am and what I am doing. Please. I couldn't bear the thought of Geoffrey finding out.'

Beth nodded. 'That would be grim. Mind you, I don't see how on earth, once we are all together again as a family, you are going to stop Anna and Tony finding out. But I promise *I* will never tell them.'

Stephanie squeezed her hand. As far as she could see, they were a very long way from being one happy family again, so that did not appear to be a problem.

'Now,' Beth said, 'let us go upstairs and sleep like ladies, in separate beds.' She got up and stalked towards the steps to the lobby.

The waiter hurried behind her. 'You forgot your napkin, madam,' he said.

Stephanie had feared that there might be some problems in emigrating to America, what with national quotas and the continuing apprehension that someone might delve too deeply into her past. But there was no problem at all, once both her publishers and her American agent, Alice Todd, were prepared to vouch for her, and once it was confirmed that in addition to her steadily building reputation and royalties, she was in receipt of a private income of twenty thousand pounds a year.

'You are a sly one,' Peter Brynne remarked without rancour. 'I really worried about you.'

Stephanie could only smile apologetically; there was no way she could tell him the truth.

'Anyway,' he said. 'I shall be sorry to see you go, although I'm sure you're taking a step forward. I hope I will continue to handle your European business?'

'Of course,' she promised.

She was on top of the world, even if she was staggered by New York rents. But she soon found herself a modest apartment across the Hudson, as she was under no obligation to go into Manhattan except when she felt like it, and settled in more happily than ever before in her life. For the first time she felt free, of her past and of all responsibilities expect George. Even the waves of depression sweeping across her new country as the Vietnam war dragged on from bad to worse, failed to deflate her buoyancy.

George was quickly placed in a nursery school, and she had all the time she wanted to write. And to sight-see, when the mood took her. And to write. And to meet the people who could further her career. And to write.

But the people were important, too. Alice, a petite, demure woman, who was yet regarded as one of the toughest agents in the country, was very ambitious for her, and invited her to every party she threw, in addition to securing for her invitations to attend every other literary party she could discover. Stephanie was reluctant at first, remembering the let-down of her first American literary party, but Alice accompanied her to the first few, carefully introducing her around, and refusing to allow anyone to talk about anything but Stephanie's last book in her presence – unless they wanted to talk about her next book instead. The parties were pretty boring affairs, and Stephanie only attended them because Alice insisted she did. Nor were there any immediate results, in either increased advances or sales, but then she met Ed Martinez, who was Managing Editor of Folsom Books, a paperback house.

He promptly invited her out to dinner, which alarmed her. The last man to take her out to dinner had been Geoffrey, and she felt that while where lunches were concerned it seemed natural to discuss only business, especially as there was only the office to return to, dinner was after the business day was completed – and there was only bed to return to afterwards.

But she accepted, because Alice had told her that Martinez was a very important publisher as well as a brilliant editor, and even more important, because Folsom Books had just bought her fourth novel.

As it turned out, Martinez did only want to talk

business. 'I like how you write,' he told her. 'Have you ever thought of branching out?'

She had no idea what he was talking about, as he could see.

'I mean, trying a different style, or at least, a different genre. The trouble with 'straight' novels is that they're difficult to market at any high level, at least for us. The hardcover boys now, they're over the moon with a ten thousand copy sale, and a few positive reviews will get them that. We really like to think in terms of six figures. Sales, I mean,' he added hastily. 'And that's difficult to achieve with a straight book unless there's been a film or it deals with a very hot subject. When it can hardly be classified as a straight book any more. Genre novels have a much more guaranteed sale.'

'I appreciate that,' she said. 'But I don't know any genre in which to write.' But she was excited. Folsom Books had actually paid ten thousand dollars for the paperback rights to her 'straight' novel, and although she would have to share that with the hardcover house, it was still the biggest advance she had ever been offered. But now he was hinting that it might be possible to make more.

'Have you ever thought of historical novels?'

'I wouldn't even know how to begin one.'

'Oh, rubbish. It's just like writing any other book, only a historical should be longer than average, and the emphasis is different. But your style would lend itself to it. You know, if you don't mind my saying so, it's a little stiff, sometimes stilted. Do you know what one of my copy-editors said the other day? "Mrs Johnson writes as if she hadn't learned English as her mother tongue, but as if she picked it up in her teens, or something." Don't take offence,' he added , as Stephanie shot him a glance – which he misinterpreted, because far from taking offence she was only worried that he might be starting to probe. 'I'm not criticising your style. I find it refreshingly different, as I said. And natural for a big, lusty historical. You see, a good bodice-ripper always does well. Maybe never as well as a novel which has everyone talking and hits the top ten, but equally it never does as badly as the average novel which sells a couple of thousand copies and is buried.'

'Bodice ripper?'

He grinned. 'It's a trade term. Historicals rely on sex as much as on action, or background, or pageantry. Don't get me wrong. The actual history needs to be carefully researched, and as accurate as possible, bearing in mind, always, that your reader will be looking for plot and characterisation and action more than history.

'After all, Shakespeare himself handed out a few anachronisms in his time, and even more, he compressed history or reversed it for the sake of the plot. The plot's the thing, eh? That's what every budding novelist should have pinned up above his or her desk. But your readers will also expect their heroines to have their clothes torn off from time to time, hence bodice-ripper. In this day and age, lusting fingers are even required to go in search of panties from time to time, although your heroines would never have worn them. So it's pure melodrama, more than great literature. It's what people want to read, and that is what writing is all about.

'You should never forget for a moment – and so many people, especially the critics, do forget it all the time – that all the really successful writers, beginning with Chaucer and coming down through Shakespeare to Defoe and Scott and Dickens and in our day Hemingway and above all, Christie, or Fleming, wrote what the public wanted to read, not what the critics of their time called great literature. So maybe you will never be called a great writer until after you're dead, as happened to most of those – but at least you'll have laughed all the way to the bank.'

She was intrigued, if uneasy about the scenario he was painting. She had never considered herself a great writer, but she had always felt her books were honest outpourings of her emotions and her experiences. To write pure entertainment seemed deceitful – to herself, anyway. 'What about Dashman?' she asked. These were her hardcover publishers.

'Oh, they wouldn't be interested. I'm thinking of a paperback original. That's good for you, you see, because you'd have the whole paperback advance for yourself, as well as the royalties, instead of having to share them with your hardcover people.'

'But wouldn't they object? They have an option on my next book.'

'They have an option on the next book by Stephanie Johnson. We'd use a pseudonym for the new line. You'd keep up your Stephanie Johnson books, of course. Alice tells me you do nothing but write. Well, hell, surely you can do two books in a year? Think about it. This could be the start of something tremendous, for you. You would double your income, maybe even treble it.'

She did think about it, but remained afraid she wouldn't be able to carry it off, quite apart from the nagging feeling that she would be prostituting her art. But then a letter arrived from Beth. After telling her what an exciting time she and Father were having settling in – she hadn't spent any time in Lorges after all, merely placed everything on the market and then gone straight on to the Riviera where she had apparently bought a villa – she wrote, 'And now I have two enormous pieces of news, one good and one bad. Although I think they are both good. The good good news is that Tony is back with us. I put an advert in the papers, just like Lawson did for me, and he answered it. I'm over the moon. So is he. He's had such a bad time, Stephanie, always hiding, knowing he was wanted by the police . . . He got out of England, of course, and has been hiding in France, making a living as a petty crook, you know the sort of thing, larceny, conning people, fencing . . . can you imagine? It must have been dreadful. As a matter of fact, between you and me, my darling, he has developed very disturbingly and has become what you would call a wide boy. But I am determined to change all of that and reform him. He wants to be helped, and has promised to stay with me, and live on the income I am giving him. I know there will be problems from time to time, but it is such fun having him around again. And at least he isn't on drugs!'

Stephanie put down the letter to stare into space. Beth could almost be considered a fool, the way she doted over her family. Giving away money left and right, taking them in from the cold as and when they felt like coming . . . She sighed, and picked up the letter again.

'And now, darling, brace yourself. The good bad news is . . . that you're a widow.'

Stephanie gasped, and nearly crumpled the sheet.

'Isn't that a relief?' Beth wrote. 'It all happened quite without warning. Your husband was released from gaol last month, after, according to the newspapers, having had the most terrible time. Apparently, as a stool pigeon, the authorities didn't dare let any of the other prisoners near him; he spent the entire five years in solitary confinement, for his own protection. Well, of course, I think he deserved everything he got. Anyway, he was finally let out, and would you believe it, was found shot through the head in some back alley just three weeks afterwards. Now there is justice for you. Obviously Bertie still commands some respect, even inside Dartmoor, although the police don't seem able to relate it back to him. So my darling, you are at last a free woman.'

There was a lot more, but Stephanie had stopped reading. A free woman. My God, she thought, but that is perfectly true. Because suddenly she did feel free; she had not hitherto understood how heavy a weight Geoffrey had been on her mind. Did she feel no regret, no remorse, no grief? Then she would indeed be like Beth. She found it difficult to recognise any emotions at all, other than relief. Geoffrey had been her husband for three years, and she had given him every single thing, physical and emotional, that she possessed. He had made her happy during those three years, and out of their union had come George, the most valuable creature in the whole world, to her. Yet throughout those three years he had also deceived her without blinking an eye-lid, and in addition to his drug habit he had been a cold hearted thug, who had smiled at people while he had been condemning them to the loss of their businesses and even, as with men like Alberto, to grievous bodily harm. And finally had committed murder, at the behest of his employer. His defence lawyer had made much of that at his trial, that he had been commanded and obeyed, that the real crime had been Szabo's. Yet Geoffrey had even then been engaged in betraying that employer, in an attempt to save his own skin.

No, she thought, she could feel no grief. Yet she found herself weeping as she recalled those years together. She would never be as hard as Beth. She lacked the mental equipment.

But she felt free, and keen to earn all the money she could from her profession. She agreed to write what Martinez wanted, and got to work. He told her to be as far out as she liked, sexually.

'If it's a shade too hot, I'll ask you to cut bits,' he said. 'But write them first. Okay?'

'Okay,' she agreed. And was amazed at the outcome as she wrote a swashbuckling adventure about Poland and Germany and Hungary in the eighteenth century, with damsels in distress and gallant young officers in Hussar uniforms and roguish old lechers with sadistic tastes, and floggings and rapes and tortures and battles and dramatic confrontations . . . It was tremendous fun. More to the point, it was tremendously successful. If not appreciated, or even noticed, by the critics, who had always previously approved of her books, it was lapped up by the public, and earned seventy-five thousand dollars in royalties. Ed had paid her twenty thousand as an advance, far more than she had even been offered before. Now he was so pleased he offered her a hundred thousand for a sequel. Combined with the steady ten to fifteen she was now pulling in, world-wide, for her straight novels, she suddenly found herself a wealthy woman.

But before *The Woman on Horseback* was even published, she was again reminded that she was still a member of a family, and therefore could never be quite free. A letter arrived from Beth announcing that she was returning to England the following week, to greet Anna on her release from prison.

'Oh, Stephanie,' Beth wrote. 'Would you believe that I am quite nervous? How I wish you were here.'

Beth had hoped Tony might be able to accompany her, but as he did not dare return to England, even after six years, she left him in France in charge of Father. Not that he needed a lot of looking after. He did nothing but sit on the verandah of the house she had bought – it was virtually on the beach – watching the topless sun-bathers through binoculars and drinking wine – she wouldn't allow him spirits.

Father was in many ways a mystery to her. He would never talk of the years he had spent wandering over Europe after the collapse of Germany. Clearly he had not been looking for them. He had never spoken either of his life in England before he had discovered his children were still alive. She had the evidence of her eyes that he had been very poor, and her eyes could also tell her that he had suffered physically; the tremendous strength she remembered had disappeared. She also believed that he had been afraid of something. Even in the bright sunlight of Cannes he would occasionally twitch with mysterious anxiety. But she had no idea what he thought about as he stared at the beach; what secrets were locked away in his brain, even if he got any kick out of the naked nipples he stared at. And she did not really want to find out. Like Stephanie, her instincts warned her that Father was not really an admirable man, perhaps even that in saving their lives by taking them from Warsaw he had been more interested in saving his own. Unlike Stephanie, however, she was content to recognise that he was her father, and thus her responsibility. Accepting that, and more, being able to do something about it, made her feel good in herself, just as accepting Tony back and forgiving him and caring for him had made her feel good.

And now Anna. Beth put her Rolls on the ferry from Boulogne, having driven up from the south, disembarked at Folkestone, and drove up to London. The prison governor had been good enough to inform her the exact hour of Anna's release, and she left the car down a side street and walked to the prison gate, wrapped in her mink, attracting envious and startled glances from passersby, busily suppressing her nervousness and reminding herself that she held all the aces nowadays, and that it was simply a matter of being forceful and confident . . . as she always had been.

Anna registered consternation. 'Beth?' she whispered. 'Is it really you?'

Beth felt she could more appropriately have asked that question of her sister. Anna's magnificent hair had been cut short, and she had lost a lot of weight. The result was not unattractive, as Anna had always had a tendency to plumpness, but more important, all the ebullience had left her. Beth, having experienced prison herself, did not suppose the change had been caused by Anna's having been locked up for five years; the facts of her drug habit had been brought out in court, and she had clearly been given the coldest of turkeys.

But also a long time ago. She looked perfectly fit. 'Of course it's me, my dear girl,' Beth said, giving her a hug. 'Come along, I've a car waiting.'

'But where are we going?' Anna asked.

'To my home,' Beth said.

'But . . .' Anna stopped, goggling at the Rolls. 'We're not going in that?'

334

'Of course we are.' Beth opened the door for her.

'You mean Bertie sent for me?' Anna cried in delight.

'No,' Beth said coldly. 'Bertie did not send for you. Bertie is never going to send for you again. This is my car.'

'I don't understand,' Anna said.

Beth explained all she thought necessary on the drive back down to Folkestone. She didn't intend to spend a day more in England than she had to.

'You were born lucky,' Anna commented when she had finished. 'If you fell off the top of Mount Everest you'd land on your feet.'

'I'm sure I'd break my ankles,' Beth pointed out. Then she told her about Father and Tony.

Anna didn't seem the least impressed, or even interested, that Father had turned up. But Tony ... 'That little rat,' she said. 'Beth! I want to go and see Bertie.'

'Now, darling,' Beth said, 'don't be ridiculous. Bertie is in Dartmoor. That's the other end of the country.'

'Can't we drive down there? I have to see him, Beth. Please.'

'Why do you have to see him?' Beth asked.

'Because I love him. He's my man. He's all I want in this world. Please, Beth.'

'You are being ridiculous,' Beth told her. 'That man is a thug and a murderer. I am going to have to be very straight with you, Anna. I am in a position to offer you the very best things in life, at last. For the rest of your life no one is ever going to harm you or trouble you again. But that will only happen, I am only going to protect you and help you and keep you out of trouble, and make you happy again, if you do as I say. If Tony can do it, so can you. And the first thing you have to do is forget about Istvan Szabo. He was a disaster for you. For us all.'

Anna did not reply to that, but her face settled into an expression Beth knew very well; Anna was making plans. But Beth was not overly worried. She intended to watch her sister like a hawk, and she also felt sure she would not have to act the gaoler for very long. She meant to dazzle Anna with the quality of the life she could live – if she stayed with her sister.

Her success was even more immediate and complete than she had dreamed. On the drive down, Anna was clearly impressed, both by the car and the quality of the two hotels they used for overnight stops. But that was nothing to her reaction when she saw the house outside Cannes, with its Moorish arches and its brilliant white stucco, its cooling breezes and its views over the beach and the Mediterranean, its white-jacketed butler and its attentive housemaids. Beth had reconstructed the Hertfordshire scenario, in a much more beautiful setting.

But she only gave Anna time to be thrilled with the house before she whisked her off on the boat. This was a Baglietto, a large, very fast, and beautifully appointed Italian-built motor cruiser, the last word in elegant power, from the huge curved double bed in the master cabin to the spiral staircase, from the bridge deck which looked like the cockpit of a spaceship to the two five-hundred-horsepower diesels which pushed her along at a comfortable twenty-two knots. The yacht was more than Beth could strictly speaking afford, and cost a fortune to run and maintain, for it required a crew of four, a captain, who wore a white cap, an engineer, who touched his blue cap and said, 'Ready for sea, madame,' whenever she looked at him, a pretty little girl who acted as deckhand and maid, and a barman-cum-chef, who wore a red jacket when serving drinks and a white hat when cooking.

Anna was fascinated, and Beth was delighted. She was equally delighted that Tony had also fallen in love with the yacht, which she called *Poseidon*, and liked nothing better that to helm it, the captain standing indulgently at his side. They would pop down to Corsica or the Balearics for the night whenever they felt like it, Anna and Beth stretched out on the after sundeck in the nude while the sun gave them golden tans, anchoring for the evening in sheltered bays like Calvi or Girolata or Cabrera, and sit out beneath the stars to be served their aperitifs and gourmet dinners.

Anna was in seventh heaven, and Beth humoured her in every way she could, raising no objection to her going topless on the beach. Beth went topless on the beach herself to keep her company – and even Stephanie, when she flew across from America for a visit, surprisingly agreed to go topless in public.

Stephanie, even more to Beth's surprise, was now doing very well and earning a fortune, even if her books weren't terribly well known in Europe as yet. Beth was delighted that she had at last visited with them, and seemed prepared to be friends with Anna and Tony; she had had to work very hard to reconcile Anna and Tony in the first place, and now she felt the family was again complete, a single unit, able to take on the world once more ... and now from a position of enormous strength. She was tremendously proud of Stephanie, and relieved when Stephanie accepted that it was no longer possible to conceal her success or her pseudonym from her brother and sister – nor was there any reason for it now that Geoffrey was dead. Of course the old intimacy was gone, especially with Tony, but Stephanie would have been less than human had she not been pleased to illustrate her success, especially as, in real terms, she far more than Beth had earned that success.

Even Anna had to accept that Stephanie was a changed woman, for the better. Not only had she resumed wearing her hair loose, and the only spectacles she ever used nowadays were Gucci dark glasses, and her clothes were more expensive and elegant than Anna remembered from before the trial, but she had gained enormously in confidence, had lost that 'Is this really me?' look which Anna remembered so well. And all without any physical evidence of the traumas she had gone through. It was actually impossible to believe, in the summer of 1971, that Stephanie was thirty-five years old, or that she was the mother of a seven-year-old boy. But George was a joy to have around, a bubbling, happy child who basked in his mother's love and might never have known a hungry day in his life.

'There is no reason why you should not do as well,' Beth told Anna, as they waved the jetliner away from Nice airport. 'For heaven's sake, you are better educated than Stephanie. She never even got to finishing school, much less university.'

'Not like Tony,' Anna muttered, because she had not entirely lost her sly ways. And anyway, Beth knew, she was thinking less of Tony than that she was thirty-nine years old, rapidly approaching the dreaded demarcation line of forty. As if forty was an obstacle, she thought, with a squaring of her magnificent shoulders.

Oddly enough, although she well understood the point Anna had been making about Tony, Beth did not worry about her brother, mainly because she had no ambitions for him. To some people it might indeed have seemed a tragic waste of a young man with undoubted brains, Cambridge educated, having degenerated into a useless layabout. But he filled her ideal of a brother perfectly. Whatever his crimes, he appeared to have reformed, and all she now wanted from him was what she was getting, his constant support and attendance.

He received a handsome salary from her, and had the freedom to pick up any of the huge migrant and drifting population of young women who flowed to and fro along the Riviera. Sometimes he even brought one home to dinner, to have her impressed with the standard of Beth's household and cuisine, the elegance of his sisters – and as part of a bed bargain.

Beth didn't really mind that either. She was rather pleased about it. Tony was proving the perfect Father-minder, as there seemed to be a real affection between the two men, and that gave her a lot more time to forward her own plans. That he might only be recuperating from his grim existence of the previous seven

338

years, be content to mark time until he found something he wanted to do, did cross her mind – but she was content to face that problem when she came to it.

Beth had a great many plans still waiting to be implemented. At forty-one she was a very handsome woman, with the figure of an Amazon. Walking the beaches topless she could not help but attract attention, and she amused Anna and herself by occasionally taking the Baglietto across to the Iles de Poquerolles, and joining the nudists in Levant or Port Man. As she was also manless, the attention had crystallised into a wide choice of eager squires, out of whom she had allowed John Alten to be her most constant companion. Alten was taller than she, an important consideration, good looking in a battered fashion, and very wealthy, as well as being a witty companion. Once Beth gave him a little encouragement, such as allowing him to coat her with sun tan oil, front and back, he rapidly fell in love with her and asked her to marry him.

Nor did she immediately refuse him, because he possessed another asset which was far more important than his money or his looks or his devotion – he was an American, a retired oil dealer, who had made his fortune very young, and was currently enjoying the flesh-pots of the Mediterranean before returning to his native Los Angeles. He had been married once, but had been divorced for several years. Beth had never given up her dream of getting to America. Of course, it was no longer necessary, in terms of achieving worldly success, or even safety. As far as she could see there was no one left in all the world to trouble her, and she had all the money she could possibly use, especially since she had at last sold Château Lorges to an hotel chain for her asking price. She was pleased about that, and not only because of the money. The only possible use for a building like the château was as an hotel, and its sale severed her last link with that village she regarded with nothing but unpleasant memories.

But America remained a dream. If it could be accomplished, with her past. Because it could not only be accomplished for her. If she went, Tony and Father and Anna had to come, too, and that might not prove very easy, she knew. Having Stephanie firmly installed over there seemed her best bet at the moment. Unless something could be done with Alten.

She was still mentally debating the matter, and slowly coming to the conclusion that her best prospect was to confide in him, at least up to a point. If he loved her as much as he pretended he would surely be able to find a way round the rules. The real question was whether he loved her enough to overlook a bigamous past. But she did not think that should prove an insuperable handicap, as she could swear that she had been led to believe that Georges was dead when she had married Paine. But then it seemed that not only would Anna's future be settled first, but that she could be used as a test case.

As had been the case ever since Beth could remember, Anna remained the number one problem in her life. If she seemed to have accepted that Szabo would never again be allowed into *her* life, unless she intended to give up the luxury in which she now found herself, that was no guarantee that she had forgotten him. Beth was also worried about the drug habit. Anna had been wrenched away from it in prison, but was the cure permanent? There were other aspects of the Anna which emerged from prison which also bothered her. The old Anna had been impulsive rather than introspective. This new Anna had become a brooder, a dreamer of dark dreams, Beth suspected. Stephanie had also been a dreamer, but no one could ever have doubted that Stephanie's dreams were of light and air, laughter and adventure – as was proved by her books, even when she was trying to write seriously. But Anna had become an altogether more sombre character than she remembered, or wanted around the place.

She had worked away at tying up all the possible loose ends which could conceivably interfere with

340

anything Anna might want to do, or need to do. Beth had done this for all of them, and Anna had been by far the least trouble. She had restored her French nationality, as Tony had regained his. Thank heavens, Beth thought, that whatever the life he had led since fleeing England, he had kept himself clear of the law. Now there was a continuing hassle as to whether or not he was still eligible for military service, but she had lawyers working on it, and as he was thirty-seven and had done some national service with the Royal Navy, she was confident of winning her point.

Father, who had never had a passport as he had entered England illegally, had been more difficult. But she had solved that by taking him out of England just as illegally – on what had ostensibly been a day trip to Boulogne, from which he had simply not returned. Then she had told the French authorities that her father had only just reached France from Poland, having escaped the Communists to be with his daughter. Father had been very anxious about that, as he seemed terrified to have any links with Poland revealed to anyone, but Beth had reassured him, and the French had been their usual understanding selves, and given him nationality and a passport.

They could all therefore claim to have maximum mobility, but while Beth was resolved that Father and Tony should accompany her wherever she went, she was equally determined to have Anna off her hands by then, providing she could be sure that Anna, like a pet dog, went to a good home. And that needed some co-operation from Anna herself.

Obviously, the answer to all these problems was an even deeper immersion in the voluptuous life of the Riviera – as long as there were no drugs involved. Beth began to entertain on a great scale. She held luncheon parties at her house where everyone was supposed to strip off and plunge into the pool. She held midnight dinner parties-cum-cruises on board *Poseidon* at which, once the yacht was several miles offshore, the engines were stopped and everyone stripped off and plunged into several hundred fathoms of dark water. On every occasion the champagne flowed and men of all ages and nationalities swarmed around the beautiful Janska women.

When, early in 1972, Stephanie returned for another visit, even more flushed with success and confidence – and with her magnificently mature figure and her huge eyes and her wealth of dark brown hair, Stephanie was even more beautiful nowadays than Anna – the Mathieu mansion really hummed. It was a treat to see Father looking so well and happy, wearing his blue yachting cap and blazer and his white trousers, smiling benignly at the guests as he quietly got drunk.

Beth supposed Stephanie could have had her pick of any man on the coast. But Stephanie wasn't interested. She didn't appear to need a man; she got her kicks out of the books she wrote. And Anna was still lovely enough to be intensely attractive, however old she might be. The problem was in getting Anna attracted back.

Beth was nearing despair when, in the spring of 1972, just after Stephanie had returned to America, and when Anna had been out of prison for some three years and surely should have recovered from that experience, she received information from England, where she employed a lawyer to keep an eye on things. Istvan Szabo had been paroled from prison to hospital, despite having served less than nine years of his sentence. Apparently he had heart trouble. But then he had disappeared from hospital, and had not yet been found.

The manhunt had not been carried out very vigorously, so far as Beth could make out from reading the newspapers, because the doctors had told the police that Bertie did not have very long to live. Beth was relieved about that, but disturbed that there was no definite news of his death, and beside herself with worry that Anna might find out. But Anna never read any newspapers or watched any television. She spent

342

her days either entertaining or sunning herself, dreaming her dark dreams.

A week later Lionel Hunt came to one of Beth's parties. He was a well known London neurosurgeon, taking a Riviera holiday, and a handsome, attractive bachelor. And he was immediately smitten with Anna. Anna's response was as negative towards him as towards anyone else, but when Beth heard that he had just been offered and accepted a post in the United States, she decided that there would never be a better prospect for Anna, or a better opportunity for her to test the temperature of the water for herself.

Hunt was invited to the house or out on the boat with great regularity, and two days before he was due to return to England to wind up his position there, Beth cornered him for a tête-à-tête, which flattered him enormously, and convinced him that Anna was really very fond of him but was too shy to say so. Mainly because, Beth explained, she felt it would be pointless.

'But I do love her,' Hunt protested. 'I have asked her to marry me, and she has refused.'

'Oh, she doesn't doubt your love,' Beth told him. 'It's because of the court case.'

Hunt raised his eyebrows, and Beth told him as much of the truth as she felt was necessary. She had calculated things as best as she was able, which was why she waited until he was on the point of leaving France. She reasoned that if he was shocked and horrified that Anna could have been the mistress of a man like Szabo, they would have lost nothing; he was off to the States anyway in a few months and would disappear from their lives. Whereas, if he really did love Anna . . .

It turned out that he did. 'The poor girl,' he said, several times. 'The poor girl. What a sad world it can be.'

'Tragic,' Beth agreed, suppressing a sniff. 'But what's done is done, and there is an end to it. I don't see any way round it.'

'Nonsense,' he declared. 'Of course we can get round it. She will be going to the States as my wife.'

'That isn't going to matter to the Americans,' Beth pointed out.

'She will go as my French wife, Anna Mathieu, from Lorges and now Cannes,' he explained. 'I know a bit about bureacracy, Beth. It is extremely unlikely that anyone at the United States Embassy in Paris, at this distance of time, is going to relate Anna Mathieu, of Lorges in France, to a woman who by coincidence happened to be named Anna Mathieu, of London, who was sent to prison nine years ago, especially when she is presented to them as the wife of Lionel Hunt.'

'Do you really think it will work?' Beth asked.

'Of course. If they want me, they must want my wife.' Hunt said confidently. And he was a very confident man, like most successful surgeons. 'The only question is, will Anna be my wife?'

'Leave that to me,' Beth promised.

Anna was far easier to convince than she had anticipated. She was not only becoming increasingly fed up with living like a bird in a gilded cage, she had also become intensely jealous of Stephanie's success. When Beth pointed out that as Hunt's wife she would also be going to the States to live, and that a successful neurosurgeon had to earn more money than a reasonably successful author, Anna became very interested indeed. Besides, Lionel Hunt was a very attractive man.

They were married in the Cannes house, Beth throwing the most lavish of her parties. They looked so handsome together, and Lionel was such an upright, capable, an clearly loving, character, that Beth almost wept herself. Her only disappointment was that it had to happen so quickly, all within forty-eight hours, that it proved impossible for Stephanie to make the wedding as George had flu.

Truly, Beth thought, the way she dotes on that child ... But despite Stephanie's absence, she knew that slowly everything was falling into place. Only Tony and Father and herself were left.

That evening, after the guests had gone, she accepted

John Alten's proposal of marriage, and for the first time let him spend the night with her in the huge bedroom overlooking the sea. She felt as she had done on that first married night with Georges, more than twenty years ago, lying in the turret room at the château. And as she was at once full of champagne and this was the first man she had been to bed with since before going to prison, it was like that night in other ways as well. She really let herself go, remembered everything she had been taught at Madame Suchet's, and left Alten both an exhausted and happy man.

Then she confessed her bigamy to him, stressing how it had been accidental, and how she had suffered. He held her tighter than ever, and kept muttering, 'Oh, you poor darling.'

She supposed she might have made another step in the right direction.

Next morning she was awake early, and left John asleep to go downstairs and supervise the cleaning up of the colossal mess left by the revelry. The post had already arrived, and after setting the entire staff, and those she had hired especially, to work, she took it on to the patio and sipped her coffee while she sorted it. At the bottom there was a letter addressed to her in a handwriting she had never seen before. Idly she slit the envelope and took out a single sheet of paper.

'I know all about your father,' she read. 'Anna told me sufficient to make me suspicious, and my investigations have brought results. Now I have found out that he is alive and well and living with you. I am happy for him, but even more for myself. If I were to tell the Israelis where Josef Janski can be found, they would have him in a moment. Remember Eichmann! Josef Janski would also be executed. Only your money can save him. Wait for my call, and do nothing stupid, or your father will die. Bertie.'

THE THIRTEENTH CHRONICLE

June 1985

'Mr Hunt will see you now, Mr Meyer,' said the nurse.

Meyer raised his eyebrows in her choice of titles, although he knew that in England surgeons preferred to be called mister, and Hunt might have insisted on the same procedure over here. But he was too aware of being virtually at the end of his quest to bother about trifles like that.

He followed the white-clad girl up the stairs and along a corridor, almost bumping into her when she suddenly stopped.

'You will be careful,' she warned. 'Sometimes any mention of his wife can have a very bad effect on him.' She gave a bright smile. 'But I think he is in one of his better moods today.'

She opened the door and stepped inside. 'I'll leave this ajar,' she said in a stage whisper. 'Mr Hunt? Doctor? Here's someone to see you.'

Meyer stepped inside, struggling to get his bearings. He was not in an office, as he had expected, but in one of the hospital rooms. It was a very nice room, with windows opening on to a terrace, which in turn overlooked a lawn. Down there people were being pushed or walked to and fro by white-coated men and women. Up here a man sat in an easy chair, just inside the terrace door, enjoying the hot breeze which came out of the Everglades. He wore pyjamas and a dressing gown, but otherwise looked perfectly healthy, although much older than Meyer had expected; his hair was quite white.

Now Lionel Hunt slowly turned his head. 'A visitor?' He seemed surprised.

Meyer glanced at the nurse. She gave him an encouraging smile, and left the room, but Meyer was so taken aback by the situation he couldn't think of what to say for several seconds.

346

Hunt waited politely. 'I don't get many visitors,' he said, and gave a twisted smile. 'As a matter of fact, I don't get any visitors. What did you say your name was?'

'Bob Meyer,' he said, and held out his hand.

Hunt looked at it curiously for a moment, then grasped it; his fingers were limp. 'I'm Lionel Hunt. Do sit down.'

There was one other chair in the room. Meyer placed it alongside Hunt's and carefully sat down. He now understood what the nurse had meant; this was going to be tricky, and he didn't even have a starting reference, such as knowing what had become of Hunt's wife.

'Nice place here,' Hunt remarked. Even after twelve years he still retained his British accent. 'I've always liked it. I used to work here, you know?'

'Yes,' Meyer said.

Hunt turned his head. 'Did you? How?'

'Ah,' Meyer said. 'Your wife . . .'

He paused, because Hunt had turned his head again. But Hunt was looking animated, rather than upset. 'My wife sent you?'

Meyer swallowed; the man was so eager. But he was here to learn, not to be sympathetic. 'No,' he said. 'I am looking for her.'

Hunt seemed to sag. 'You'll find she's changed,' he muttered.

'I have some information for her,' Meyer lied. 'Information which may well make her wish to see you again.' He was taking a stab in the dark, and being inexpressibly cruel to this shattered hulk of a man, but he was also playing a hunch.

'What sort of information?' Some of the animation returned to Hunt's voice and eyes.

'First tell me where she is,' Meyer said.

Hunt's shoulders rose and fell. 'She could be dead, for all I know.'

Meyer frowned at him. 'Dead?'

'Oh, she won't be dead,' Hunt said. 'Her sort doesn't

347

die. I loved that woman, Mr Meyer. I loved her.' His hand caught Meyer's; his fingers might have belonged to a skeleton.

Meyer resisted the temptation to pull away. 'I know you did, Lionel,' he said. 'Tell me what happened between you.'

Tears dribbled out from Hunt's eyes. 'I loved her,' he said again. 'I lied for her, to get her into this country. And then ...' he sighed. 'She was rotten to the core. They both were. Maybe they all were.'

'Rotten?' Meyer asked gently.

'She was on drugs,' Hunt said. 'Christ, she was on drugs. And booze. She didn't seem so when we married. Nobody told me she'd been using heroin before her gaol term. That sister of hers told me everything else, but not that. We hadn't been here a month when I knew the score. You know what Miami is like. You want it, you can get it. I don't know who she contacted, but she must have started looking for it almost the moment we landed. She'd just cut loose, and go wild. There were men, God knows how many men. There were ... oh, Christ, I don't want to talk about it.'

'Why didn't you just throw her out?' Meyer asked, this time with genuine sympathy.

Hunt raised his stricken eyes. 'I loved her, Mr Meyer.'

'So you let her ruin you.'

Hunt uttered another sigh. 'I loved her,' he repeated. 'I didn't want to see her hurt. I tried to cope with her. I tried everything I knew. I let her call me names ...'

'And you financed her habit,' Meyer reminded him. 'You could have put her in a clinic. You could have put her in this clinic. That would have been the best thing for her.'

'I didn't want to do that,' Hunt said. 'She could be so alive, so vibrant. And she was so beautiful ...'

'But eventually she left you,' Meyer prompted. 'And you had a breakdown.'

'I followed her all over the country. I couldn't eat, couldn't sleep, God, how I loved that woman.'

And still do, Meyer thought, or you'd have chosen a different word to woman.

He leaned forward. 'What happened in the end, Lionel?'

Hunt's shoulders rose and fell once more. 'I don't know for sure. I don't remember. I . . . I remember being in New York, at a house . . . There was a party, and I went in, and there she was, and her sister was there too, and somebody else . . .'

'Where was this party?' Meyer asked. 'What was the address?'

'I don't remember.'

'Try,' Meyer said.

Hunt shook his head. 'It all seemed to go black. I remember a lot of noise. Then there were the police. They said I'd smashed the place up. I don't remember.'

'They arrested you?' He'd be able to get the address from the police.

Hunt shook his head. 'The sister settled the matter. I don't know how. I believe that, anyway. I remember waking up here.' He looked at Meyer with enormous eyes. 'I've always been here. Maybe there wasn't a party at all. Maybe there isn't even an Anna at all. They say I'm mad, Mr Meyer. Do you think I'm mad?'

'I wouldn't say you're mad,' Meyer said carefully. 'Why don't you just get up, get dressed, and walk out of that door.'

'Leave?' Hunt shuddered. 'Go out there? Where is she? I don't know. I don't think I could do that.'

'And you have no idea where Mrs Hunt is now?'

'No.' Hunt's shoulders slumped, then he gave an appealing little smile. 'But I know she'll come back. I know she will. Some day. She really loved me, Mr Meyer. I know she did.'

'I'm sure you're right,' Meyer said, and went downstairs. He stopped at the desk. 'Is this a charity hospital, Sister?' he asked the woman in white.

'Oh, good heavens, no,' she replied, looking shocked at the very suggestion.

'Then tell me who's paying for Mr Hunt, in Room Fourteen.'

'Mr Hunt used to be a member of the faculty here, Mr Meyer,' she said sternly. 'He was our chief surgeon, once.'

'So when he had his breakdown you couldn't throw him out in the street,' Meyer remarked. 'So what happens at the end of every month? You hold a whip around the staff?'

'I'm really not at liberty to say,' she said.

'I think you should be,' Meyer suggested. 'To me. Or I might just get hold of a hunch that you're being paid to keep him here.'

She glared at him. 'Mr Hunt is suffering from a complete rejection of the outside world,' she said. 'It's not just agoraphobia, believe me. He is afraid to go to the toilet without someone at his side.'

'A condition aided no doubt by the drugs you keep pumping into him,' Meyer observed. 'Did I ever tell you that I'm a close personal friend of the Miami District Attorney?'

The nurse made a move. 'You are asking for confidential information, Mr Meyer. But since you are pushing, I'll tell you, in the strictest confidence, that Dr Hunt's expenses are paid by Mrs Vernon Latchman.'

'Mrs who?'

'You must have heard of Vernon Latchman, the industrialist?'

'Oh, that Latchman,' Meyer said. 'Stupid of me.'

'Mrs Latchman is the sister of the novelist. You know, Stephanie Johnson.' She took a copy of *Where the Sun Never Shines* from beneath the counter. 'It's all the rage, right now.'

CHAPTER 13

The Riviera, 1972

Beth stared at the letter for several minutes, while her brain seemed to glow with molten anger. Anna, she thought. Once again Anna had brought disaster on them. The little bitch, she thought. If she had had her in front of her at that moment she would cheerfully have broken her neck. And once she had thought there was no one left in the world who could trouble her.

But the angry heat was still surrounded by the icy cold of her personality. Anna was safe from her, for the time being; she had already left on her honeymoon and she and Lionel were going straight on to the States afterwards. There had been, as Lionel had promised, no problems whatsoever with Anna's visa . . . as Mrs Lionel Hunt. And losing her temper was not going to help.

Rather she reflected, she should be pleased that Anna was not there, because she had no idea what Anna's reactions might be to knowing that her Bertie was again in touch with them, however criminally. In fact, she realised, this was something that Anna could never know about at all. She would have to see to that.

She got up, went upstairs, and into father's bedroom. Josef Janski was sitting up, drinking coffee and eating croissants. 'Why, Beth,' he said. 'You're up early. What a lovely wedding that was.'

'I enjoyed it,' Beth agreed. 'Here's your post.'

He frowned at her – he had never received any post before – and took the letter, while Beth removed the coffee cup from his hand. Wisely, as it turned out, for he would certainly have dropped it; he dropped the letter.

'Oh, God,' he whispered. 'Oh, God in heaven. Beth, they're after me. Beth . . .' He caught her hands. 'We must pray to God.'

'Nobody is after you at this moment,' Beth told him. 'But they will be, if Szabo starts talking. And God has a habit of helping those who help themselves.' She sat on the bed. 'Now tell me, Father, just what he has to talk about.'

Josef Janski gazed at her, then looked away; without actually moving, he seemed to shrink into the bed-clothes.

'I will not be angry,' Beth said. 'I promise. And I am not going to let anyone harm you. I promise that, too. But I must know what I have to fight.'

He sighed. 'When the War started, the Germans ...' Another sigh.

'They occupied Poland and destroyed Warsaw,' Beth prompted. 'They deported the Poles. But they didn't touch us. Why, Father?'

'I knew them before,' he explained. 'I used to go fishing with them, and sailing, and I even stayed with them in Berlin.'

'Who?'

'Oh, men like Riedeler. And Kaltenbrunner. High men in the SS. I even knew Frank, the Governor General of Poland. We were friends. So when they invaded Poland, they came to me, as friends. You remember how kind they were to us. But they also wanted me to help them. They wanted to discover all the Jews in Poland, so they could be expelled. Even those who were only part Jewish had to go. But they knew they would have difficulty in locating them all. They wanted me to help them find all these Jews.'

'And you did,' Beth said, half to herself.

Josef Janski might not have heard her. He was speaking more confidently now, perhaps relieved to have got it off his chest after so many years. 'So I advertised, in apparent secrecy, that I knew a way of getting Jews safely out of the country, with all of their money, before the Nazis found out about them. Many came to me.'

'And you identified them to the Gestapo,' Beth said. 'And kept their money.'

'It was very expensive,' he muttered. 'And there were all of you to look after. Without that money we would have starved. Who needed a lawyer in Warsaw, in 1940? And Beth . . .' He caught her hand. 'I didn't know the Jews were going to be sent to death chambers. I swear it. I believed what the Nazis told me, that they were going to be resettled in the south. I swear it.'

Beth wondered if that were true. Yet it was still a ghastly act of betrayal, of hundreds, perhaps more, innocent men and women, and children. My father, she thought. The man who gave me life, and who preserved that life . . . by condemning others to death. Yet he had done that when he had shot that man on the walk away from Lódź. She had been shocked by that, but she had been grateful, too. She had even admired him for his courage and resolution.

Could she possibly admire this broken old man who was also a mass murderer? Could she ever have admired him? Then a terrible thought crossed her mind. 'Did Mother know about it?'

Another sigh. 'She found out,' Josef Janski said miserably.

'And that's why she joined the Home Army,' Beth said thoughtfully. How she had hated Mother at that moment, because she had trusted Father, had worshipped Father. 'And she got herself killed,' she muttered.

'It was an accident,' Josef Janski snapped. 'I am sure it was an accident.'

Beth frowned at him.

He lowered his eyes. 'The Germans did not know it was her,' he said.

'She was a heroine, after all,' Beth said. 'A true heroine.'

'Oh, she was,' Josef agreed eagerly. 'A true heroine. I . . . I only sought what was best for the family.'

'Yes,' Beth said drily. 'Well, Father, you probably do deserve to be handed over to the Israelis to be hanged.

Oh, don't worry,' she added as his face blanched. 'It won't happen. You're my father.'

'But this man Szabo, who knows . . .'

'Szabo is interested only in money,' Beth told him, 'not justice. I can handle Szabo. But you must swear to me that you will never mention this letter, or this Szabo, to a soul. Especially not Johnnie Alten. Do you understand that?'

'Me? Mention it? God knows I'd never mention it to anyone.'

Beth knew he was telling the truth. She patted his hand. 'So just relax. Leave it all to me.'

There was nothing she could do about Szabo until he called, because she was unable to cut and run. At least, to anywhere she wanted to go. She had too much money tied up here in the Riviera, and she was more than ever convinced that true safety could only lie for her father if she buried him in the huge mass of the American people. But it was still necessary to make plans for the moment she could move.

She returned to the bedroom and John, took off her dressing gown and lay beside him, and asked him how soon they could get married.

'That depends on you, my angel,' he said, stroking her. He loved stroking her. 'If you want a big wedding . . .'

'The hôtel de ville will do,' she said. 'But I am thinking of my visa.'

'You leave the visa to me,' he promised. 'I know a man in the Embassy in Paris. There'll be no trouble about that.'

'There are other things, too,' she said. 'I will have to sell this house, and the boat, and the car, and other things . . .'

'An agent can handle that for you. Or we could go on living here for awhile.'

'No,' she said. 'I want to get to the States, just as soon as possible. I've always wanted to go there.'

'Then you shall. Next week.'

354

'What about Father and Tony?'

For the first time some of the adoring good humour left his eyes. 'Am I marrying them, too?'

'Oh, heavens, no, darling, but you must see I can't just abandon them. I'm Tony's employer, and Father can't be out on his own. I'm not suggesting they come and live with us, or anything like that. I'll set them up on their own somewhere. But I must be able to go and see them without having to cross the Atlantic. I don't think that's being unreasonable.'

She was stroking him now, and that he could not resist. 'I guess not,' he said. 'Just as long as they never have to get into bed with us.'

'My darling,' she smiled, kissing him. 'Then you think you can get them visas too?'

He sighed. 'I reckon so. I'll work on it. But . . . don't tell me either of them has ever been to gaol?'

'Heavens, no,' Beth cried.

'Then leave it with me,' John promised. 'I'll get on the phone today.'

Actually, he needed to go up to Paris to see his friend personally, and while he was away Beth not only put the boat and the house and the car on the market, but told a mystified Tony what was happening, and showed him Szabo's letter, after swearing him, like Father, to absolute secrecy, even as regarded Anna or Stephanie. Especially Anna.

'By God,' Tony said. 'That lousy swine. Christ, it was an unhappy day for us when he came along. What are we going to do?'

'Pay him off,' Beth said.

'Pay him off? But Beth, you know as well as I that once you start paying a blackmailer you're hooked for life.'

'I'm only going to pay him in exchange for the information he has.'

'Oh, big deal. Of course he'll give it to you. After having taken a copy. Several copies.'

'Well, I don't see what else I can do,' she said. 'But

355

that's why I'm making plans just to sidle away from here, where he won't be able to find us.'

'In the States? Don't you think he'll be able to find you over there? Or if he can't, that he'll give his information to Mossad or whoever it is?'

'That's a chance we have to take. But I don't see any other way to do it. Tony ... you are one hundred percent behind me in this?'

'Of course I am, sis. He's Father.'

'Yes. But what do you feel about what he did?'

Tony brooded for a while. At last he said, 'God knows. Of course he was wrong. But he did it for us. I don't know, Beth. I just don't know.'

'He's Father,' she reminded him. 'That's what counts. And no nasty little Hungarian pig is going to have him executed.'

'No way,' Tony agreed. 'Has Bertie called yet?'

She shook her head. 'I suppose I'm still half hoping it was only a nuisance letter.'

'It wasn't,' Tony assured her. 'Not if it was from Bertie.'

He was right. The following evening the telephone rang, and the butler brought it to Beth on the patio, where she and Tony were playing backgammon. 'The gentleman won't give his name, madame,' he explained. 'But he says you are expecting his call.'

'Oh,' Beth said. 'Oh, yes.' She gazed at Tony, who gazed back, then she took the receiver, aware that her heart was pounding like a bass drum. 'Hello?'

Tony picked up the extension receiver.

'Darling girl,' said that all too familiar voice. 'I assume you got my note?'

'I did,' Beth said.

'Then you will have had the time to consider all the possible consequences of non-co-operation. I will not delay you, just in case you have put a trace on this call. I wish the equivalent of one hundred thousand pounds in Swiss francs. You may have tomorrow to obtain the money. Then you will place it in an attaché case and take it to the Port of Cogolin, you must know it, as you have a boat of your own, at the head of the Gulf of St Tropez. You will take a seat at one of the dock-side cafés, they are all in a row, and wait there, asking no questions and sipping a Pernod. Someone will contact you. Oh, and by the way, darling, my information on your father will be in a safe place, with instructions for it to be delivered to the Israelis should I not come to collect it within a specified time. So it would be very foolish of you to try any tricks.'

'Now wait just one moment,' Beth said. 'If I pay you a hundred thousand pounds, I want that information in exchange.'

'You will have it, darling girl. But I certainly am not going to have it on me when we meet. I was hardly born yesterday, and I have had dealings with you before. I hope you will not be as absurd this time, because if you try anything foolish, your father will surely hang. But if you do exactly as I say, all will be well. The day after tomorrow, at about five in the afternoon, mind.'

Beth replaced the receiver, and Tony put his down as well. 'One hundred thousand pounds,' she said. 'Do you know, I had thought he would aim much higher?'

'He doesn't need to,' Tony told her. 'That is only a first demand. He means to bankrupt you.'

'We will have to see about that,' Beth said. 'Well, I had better go into town first thing tomorrow and have a chat with my bank manager. You look up the best road to Cogolin; I've only ever been in there by boat.'

She got up, and Tony caught her hand. 'I will take the money to Cogolin.'

'You?' Beth frowned at him. 'But Szabo will expect to see me.'

'He'll expect to see one of us. He knows me. If I am there with an attaché case he will know I have brought the money.'

'Yes, but why should you take a chance like that? He loathes your guts. He may want to fight you, or something. He's a very vengeful man.'

357

Tony grinned. 'Bertie only hates people in relation to money, Beth. He wants that hundred thousand. If he's really on the run he probably needs it desperately. He's not going to fight with me, and if he does get aggressive, it's better for me to handle it than you. I don't have your trusting nature. I won't let him step out of line.' He winked. 'And I'll bring his documentary proof back with me.'

Beth considered. But although she would not admit it to Tony, she was a little afraid. Blackmail was something she had never before got into, not like this. She supposed she had blackmailed Georges, just as Georges had blackmailed Madame Suchet into letting them go, and Madame Suchet had blackmailed her into becoming a prostitute in the first place. It all seemed part of a chain, But her other attempt at blackmail, with Szabo himself, had turned out disastrously because she had lost her temper. It would be an even greater disaster were that to happen again now. Tony was experienced at this sort of thing and she knew he could take care of himself. Most important of all, he certainly knew Szabo.

'Well,' she said, I'll admit I'd be grateful, Tony, really I would. Providing you give me your solemn word you'll do nothing foolish.'

'I'm not going to take any risks at all, sis. Believe me.'

'Then you get Bertie off my back,' Beth said. 'And we'll all push off and leave this benighted continent behind us.'

THE FOURTEENTH CHRONICLE

June 1985

Meyer bought a copy of *Where the Sun Never Shines* at Miami Airport. He had heard of the book, as it was indeed all the rage, and had even seen it on various news-stands. But he had never thought to pick it up. He was not into books by women or very big books; his life of constant travel interspersed with bouts of total relaxation had precluded his ever settling down for a good long read, and he had always indulged in thrillers. Now he could kick himself. If he had looked at the book when it had first come out, the previous December, he might have saved himself six months of hard work.

It wasn't even necessary to read the novel, although he intended to do so. But for his purposes, the photograph on the dust jacket was sufficient. Stephanie Johnson was clearly a very successful, and very confident woman. She would be in her fifties, he knew, although there was no information as to her age or domestic situation on the blurb, only a list of her previous successes and the information that she was also a highly successful writer of historical novels under the name of Michelle Durand – but there was little to suggest her age in the photograph. Maybe she dyed her hair, but it was still worn full and long, and still possessed a gentle wave. Her forehead was high, her nose straight and perhaps a trifle long, her mouth wide, her chin pointed. She had a long neck but with no trace of a wrinkle. It was a lovely face, and a calm one.

He took the photograph of Beth's wedding to Georges Mathieu from his wallet, and compared the Stephanie of 1948 with the Stephanie of 1985. Thirty-seven years. And from all he had gathered about this family, thirty-seven fairly traumatic years. But it was the same woman.

He had read half the novel by the time the jetliner

touched down in Kennedy. By then he was in a hurry to read the rest. Because it was all here. Obviously Stephanie Johnson, as a skilful novelist with aspects of her life she wished to keep private, had not told her autobiography. But the book was still the story of a young girl who escaped from Warsaw in 1945, and who after half a lifetime of misadventures, eventually married and lived happily ever after, some thirty years later.

As a refugee she had wandered across Germany and France and England, had been incarcerated in a DP camp, had been forced to earn her living in a Parisian brothel before marrying a wealthy French farmer, had eloped with an Englishman who had turned out to be a crook, had been sent to gaol as an accessory after the fact of a murder he had committed, and had received a strange inheritance soon after her release which had enabled her to take up a writing career.

There was no mention of any sister or brother, and at first glance the book might have appeared, to anyone with Meyer's background knowledge, as the story strictly of Beth. But it wasn't. He suspected that it had bits of the experiences of all three of the girls in it, seen through Stephanie's eyes, strained through the ebullient beauty of her personality. If the sun had never shone in that nightmare world of the refugee – and he could believe that – it had done enough shining from the eyes of Stephanie Johnson to illuminate the pages of the book.

Only the end was disappointing. In the last couple of chapters, when she was describing her heroine's romance with a marvellous man who had suddenly swum into her live in the Riviera, and with whom she fell instantly in love, was Stephanie Johnson's writing less than sure. Meyer supposed he alone of all her readers would know why: for the first seven-eighths of her book, she had been recalling past events, even if at second hand – but the ending was pure fiction. She had not yet lived that part of her life.

He lay in bed after he had read the last page, at two o'clock the next morning. The Riviera! That was where Anna Janska and Lionel Hunt had been so unluckily married, according to Clive Carter's secretary. It was where Stephanie Johnson's heroine had got married as well. But that had been a happy marriage, of a successful novelist with the man of her dreams. Had Stephanie been retelling the Anna story as she would have liked it to be? Or had she really been telling the story of Beth?

And was Beth really this Mrs Vernon Latchman? The nurse at the clinic had suggested so. But the person paying for Lionel Hunt's keep, and incarceration, could easily have been Stephanie herself, pretending to be her own sister. That would not have been strange, granted the convolutions of this family. Indeed, except for the certainty that she had not yet met her man, he would have plumped for the latter. But that was because he did not want Beth Janska to be married.

Either way, he was home and dry. He felt a curious mixture of anticipation and apprehension. Real butterflies in his stomach. There were so many things he did not want to discover now, because certain of the answers he sought might disrupt his own private dreams, his concept of how things should be with these three beautiful, but haunted sisters. The whereabouts of Josef Janski scarcely seemed relevant beside the possibility of at last coming face to face with Beth Janska, and finding that she was everything he wanted her to be. Or the catastrophe of finding she was not.

But he was a professional, and he knew the chase had to be completed. Next day he went to see a friend of his who was a Manhattan literary agent. 'Martin,' he said, 'I need an introduction to Stephanie Johnson.'

361

CHAPTER 14

New York 1972–85

'That was a magnificent dinner, Stephanie,' John Harper said. He was her accountant, and had become in many ways her business manager, since her success and her move into Manhattan itself. Also present were Alice Todd and Ed Martinez, and a few other close friends in the writing business. Her little world, into which no outsiders, not even members of her own family, were allowed to wander. Or would ever be allowed to wander.

It was also a world the privacy of which her friends, intelligent people all, respected and understood. Yet, being human, they could not avoid being curious at the way their hostess remained an almost disembodied entity, with no background, no family . . . only a son.

'Almost,' Martinez remarked, 'I would have supposed we were celebrating something.'

Stephanie merely smiled at him. 'Of course,' she agreed. 'I am celebrating your company.' Yet even she, tonight, felt called upon to celebrate publicly. She raised her glass. 'I would, however, like to drink a toast to absent friends.'

They drank readily, and enjoyed their coffee and cigars and brandy, and about midnight made their way down on to the crowded precints of Fifth Avenue to locate their cars and wend their ways home. Martinez remained. He often did. Stephanie was well aware that he would like their relationship to broaden beyond that of author and publisher, and even of Pygmalion and Galatea; Ed certainly regarded her as his fair lady, whom he had remodelled into the facsimile of a very successful novelist. Nor did she mind his hankering. Sometimes she had half a mind to encourage him. But Ed, being both old-fashioned and honourable, would then propose marriage, she knew. Even that would have been a pleasant prospect, had all else been equal. But marriage, for her, would mean an end to secrecy.

In so many ways she was unlike Beth, who should surely have been on the stage. Beth could pretend with her entire being, while keeping aspects of herself firmly under lock and key. Stephanie knew that for her that would be impossible. Marriage would have to be a total sharing, and that she simply could not risk, with anyone.

And on nights like tonight, when she was celebrating Anna's marriage to Lionel Hunt at a distance of over three thousand miles, she was at her most vulnerable.

'If you ever fire your cook,' Ed remarked, pouring himself another brandy, 'you must give me the first option on her.'

'I promise,' she agreed. She knew that he knew she did all of her own cooking.

'And how's the boy? I half expected you to cancel the party.'

'Oh, his temperature's down. I think he's just been working too hard. He does, you know.'

'George?'

'He takes his studies very seriously. I think he means to be president. Of his class,' she added. Ed knew that George had not been born in the United States.

He sat beside her. 'So, what's next on the agenda?'

'I'll be submitting the treatment for the new book by the end of next week,' she promised.

'I've been meaning to talk to you about that.'

'Yes?' She could not prevent the wariness from entering her tone.

'Writing is like any other business,' he said, peering into his glass. 'One doesn't stand still. One either advances or slides backwards. Oh, I know we can both think of a lot of authors who appear to stand still, and quite successfully. But they don't really. There are no plateaux which stretch forever.'

'Meaning you think my historicals are getting stale?'

'Nope. They get better and better. Maybe I think you are ready for bigger and better things.'

'I'm content with my lot.'

'Never! Never be content with your lot,' he said. 'Especially when your lot depends on your brains. The human brain needs to be stretched, time and time again, to its limits. When you stop doing that, you're getting ready to be old, and that's a stupid thing to do until the day you die. Anyway, I'm not suggesting for a moment that you give up writing historicals.'

'I'm glad of that,' she said. 'I'd hate to starve.' She nearly added 'again' without thinking, and she had an idea he realised that.

'It would make a dent in my sales figures, too,' he agreed. 'But I have an idea that if you could combine the pace and the action and the sexiness and the sheer joie de vivre of your historicals with a big modern subject, you could have that bestseller you want.'

'Do I want a bestseller?'

'Doesn't every novelist?'

She gave a mock shudder. 'Another pseudonym? I have enough on my plate.'

'I don't think you should use a pseudonym at all.' He paused, to let that sink in. 'I think it should be written under your real name.'

Now he was definitely probing. But she wasn't going to take the bait, or make any mistakes. 'Stephanie Johnson?' she asked. 'Oh, no. When it falls flat, I've lost a publisher.'

'It could fall flat,' Ed agreed, temporarily abandoning his quest. 'But right now, you can afford that. Your historicals pay for your living, on a pretty good scale. If you are ever going to strike out in a new direction, now is the time. Go for broke. If it fails, well ... just go back to square one. But if it comes off, bingo. You could be up there amongst the big boys and girls.'

Stephanie scratched her nose. He certainly could make his ideas sound attractive, and she remembered how reluctant she had been to attempt her first historical novel. 'Would you commission such a book?'

'Nope. I don't think it should be written to a commission, or to a synopsis. I think it wants to come right out of the heart as well as the head.'

'What sort of subject did you have in mind?'

'That has to be your decision, but for starters, I think that if you could combine the intensity, the almost reportage of books like your early novels under your own name, by all means set in Europe as they were, but as I say, written as you write your historicals, you would have a winner.'

She stared at him. Was he really saying, write an autobiographical novel? The odd thing was, she had always wanted to do that. But was he actually wanting her to write a novel, or trying to probe into her past? She could not get that fear, that suspicion, out of her mind, even with men like Ed, who in every other respect she both knew and trusted.

'I'll think about it,' she promised.

But of course the whole idea was impossible, because that background she had kept so carefully hidden from her literary friends, and her public, was suddenly threatening to cluster around her. She had had quite a shock when she had received the telegram from Beth announcing, quite out of the blue, that Anna was getting married, and would be coming to live in America. That was one eventuality she had never supposed could be possible. Her only comfort lay in the additional information that the Hunts were taking up residence in south Florida, which was a long way away from New York. But in her confidence that a whole ocean would always separate her from the family, she had foolishly agreed to tell Anna that she was really Stephanie Johnson, as well as Michelle Durand, her pseudonym for the historicals. Anna could easily find her if she wished to.

The very next day after her party, she received another amazing telegram from Beth, this time announcing that they were all coming west. She was marrying, too, someone called John Alten. Stephanie remembered him vaguely from her last visit to Cannes, but she had never supposed Beth intended to marry any of the men she had always had clustering around her. Nor could she understand why both Anna and Beth had found it necessary to make such sudden marital decisions, in each case preventing her from being present. Of course she welcomed the idea of Beth being once again in the same country. Beth she trusted above anyone else in the world, with family secrets, anyway. But the idea of Tony and Father . . . She just didn't see how it could be done. And she certainly didn't want them anywhere close to her.

In fact, even Beth did not find it so easy to bring Tony and Father across. About a week later Stephanie received a telephone call from her sister, in New York, asking if they could meet for lunch. So Beth was already being discreet. They met in a sushi bar just off Broadway, where no one was likely to know Stephanie.

'Well,' she said, giving her sister a big hug and a kiss. 'Marriage agrees with you. Legitimate marriage.'

'Ha,' Beth commented enigmatically, and ordered sake.

'Now, you have to tell me what this is all about,' Stephanie said.

'What?' Beth asked.

'Leaving the Riviera. I thought you were settled there for life.'

Beth toyed with the plate of Japanese pickles. 'Well, I thought so, too, and then I met Johnnie, and I allowed him to sweep me off my feet.'

Beth never seemed to realise that Stephanie could tell when she was lying. But Stephanie preferred not to comment. Beth had obviously done the sweeping bit. But why? Only patience was going to find that out. 'But what about the house, and the boat, and the car?' she asked.

'They're up for sale,' Beth explained. 'I'm going to live in California. That's where Johnnie has a house. Los Angeles.'

'Oh, how splendid for you,' Stephanie exclaimed

with genuine pleasure; Los Angeles was farther away from New York than London.

'I'm looking forward to it,' Beth agreed unenthusiastically. 'If I can just get Tony and Father over here, then our problems are over.'

'Do we have problems?' Stephanie asked.

Beth gazed at her, then attacked her raw fish. 'Of course we don't, my darling girl. But I don't intend to be separated from my own father by an ocean.'

Once again, she was lying. 'I don't see how you're going to do it,' Stephanie remarked.

'It's proving difficult,' Beth acknowledged. 'And Johnnie isn't helping matters much. So I've had to leave them behind temporarily. But Tony is organising things.'

'What kind of things?' Stephanie wanted to know. Where she felt she could at least trust Beth in regard to family affairs, she didn't feel she could trust Tony in any direction at all.

'Well, it's necessary to fake a few papers, and cross a few palms with silver, and that sort of thing. Oh, Father is in the clear, really. He's a refugee from Communism. God knows he was never a Red himself. He only pretended to be one for a day or so to get us out of Warsaw. But the American Embassy does like to have backgrounds filled in and that sort of thing ... They'll be here.'

After lying and faking, where necessary, Stephanie thought. But hadn't she done the same thing, to reach this haven for all refugees? Yet there was one thing she had to be certain of. 'In California,' she said.

'Um.' Beth said. 'Somewhere like that.'

'What do you mean?' Stephanie asked anxiously.

'Well, Johnnie isn't keen on them being with us, or even too near to us. I thought he'd be more reasonable about it, but he is really being rather a shit. I'm going to have to set them up in a place of their own, but it will probably be in California, yes; it has to be somewhere I can keep an eye on them.'

'It's never occured to you to let Tony go out and get a job and stand on his own two feet?'

'I don't think he wants to stand on his own two feet,' Beth said.

'Beth ...' Stephanie squeezed her hand. 'You really can't treat us all as small children for the rest of our lives.'

Beth frowned at her. 'Do I treat you as a small child?'

'You would, if I gave you an inch.'

Beth smiled. 'But you don't give me an inch. You're settled, and successful. And now Anna is settled, and married to a successful man. But Tony and Father are lame ducks. Don't worry, I'll look after them. Anyway, Tony has a job, looking after Father. He enjoys it. They get on so well.'

'Beth,' Stephanie said, 'why not tell me all about it?'

'All about what?'

'Whatever it is eating you. Something is.'

Beth considered while she finished her sake. 'Can we go somewhere private?'

They went for a walk in Central Park, which Stephanie reckoned had to be the most private place in New York. Besides, ever since she had first come to America six years before she had dreamed of walking in Central Park with Beth. But not to hear the horror story Beth proceeded to unfold; she even had the letter with her. Stephanie got the impression that it never left her handbag.

'But my God,' she said. 'What did you do?'

'I paid up,' Beth said. 'What did you expect me to do?'

'But ...'

'Oh, I know,' Beth said. 'Tony kept carrying on about how I'd be hooked for life. But he was wrong. He admits it now. He did the transacting for me. He went along to meet Szabo, gave him the hundred thousand, and Szabo handed over the document that he actually did have with him, after swearing he didn't, mind.'

'Tony went to see Szabo?' Stephanie could not believe her ears. 'I would have thought that was highly dangerous. Doesn't Szabo hate his guts?'

'He certainly did once. And I thought it was dangerous, too. But Tony wanted to do it. And as it turned out, all was sweetness and light. Would you believe that they even had dinner together? Can you imagine the pair of them, sitting at a candle-lit table, drinking their cognac, and reminiscing about old times?'

'No,' Stephanie said. 'I can't imagine that at all.' She felt as if she were listening to one of her own less successful novels, where people are manipulated for the sake of the plot.

'Well, that's what happened,' Beth insisted. 'Tony says he has seldom enjoyed an evening more. I suppose he was pretty nervous about the meeting himself, although you would never have guessed it. Anyway, he didn't get home until about three in the morning. And as I said, Szabo handed over the document without any fuss, said he just needed the hundred thousand to get a fresh start, and went on his way.'

Stephanie frowned; the story was getting more and more unreal every moment. 'That doesn't sound the least like Bertie to me,' she ventured.

'It didn't to me, either, at first. And even Tony confessed he was surprised. But he says that it was clear the combination of prison and then the heart trouble had softened Bertie up, made him look only for survival. That makes sense to me. Of course Tony still doesn't altogether trust him. He's sure there is a photostat of the document somewhere, and that we'll hear from him again. Well, we'll cross that bridge when we come to it; he's going to have to find us again first. But you'll appreciate why I'm in a hurry to get Father out of Europe.'

'I don't, actually,' Stephanie said. 'You haven't told me what was so incriminating in this document of Szabo's. Was it really worth a hundred thousand pounds? What could Father possibly have done to

369

make the Israelis want to hang him?' As far as she knew, they hadn't even known any Jews as children. But then, of course, there had been no Jews to know.

'Um,' Beth said. 'You once told me you didn't really like Father.'

'Well, that was when he was down and out. He gave me the creeps.'

'So you said. Well, maybe your instincts were right. He *is* a war criminal.'

'Father?' Stephanie stopped walking. 'I don't believe it.'

Beth told her what Father had confessed.

'Oh, my God!' Stephanie gasped. 'How awful! And we never knew! But Beth, if that is true, then he should be handed . . .'

'He should not,' Beth snapped. 'And he will not. He's Father. Nobody is ever to know.'

'But if Szabo could find out . . .'

'Others can too. They already have. But they don't know where to look, or even if Father is alive. Think how Szabo found out. It was just a series of unlucky coincidences, if you ask me. He happened to have Father's daughter as his mistress, and she, the silly little bitch, told him that Father had something to hide. Just as she told him about my bigamy,' Beth brooded.

'Anyway, that was when we all supposed Father was dead, remember? Szabo thought nothing more of it, so he told Tony, until he escaped from that hospital. Then he immediately hightailed it out of England to the continent, to hide, and worked his way down to the Riviera because he'd seen photographs of Anna and myself in some society magazine. He meant to touch us for some money, maybe get together with Anna again. But when he looked the house in Cannes over, the first person he spotted was Father. And I suppose we all always called him Father, even in public. So old Bertie put one and one together and came up with an idea. He didn't know if Anna would still go for him, but he was damned sure I would pay up to keep the old man alive

370

and free. I suppose we were lucky there, in that he is so crooked he preferred that approach to chancing his arm with Anna, or the whole thing between them might have started up again.'

'But all he had was what Anna told him, and she didn't know anything important,' Stephanie objected. 'None of us suspected anything about Father. So how did he find out?'

'He used his head. Apparently he has contacts all over the world, certainly all over Europe. One of these contacts was able to give him the information that the Polish police still have an unexecuted warrant out for Father for all of those crimes. The Poles think he's dead, actually. But Bertie knew better.'

'I wouldn't exactly call that documentary proof.'

'But it's true, don't you see. As Szabo knows, and as Father has confessed to me. If it were to get into the hands of the Israelis, the information that he is still alive, they'd put their sleuths on his trail.'

'But in that case, you've paid all that money for nothing,' Stephanie said. 'Even if he did give you his "proof", if there really is a warrant in existence for Father's arrest, or was once, all Bertie has to do is to tell the Israelis where he can be found.' She shuddered. 'Suppose they are already on his trail and we don't know?'

'I think we'd have found out by now,' Beth said reassuringly. 'Anyway, we are doing the best thing possible, by doubling to and fro, changing names, and addresses, and those sort of things.'

'It's a terrible way to live,' Stephanie said. 'My God, will we ever stop being refugees? Is it possible to have one's past always at your heels ... I really thought I could turn my back on all that when I changed my name and emigrated here.'

'I guess everyone is always a refugee from their past,' Beth mused. 'Ours is just more lurid than most, I suppose.'

'Lurid? To have a father who is virtually a mass murderer ...'

371

'That cannot be your responsibility, Stephanie, any more than it is mine. I happen to believe that it is my responsibility to care for Father for the rest of his life, just as I'm prepared to care for any of you who may need my protection. As for Father's crimes, if you believe in God you must also believe he'll be punished for those after his death; the important thing is that his death will never be on our consciences.'

Which was easy for Beth to say, Stephanie reflected, because she was by now perfectly certain that Beth did not believe in God any longer.

But she could certainly be reassuring. 'As for our past,' she went on, 'we'll beat it, Stephanie. You and me, because we have what it takes. You'll see. But you must swear never to tell anyone what I have told you today. Not even Anna. Especially not Anna.'

'You can believe that,' Stephanie said.

She actually had no desire ever to see Anna again. At that moment she wasn't sure she even wanted to see Beth again. She knew it was selfish of her, and she wished she possessed Beth's resoluteness and determination, always to force her way through whatever obstacles lay before her. She only wanted to live the life she now had, to write books which were at once enjoyable to put together and which earned her a good living, and to protect and enjoy George.

As he moved through his high school grades he became ever a more enjoyable companion. She would have been less than human had she not kept looking for signs of Geoffrey in him, but she could see none. Nor did she ever want anything to happen which might bring out any latent traits which he might have inherited from his father. But now she had to worry about traits he might have inherited from his grandfather as well. At least as regards Geoffrey she could be sure he could never come back into their lives. But Father . . . She could only pray that he never did get his visa. Nor could she convince herself that he shouldn't be punished, right here on earth, even if he was their father. It was a horrible decision to have to consider; once again she could only thank God it would never be hers to make.

But of course, with Beth working on it, there was no way Father was going to stay on the other side of the Atlantic. That autumn a letter arrived from Los Angeles informing her that Father and Tony were now in the States.

'Would you believe,' Beth wrote, 'that those silly people at the Embassy in Paris would only give them a three months visitors' visa? Of all the rubbish. Still, they are here now, and that is all that matters: they won't be going anywhere again. And before you fly up into one of your hysterics, my darling girl, let me tell you that it is done all the time. There is nowhere anyone can trace them to me, and there is no way anyone can trace them anyway, as I am paying their way, so there is no business of involvement with social security or job hunting or medical bills or anything like that. Josef Janski left France to go to America, and has simply disappeared off the face of the earth. So if the Israelis or the Poles or the Russians are after him, they're just going to have to give up. That's what I always planned to happen anyway, even if he'd been able to come here legally. And here we are, all together once again. And safe!'

It seemed that Beth did not have any moral values left at all. Although sometimes Stephanie wondered if Beth hadn't left all of her moral values in Warsaw at the age of fifteen. What was more surprising, and more disturbing, was her sublime confidence. As she had said, they had never made any secret that Father was Josef Janski, in Cannes; there had never seemed any reason to. Equally, it was true that Bertie discovering he was the Josef Janski wanted for war crimes was a coincidence. And she might even be right in assuming that no one was looking for Father because he was supposed to be dead. But Bertie was very much alive, and whenever he needed money all he had to do was turn the screw; he would certainly be able to find out that Beth had married John Alten, and armed with that information, she would not prove difficult to find.

Yet the following summer, when George had gone on a camping holiday with school friends, she went to the West Coast. This was partly duty, but it was also partly curiosity; she wanted to know just how Beth had arranged things.

Security was certainly tight. While Beth happily told her how she had refrained from meeting Father and Tony in New York, had told them to go to an hotel and then to a secret place where she had met with them and taken them to a hideaway she had prepared, so that, as she said, no one trailing them could ever link them to Mrs John Alten, she again swore Stephanie to secrecy as to their present whereabouts.

Stephanie almost felt her sister wanted to blindfold her as they drove into the mountains behind Sacramento. Here Father and Tony were installed in a very comfortable cabin, with all mod cons, although Stephanie was shocked to be greeted by a Tony armed with a revolver, and to see the hunting rifle waiting beside the door. When she commented that this seemed a dreadful way to live, Tony claimed it was fun.

She wasn't sure Father found it fun. He had suffered a stroke on the boat crossing, and although he had been treated by a friendly passenger, a doctor whose help Tony had enlisted to avoid any risk of publicity, Stephanie found him very frail even if Beth claimed he had made a full recovery.

Beth also considered it was fun, to live like a bandit queen of the 1870s, as long as she could at the same time drive a Cadillac and own a beach house on Malibu and entertain lavishly and in every way carry on her unlawful activities in the lap of luxury.

On their return to Los Angeles, however, where Stephanie stayed for a few days, she noted that Beth and her Johnnie did not exactly seem to be getting on like a house on fire. Stephanie wondered if he knew that Father and Tony were illegal immigrants, and worried about it, or if he was just finding living with a ball of unpredictable energy like Beth more wearing that he had anticipated.

Or if, most likely of all, he was aware that since the outbreak of the Arab-Israeli war, and the jump in inflation caused by the gas shortages, especially in Europe, even Beth, most of whose money was invested in France and England, was feeling the pinch. She joked about it, of course, remarked how fortunate she was to have enjoyed those years in Cannes and with the yacht, as she doubted she would be able to afford them now – but she obviously had a lot on her plate maintaining the secret house and supporting Father and Tony.

Stephanie had already ceased to accept her twenty thousand pounds a year, and now she tentatively offered to help, but Beth would not hear of it. Stephanie was rather relieved, not because of the money, but because she did not really want to become involved in anything as shady as maintaining two ex-criminals, even if they were her father and brother. She felt she had done her duty in visiting them, and reflected with some satisfaction that if Beth was going to keep them hidden away for the rest of their lives, they could hardly interfere with her life, while Anna had completely disappeared into the Florida scene – she did not even write to Beth any more.

Stephanie almost felt she could relax, until in the late summer of 1975, the family once again erupted into her lap.

She was fast asleep when the doorbell rang, just after seven one morning. She was having a dinner party that night, and had spent most of the previous evening preparing her favourite marinated steaks.

Drowsily she got out of bed and pulled on her dressing gown, but George was there in front of her, opening the apartment door, and saying, 'Hello?'

'You'll be George,' said a familiar voice. 'My, how you've grown. Is your mummy awake?'

Stephanie pushed hair from her eyes and hurried into the hall, still too sleepy to feel alarmed. But she felt alarmed when she looked at her sister. Anna was hardly recognisable, because she had lost weight, and if she had grown her hair again it was straggling in an unwashed fashion past her shoulders. Her face was blotchy and Stephanie didn't think she had washed her clothes, which were crushed and sweaty, or her body too recently. Nor did she have a suitcase, or even a handbag.

'Anna?' she asked.

'Everyone always seems so surprised to see me,' Anna complained. 'Won't you introduce me to your son?'

'You remember Aunt Anna, from Cannes, George,' Stephanie said briefly.

'Hello, Aunt Anna,' George said, and held out his hand. But he was an observant boy; questions would no doubt come later.

'Hello, George,' Anna said again. And looked at Stephanie. 'Aren't you going to invite me in?'

'George,' Stephanie said. 'I'm sure it's time you got ready for school.' She led Anna into the lounge. 'This is an unexpected pleasure. Where are you staying?'

'This is a super flat,' Anna remarked. 'Beth said you were doing well, but I had no idea . . .'

Lumps of lead began to accumulate in Stephanie's stomach. She went into the kitchen and brewed coffee. 'Thank you,' she said, and tried a different approach. 'What brings you to New York?'

'You're so hostile,' Anna complained.

'Well, you turn up here at the crack of dawn, looking as if you've been run over, without even a handbag . . .'

'I lost it,' Anna wailed, and Stephanie looked up to see tears beginning to well from her eyes.

'Oh, Anna,' she hurried to the doorway, put her arm

round her sister's shoulders, guided her to a settee. 'Whatever is the matter?'

'Everything,' Anna sobbed, her composure now entirely disappeared. 'Nobody loves me. People are always chasing me, and beating me, oh, God, life is so frightful.'

Stephanie supposed she must be having a breakdown; she had never encountered a mood like this since the night Bertie had been arrested. After the glowing description Beth had given her of Lionel Hunt, so kind and thoughtful and gentle, what Anna was saying sounded like gibberish.

'I'll get the coffee,' she said.

Anna ran to the breakfast bar behind her. 'Stephanie,' she whispered. 'You wouldn't have ... ?' She licked her lips, and the tears returned as Stephanie stared at her. Then she tossed her head defiantly. 'No,' she said. 'You wouldn't. You're Miss Goody Two Shoes. Miss Goody Two Shoes.' She stuck out her tongue and returned to the settee.

Stephanie was too concerned that Anna might have gone mad to feel offended. Carefully she poured coffee, wondering how she could phone Beth. If there was any time she had ever needed her sister, it was now.

'Oh, Stephanie,' Anna wailed. 'I'm so sorry, Please forgive me.'

'Forget it.' Stephanie placed the two cups on the coffee table.

'Stephanie ...' Anna caught her arm. 'Have you any money? I ... I lost all mine when my handbag was stolen. But you must have money, with a place like this. Stephanie, can you lend me two hundred dollars?'

Stephanie gazed at her, the lead growing heavier. As Beth had once accused her, she did get most of her knowledge of life from the researches she did for her books, and two hundred dollars happened to strike a memory chord. Anna was wearing a long sleeved dress. Stephanie seized her wrist and pushed the material back above the elbow. Anna gave a gasp and jerked her hand away, turning her whole body as she did so, and drawing up her knees as if she were cowering from a blow. But Stephanie had seen the tell-tale punctures. 'Oh, God,' she said.

'Look,' Anna said, twisting on her knees to face her. 'Just lend me two hundred dollars. Please, Stephanie. I'll pay you back. But right now I have to get a fix. Once I've done that I'll be all right. Please, Stephanie.'

Her fingers were like claws.

'Where is Lionel?' Stephanie asked.

'I don't know. But he's following me. I know he is. I couldn't live with him any more. He was going to put me in the clinic. I couldn't stay there, Stephanie. I couldn't. I'd go mad if I were ever locked up again.'

'Drink your coffee,' Stephanie said, her brain doing handsprings. 'You say you lost your handbag. Where are your clothes?'

Anna shook her head in a bewildered fashion. 'I don't have any clothes.'

'Oh, God Almighty!' Stephanie exclaimed. She got up, paced to and fro. 'Listen,' she said. 'You can't stay here.'

'Oh, Stephanie, I have to stay somewhere. I don't have any money. I ...' she paused, staring open-mouthed at the door as George appeared.

'Shall I skip breakfast, Mom?' George asked, aware that he had interrupted a crisis.

'Certainly not, if you don't mind getting it for yourself. Your aunt and I will go into the bedroom. Come along, Anna.'

She held the door ajar, and after a moment's hesitation, Anna followed her. 'You can't throw me out,' she begged as Stephanie closed the bedroom door on them. 'You just can't. I've nowhere to go. I've no money. And I need a fix. Oh, Stephanie ...'

Stephanie thrust her fingers into her hair, wishing she possessed Beth's powers of instant, and ruthless, decision. But Beth had to sort this one out. 'Listen,' she

378

said. 'Go and have a bath. You stink. And be sure you wash your face and try to stop crying. By the time you've had a bath I'll know what to do.'

'If I have a bath, will you give me the money for a fix?'

'Yes,' Stephanie promised. 'Just go and do it.' She half pushed Anna into the bathroom, then closed the door and dialled Los Angeles. She was through almost immediately, but the phone rang for nearly a minute before it was answered.

'Who is it?'

'Beth! Stephanie.'

'Oh, for God's sake,' Beth snapped. 'Do you realise what time it is?' Then she must have looked at her watch, because her voice rose an octave. 'It's five o'clock in the morning!'

'Well, it's a lot later than that here,' Stephanie told her. 'In every way. Listen, Beth, are you awake?'

'Do I have a choice?' Beth groaned. 'Whatever is the matter?'

'Just listen,' Stephanie said, and told her the situation. By the time she was finished Beth was entirely awake. 'Oh, Christ,' she commented. 'All right, keep her there.'

'Here?' Stephanie shouted.

'Until I get to you. I'll catch the first plane east.'

'She wants heroin,' Stephanie said.

'You'd better give her some, then.'

'Me? Where do you suppose I keep it?'

'Well, give her the money. I'll refund you. If you don't she'll have the screaming heebie-jeebies, and maybe rush off somewhere.'

'You don't think she's going to rush off somewhere if I give her money?'

'Sure. But if she thinks you're a soft touch she'll be back. I'll be there by this evening, and I'll sort everything out then. But Stephanie, don't tell Anna I'm coming.'

Presumably she could hope for nothing better than

379

that, Stephanie realised as the phone went dead; Beth was at least coming. And in all the circumstances Beth would not be interested in hearing that what Stephanie feared was the imminent collapse of her private world. She could only thank God that Ed Martinez was not amongst the guests for dinner.

She got Anna out of the bath, got them both dressed, went with her to the bank, and drew out a thousand dollars.

'For heaven's sake don't lose it,' she warned. 'Go and get yourself something decent to wear. I'm having people to dinner tonight.'

'Are you?' Anna cried. 'Oh, how splendid. Am I invited?'

'You're here, aren't you?' Stephanie pointed out. 'Now, off you go and get whatever it is you have to get. But Anna, I want you home by five this afternoon at the latest.'

'By five o'clock,' Anna promised humbly. 'I'll be there.'

'And Anna, you are going to behave yourself tonight, I hope?'

'Well, of course I am,' Anna said, and hurried down the street.

Stephanie wondered if she would ever see her again, or her money. Actually, she felt it would be a worth while investment to have paid a thousand dollars to be rid of her, except that Beth would be furious. But as Beth had suggested would be the case, Anna was home by five, looking a different woman. She had had her hair done and had bought herself a dress and some clean underclothes. And undoubtedly she had had her fix; her eyes were bright and she bubbled, just like the old Anna. She even helped Stephanie make the final preparations for dinner, and when George came in from school, sat and watched TV with him for an hour before going off to dress.

It was quite fun having a helpful sister about the place, Stephanie thought, although she still anticipated the evening with dread.

But Anna was the life and soul of the party, flirting with the men just sufficiently to arouse their interests and not sufficiently to arouse their wives. She was very good, too, and obeyed Stephanie's instructions not to reveal their relationship, but to pretend she was an old college friend. Of course there was a certain facial resemblance between them, but far less now than there had been when they were girls, and no one commented on it, although Stephanie had no doubt Martinez would have, and once again thanked God he was not there.

The evening went off very well, and she was just beginning to relax, when there was a knock on the door. That'll be Beth, she thought, and excused herself. She opened the door, and was almost knocked over by the man who stormed into the apartment. 'Where is she?' he demanded.

Stephanie knew at once who he had to be, even if Beth had not sent her a photograph of the wedding; not that Hunt looked much like his photo at this moment. He looked scruffier and more distraught than Anna had done several hours before.

'Hello,' Stephanie said, having recovered her balance. 'You'll be Lionel. I'm Stephanie.'

He ignored her proffered hand. 'I know she's here,' he said. 'I'm going to find the little bitch, if I have to tear this place apart.'

Stephanie was determined not to lose her temper. 'I think you had better come in,' she suggested, 'and have a drink, and behave yourself.' Where, oh where, was Beth? She could have walked from Los Angeles by now, surely.

She opened the dining room door, and he stepped past her, stared at the guests, who were sitting about enjoying their coffee and brandy, and who all turned politely to face the doorway, looking surprised at the slipped tie knot, crushed jacket, and unshaven chin of the latest arrival.

'This is,' Stephanie began, but Hunt was pointing at Anna.

'You,' he commanded. 'Outside!'

'My God!' Anna screamed, only just realising that it was her husband. In addition to her fix, she had had a lot to drink, and Stephanie hadn't known how to stop her without risking a scene. Now she dropped her coffee cup and clambered backwards up and over the settee on which she had been sitting, kicking the coffee cup from the hands of the astonished man sitting beside her, and splitting her new dress as she did so.

'Don't let him near me. Stephanie!' she shrieked. 'Don't let him touch me.'

The other guests also scrambled to their feet uncertainly. Stephanie tried to catch Hunt's arm as he started across the room, and he shrugged her off so violently she fell into a chair.

'Aaagh!' screamed Anna, now on her feet behind the settee. 'Help me!'

'You'd better call the police,' one of the women told her husband, and he nodded and ran for the telephone in the hall.

'Oh, Christ,' Stephanie muttered, regaining her feet and grabbing Hunt by the collar as he started across the settee.

'You beast,' Anna shouted, finding herself against the sideboard and picking up the brandy decanter – it was cut glass – and hurling it with all her strength. She missed her husband, but hit one of the other guests, who had unwisely strayed into the line of fire. He gave a shout and fell over as his wife started to scream.

Stephanie still had Hunt's collar, and exerting all her considerable strength, pulled him back across the settee. He hit the floor with a crash which broke another couple of coffee cups, while his weight took Stephanie to the floor with him. Anna, sweeping her hand over the sideboard, located the whisky decanter and sent that flying behind the first. It hit Hunt on the chest, the stopper flying off so that Stephanie was showered in alcohol. Hunt gave a roar of rage, caught the decanter before it hit the carpet, and threw it back.

Anna sidestepped, and the glass shattered against the wall.

'Help me,' Stephanie gasped, again trying to grab Hunt's arm as she had lost her grip on his collar.

The man who had been knocked over and the one returning from the telephone ran forward, and between them they pinned Hunt to the floor. By now all of the women, as well as Anna, were screaming, and it was quite a relief to hear the wail of a siren. Either a squad car had been very close or the doorman of the building, who usually kept himself informed of what was happening on his premises, had sent for one the moment Hunt had entered the street door.

A few moments later two patrolmen bustled inside, enabling Stephanie and her friends to release Hunt. Stephanie sat up, straightening her dress, wiping whiskey from her face, seething with anger and outrage and a sense of despair, to gaze at Beth, who had followed the policemen into the room.

Beth, of course, being Beth, took immediate charge of the situation and handled everything. She convinced the patrolmen that she was responsible for both Hunt and Anna, with no argument from either of them, as they both seemed at once exhausted and in a state of emotional collapse, Hunt hardly appearing to know where he was. She had her good friend Mrs Johnson agree not to press charges, persuaded them to put the unresisting Hunt into handcuffs just in case he became violent again, and then gave him a sedative she just happened to have with her, apologised to everyone, and left with the patrolmen and her two prisoners.

Her calm had been as massive as her total authority, and calmed everyone else, as well. In fact the evening turned out to be almost a success, as Stephanie's guests were most sympathetic on the subject of how old school friends could change. Not one of them seemed to suspect that Beth and Anna were Stephanie's sisters, even if they were obviously mystified by Beth's role in the whole business.

383

George, too, awakened from his sleep by the banging and crashing, accepted that it was a case of adults having too much to drink and 'enjoying' themselves. He could remember some of the wild parties his Aunt Beth had thrown in Cannes, and if he too, was mystified that Aunt Beth and Aunt Anna should suddenly have become Mrs Alten and Mrs Hunt, he was patient enough to wait until the next morning for his mother's explanations. And Beth sent a cheque to cover both the thousand dollars Stephanie had loaned Anna and the damage to the apartment. The whole incident might never have happened.

But for Stephanie it had been the last straw, however Beth might have tried to put it right. She had no desire ever to see any of the family again, except maybe Beth, and that very occasionally. She had no immediate idea of what Beth did about Anna or Hunt, and she didn't care, was only happy that they had been removed from New York without any further fuss.

And the following year she was even happier to be several thousand miles away from California or Florida, as Beth and John Alten got a divorce.

'John says I spend more time with my family than with him,' Beth complained in her letter. 'Well, for God's sake, does he expect me to neglect them?'

Within another year Beth was married again, this time to Vernon Latchman, the millionaire industrialist.

'My dear, he is a dream,' she wrote to Stephanie. 'Of course he's no spring chicken, but he's very virile as well as very rich. I put my cards on the table, and he wasn't bothered at all. "Spend as much time as you like with your family," he told me. "Just be where I can see you and get at you from six in the evening until six the next morning." Well, that's perfect, isn't it? Of course I shall have to move the herd closer to home, as Vernon doesn't want me to spend any nights away, but Stephanie, I have the most tremendous news: Vernon lives on the East Coast. He actually has his main office in New York. I'm going to have a Manhattan apartment. We'll be able to throw stones at each other's windows, well, practically. Anyway, it should be easy enough to find somewhere for Father.'

'Oh, my God!' Stephanie shouted in despair.

But the move East did not appear to be going to interfere with her life at all, because Beth kept her word, and remained utterly discreet as regards her sister's real identity. She invited Stephanie to the occasional dinner party – and her Manhattan apartment, which occupied the top two floors of a very tall building, and had cost something over a million dollars, made Stephanie's modest home look like a coal scuttle.

Stephanie began to enjoy these excursions into the higher echelons of business and finance, and occasionally politics, and met a lot of interesting people, the masculine half of whom were all very interested in her. But she was always Stephanie Johnson the novelist, and Beth quite understood when she explained that she could never have them back. 'My dear,' she said. 'Think nothing of it. Vernon doesn't like eating out.'

Stephanie's real concern, had been that where Beth went so did Father and Tony . . . and Anna, as it turned out. For Beth would not consider putting her into a clinic. 'I wouldn't lock up a dog, after my experiences,' she told Stephanie, although she had certainly incarcerated Hunt in a clinic and meant him to stay there for a long time.

There were sound reasons for this; Hunt had apparently suffered a total mental collapse, which had taken the form both of amnesia and a fear of crowds, or indeed of people in any form. He did not seem to have any family, and therefore Beth could be said to have acted out of charity in having him examined, and then certified as needing treatment, by a doctor, and sending him back, all expenses paid, to his very own hospital to live in luxury until he got better – if he ever did.

But Stephanie felt this was just another example of Beth's growing tendency to shape the world about her for her own purposes, as Hunt's mania had undoubtedly been induced by the strain of trying to cope with Anna's problems and tantrums while holding down an exacting job. But in Beth's eyes, Hunt was no longer of importance because he was no longer family, even though she would not let Anna sue for a divorce because she did not want any publicity.

And for all Beth's words, Anna was, to all intents and purposes, locked up as well. Beth had bought a house in a remote area of upstate New York, close enough to be reached by three hours of hard driving from Manhattan, so that most days she could be out there by eleven – as Vernon was always in his office by eight she could leave then, too – and yet be back in her apartment by six that evening, after having lunched with the family. Her devotion to their well-being pricked Stephanie's conscience, except when she reflected that they had actually become Beth's hobby, her sole interest in life, and that she manipulated them as if they were her puppets.

The house was a very nice one, close to a lake, and there her three problems lived in the height of luxury, with Tony in charge during Beth's absences, with the strictest instructions that none of them, and especially Anna, were to venture out of their immediate area. If Stephanie was appalled at the way Beth was attempting to run their lives, she could not help but be grateful that they were being kept so much under wraps.

The amazing thing was that none of the three of them seemed aware of that; they just seemed grateful to Beth for looking after them. Father, of course, was practically in his dotage and did little more than stare into space, Anna had all the drugs she wanted, bought for her by Tony, who was allowed excursions into town for that purpose, and seemed content to moon about the house, swim in the lake in the summer, and generally do nothing.

When Stephanie remonstrated to Beth that she was slowly killing her sister, Beth said, 'Well, it's what she wants to do. Anyway, most junkies die either of overdoses or dirty equipment. Anna's doses are carefully controlled, and her equipment is always clean; Tony sees to that. She'll be around a long time yet.'

Tony was the real enigma. Stephanie felt compelled to visit them occasionally, and soon she started spending every Christmas Day with them, as did Beth, having lunch. Apparently it made little difference to Latchman what day of the year it was – he worked from dawn until dusk three hundred and sixty-five days a year, except when he would suddenly decide to take a trip somewhere and whip Beth off to the Antarctic or Burma, or somewhere like that, and he normally only wanted his wife around from dusk until dawn, as he had said at the beginning, either for sex or to hostess his parties. It seemed a soulless relationship to Stephanie, but it suited both Beth and her husband admirably.

Naturally Stephanie took George along for Christmas lunch, and she began taking him on most of her visits, having explained the situation as fully and carefully as she thought necessary, and having sworn him to secrecy. He seemed more amused than alarmed and also to look forward to the visits; he got on very well with his aunt and uncle, and especially his grandfather. Stephanie had not confessed to him that Father was a war criminal, but merely said he was a defector from Communist Poland, a situation George could quite understand and even found exciting.

His true attitude to the family was summed up one day when Stephanie overheard him chatting with one of his school friends, who had asked why he had never met any of his family except his mother. George replied, 'I guess because they're such a bunch of weirdos. Nice weirdos, sure, but definitely way out.' But even George found it difficult to understand Uncle Tony.

Unlike either Father or Anna, who were definitely invalids of one sort or another, Tony was in the best of health, and proceeded through life with an air of tense introspection. It was difficult to decide what he did with himself most of the time, althought he kept the house immaculate, and the garden, chopped the logs for the fires, looked after and enjoyed the small runabout he kept on the lake. He certainly lived well, on Beth's money, and he was no longer a boy or even a young man, yet he never seemed to need any intellectual stimulation or the company of women. Beth claimed he did, and would sometimes drive into the nearest village to pick one up, but it still seemed an incredibly narrow existence for one who had once been so lively and ambitious.

The short answer was that he had to be on drugs himself, but Stephanie doubted this; not only did Beth still seem prepared to trust him and leave him in complete charge in her absences, but he showed none of the tell tale signs, such as the up and down moods, depending on the proximity of a last, or next, fix which she had come to look for, while observe him as carefully as she might she had never seen any puncture marks on his arms.

She suspected that there was an even more sinister reason for her brother's willingness, indeed eagerness, to bury himself away in the woods like some latterday Thoreau: Tony was a man with something very heavy on his mind. Indeed, it was possible to say that Tony was every bit as afraid as Father. But of what? She simply could not imagine.

And as the decade came to an end, Stephanie discovered problems of her own. She was keenly aware of having past the meridian, and had the change rather early. But without great difficulty; she simply refused to let anything like that upset her, and was looking forward to a graceful descent into old age, able to fill her life with the vicarious enjoyment of George's career. Certainly she had no financial worries; her historicals continued to sell like hot cakes throughout the seventies. But in 1980 there came a change, which accelerated downhill over the next two or three years.

The trouble had been brewing for some time, and visibly, although Stephanie had resolutely refused to accept it: historicals as a genre had become so popular that everyone was trying to do it, and the market had been flooded with a good deal of cheap trash. Then at the end of 1980 Ronald Reagan took office as President, and immediately made his number one objective the determination to put an end to the inflationary spiral. This was an admirable platform, but the result was an immediate recession, which soon went very near to a depression such as America had not experienced since the early 1930's.

From the publishing point of view, it became a full depression very rapidly, as not even those whose memories could reach back to the Great Depression had experienced anything like this in the book trade before. Sales of all kinds of books dropped off alarmingly, the collapse being assisted by the over-production of genre novels, as Ed Martinez had warned was happening some time before.

Stephanie's own American sales fell by half. She still retained a good British and European market for her work, and everyone insisted there would soon be an upturn, but it was slow in coming.

'I suppose it's because publishing really became big business during the seventies, with the multinationals interested in each owning a publishing house,' Ed explained over lunch. 'The result has been that in the book trade, and in mass marketing even more than hardcover, the fate of a novel has been taken out of the hands of editors and put in the hands of accountants, who are interested only in profits, preferably instant profits, as opposed to the production of novels which might possibly have something to say. This goes right through the whole business, alas, down to the wholesale and retail outlets. In addition, of course, the fact is that when people are worried about money, and everyone is worried about money right now, the last thing they want to spend several dollars on is a book, unless it's something everyone feels they must read.'

'I have a feeling you're trying to tell me something,' Stephanie remarked.

'Well ...' He pulled his nose. 'I'm afraid I can no longer go on paying you six figure advances. Sales just aren't reflecting that kind of level right this minute.'

She nodded. 'I guessed that was on the cards when I looked at your last statement. Well, I can't pretend I'm not upset. I was even thinking of cutting back my writing a little, now I'm approaching fifty ...'

'You, approaching fifty? I can't believe that.'

She blew him a kiss. 'You darling man. But I'm afraid it's one of the facts of life. Now it looks as if I'm going to have to write even more to keep up the income.'

'Do you have to? You must have salted away quite a lot over the past ten years.'

'I'm not a great believer in salting away, I guess. There never seems to have been any need. I've played the stockmarket once or twice, and always lost my shirt. Then George is going to Harvard next year, and then hopefully into a law practice. These things cost money. So it's back to the old typewriter.'

'There are alternatives.'

She squeezed his hand. 'Marriage? I don't think I'd make anyone a good wife, Ed; I'm too set in my bachelor girl ways.'

'Well, that was certainly what I had been going to suggest,' he agreed. 'To the right man, of course. But there is another alternative. As I said, the very top books are still doing as well as ever. You just never managed to get into that echelon. Maybe you never tried hard enough. Now would be a good time.'

'Easier said than done. Jonathan Price once told me that one doesn't write a bestseller; it just happens.'

'Very true. But you can give it a push in the right direction by choosing the right subject. Okay, so I talked you into the genre business. It was good at the time, and it'll come again; the one good thing about a recession is that it does weed out all the also rans, the guys who are just in it for the quick buck. But you're a professional. Your work will always sell. On the other hand, a professional also has the discipline to go where the most profit is. I would strongly recommend that now is the time for that really big book you and I talked about . . . my God, it must have been ten years ago.'

Stephanie gazed at him. If the idea had sounded alarming ten years before, it sounded even more alarming now that the family were all in the States. On the other hand, they were all busily living their lives with no thought for her. Beth would help her out financially, of course, whenever she chose to ask – but she had no intention of ever being beholden to Beth again. For the rest, she did not see how she could possibly harm them, as long as she didn't identify them. In fact, she already had some ideas on how to tell their story without involving them at all; between the three of them, she and Anna and Beth had lived a pretty full life. If one woman had lived all of that, she would indeed have a formidable story to tell. And it could have a happy ending, as well, whereas none of their lives indicated such a prospect in the least. And if it would put her back on top . . . She smiled. 'You're on,' she said.

It was like starting all over again, writing the story of the children who had featured in her very first novel. Because it began in the same place and with the same scenes – Ed said that didn't matter, as no one could stop an author plagiarising her own books and anyway that first novel had been out of print for years.

She wrote and wrote and wrote, and Ed collected the chapters as she finished, read them, and offered criticism where necessary. It was immensely flattering to have such close editorial assistance from so expert a man, and their friendship grew even more intimate – but he never crossed the bounds of mental into physical intimacy, no matter how much she knew he wanted to do that.

Anyway, as the book progressed, his interest in it as a novel began to overtake his original interest in it as the story of her life, which he undoubtedly suspected it was. This disturbed her a little at first, but then she thought, if he thinks I was once a whore and bigamously married to a London gangster, well . . . that's more than a little true, and if it decides him against ever wanting to ask me to marry him, that'll be the best thing for both of us.

But she wondered what he would make of the ending, which was pure fiction, as she allowed herself to dream, even at her age, of at last meeting a man who would be entirely right for her, and whom she could love with her whole being.

She wasn't sure whether Ed saw himself as that man or not, but he was certainly pleased with the finished book, as was Alice. She insisted on selling it to hardcover first, for the maximum publicity, although with a presale agreement that Folsom Books had the reprint rights. And it was a bestseller. Stephanie had hoped it would do well, but she had never expected it to hit the top, and kept feeling there had to be some kind of a mistake. But apparently there wasn't, and suddenly there was a real film interest again, and huge overseas sales, and she was back on top of the moon. It was the first time, she realised, she had ever really been on top of the moon – the others had all been illusions.

Most remarkable of all, having reached the top of the bestseller lists, the book stayed there, for week after week after week.

'I tell you what,' Ed said, 'if it makes fourteen weeks up there, which is longer than any book I've had the rights to has stayed number one before, I am going to throw the biggest party you ever saw, with you as the guest of honour.'

'I think Dashman should throw the party,' Stephanie objected. 'They're raking in the sales.'

'Oh, they'll go halves with me,' he said. 'But with hardcover sales like this, and a film to follow, I know we have a paperback blockbuster.'

'Do you think the film will come off?'

'No doubt about it. They'd be crazy not to. You're at the top, Stephanie. The very top. And I want to make sure the whole world knows about it. Now, if there's anyone at all in New York, or anywhere in the world, that you'd like to invite to the party, just tell my secretary. Anyone at all.'

Well, Stephanie thought, maybe it would be nice to have Mrs Vernon Latchman looking up at me, just for a change.

THE FIFTEENTH CHRONICLE

July 1985

It was the strangest sensation, Meyer thought, to have actually shaken the hand of Stephanie Janska. He had now been pursuing her, and her sisters, and their father, for nine months, and had come to feel that he had known them all their lives. During the last week, while he had been awaiting the invitation his friend Martin had promised to obtain for him, he had, now that he at last had a living, breathing target, so to speak, in his sights, completed his investigation, followed her on the street, discovered her bank, made discreet inquiries about her both there and of the doorman at her apartment building, studied her from a distance. And here she was in the flesh, close to, twice as lovely as he had imagined she would be, a woman with the world at her feet. Was he about to roll that world away?

He had already formed a plan of campaign, evolved a cover story, which he had no doubt would take him towards his goal without revealing his purpose. For while he no longer agreed with Stein's hypothesis, that Anna Hunt could have been the security towards which Josef Janski had been fleeing in 1972, he had a shrewd suspicion that as Stephanie was currently on top of the world, through her he could locate both Anna and Beth, and that where Anna was being kept hidden – obviously by her sisters if they were keeping Hunt in Miami – there, too, he would find Janski.

And if he still wasn't sure that he wanted to do that, to complete this investigation, and bring this lovely woman's life down in ruins, if he still hoped and prayed that Janski might have died and be buried in some unnamed grave, he had no doubt at all that he wanted, through Stephanie, to come face to face with Beth Janska.

He obtained a glass of champagne, and gravitated to

the sides of the room. The talk was all books and writing, as was to be expected at a literary party, and although he was sufficiently practised a conversationalist to keep his end up even at a subject of which he knew so little, he wasn't really interested in conversation, as he preferred to watch Stephanie acting the gracious hostess. He had been in the room for about half an hour when the guest line came to an end, and she started to circulate. He followed her with his eyes, and his heart nearly stopped as he saw her talking to ... Beth. It had to be Beth Janska. And she must have arrived before him, and been there all the time, without his noticing it.

Seen together, the two women were clearly sisters. And yet, they were so very different as well. Beth had technically the more beautiful face, her contours as crisp as they had been in the two photographs he had carried in his wallet for so long. She also had the fuller figure, and in the glitter of her clothes and her jewellery and her personality she was by far the more dominating. Those were all things he would have expected of Beth Janska, the Beth Janska he had studied so carefully. They made a most attractive package. But there was also a coldness about Beth's expression, an almost harshness to her mouth, which he found offputting. He knew he was being less than just. No woman could have experienced what Beth Janska had endured and might still be enduring, for all he knew, and not become as hard as nails. Yet the disappointment was there.

He half turned away, so that they would not see him staring at them, engaged the woman beside him in animated conversation, waiting his opportunity to turn back, and watching the door to make sure neither of them left without his knowing it – although if they did he had no idea what he could immediately do about it, save follow them – and was thus taken by surprise when he heard a voice at his elbow, saying, 'Mr Meyer? Mrs Johnson would like to have a word with you.'

CHAPTER 15

New York, July, 1985

Stephanie realised she was tense, but at the same time, exhilarated. Throughout her life she had retreated from conflict wherever possible, content to let Beth take over and deal with each crisis as it arose. But tonight, to have someone turn up on the biggest occasion of her life, to threaten Beth ... Because she no longer had any fears for herself – she had never committed any crime that she knew of – she was quite prepared to take on the world.

Actually, Robert Meyer did not look in the least threatening, rather embarrassed that he should have been singled out to meet the guest of honour. And, as she had remarked to herself when meeting him in the reception line, he was an attractive and good looking man, of about her own age, she estimated. But he was obviously Jewish ... and suddenly the fact that he was about her own age was no longer the least reassuring.

'Mrs Johnson,' he said. 'This is the greatest pleasure of my life.'

Surprisingly, she thought he might have meant it.

'I've read your book,' he said. 'And I just had to meet you. So I'm afraid I rather inveigled an invitation to this party.'

'Then you are not in writing yourself?' asked John Harper, who had made the introduction.

'I wish I were,' Meyer confessed.

'I see,' Harper said thoughtfully.

'What line of business are you in, Mr Meyer?' Stephanie asked.

'It would be difficult to explain, Mrs Johnson,' Meyer said.

'Yes,' Harper remarked. 'Well, it's been a great pleasure meeting you, Mr Meyer. Now, Stephanie, Harry Edmonds is wanting to have a word with you about ...'

'Later, John,' Stephanie said. 'Mr Meyer's glass is empty. So is mine.' She drained it. 'Do you think you could find us a refill?'

Harper hesitated, trying to catch her eye, and then gave up and went in search of the wine waiter.

'I suspect he feels I'm an imposter,' Meyer said.

'I suspect I agree with him,' Stephanie said, looking into his eyes. 'But I am intrigued as to why you should be imposting, if there is such a word, at so limited a gathering. There are scarcely any trade secrets to be gathered here, Mr Meyer.'

'I told you that it was a long story, Mrs Johnson,' he said. 'And an involved one. But one which you might like to hear. Perhaps over dinner?'

Stephanie continued to gaze at him. He gave the impression of being as cool as a cucumber, yet she suspected that he wasn't. But he certainly had tremendous confidence in himself, and a cheek to equal it. He could be a very dangerous man ... and she just had to find out in which direction he intended to be dangerous.

Her immediate supposition was that he might be an envoy from Bertie. But the fact that he was an Israeli could have a far more sinister explanation: that Bertie had after all spilled the beans. Either way, someone had to find out. And in this case it would have to be her. Besides, her sense of exhilaration was growing.

'I might just take you up on that, Mr Meyer,' she said. 'But I think if we were to leave together, in the middle of my party, my faithful friends might lynch you before we reached the street.'

He smiled. 'That must be a solid position to be in, Mrs Johnson. Very reassuring, for you. Then perhaps I could call you.'

'No,' she said. She wasn't prepared to wait, a moment longer than she had to. 'I have to sit this party out, but it should break up by nine. Why don't you leave in about half an hour? Then I'll meet you at ... say the Four Seasons for supper, at half past nine.' She smiled

397

at him, unable to resist the temptation to let him know that he was playing in her backyard. 'If you have any problem getting a table, tell them you're dining with Mrs Johnson.'

'The magic words,' he riposted easily.

'Oh, thank you, John,' she said, taking her glass of champagne as Harper returned to them. 'Mr Meyer is most interesting. So glad to have met you, Mr Meyer.' She walked away from him, feeling his eyes on her back.

A moment later Beth joined her. 'Now there's a tall, dark, handsome stranger,' she said. 'Who's crazy about you.'

'Don't be absurd,' Stephanie said. 'We only just met for the first time.'

'You haven't been watching the way he's been looking at you, since coming in,' Beth said. 'Hungry is hardly an adequate description. You want to take his telephone number.'

'Anyone would think you were trying to marry me off,' Stephanie remarked, hoping her cheeks weren't as flushed as they felt. 'Beth . . . about supper . . . do you think we could make it another night? All of this noise and champagne is giving me a headache.'

'Even adulation can get on top of you,' Beth agreed sympathetically. 'Of course, darling. Give me a ring when you're feeling better. And come to dinner with us on Saturday. Vernon wants to talk. He says, now that you're a wealthy woman, I mean by his standards, he has some stock exchange details which might interest you.'

'No way,' Stephanie laughed. 'But I'm always prepared to listen.'

Ten minutes later, Beth was amongst the first to leave. And it occurred to Stephanie that she had never lied to Beth before.

'Mrs Johnson.' The maitre d'hotel took her fur reverently. 'How nice to see you. Mr Meyer is waiting for you.'

So he had used her name. She went into the dining room, conscious that she was being recognised by more than one person present. The result of the TV interview she had given a couple of days before, she supposed; it was a comforting and reassuring feeling.

Meyer was on his feet to greet her. 'I'm a few minutes late, I'm afraid,' she apologised. 'These parties always contain one or two hangers-on, and I had to stay until the bitter end.'

'I'd have waited all night.' He held her chair for her.

She studied him. Had he really been watching her, all evening, hungrily? Her exhilaration began to translate itself into excitement. Her instincts kept telling her that he was dangerous, that if Beth knew what she was doing she would have a fit; her femininity kept pointing out that he was the most attractive man she had met since Geoffrey Trene ... and look where that had got her.

She declined an aperitif, having had more than enough champagne, and they ordered.

'Now,' she said, when they had started into their entrées. 'You had a long story to tell me.'

'Less long than involved,' he said. 'Do you mind if I call you Stephanie?'

'Please do. And you're Bob, right?'

He nodded. 'I suppose I should begin by saying that you and I share a common heritage, to a point.'

Stephanie raised her eyebrows.

'I was born in Warsaw, too,' he explained. 'On 15 April 1936. Your birthday was 6 November 1936.'

Stephanie swallowed a piece of veal without chewing it, had to wash it down with a gulp of wine. Oh, my God, she thought, why didn't I bring Beth? She had a terrible feeling that she was rapidly drifting out of her depths.

'We were lucky, I guess,' Meyer said. 'We both got out. But I'm afraid my sister may not have.'

'Sister?' Stephanie asked, trying to put her thoughts in order.

399

'Gertrude. She was four years older than I.'

'Oh,' Stephanie said. 'When you say she didn't get out, you mean . . ?'

'Oh, no, no,' Meyer said. 'I didn't mean she died in a gas chamber, or anything like that. Well . . . let's say I have no proof that she did. But when I returned after the War to find her, she had disappeared. No one knew what had become of her. I have spent most of my life searching for her.'

Stephanie had by now recovered, and was prepared to pick holes in his story. 'That's terribly sad,' she said. 'But searching for her must have cost a bit, if it's taken you all over the world.'

'I inherited a private income,' Meyer said, gazing into her eyes.

Every instinct she possessed told her he was uttering a pack of lies – but she so wanted to believe him. On the other hand, she didn't dare lower her guard for a moment. Obviously he had to be met with a blanket refusal.

'I still don't understand what brings you to me. Or where you got the idea I was born in Warsaw. I'm Stephanie Johnson, remember? I'm British. Or I was until I came over here.'

Meyer gave a quiet smile. 'My impression is that your real name is Stephanie Janska. I'm sorry,' he hastily added. 'I know it is very presumptious of me to come at you like this, but I want you to believe that in my desperation to find my sister, I left no stone unturned, as it were. The Polish authorities were quite co-operative, really, even if I was a Jew and they were Communists. They let me look at records, and things like that; such as were available. I know Gertrude was at school in Wrakinow at the beginning of the War; they allowed me to see a list of the names of all her classmates . . .'

'There was no Gertrude Meyer in my class,' Stephanie interrupted without thinking. That would have been impossible, anyway, in her German controlled school.

'Of course not,' Meyer agreed easily. 'As I said, she was four years older than us. But there was an Anna Janska in her class. I cannot help but wonder if she might be a relative of yours.'

Stephanie had stopped making any attempt to eat. She was aghast at what she had just virtually admitted . . . But could it possibly be true that he was seeking a sister? And not her? Or Father? Logic told her there could not possibly have been a Jewish girl in Anna's class either, except that he had said the beginning of the War. Anna had first gone to school then, a good four years before herself. She couldn't remember much about those early years – she had only been four – but perhaps the German's hadn't been as strict then. Beth would know, of course. Oh, why hadn't she brought Beth?

And until she could discuss the situation with her sister, she simply had to keep up the straight denials. She kept her voice quiet and amused with an effort. 'I really hate to disappoint you, Bob,' she said. 'But I simply have no idea what you are talking about. I am Stephanie Johnson, from London.'

He gave a little sigh. 'I suppose it was a very long shot. You see, I did manage to find out that there were three Janska sisters, Elizabeth, Anna, and Stephanie, and that they, too, disappeared from Warsaw at the end of the War – at least, no trace of them was ever found, and they were officially considered dead, as were so many people who had simply disappeared. However, I am fairly sure the three Janska girls did not die. In my hunt for Gertrude, I naturally went through the records of every Displaced Persons camp I could find, just in case she had made it to the West. Well, I never did find a Gertrude Meyer, but I did find the names of three Janska sisters. So they managed to get away from Warsaw and the Communists. Of course, I have no idea what happened to them after they left the camp . . .'

Stephanie continued to gaze at him, keeping her face

401

still with an immense act of concentration. 'But your sister didn't. How terrible for you.'

Meyer shrugged. 'I didn't want to give up, I guess. I just had this crazy idea that if the three Janska girls got away, Anna might have taken her classmate with her, or at least been accompanied by her for part of the journey. As you say, Gertrude doesn't seem to have reached the DP camp. But if I could just know that she is dead, and how and where, and escape this feeling that she may be alive somewhere, believing me to be dead, perhaps . . .'

He gave another sigh. 'Anyway, that was that, and I had to give up. Until I read your novel. Of course I understand that it is a work of fiction, and yet, however brilliantly you have embroidered the facts and spiced it up, such as adding the brothel scenes and the London gangsterism and that sort of thing, I gained the impression that in certain places, and especially the story of the escape from Warsaw and life in the DP camp, that you were recalling events which you had actually experienced. And then, Stephanie Johnson, Stephanie Janska . . . It was a pure stab in the dark, but I just had to try. I love my sister, Stephanie. So I secured an invitation to your party. Now . . .' he gave a sad smile. 'You will be quite within your rights if you feel like slapping my face for an unutterable cheek for attempting to interfere in another person's life, and I shall apologise and go home. Sadly, but immediately.'

Stephanie continued to gaze at him. Beth would say that it had to be pure coincidence, that someone searching for a long-lost sister out of Warsaw should have read her book. The fact remained that she had supposed the novel would never be related to any of them. Certainly she could never let him further into the secrets of her life; now for the first time she was thankful that she had not brought Beth along.

She smiled. 'I am terribly sorry, Bob, but you have made a mistake. I'm afraid I don't have any sisters, and

402

I really only know about Poland and DP camps and things like that from reading other people's accounts of them; as a young woman I happened to be engaged in refugee work, and some of the tales I had to listen to were so harrowing I just knew that one day I would put them in a book. I do wish I could help you, but I simply can't.' That at least was true.

Meyer drank some wine. 'Then I do apologise, very sincerely. It was a very long shot.' He summoned a smile himself. 'At least you haven't slapped my face. Do you want me to walk away?'

'Oh, not in the midst of a lovely dinner,' she objected. 'I might have to pick up the bill.'

They gazed at each other. And Stephanie knew he knew she had just lied to him. But then, she had suddenly become sure that he had been lying to her as well. He had not confessed that he had been following her about, making enquiries of her bank and doorman – he didn't know she knew about that.

'In that case,' Meyer said, 'how about letting me pick up some more bills, from time to time?'

Sitting at home that night Stephanie thought over that eventful day. She had every reason to congratulate herself. She had, as Ed Martinez had said, tonight reached the pinnacle of her profession. But she was pleased with herself for an entirely different reason: she had this time stepped in front of Beth, to fight for the family on her own two feet. But having done that, when she could indeed have accepted Meyer's invitation to slap his face and tell him to stop cluttering up her life, she had agreed to see him again.

She could pretend there were logical reasons for this. If he had been lying, and was really seeking the Janska sisters for some ulterior motive, which could only be to do with Father, then she had to find out. If she had turned him away he would have turned his attention to finding Beth, which would not have been too difficult

403

once he was sure she was the Stephanie Janska he sought, and that could have led to endless trouble. She dared not imagine what Beth's reactions might have been to discovering there was an Israeli pursuer on her heels.

This way, she would absorb him and make him think he was on the verge of a breakthrough, while keeping him surrounded by brick walls. Thank God he did not seem to realise that Beth had been at the party tonight.

But the truth of the matter was that Meyer attracted her. Attracted her! She had not felt so excited since the night Geoffrey had taken her to Alberto's. Thus she was being as foolish now as then. Far more foolish, because then she had been a foolish virgin of twenty-three and now she was a hard-bitten matron of forty-eight. She was being absurd. She knew the man was a liar, and probably a sworn enemy of everything Janski. She knew she was risking everything Beth had so carefully put together. And she might even be risking George. But it was so terribly long since she had been attracted by a man, or attracted at all. She loved Ed Martinez like the brother Tony should have been, but she could not see herself ever feeling the least turned on by him. The same went for John Harper or any other of the men who had taken her out over the past fifteen years. Then why Meyer?

She just did not know. Save that he suggested tension, and yet sophistication, danger, and yet superb physical pleasure, tragedy, and yet strength, experience allied to determination, all rolled up into one and concentrated in a way she had never known before. So he might be an enemy. Then she could enjoy him to the hilt, and still discard him, coldly and cruelly, whenever the necessity arose.

And she need tell him nothing about the family.

She felt like the heroine of one of her own books. It was going to be an exciting autumn. If he lasted that long.

THE SIXTEENTH CHRONICLE

December 1985

Meyer entered his rented apartment on lower Park Avenue, threw his hat in a corner and threw his topcoat behind it. Then he poured himself a scotch and water, sat in an easy chair and stared at the ceiling. When he at last lowered his eyes, he saw the pile of mail which his cleaning lady had kindly accumulated on the coffee table; both letters bore a Jewish postmark. Well, he had known they had to come.

But he didn't want to open them right this minute. He wanted to savour the afternoon he had spent, as he enjoyed savouring most afternoons nowadays. If this was the best of them all, they had none of them been less than entrancing, whenever Stephanie was available, which was only a couple of times a week. She worked extremely hard most afternoons on her next novel. Nor would she allow herself to go out to dinner more than twice a week, and never at all when George was home from Harvard. This was because she liked to spend her evenings with him, and because she was as careful about her sleep as she was about everything else. She reckoned that she always needed a clear brain to write with first thing in the morning.

The information he had gathered over the years had been no more than scratches on the surface. Stephanie Janska was a remarkable woman. He had soon learned that, without wearing it up front as Beth so obviously did, she was a very strong, tough woman. Well, it

405

would have been surprising had she not been, given her present circumstances. No one who could surmount all of her setbacks and disasters and rise to the top of probably the most competitive vocation in the world could have done it without possessing a very tough streak.

What really surprised him was the absolute determination with which she had set out to protect her family, and which she had now maintained for five months. She was Stephanie Johnson, and she would admit to nothing different. Indeed. had he not known positively that she was also Stephanie Janska, he would long ago have accepted that he was following the wrong scent. What was more, she had trained her son in the same mould. George was a splendid fellow, big and strong and handsome and talented, but he, too, presented a brick wall when it came to releasing any information about the family.

Mother and son were so obviously in complete rapport with each other that it would have made them a most attractive prospect, save to a man who desperately wanted to come between them, for a variety of reasons.

And had now done so?

He leaned forward to pick up the letters. The first was his pay cheque, and he let that fall back to the table. The other, predictably, was from Isaac Stein.

'May I ask what the hell is going on?' Stein began. 'Last July you were virtually home and dry. You just needed a couple more weeks, you said. In August, you were just about there. In September, ditto. It is now December. Maybe you don't have a calendar. But I would like to know what you have been doing these last three months.'

Meyer leaned back again, and resumed gazing at the ceiling. What have I been doing? he asked himself. Not a lot he could possibly tell his boss. He had been dating the most magnificent woman he had ever know. No doubt, after the long years when his profession had kept him apart from women except on the most casual basis, he had been something of a pushover, and no doubt he had been falling in love with this woman for a year, while he had painstakingly put her life together – except that he had always supposed he had been falling in love with Beth.

The truly remarkable thing, the fact which had caused the mutual spark which he felt had existed from the moment of their first meeting to burst into flames, was that she had been in exactly the same position.

He presumed that she might also have had the odd casual fling over the twenty-odd years since her marriage had ended in disaster, although he doubted even that, now; certainly he was't concerned about it. What mattered was that from the start, and notwithstanding the fact that she immediately recognised that he might be a threat to the safety of her family sufficiently to lie to him, she had seemed to enjoy his company, and had gone on enjoying it, more and more.

Not things he could tell Isaac Stein; those unfortunates pursued by one of Stein's agents were not supposed to enjoy it. Stein would ask, very correctly, why, if he was getting nowhere with Stephanie Janska, he had not switched his attention to her sister. He knew Beth Janska's married name and address, and he was now quite sure that if anyone was concealing Josef Janski, and perhaps Anna Hunt as well, it would be Beth and not Stephanie. What could he reply to that, save to admit that he no desire to chase Beth Janska any more? He had found the Janska he wanted.

Well, then, Stein would say, were he in possession of all the facts, what about those days every week when Stephanie Johnson mysteriously goes out of town? There can only be one place she visits so regularly and so secretly. Any competent detective would have tailed her and found out exactly where that place was – and who lived there.

So, would he tell Stein that he had no desire to complete this assignment? That he was afraid even to push too hard in the direction of discovering that Josef Janski was dead, in case the moment of discovery might lead Stephanie to deducing who and what he really was?

Stein would blow a gasket.

But what would happen now, because of what had happened that afternoon? He was crazy. But then, so was she. He knew she was living a lie, certainly to him. He felt she knew he was living a lie, at least to her. Yet the mutual enjoyment they had found in each other had made those two sinister facts seem irrelevant.

So they had done nothing more than enjoy themselves for four months. He had maintained the mental reservation, and escape clause, that he was pursuing an assignment, and that sooner or later she would make the slip which would give him everything he wanted to know . . . while always praying that she wouldn't. Their relationship had been fun. They had not kissed each other until their fifth date, but that had been a mutually hungry moment. He had thought, then, she would be an easy woman to seduce, because she wanted it, despite all . . . and he had always been taught that the easiest and quickest way to get through a woman's mental defences was in bed. Thus he had determined not to do it, had held back time and again when she had expected it and had been looking forward to it, he thought.

Yet it had eventually happened, and been the most wonderful experience of his life, while her mental defences had not lowered an inch. So, try again, Stein would say. But that evening had sealed his defection from the cause he had always hitherto held sacred. And when it had happened again, this afternoon, it had sealed something else: the fact that he was utterly and totally in love for the first time in his life. He was also sure she felt the same. So he had said, 'I'd like to do something about us.'

It had been a tentative proposal, because even as he was uttering the words he had known it was probably the most absurd statement ever uttered by a pursuer to the pursued. This woman's father had in all probability murdered his mother and father, at least by proxy, and here he was suggesting marriage.

The incongruity of the situation, even if she might not yet have worked out the truth of it, had not escaped Stephanie. She had stretched those splendid legs, and sighed against his chest, and replied, 'I'd like that, Bob, more than I can say. But let's think about it for a while.'

Because marriage would necessitate an end to lying. She had recognised that right away. He had been prepared to let events take their course. So, when she said yes, would she then tell him the truth about her family?

What then? Would he ever tell her the truth about himself? Could he?

He picked up Stein's letter again.

'I feel we have to have results, right now,' Stein wrote, 'or accept that the trail has grown too cold. You have now been on the Janski case for one year. This is a long time. Too long a time to waste on a not very important target, and especially one who may be dead in any event. I await your comments, but as of this moment, unless you are about, and I mean, about, to close on Janski, I intend to close his file.'

Meyer laid down the letter again. Hallelujah, he thought. Yet, it wasn't really an out. It didn't really alter the reasons why he had tracked Stephanie and her sisters so remorselessly for a year. If he intended to live with her, he would have to tell her the truth. There was only one course of action which would permit that.

He got up, went to his desk, placed a sheet of paper in front of him. He had no time for a further exchange of letters. A telegram would reach Stein tomorrow. He wrote: 'LETTER RECEIVED AND UNDERSTOOD STOP AGREE ALMOST CERTAINLY TARGET NOW DECEASED STOP IN ANY EVENT I RE-SIGN STOP BEST MEYER.'

As he wrote his name, the doorbell rang. He got up and went to it, opened it, and stared at Beth Latchman.

Meyer was so surprised he forgot his manners, and just kept staring at her.

Beth smiled. 'Mr Meyer, isn't it? We have never actually met. But I do feel I know you so well. I am Elizabeth Latchman. Won't you ask me in?'

Meyer stepped backwards, and Beth entered the apartment. More accurately, she swept past him with a burst of *Adoration* perfume and a swish of her mink coat. He supposed there was no other way Beth Janska could enter a room.

He followed her into the lounge, still unable to think of anything to say. His mind continued to be in a total jumble, his attempts at coherent thought obscured by the realisation that in some inexplicable manner he was alone in his apartment with the woman that for nearly a year he had supposed himself to be in love with, after having only two hours before left the bed of the woman he now knew he was in love with . . . her sister.

Beth sat down and crossed her knees. 'You don't mind, I hope?'

Meyer found his voice. 'Be my guest.'

'Thank you. I felt that you and I should have a little chat,' Beth explained.

'You and me,' Meyer said thoughtfully. 'About what? Would you like a drink.' He certainly felt like one.

Beth looked at her gold Rolex. 'Why not, it's all but six. Vodka on the rocks.' Meyer poured, took one for himself.

'Ciao,' she remarked, and sipped. 'I imagine you are totally mystified by this.'

'Interested,' Meyer corrected cautiously.

'I wish to talk to you about my sister,' Beth said.

'Your sister?'

'You mean Stephanie has not told you I'm her sister? I suppose I should have expected that. She's very secretive. Well, I am Stephanie Johnson's sister.'

'You are Stephanie's sister?' Undoubtedly his best course lay in feigning utter ignorance of, and surprise at, everything she might say.

'Oh, come now, Mr Meyer, surely you can see the resemblance. I am her elder sister, by several years. I am also the de facto head of our family.'

Meyer's heart gave a lurch; the slip he had been waiting for Stephanie to make for five months. De facto! Therefore there was a de jure head of the family still around, and it could only be Josef. God, why had Beth of all people turned up at this moment to tell him something like that?

If she had made a slip, Beth showed no sign of realising it. 'Thus,' she continued, 'I am interested in your plans for my little sister.'

'Plans?' Meyer asked.

'Stephanie rang me not an hour ago,' Beth told him, 'and announced that she thought she was going to get married again. Stephanie! She was quite unlike her normal self. I thought she was drunk. And then I realised she was merely in a state of euphoria. Because I assume you had just left her bed. Four o'clock in the afternoon. I never enjoyed sex in the afternoon. However, I also realised that she was very serious.'

'Stephanie said she was going to marry me?' Meyer asked, and now he was not feigning amazement at all.

'Oh, indeed. Well, she didn't say she was going to marry *you*. She refused to tell me who she was going to marry. But of course I knew it was you.'

'How?' Meyer asked, with genuine interest.

'My dear Mr Meyer, I have had you under surveillance ever since Stephanie's party at the Waldorf.'

'You have ...' God, had he given himself away? 'May I ask why?'

'Because I was at that party. Perhaps you didn't notice me,' Beth said, without total belief. 'But I noticed you, and I noticed the way you were looking at Stephanie. It so happened that Stephanie and I had arranged to have supper together afterwards. But on

411

leaving you, she cried off because of a headache. It is continually amazing to me how someone who can write as imaginatively as Stephanie can at the same time be so totally lacking in imagination in her own affairs. Of course I knew right away you and she had made a date. So I left the party early, and sat in my car, and waited. Ten minutes later, you came out, by yourself. The doorman called you a cab, remember? I waited until you had driven away, then went across and asked him where you had gone; he told me, the Four Seasons Restaurant. I went back to my car and waited for Stephanie to come out, after the party ended. Then I followed her. To the Four Seasons, headache and all.'

Meyer scratched his head. Once he had supposed this woman would prove a worthy adversary. He had been right.

'After that, as I have told you, I hired a firm of private detectives to check up on your activities, and they have had a lot to report, about you and Stephanie. So I have to ask you to come clean with me, Mr Meyer. You may suppose that Stephanie is a lonely middle-aged woman who will fall for the first man who flashes his teeth at her. I may agree with you. But that does not mean I am going to let her be taken for a ride by a man who is either after a free fuck or her very hard earned fortune. She obviously thinks you mean to do the honourable thing. I would like confirmation of that.'

She had spoken for long enough to allow Meyer, who had at last got his brain working, and now had it whirring as hard as if he had found himself engaged in a five-minute chess game against a grand master, the time to consider various possibilities. All based on his knowledge of this woman, which was the one real advantage he possessed – simply because she was unaware of that knowledge. Thus, while it would be in character for Beth Janska to appear as the protector of the happiness of her forty-nine-year-old sister, presuming that she was still protecting the other members of her family, it would be more in character for her to have some deeper motive for this call than that.

She could see that he was Jewish; she would certainly have established through her private detectives that he had appeared in New York from nowhere and possessed no visible means of support; if she had any idea of what her father was guilty, and he was still around ... But wouldn't it have been safer for her just to keep her distance, and rely on Stephanie's not having confessed her true identity? Perhaps she didn't trust Stephanie. ... She had certainly been momentarily surprised to learn that Stephanie had not told him she was her sister.

Equally, perhaps, it was not in Beth Janska's nature to do anything less than charge an opponent. Because if she had been surprised, she had not allowed it to change her plans in any way.

But there was another possibility, which was quite terrible to consider, but which he had to take into account.

He could only play her along and see what devolved.

'I do certainly mean to marry your sister, Mrs Latchman,' he said, 'if she'll have me. If I was taken aback just now, it's because I have already asked her to marry me, and she said she wanted to think it over. I guess I'm still a little dazed that she should be saying yes.'

'Yes,' Beth agreed sceptically, 'Well, I should be delighted, of course. Stephanie has long needed a man. But he has to be the right man, and the right sort of man. I hope I am not being offensive, Mr Meyer. But would you mind telling me what you do for a living?'

'Not a lot,' Meyer said.

Beth raised her eyebrows.

'I have a private income,' Meyer explained, deeming it best to stick to that story for the time being, just in case the sisters had exchanged notes at any time.

'How convenient for you,' Beth said. 'So do I. And is it concerning this private income that you have come to New York? And stayed for five months?'

Meyer shrugged. 'Mrs Latchman, I guess I'll have to be honest with you. The fact is, I happened to pick up a copy of Stephanie's book, back in July, and was utterly fascinated. By the woman in the book as much as by the woman on the dust cover. I guess it sounds foolish to admit it, but I fell in love with her there and then. I've always been an impulsive fellow. So I came to New York in the hopes of meeting her, and a friend of mine wangled me an invitation to that party. I still find it difficult to believe that it has all worked out so well.'

'Yes,' Beth agreed, more sceptically than ever – she obviously found it impossible to believe anything he had said. But she gave him a reassuring smile. 'Well, that sounds delightfully romantic. I do hope you will forgive my barging in like this?'

'I think you had every right to, in the circumstances,' Meyer said.

'Do you? I'm so glad. Well, Mr Meyer, while I am perfectly willing to give you my blessing, in view of what you have told me so frankly, I think we are going to have to go along with my sister's secretive ways for the time being. She would be furious if she found out, for instance, that we even knew each other, much less that we have had this little chat. So I would be so very grateful if you didn't mention it to her.'

'Of course,' Meyer agreed.

'That's so good of you. When were you thinking of getting married?'

'Well, Stephanie hasn't actually said yes to my proposal as yet. Supposing she does, there'll be things to arrange . . .' Beth clearly needed the time to do some arranging herself. 'I would say early in the New Year would be best.'

'How right you are,' Beth said. 'I adore January weddings. But I think that we must make it a family occasion, whether Stephanie wants that or not. I know that my brother and sister will be so happy to know that little Stephanie is going to settle down at last. So I think we should plan a little surprise engagement party for her, don't you?' She arched her eyebrows at him; she had a way of creating an amazing feeling of intimacy, merely by her facial expressions.

'I think that would be a great idea,' he murmured, wondering what was coming next.

'So ...' Beth appeared to consider. 'I know, why don't you come down to my country place and have Christmas lunch with us all?'

'Christmas lunch?'

'Oh, I know that isn't a big occasion for you, Mr Meyer, but we do like it so. We are Catholics, you know. I am sure Stephanie must have told you that. Yes, you can meet my brother and sister, and you can also meet my father. Poor old dear, he's eighty-four, you know. I shouldn't think he'll be able to attend the wedding. But I know he would love to meet you.'

Meyer stared at her in consternation. He could not believe his ears.

'Stephanie and George are always there as well, of course. But Mr Meyer ... do you mind if I call you Bob, as we are going to be related? Stephanie is very secretive about the other members of the family. I'm afraid she doesn't altogether approve of them. Well, frankly, there are times when I feel she doesn't altogether approve of me, either. So again I must ask you to preserve a complete secrecy about this. We'll surprise her. Believe me, me when she sees you there in the bosom of her family, she will be as happy as anything.'

'Well,' Meyer said, with more than a little truth in his pretended doubt. 'If you're sure she won't be mad ... Where exactly is this country house of yours?'

Beth's mouth assumed a peculiar expression for a moment, then she was smiling again. 'You'd never find it on your own, Bob. I'll pick you up, on Christmas morning, that's December 25, you know, and drive you down there myself. Stephanie and George usually come down a little later. It'll be a real lovely surprise for her. Shall we say eight o'clock on the morning of Wednesday 25?'

'That'll be lovely,' Meyer said.

He closed the door behind her, and leaned against it for several seconds, still inhaling her scent. Beth Janska, he thought. A worthy opponent. Yes, but not quite as worthy as he had feared, and anticipated. She knew just who and what he was, but she had invited him to meet her father at a lonely country house. Presumably, if Beth Janska had a weakness, it was a tendency to regard everyone else in the world as a fool; but this he had realised during his pursuit of her.

The question was, what was he going to do about it? But that was connected with and overlaid by that other question which had occurred to him when she had first appeared, and was far more interesting and disturbing to him: was Stephanie involved?

Logically, she had to be. His researches had proved one thing beyond a shadow of a doubt, that the Janski family always stood shoulder to shoulder when the chips were down. And he knew that Stephanie had been resolutely lying to him from the beginning, however much she had appeared to enjoy his company. While he had only Beth's word that she had him followed; Stephanie could easily have been relaying everything that had happened between them to her sister from the very beginning. It was a terrible thing to believe of a woman he felt genuinely in love with, genuinely wanted to live with and care for throughout the rest of her life. But he had spent so much of his own life probing into the most unsalubrious places and people on earth, that he was conditioned to suspect everyone and accept nothing as being what it seemed on the surface.

Then he had better stop being the lover and become the cold blooded avenger once more. Whether after consultation with her sister or not, Beth Janska had decided he was too big a risk to be ignored, and thus she was making a play. Either he was what he claimed

416

to be, in which case what could be nicer than a family get-together with the man Stephanie was going to marry, champagne and congratulations all round, or he was what she suspected him to be, in which case she felt confident he would betray himself when he came face to face with the man he was hunting.

In which case she would have made some contingency plans for when that happened. In which case, she might just have invited him to attend his own execution. He did not doubt that Beth was ruthless enough even for that, when it came to protecting her own father. The prospect did not unduly alarm him. He had been invited, if perhaps not quite so openly, to attend his own execution in the past, and he was still around. But Stephanie . . . he could not believe that of her. He did not want to believe she had betrayed him to Beth. Yet he had to find out. He might be going to lose her anyway, even if she were innocent of the plot against him, if she chose to side with her family against him. But he knew he couldn't just walk away from her; he had to a accept the risk.

But if she did choose her family, then he couldn't walk away from his profession, his oath, his determination to avenge his parents, either. His determination to do those things had been based on the wild dream that he had found something, something, someone, to replace them. Nor could he, in those circumstances, walk away from the only true friend he possessed in the world, Isaac Stein. He went to the desk, and tore his drafted telegram into strips. Then he sat down and wrote out another message:

'HOLD ON FOR TWO MORE WEEKS STOP WILL POSSESS POSITIVE INFORMATION RE TARGET AND WHEREABOUTS BY MONTH END STOP MEYER.'

CHAPTER 16

New York and Environs, 1985

George said, 'Who's in love, then?'

'Don't be absurd,' Stephanie objected, but she had been caught singing as she put away the dinner dishes, a pastime she seldom indulged in.

'Well, then, you should be,' George pointed out. 'Bob's a nice guy, Mom. I mean, really.'

'Do you really think so?' Stephanie asked, aware that for a best-selling novelist, she could hardly engage in a more banal conversation.

'Really,' he agreed kindly.

'Well, I'm glad you feel that way. Because I think I am going to marry him, if it's all right with you.'

'You think?'

'I am,' she said decisively. 'And you're the first person I've told. About Bob, I mean. But I don't want you to tell a soul. Especially Aunt Beth. No matter how she presses.'

Because Beth would. She had had some vague idea of telling Beth everything, when she had dialled the number, in the expectation that Beth might be able to talk her out of it. Beth would have talked her out of it, had she identified the man. So she hadn't, just said she was the happiest woman in the world. To her relief, Beth had taken it all in good part.

Stephanie knew she was in love. She had loved Geoffrey, and would have loved him to the end, had he not lied to her. Which was what made her love for Bob Meyer so absurd; she knew in advance that he was lying to her, and had from the moment of their first meeting. Yet she had fallen in love with him. Beth would make a meal out of that.

If she ever found out. But she needn't. Stephanie intended to find out the truth for herself, first, when she said yes, officially. And if he didn't measure up, she would draw back. But she didn't truly care what he was, or what he was pretending to be. He had made her happy. Happier than she had even been in her life before. And she was no twenty-three-year-old virgin innocent, as she kept reminding herself, as when she had fallen for Geoffrey. Although she had felt like one when she had gone to bed with Bob for the first time.

She was not sure she had intended to do that, because it had been an irrevocable act for her; he was only the second man to whom she had ever extended that privilege. If Bob had proved the least inconsiderate or aggressive or incapable, she felt that she would have been able to end it there and then. Instead he had proved the most wonderful experience of her life.

So the decision had been taken at that moment, even if she had waited to make sure. But now she was sure. Tonight was going to be the happiest night of her life.

'Have you told the family?' George asked.

'Not really,' Stephanie confessed. 'Aunt Beth has an idea what's happening, which is why I want you to be very discreet with her.'

'So when are you going to tell them all?'

'Well ... I know, on Christmas Day. I'll announce my engagement on Christmas Day, to the whole family. Don't you think that's a good idea?'

'I think that's a great idea,' George said.

And by then, Stephanie thought, I'll know all about him.

But it didn't work out that way. The following night they went out to dinner, to the Four Seasons at her suggestion, because that was where they had first dined together. They had champagne, and she looked into his eyes, and sensed for the first time in a very long time, that the tension of their first meetings was back.

'What's on your mind?' she asked.

'Should there be anything on my mind?' he countered. 'Other than you?'

'I guess I'm quite a weight,' she agreed, determined not to be put off tonight of all nights. 'I was just wondering if you'd changed your mind about wanting to marry me.'

'Do you really think I'd do that?' he asked.

Once again she stared at him. The tension seemed to be growing. But perhaps he was just upset because she hadn't immediately said yes. Now was the time to put that right. 'Because I've been thinking,' she said. 'That I'd rather like to do that.'

'Oh, my darling girl,' he said. 'You have made me so very happy.'

He might be reciting, very badly, the lines in a play.

'Now,' he went on, 'when shall we do it?'

'Well . . .' she began.

'I rather thought immediately after Christams,' he suggested. 'In the New Year.'

It was time to shake him up a little, get him out of this strange mood. 'You have it all planned,' she accused. 'You mean you never had any doubt that I would say yes?'

'I was keeping my fingers crossed,' he smiled, and for a moment was the man she had fallen in love with again. But then he changed once more. 'There is a lot of arranging to be done. I mean, how will your family feel about your marrying a Jew?'

'George is all for you,' she said.

'That's terrific. I love him, too. But aren't there any other family?'

'None which matter that much,' Stephanie said.

They gazed at each other. 'Then there's no problem,' he said easily.

How she wanted to tell him the truth. Because she felt that a lot of his coolness might be being caused by his own awareness that she was holding part of herself back.

'But I'm sure you'll have to do some convincing of your old Irish priest, or whatever,' he went on. 'I know I'll have to do some convincing of my rabbi. But we'll manage. And I promise that whatever he says, I'm going to start being a good Christian as well as a good

Jew. I want to have Christmas lunch with you.'

She had the oddest feeling that he had been leading up to that request all evening.

'Why?' she asked. 'There isn't anything very Christian about Christmas lunch, believe me. It's just one long exercise in gluttony, which leaves everyone with galloping heartburn.'

'Sounds rather fun to me.'

Stephanie hesitated. It was such a temptation to invite him down for Christmas lunch with the family. After all, they were going to be married. But she didn't dare risk it. She had to tell them first, and discover their reactions to the idea – especially Beth's.

She leaned forward and held his hand. 'Bob, darling, darling Bob ... would you take it terribly amiss if we skipped Christmas lunch? Just this time. We can have all the Christmas lunches you wish after we're married, but ...'

'This one is bespoke?'

'Well, I'd sort of promised George a special thing, just him and me. Believe me, he is terribly fond of you. I told you, he's all for us getting married. But you know, he's only twenty-one, and the realisation that his dear old mom, who's been a widow ever since he can remember, is about to get hitched again, is proving a bit hard to assimilate. I really would like to ease him into the situation slowly.'

'I never knew you were a widow,' Bob remarked. 'You never told me.'

'Oh? Well, as I said, it happened a long time ago.' But she had been given a cue. 'I guess there are an awful lot of things we haven't told each other, simply because we haven't thought of it. I suppose that's a concomitant of getting together in a ripe old age.' She squeezed his fingers. 'What haven't you told me? I'm sure there must be lots. I'm sure you have a family.'

'They're all dead, remember?'

'I hadn't realised they were all dead. Oh, Bob, how terrible for you.'

'I don't really want to talk about them,' he said. 'My family is in the past. I have an idea from what you just said that yours is in the past, too – except for George, of course. And you and I only have the future. That's all that matters. Now, first thing tomorrow morning we go and buy your engagement ring.'

He had switched into high gear, was smiling and again the man she loved. She spent the rest of the evening high in the clouds, indeed the night, because he went home with her. Only after he had left her in the morning, and she was getting dressed to meet him for the ring buying exercise at Tiffany's, did she remember that she hadn't got any further towards finding out the truth about him.

But suddenly she no longer wanted to. There was clearly something in his past which he didn't want to talk about. Well, there was a lot in her past she didn't want to rake up. And she loved him and wanted him. So she was being just as foolish now as she had been over Geoffrey, in cold terms. She didn't care. She had lived alone and been lonely for too long. Now she had found the man she wanted to share her life with. She didn't really care what he might have done, what skeletons might be lurking in his cupboard. Or even what he might still plan to do. Because she was invulnerable. That was the most reassuring thought she had ever had. But it was true. He could not even rob her, simply because all her money, even what she carried around in cash, was controlled and paid out by John Harper. Of course Harper would scream in agony when she told him what she was going to do, but as long as she promised never to change the financial set up, he would have to be reassured. As for her reputation, that rested securely in her books. That was the truly reassuring thought.

And the family? Oh, they would undoubtedly scream in agony, too. Beth loudest of all. But they didn't ever have to see Bob, if they didn't want to. That would almost certainly be the best solution. He knew nothing

422

of them, there was no need for them to have anything to do with him. On Christmas Day she would put the facts squarely to them, and let them choose. But whichever way they chose, she was going to live her own life, without looking over her shoulder. Just for a change. She intended to be utterly, irresponsibly happy. That was what being successful was all about.

It occurred to her that after Christmas Day, she would be truly free, for the first time in her life. She might even be able to stop being a refugee.

They spent Christmas Eve together, as they spent most evenings together, nowadays; the tension of that night had quite disappeared. 'I feel so bad about tomorrow,' she said.

'So do I,' he agreed.

'But it's something I feel I have to do. Just this last time, Bob. Say you understand.'

'Of course I understand. Are you taking George out of town?'

She glanced at him. 'We usually do. Why?'

'I'd just like you to be careful, that's all. There's a Travellers' Advisory out for snow and ice.'

'I've driven on snow before,' she assured him. 'And I'll be back by six in the evening. How about having Christmas dinner with me?'

'I'd like that,' he said. But suddenly the tension was back. He was still offended at being left out of even this last part of her life. But she knew he would understand and accept it when she could explain it to him – and besides, there would be other private parts of her life he would have to accept; her work would make that necessary.

And he was more loving than ever that night in bed.

When he left, at seven the next morning, it was already snowing, lightly. He held her very close and tight. 'Happy Christmas, darling. I'll have your present waiting for you this evening.'

423

'Happy Christmas,' she said and kissed him.

'It must be,' he said, with strange determination. 'It must be. But Stephanie, for God's sake take it easy on those roads.'

She and George drove carefully through the heavily falling snow. She was extremely relieved when eventually they came to a little gate leading to the yard and then the old timber house, two storied and originally box-like, but with wings built on to each side by previous owners, one to provide a TV den and the other a self-contained guest apartment. From the front porch, the grassy meadow – it could hardly be called a lawn – sloped back down to the edge of the lake. Here there was a little dock surrounded by ice and covered in snow. Tony's boat had been pulled up and lay upside down at the inner end of the wooden platform.

To Stephanie's surprise, Beth had not yet arrived; the only car to be seen was Tony's old Buick, in the lean-to garage. Tony himself was waiting on the porch to greet them, with Anna. Father seldom left his chair by the fire unassisted nowadays, and she stooped to kiss his cheek before taking off her mink and handing it to Tony to hang up. Then she gave Anna a big hug and a kiss.

Anna was properly dressed and even looked clean – she had obviously had her fix for the morning, was in a bubbling mood, and insisted on showing Stephanie the dining room, already set, as well as all the dishes she had prepared for the meal, and the bird, roasting away. She claimed to have done it all herself, although Stephanie had no doubt Tony would have done most of the cooking.

Tony appeared more highly strung and nervous this morning than usual, but he helped George bring the presents in from the car, and attempted to be light-hearted.

'Some car,' he commented. 'The wages of sin, eh, as lucrative as ever.'

'The wages of my typewriter,' she pointed out. 'I wonder why Beth is so late?'

424

'She only seems late, because we left early,' George suggested.

'I hope she gets here,' Stephanie said. 'It's really coming down.'

'Beth always gets wherever it is she's going,' Tony reminded her. 'And here she is.'

They watched the Cadillac pulling through the gate, windscreen wipers whirring furiously, and slither to a halt.

'You'd better give her a hand, George.'

He nodded, began to descend the steps, and checked as Beth, almost invisible beneath a volumious mink, got out – because the other door was opening as well. 'Holy smoke,' George remarked. It was unique to have an outside guest at this house at all, much less for Christmas lunch.

While Stephanie stared at Bob with her mouth open.

'Surprise!' Beth smiled. 'Don't look so dumbfounded. Isn't that what Christmas is all about?'

'Bob?' Stephanie went out on to the porch, despite the cold. 'But . . .'

He gave an anxious smile. 'It was Beth's idea.'

'Of course, darling,' Beth said. 'You didn't really suppose you could keep a secret from me, did you? Now, come along, Bob, I want you to meet the family.' She tucked her arm through his, almost, Stephanie thought, as if he were her fiancé. 'This is our brother Tony,' she said.

Tony had reached the bottom of the steps. 'Hi,' he said, and shook hands. Then he looked at Beth. It would have been the natural thing to do, Stephanie realised, seeking some explanation of this break with tradition, except that his eyes were not asking a question. In fact, he looked totally unsurprised by Bob's appearance. Unease began to grip her.

Beth smiled at her brother; she seemed to be on top of the world. 'The boot is packed with presents,' she said. 'Be a dear and unload them.'

'I'll give him a hand,' Meyer said.

'Oh, no,' Beth said, marching him towards the steps. 'You have to meet the family. But you may kiss your future bride.'

'May I ask what is going on?' Stephanie demanded, determined to be annoyed. 'Beth . . ?'

'I told you, I planned this as a surprise,' Beth told her, propelling Meyer up the steps.

'And you?' Stephanie looked at Meyer, and held him away as he would have taken her in his arms. 'You knew about this all the time?'

'Beth said you really wouldn't mind,' he said. But the tension was back, and more than the tension; she felt that he was coiled like a steel spring, as she finally allowed him to kiss her. Her feeling of unease deepened.

'I think you and I should have a little chat, in private,' she decided.

'Now, Stephanie, you can't be meaning to quarrel on Christmas Day,' Beth protested. 'Not with Bob. Quarrel with me, if you have to quarrel. But later. Bob, you know George, of course.'

'Hi, Bob,' George said, looking bewildered.

'Now come in out of the cold,' Beth said, half pulling Meyer through the front door; he obviously would dearly have liked that chat with Stephanie. 'Father, this is Bob Meyer.'

Stephanie, hurrying through the doorway behind them, saw her father's tired eyes gazing at Meyer, and Meyer gazing back at the old man. Neither man's expression revealed any particular emotion.

Beth was presenting Anna. 'Bob Meyer,' she explained.

'Well, hello,' Anna said, tossing her golden curls – nowadays she dyed them the same colour they had been when she had been a girl, to disguise the increasing number of grey strands – and coming forward to shake his hand. 'You look kind of nice. Are you . . ?' she looked at Beth, and her look was definitely seeking information. Presumably she expected to be told that

426

Beth had shed Latchman and was preparing to marry for a fifth time.

Beth smiled at her. 'Oh, no,' she said. 'Something far more exciting. Everybody, listen.'

'Beth, please,' Stephanie protested.

'They have to know, darling.' Beth said. 'Bob is going to marry Stephanie,' she anounced. 'Isn't that exciting?'

Everyone stared at Bob, and Anna clapped her hands.

'So he could become one of the family,' Beth went on. 'Unfortunately, he is also an Israeli agent, charged with hunting down Josef Janski.' She released Bob's arm and stepped away from him. 'Don't make any mistakes, Meyer. Tony is a very good shot.'

Their heads turned as if someone had jerked on a string, an they gazed at Tony, standing in the doorway, carrying, not the presents from the boot of Beth's car, but his deer rifle, which he had levelled at Meyer.

Meyer stood very still, looking from Tony to Stephanie, his expression more one of self criticism than alarm. He had come here expecting something, but nothing as sudden or decisive as Beth's announcement, and was mentally kicking himself.

Stephanie looked from him to Tony and then to Beth, and exploded. 'Are you mad? Is this some kind of stupid joke? My God . . .'

'Joke?' Beth asked. She opened her handbag and took out a small automatic pistol. With this in her hand, she stepped against Meyer, thrusting the muzzle into his ribs. 'Move and I'll kill you here and now,' she said, her tone leaving no doubt that she meant what she said. Then she thrust her other hand into his left armpit, beneath his jacket, and pulled out a thirty-eight revolver. 'Is this what a man usually carries to Christmas lunch?'

Stephanie stared at him, as Beth retreated across the room, carrying both guns; Meyer's she thrust into the pocket of the mink she still wore.

'Bob?' Stephanie whispered. 'I don't believe it.'

427

Meyer sighed and shrugged. 'It is true, Stephanie. I came looking for you, to get a lead on your father. But I swear to you that I abandoned the chase last July. Hell, you must realise that.'

'Abandoned the chase?' Beth sneered. 'Do you think we are fools, Meyer? Or frightened little people? Don't you think the moment I realised you were after Stephanie I had you investigated? It wasn't difficult, you know; my husband has business connections with every country in the world. You work for the famous Isaac Stein. But you're quite famous yourself. Robert Meyer! Oh, I found out all about you. M for Mountie is what they call you, isn't it, because you always get your man?'

Meyer shrugged again. 'It's a nickname. Nonetheless, I am telling you the truth. I abandoned the hunt when I realised I was falling in love with Stephanie.'

'But you were eager to accept my careless invitation to come down here today,' Beth reminded him.

'I wanted to meet you all,' Meyer explained. 'Heck, I've been tracking you for so long I feel as though I've known you all of your lives. That's all.'

'Oh, Bob, that's why you've been acting so strangely,' Stephanie said, and ran to him. 'I was so afraid.'

'But you do believe me?' His arm went round her.

'Of course I do. Oh, Bob . . .'

'Thank God for that. Just as thank God you had nothing to do with this charade.'

Her head went back. 'You thought that I . . .'

He kissed her nose. 'Only for a moment, my darling.'

'For God's sake,' Tony snapped. 'Are we going to have to listen to this lovey-dovey drivel all day? Let's get it over with. Stand away from him, Stephanie. And you, Meyer, outside. I don't want to mess up the house.'

Meyer raised his head, and Stephanie turned to face her brother, still in Meyer's arms. 'What did you say?' she asked in a low voice.

'Well, hell,' Tony pointed out. 'Why else do you think Beth invited him down here?'

Stephanie stared at Beth. 'You meant to *kill* him?'

'My darling,' Beth said reassuringly, 'what else can we do? It's the family, remember? Us against the world. This man represents all those forces in the world who have been hounding us all our lives.'

Stephanie looked from one to the other. 'I just don't believe it,' she said. 'You have got to be mad. Both of you. You think you can just kill someone because you regard him as a nuisance?'

'There is no risk,' Beth pointed out. 'Nobody knows he came down here today. And we can sink his body at the bottom of the lake, the moment there's a thaw. Nobody will ever find him. Nobody will ever even look for him, except his Israeli friends, and they won't know where to look.'

'My God,' Stephanie said. 'You can just stand there, and talk about killing someone, as if it were a game.'

'You're being childish, Stephanie,' Beth snapped. 'Didn't Father kill those people outside Lódź to save us? Don't you think I'd have done the same if he hadn't been there?'

'That was different,' Stephanie insisted. 'That was war.'

'Do you suppose the war has ever ended, for us?' Beth demanded. 'Then you are even more innocent than I had supposed. Who do you think saved us from Szabo?'

Stephanie could not believe her ears. She stepped away from Meyer. 'You killed Bertie?'

Beth made a face. 'No, I didn't. Tony did.'

'Beth,' Tony protested. 'You promised . . .'

'Oh, for God's sake, Tony,' Beth snapped. 'She has to know.'

'But the boy . . .'

Beth looked at George, who was standing to one side as if turned to stone. Stephanie knew that, however confused he might be by the bizarre events taking place around him, he was awaiting a lead from her, and would react to it. But she didn't dare give him a lead at

429

this moment. Besides, she also was too confused.

To this moment Anna, like her father, had remained a bemused witness of the scene, but now she stood up. 'What are you saying?' she shouted, her voice rising into a shriek. 'You killed Bertie? My Bertie? You . . .'

'Now look what you've done,' Tony said plaintively. 'I told you she must never find out. She has a real fixation on that character. It seems to have grown with the years. I guess when she was with him was the last time she was ever really happy.'

'Oh, pull yourself together, Anna,' Beth ordered. 'You're just as dumb as Stephanie. He was blackmailing us. And he was a thug. And he possessed the evidence to send Tony to gaol. I take full responsibility for what he did. I didn't tell him to do it. It just never crossed my mind, I suppose. But when Tony confessed to me that he'd done it, I realised it was the only way. Tony was so distraught about it. Weren't you, you poor boy. But you had done the right thing. And the proper thing. He sank Bertie's body into the sea, and do you know, the French police never identified it when it was washed up a few days later? Well, I don't suppose they tried very hard; people are always getting drowned along the Riviera, and Bertie had nothing on him to indicated he had any connection with England or with us. Tony had seen to that. But even his clothes had been bought in France. They put him down as some tramp who had fallen into the water and died.

'Of course,' she added, 'we took a risk, that he *had* left instructions that his information should be forwarded to Isaac Stein in the event that anything happened to him, but Tony was sure that was just a bluff, and he was right.'

Stephanie was still staring at her. 'Then all that rubbish you told me about them having dinner together was a lie?'

'You didn't really believe it, did you, my darling girl? But it was the story we had agreed upon. The important thing was that we were free of that pest, and that

Tony ...' she smiled at her brother, 'having told me what had happened, agreed to work for me so we could keep his little secret our little secret.'

'And now you've told everybody,' Tony grumbled.

'Well, because now the whole family has to stand together. It's all Stephanie's fault. I don't really believe she would have been so stupid to tell this man the truth about us, but I think he was telling the truth when he said he'd got the idea from reading Stephanie's book. God, the things I have to put up with.'

'Watch out!' Tony shouted, and Beth turned in time to catch Anna's arm as she rushed at her, sobbing and swinging her fists.

'You killed Bertie,' Anna howled. 'My Bertie. The only man I've ever loved. And you killed him. We were going to be married. And you killed him.'

Beth held Anna off with one hand while she pocketed the pistol, then she slapped her sister so hard across the face that Anna fell over into a chair.

For the moment she was the centre of attention. Stephanie turned to George, who began to move forward, to be checked by a command from Tony, as the rifle swung to and fro between him and Meyer.

'I've seven shots in this magazine,' Tony said. 'Don't make me waste you, too, George.'

George hesitated, and Meyer shook his head. 'Don't take any risks, George. This is my problem.'

Beth was still concentrating on Anna. 'Get up,' she was saying. 'And stop that snivelling. Get upstairs and wash your face. Pour yourself a drink, for God's sake.' She pulled Anna to her feet and pushed her from the room, closing the door behind her.

Josef Janski appeared to be trying to say something, and Beth patted his hand. 'I know, Father, it's all being a bit much, isn't it? But you know what Anna is like. We'll just finish this business and then we can have lunch.' She straightened, looking at Stephanie. 'I hope you are prepared to come to your senses,' she said. 'And tell George to come to his. This man you so stupidly picked up is here to destroy the family.'

'That's crazy rubbish,' Stephanie shouted. 'You heard what he said.'

'I heard what he said. I also know that he will say anything to get out of here alive. But he's not going to succeed. What is more, Stephanie, you and George are going to help us, so there can be no question of you running off to the police afterwards, although if you did that you would be the most foul traitors to the family.'

'Beth,' Stephanie begged. 'Listen to me. Can't you see how wrong you are? You keep carrying on about the family. My God! That man ...' she pointed at her father, 'is a mass murderer, to all intents and purposes. Yes, he is,' she told George, who had looked at her in consternation. 'Don't think I haven't had that on my conscience for more than ten years. I kept trying to believe Beth, that it didn't matter what he had done, he was still our father. But he deserves to be arrested. God knows, he even deserves to be hanged. And you are going to kill again to protect him, Beth?'

'It is you who are wrong, Stephanie,' Beth said. 'I have always been right. It does not matter what Father may have done. Whenever he killed, even the Jews, it was for us. He has spent his life fighting for us, for the family. That is all that matters.'

'I had to do it,' Josef Janski muttered. 'I had no choice.'

'Of course you had no choice, Father,' Beth agreed. 'Or we would have starved. Or been sent to a death camp ouselves. Now ...' She drew her pistol and pointed it at Meyer. Stephanie could almost feel the tension building in the room. This far Meyer had been content to remain still and let the family conflict flow around him. He had been reluctant to attempt to seize control, because once he had started on that, he knew, and she understood, there could be no stopping. But if he felt he was running out of time, he would have to act. And she would have to help him, and pray that George would not be hurt.

She tensed her own muscles, and the inner door burst open. Everything happened so quickly that no one, not even Meyer, had the time to move or say anything. Anna leapt into the room, brandishing a carving knife she had taken from the dining table, and in a single vast lunge buried it in Tony's back.

Tony made a choking sound and fell forward, killed outright by the blow.

'Oh, my God!' Beth screamed, and hurled herself at her sister, seizing her from behind by the shoulders and jerking her backwards with such force that Anna let go of the knife and threw her on the floor. Then she knelt beside her brother. 'Oh, my God,' she said again, more quietly.

Stephanie clasped both hands to her throat. Meyer crossed the room in two strides and picked up the rifle. George held Anna's shoulders as she attempted to rise.

Beth had turned Tony over; there was blood on her hands now as well, and staining the mink she had not yet removed: blood gathered in a pool beside the body. 'He's dead,' she said. 'Tony's dead! Oh, God, Tony's dead.' Her voice threatened to break.

'He killed my Bertie,' Anna snarled. 'And you protected him. I'm going to kill you, too.'

Beth turned, on her knees. Suddenly, and for the first time in her life, Stephanie thought she looked her age. But she was rapidly regaining control of herself. She looked at Anna, and then at Meyer and the gun he held, and her lips twisted. 'She should be sedated,' she said. 'But I don't suppose you would like me to leave the room. Stephanie, my darling, there is some codeine in my dressing table drawer, upstairs. Would you fetch it for me, and a glass of water?'

Stephanie looked at Meyer, who nodded. She hurried for the door and the stairs.

'You let go of me,' Anna snarled at George.

He also looked at Meyer.

433

'You'd better hang on to her for the time being,' Meyer said.

'You keep your mouth shut, Anna, or I am going to knock your head off,' Beth told her sister, her tone loaded with such venom that Anna did close her mouth.

Beth looked at her father, who had stared at the scene in front of him with blank eyes. He seemed to be seeing some memory from his past. 'Father?' she asked, gently.

He seemed to wake up. 'I had to do it,' he said again.

Beth signed, and turned to Meyer. 'His brain has gone. Well, you have managed to destroy my family, Mr Meyer, whether you were trying to or not. As for him, can't you leave him alone, now?'

Stephanie came back into the room, and Beth ground up six of the tablets into a powder in the water. 'Drink this,' she commanded Anna.

'Are you sure that's not too much?' Stephanie asked anxiously.

'She's used to drugs,' Beth pointed out. 'And what are you so anxious about keeping her alive for? So she can be locked up for the rest of her life?'

'It's what must happen, Beth. Now we had better telephone the police, and . . .'

'I had to do it,' Josef Janski said, more loudly than before. 'Don't you see? I had to do it. She found out, don't you see. She found out what I had been doing. She wouldn't understand that I had no choice. She swore she'd denounce me after the War. And then she joined the Home Army, let them use my house as a headquarters. I was sure she'd be killed in the fighting. But I had to make sure, don't you see?' He looked from one to the other of the horrified faces in front of him. 'I came back with the Germans. You remember that, Beth. And as we crossed the garden, she came out of the back door, she had a rifle, slung on her shoulder. You remember that, Beth. But those stupid men wouldn't shoot her. They called on her to surrender, and she raised her hands. I couldn't take the risk that she might survive prison. I had to do it, myself.'

For a moment there was absolute silence in the room; even Anna was incapable of making a sound.

Then Beth asked, in a quiet voice, as if determined to make quite sure. 'You shot Mother? You?'

'I had to do it,' Josef Janski repeated stubbornly.

Beth's expression was terrible to behold. 'All these years,' she said, 'I looked up to you. I admired you. I tried to be like you. Even when I learned what you had done with the Jews, I still loved you, because of what you had done for the family. And you killed my mother!'

'You don't understand,' Josef Janski mumbled. 'I had to do it.'

Beth turned away from him; her face was again composed as she faced the other four people in the room, looked at the dead body of her brother. Anna was already half asleep from the effects of the drug. The other three could only return Beth's gaze. Stephanie could see the catastrophe in her sister's eyes. She had devoted her life to a single objective, and now realised what a tragedy that had been. Her own anger had already disappeared. She could hardly remember Mother. And even so terrible a crime did not really matter, when added to all the other crimes of which Father was guilty.

'Beth . . .' she ventured.

Beth seemed to awaken from a deep sleep. 'I want you to leave here, Stephanie,' she said. 'Take George and Mr Meyer with you. I apologise for wishing to kill you, Mr Meyer. I was acting upon a false premise, and I hope you will forgive me. Now I know that you will not wish to be involved in what has happened here, nor need you be. Go with Stephanie, and if you can bring yourself to do so after what you have seen and heard, marry her, and look after her, as I have tried to do.'

Meyer looked at Tony.

'I will call the police, and show them what has happened, and tell them what has happened as well,' Beth said. 'The moment you have gone. I give you my most solemn word of honour.'

'We can't leave you on your own,' Stephanie protested.

'You can and you must,' Beth said fiercely. 'If you stay you will be involved, and there will be scandal and God alone knows what else. There is no one in the world outside of this room who knows you came down here today, none of you. There are not many people in the world who even know you are my sister. Go back to New York and pretend you never left it. I will tell you when it is safe to come publicly to our help.'

'But Beth,' Stephanie protested. 'I must . . .'

'What can you do to help?' Beth demanded. 'Do you suppose I need to borrow to be able to afford the best lawyers? Anna is guilty, she will have to be locked up, as you say. Or do you mean to haul me before a court on a charge of being an accessory after the fact of the death of Szabo? He was a vicious scoundrel. He deserved to die.'

Stephanie looked at Meyer.

'I won't argue with that,' he said.

'So get out of here,' Beth said again. 'Quickly, for all of your sakes.'

Stephanie still looked at Meyer.

'I can't advise you,' he said. 'But it does make sense, if you trust your sister.'

'I will call the police the moment you have gone,' Beth repeated. 'I have given you my word.'

Still Stephanie hesitated; she had seen the expression on Beth's face before she had turned away from Father. 'Father,' she ventured.

Beth's smile was sad. 'Do you think I am going to scratch out his eyes the moment you leave? I will give you my word that I will not lay a finger on him.'

'And you'll call me this evening,' Stephanie insisted. 'Anyway. But if you need help . . .'

Beth held her shoulders to kiss her on the forehead. 'I'll be in touch with you by this evening, I promise. As soon as I know exactly what is going to happen with Anna. As for Father ...' she shrugged. 'He once said he would find his own way to hell. I am going to let him do that. But I really do not feel like celebrating Christmas any more.'

'And Tony ...' Stephanie bit her lip.

'There'll be a funeral date set. I'll be able to let you know about that too, when I know myself.'

Stephanie hesitated a last time, then she sighed, and put her arm round George's shoulder. 'Come along, darling.'

Beth kissed George too, hesitated herself, and then shook hands with Meyer, stood on the porch to watch them as they got into the Rolls.

Meyer drove, as the roads were still bad. No one said a word throughout the three hours it took them to regain Manhattan.

When he parked the car in the basement garage of Stephanie's apartment, Meyer said, 'Would you like me to stay?'

Stephanie shook her head. 'But maybe ... maybe I'll call you, tomorrow.'

He nodded, and walked into the snow.

Beth stayed on the front porch to watch them out of sight, then she went down the steps to the Cadillac, started the engine, and reparked it at the very foot of the steps, leaving the engine running to warm it up. She moved with all the powerful confidence she had always exuded, got out of the car, and went back up the steps. At no time in her life since her mother had died had she ever had more than a moment's doubt as to what was the best course for her to follow, and she did not have any doubts now; it was simply a matter of staring straight ahead and doing what had to be done.

She stood in the doorway, and surveyed what was left of her family. Tony lay where he had fallen, his blood starting to coagulate. Anna was now fast asleep on the settee as the codeine gripped her system. And Josef Janski watched her with anxious eyes.

'They've gone?' he asked. 'They never said goodbye. They're angry with me. Stephanie is angry with me. She's always been angry with me,' he reflected sadly. 'But I had to do it, Beth. You understand that, don't you?'

'I understand a lot of things, Father,' Beth said. She went to Tony, held his wrists, and dragged him to the door, leaving a trail of coagulated blood on the floor. Panting and sweating, she rolled him down the steps, and then lifted him, limb by limb, into the back seat of the car. Then she went back into the house, and did the same for Anna. Anna grunted as her knees and head bumped, and she half woke up, but subsided again as she collapsed into the back seat beside the body of the brother she had murdered.

'Where are you taking them?' Josef Janski asked. 'Aren't we having lunch here?'

'Now you know we can't do that, Father,' she said. 'There's blood all over the place. And there has been a crime committed, which has to be reported to the police. I promised Stephanie I would do that, remember? Come along now.' She held his arm and assisted him to his feet.

'Do I have to come too?' he asked plaintively.

'I can't leave you here by yourself, Father.'

'But I have no coat. I must have my coat, or I'll catch my death of cold.'

'The heater is on in the car,' she told him. 'Just be patient, and you'll be as warm as you wish.' She helped him down the stairs and into the front seat of the car, carefully wrapped him in his rug, and then strapped him in. 'Now, wait just a moment,' she said. 'I'll be back in a second.'

She went back into the house, picked up the telephone, and dialled the police station in the village. It took some time to get through, as it was lunchtime and everyone was tucking into their turkey, but at last the sheriff came on the line.

'This is Elizabeth Latchman,' Beth said. 'I wish you to come to my house, as there has been the most terrible accident.'

'What kind of accident?' he wanted to know.

'A fatal one,' Beth told him. 'Please hurry.' She replaced the phone, sat at her desk and wrote a short note which she left on the blotting pad, then returned to the car, sat beside her father, and strapped herself in.

'Are we going far?' Josef Janski asked.

'Oh, yes,' Beth said. 'Just as far as we can.' She turned the car and drove up the slope to the gate. There she reversed again, until she was facing the yard as if she had just driven in. Her father did not appear to notice, but his head jerked when she rolled down her window.

'You're letting all the cold air in,' he protested.

Beth smiled at him. 'On the contrary, Father, I'm making sure we all get as warm as possible as quickly as possible.' She put the car in Drive, pressed her foot on the accelerator flat to the floor, and as the engine roared and the car bucked, took off the handbrake. The heavy Cadillac shot down the slope beside the house, Beth's hands tight on the wheel. It hurtled off the snow covered grass and on to the thick ice which surfaced the lake close to the dock, and seemed to gather speed. Josef Janski gave a startled exclamation as he sat up. In the back, Anna woke up and screamed. But Beth stared straight ahead with half a smile on her lips as the car struck the thinner ice a hundred feet from the shore, plunged through it, and began to sink. The reservoir was a hundred feet deep out here. Why, she thought as the icy water poured in her opened window, that is surely half way to hell.

Stephanie made sandwiches for lunch; neither she nor George felt much like eating. And this had been going to be the happiest Christmas of her life, Stephanie thought. The Christmas which had been going to set her free.

After lunch, they sat and waited for Beth's call, and Stephanie told George of his grandfather's crimes. He listened in silence, and made no comment. Stephanie knew she would just have to wait and see what effect the news that he was descended from a mass murderer would have on him; whether it would crush him completely or whether it would make him a harder, tougher personality. She could only pray for the latter; he was all she had left.

At six o'clock she began to get restless. 'Beth should have called by now,' she said, pacing the room, and stopping to stare, at the door as the bell rang.

'I'll get it,' George said, and returned with a police inspector.

'What is it?' Stephanie asked, keeping her voice even with an effort. She dared not try to suppose what might have gone wrong with Beth's plan.

The inspector told her. As there had been no doubt, from the tyre marks, that a car had entered the lake, they had got equipment and frogmen in, and the car had been recovered an hour before. He had come to New York by helicopter. 'Some Christmas,' he remarked.

Stephanie sat down.

'I know you're feeling pretty shocked, Mrs Johnson,' he said sympathetically. 'But we have one hell of a mystery here. It just has to be suicide. I mean, no one drives a car into a freezing lake for fun. But, four people? And one of them was stabbed to death,' he added hopefully.

Stephanie said nothing.

'What brings you to my mother?' George asked.

'Well, son, we know that the driver of the car was Mrs Vernon Latchman, and we have evidence to indicate that Mrs Latchman and your mother are sisters.' He cleared his throat. 'Right now we need all

440

the help we can get, Mrs Johnson. Any information you can give us, either about your sister, or about the people she was with. We've seen Mr Latchman already, but he says he had no idea where his wife was going for her Christmas lunch. Sounds a queer set up to me, but there it is. He's pretty upset, as you can imagine. He's gone down to the village to identify her body. But the other three people in the car . . . no one seems to know who they were, really. Hermits, the villagers out there call them. Seems they've lived there for some ten years or so, but never mixed with the locals. They've always paid their bills, never caused any trouble . . . but hermits.'

Stephanie inhaled, and looked at George.

He nodded. 'One of the people in the car was my grandfather,' he said. 'The other two were my aunt and uncle.'

The inspector frowned at him. 'How do you know that?'

'I don't know it,' George said, without blinking. 'But I do know that those were the three people living in that house.'

'Holy Moses,' the inspector commented. 'Then who stabbed your uncle? It was him who was dead before the car went into the water – the other three drowned.'

'I'm afraid I can't help you there,' George said. 'My mother has been estranged from her family for some years, although she knew they were being supported by Aunt Beth.'

'Then there must have been some kind of a quarrel . . .' The inspector scratched his head. 'But to go knifing, on Christmas Day . . . it must be one of the sisters, I guess. And Mrs Latchman . . . Mr Latchman is pretty cut up. The fact is, Mrs Johnson, we need identification of the other three.'

'I'll do it,' George said.

The inspector looked at Stephanie.

'I'll come too,' she agreed.

'No,' George said. He had taken complete command,

in a way that she had always hoped he would. 'You've had quite a shock, Mom. You stay here. I'll look after everything. There's nothing you can do, now, anyway.'

Stephanie gazed at him. Does he think I knew what Beth was going to do? she wondered. In fact it hadn't crossed her mind. Yet it was all a logical development of Beth's character. 'I'm very grateful,' she said.

'Yeah, well, we'd better get down there.' The inspector got up, twisted his hat in his hands. 'Did you know that Mrs Latchman left you all her personal fortune in a will she seems to have written just before the fatality, Mrs Johnson?'

'No,' Stephanie said. 'I didn't know that.'

'I have it here.' The inspector produced the note.

It read: 'To my dearest Stephanie, who alone has nothing to answer for, I bequeath everything I possess in money, clothes and jewellery. I have not the time to have this witnessed, but I would like my wishes carried out. Signed, Elizabeth Latchman, née Janska, 25/12/85.'

'Would you have any idea what you don't have to answer for, Mrs Johnson?'

'No,' George said. 'My mother, as I have told you, has been estranged from the rest of her family for some time. She does not know what they quarrelled about.'

'Well ... this wasn't witnessed, as she says,' the inspector observed. 'But I don't suppose Mr Latchman will contest his wife's final desire – he has enough to go on with. But then, I guess you have enough to go on with as well, Mrs Johnson.'

'That's right,' George said. 'My mother doesn't have to worry about money.'

'There has to be a motive somewhere,' the inspector said as George accompanied him to the door and pulled on his topcoat. 'There always is. But I don't reckon we'll ever discover this one.'

'Not with all four of them dead,' George agreed.

Stephanie sat staring in front of herself. Her brain was quite dull, in the sense of putting coherent thoughts together. But it was yet alive in the succession of images which kept flaring through her mind. Was she guilty? If she had stayed . . . But she knew that nothing she could have done would have made the slightest difference to Beth's resolve, once she had taken her decision.

All she really wanted to do was think about Beth. Beth, accepting rape from the Russians to save them. Beth, standing in front of them with a rifle in her hands when the men came to rob them, and sending them away with the dead soldier. Beth, facing down the German girls outside Dresden, or the commandant in the DP camp. Beth, accepting prostitution to keep them free. Beth, blackmailing Georges Mathieu, with the same object in mind. Beth, confronting Szabo. All steps in the same direction. Which had led to suicide, when she realised that all her premises had been wrong.

She picked up the note, looked at it, and put it down again. Beth, who had loved them all so much. So much, that she had killed all the guilty ones rather than see them put away. And who had recognised that she was as guilty as any of them.

Beth, making her instant, irrevocable decisions, to the very end.

The telephone started ringing. John Harper, and then Ed Martinez and then Alice Todd, offering sympathy. The news of Elizabeth Latchman's death had just been announced on TV, in a car accident the report had said. Stephanie listened, and acknowledged. And at last, the doorbell.

Bob Meyer stood there. They looked at each other. 'What can I say?' he asked. 'She was one hell of a woman. But I've known that for about a year.'

'Thank you,' she said. 'Would you like to come in?'

443

'Would you like me to?'

She smiled. 'The decision has to be yours, Bob. You know what my father was.'

'I've always known who your father was, Stephanie.' He entered the apartment, showed her the telegram he had sent that afternoon. It read: 'POSITIVE INFORMATION NOW OBTAINED TARGET DEAD STOP CONSIDER CASE CLOSED STOP ALSO AM RESIGNING FOR PERSONAL REASONS STOP BEST MEYER.'

'Resigning?' She raised her head. 'What are you going to do?'

'Starve, I guess,' he said. 'Unless someone gives me a job.'

'You'd better pour us each a drink,' she said. 'And we'll talk about it. I know someone who might need a long lesson in being free.'